EROS

Helmut Krausser

EROS

*Translated from the German
by Mike Mitchell*

Europa
editions

Europa Editions
116 East 16th Street
New York, N.Y. 10003
www.europaeditions.com
info@europaeditions.com

Translation by Mike Mitchell
Original Title: *Eros*
Translation copyright © 2008 by Europa Editions

The translation of this work was supported by a grant from the
Goethe-Institut, which is funded by the Ministry of Foreign Affairs.

Library of Congress Cataloging in Publication Data is available
ISBN 978-1-933372-58-7

Krausser, Helmut
Eros

Book design by Emanuele Ragnisco
www.mekkanografici.com

Prepress by Plan.ed – Rome

Printed in the United States of America

CONTENTS

No one will knead us again out of earth and clay,
no one will breathe life into our dust.
No one.

Praise be to you, No One.
For your sake we
will bloom.
For you
to see.

Nothing
we were, we are, we will
remain, blooming:
the nothing rose, the
No one's rose.

—PAUL CELAN

Oh, one Eros sent—
see, honor notes
one honest, sore,
tho' soon serene.
The no one's rose—
O other oneness!

—INGE SCHULZ
(*checked; no action necessary*)

THE EVENING BEFORE

Without knowing much about him, apart from the few things you could read here and there, and without ever having seen him, apart from in yellowing photographs, I found him repulsive. Still I went when he called. Which of my colleagues would not have responded to his call? Every one of them, without exception, would have gone to satisfy their curiosity.

On the train taking me there I was a man whose life was in ruins going, for some unknown purpose, to visit a man of fabulous wealth.

Don't waste time with petty questions, just come, he had written, *you will not regret it and that's a promise.*

There was arrogance and magic in the way he put it. I was horrified at the fascination his seemingly bigmouthed promise exerted on me. I vowed I would not let myself be bought, not at any price—and at the same time I knew full well that anyone who made such a vow not only sensed the danger ahead, but was rushing towards it. *To play with the temptation a little, yes, that's what you have in mind. To look for, to consider an offer, no matter what kind, if only to give your vanity, your need for recognition a boost, surely there's no harm in that, you tell yourself. But to to tell yourself you will then remain steadfast, afterwards, that comes close to self-deception.* I wrote these thoughts down in my notebook while gray, swirling snow obscured the compartment windows.

The last photo showing Alexander von Brücken had been taken over twenty years ago. Since then no one seemed to have managed to get him in their viewfinder. He lived, it was said, in seclusion in his castle in Southern Bavaria, attended by a few servants.

The stormy weather only served to increase my fear of him and of myself. When I arrived at the tiny provincial station, I looked in vain for a stall where I could buy something, anything, a schnapps maybe. The only people to get off, apart from me, were three rather tipsy middle-aged ladies, in carnival costumes, giggling and bawling out songs. Envious, I watched them leave. A large black Daimler was waiting outside the station with a chauffeur who was wearing tracksuit bottoms and trainers to go with his gray jacket. He didn't wave me over or anything, just sat in the car with the door partly open, listening to pop music. It was Sunday, half past five in the evening and almost dark. I had to laugh. I did laugh, almost in desperation, at the snowbound village, its silhouette only just managing to emerge from the gray swirl of the storm. Was he, I asked the driver, without saying who I was, waiting for me? He, corpulent and dumb-looking, nodded and told me to climb in. The lighted windows of the surrounding houses seemed to be watching me. The car, scarcely managing to do two hundred meters a minute, fought its way forward through the piles of snow and turned off the road into an avenue lit by a few lamps. I was looking over the driver's right shoulder, in anticipation of the castle. What then appeared was something for which the designation castle was pretentious, a hunting lodge perhaps, an admittedly impressive country house in the neo-Gothic style surrounded by a six-foot-high stone wall.

Gates swung open, the wheels spun briefly, a garage door slid up. The garage was hardly any bigger than that of a duplex house, completely out of proportion with the building. The driver parked the car, got out slowly, and opened the door for me. Suddenly beside him, as if from nowhere, was a slim, oldish man in a gray double-breasted suit, with sharp, aquiline features and bright, blue-gray eyes.

Without offering to shake hands, he introduced himself as Keferloher, Lukian Keferloher, von Brücken's private secretary. Not a particularly warm welcome, businesslike at best. He apologized for the weather, incredible, and, asking me to follow him, opened a metal door and led the way up a stone spiral staircase for two, perhaps three storeys. Through a very narrow door we entered a high room, a grand chamber really, with a wood-paneled ceiling, lit by the subdued light of electric candelabras and sparsely furnished. Flurries of snow outside the yellow-tinted windows. A soft whistling in the rafters, like a child blowing through a gap in its teeth and fluttering its lower lip, almost a bit obscene in the overtones, though they could have been a figment of my imagination, I was freezing. Keferloher gestured toward the room and briefly closed his eyes, presumably the most succinct way of sketching a bow.

I took three steps in the direction indicated by his outstretched left arm.

And so I set eyes on *him* for the first time. Von Brücken was sitting, in a leather chair with massive ornamental carving, at a completely empty cherrywood desk. He didn't get up to welcome me, although he did put his head on one side, as if expecting something painful.

I went over to him, with rapid steps, demonstrating my self-assurance.

As if, at the last moment, he had become aware that his reception might seem insulting, he lowered his head and, without getting up, held out his right palm towards me. It was trembling slightly.

On the other side of the imposing cherrywood desk was a kind of stool, almost dainty, on which he invited me to sit down. I looked at him. Bold and brazen, as I had planned. Cool, mildly condescending. And he for his part looked at me, differently from the way I'd expected. Weary, sad, almost pleading.

According to the encyclopedia, he was over seventy, born 1930. My impression was of a determined man whose time had always been short but which now, having become even shorter, demanded a maximum of efficiency. That led me to expect him to state his request in brisk, rapid sentences. Instead he looked me up and down for a long time, in silence, before murmuring with a sigh, almost of relief, "Here you are at last. Thank you."

I didn't know what to say, I felt flattered, corrupted, and gave a nod, a knowing nod, although there was nothing to know.

"Of all the writers I know, you are the best. Allow me to say that it is an honour to have you staying here with us."

I would never have thought he had such sound judgment.

"Thank you," I replied crisply, adding, with pointed briskness, "I'm looking forward to it."

His eyelids fluttered, as if some dust had gotten into his eyes. He rubbed his right eye discreetly with his trembling hand and stared at the empty desk in front of him. Then he leant his head back and rubbed the back of his neck on the leather of the chair. There was something catlike about it and also something—vulgar, was my immediate thought at the time. Now I would say, "of a man in torment."

"It's time to get something down on paper. Not necessarily my life, but the story of a love, my love. So far it has not been told, but it must be told or it will be lost and will never have happened. I would like you to write a book for me. A novel." He made a long pause, perhaps hoping for a brisk, rapid reply. My silence irritated him. With a scarcely audible sigh, he launched into an explanation.

"Something that is written down has, in a certain way, happened, it's my way of making something very secret public. The person concerned will never hear about it, but for me it's as if they *would* hear about it if you write it down, simply because the whole world will hear about it." Another long pause, less calculated this time, he was looking for words.

"That will not excuse what I did to this person, will not make it as if it never happened—but the publication of the crime, the disclosure of a wrong, will, I feel, at least reduce the crime. You put that neatly into words once: 'the atrocity is converted into a statistic.' I liked that passage very much in your last book. You know the passage I mean."

I nodded. He nodded.

"But that's as may be. For some reason or other I trust you. If you should complete the commission to my satisfaction, I will disappear. It will be as if we'd never met. I haven't long to live. You can publish the manuscript after my death, changing the names, after a certain time has elapsed, it will be seen as a product of your creative imagination, free from the stigma of hired labor. You will be grateful to me, you can trust me as well."

Something odd was happening. Von Brücken had stood up and slowly walked around my stool. His voice had steadied until it took on the persuasive tone of an executioner assuring the condemned man he was going to make it as easy for him as possible, there was nothing for it, they just had to go through with it.

He was capable of being very direct, even coarse at times, but to withdraw the coarseness immediately, to help the one he'd insulted recover until he not only forgave the insult, but almost took the ensuing apology as an honor. A tactic I was familiar with from various publishers.

At times his right eyelid didn't function properly, it hung down, slack, half covering the eye. Otherwise he was the picture of health—slim, tall, his face smooth and bronzed. A little dandruff fell out of his granite-gray hair, now and then he gave one of his shoulders, always just the one, a quick wipe with a casual gesture that was meant to go unnoticed. He was wearing a blue suit of studied plainness, no tie and a collarless gray shirt of almost priestly cut.

Was it up to me to say something? Von Brücken opened one of the drawers and placed two red-wine glasses on the rectangle of leather let into the wood of the desktop.

Did I fancy a drop of fine wine, he asked and, without waiting for me to answer, suddenly waved a bottle which must have been there on the floor.

"*Petrus 1912*. Have you ever had anything like that before?"

No, I hadn't. To me the question seemed somewhere between vulgarly show-off and humiliating until his smile told me it wasn't meant like that. He half filled both glasses and handed me one.

"I drank this wine once before, almost sixty years ago, my father let me have a mouthful on the evening of 14 November 1944. What a waste, in those days! I drank it, not appreciating what it was, afterward I was slightly tipsy, no question of enjoyment. I'm not a man for metaphors, you know, but—"

He took a sip. "It often seems to me that most people drink life the way I drank this wine as a fourteen-year-old. You're told it's something very special, very precious, and you do your best not to seem ungrateful or too young, but—"

He didn't finish the sentence. Nor was it necessary. Perhaps it was more necessary to mention that the taste of the wine, the legendary 1912 Petrus, was delicious, but not as ambrosial as its legend would have it. It goes against the grain to admit it, but the wine left me pretty cold. Von Brücken immediately saw the disappointment in my eyes, grinned and said, "It's just *wine*, isn't it?"

"So what?"

How pigheaded I was. How vain.

Von Brücken put a tape recorder on the desk, switched it on. And switched it off again.

"I'm impatient. This evening's not the right time. Lukian will show you to your room. Should you need anything you can't find there, Lukian will get it for you. Don't be shy about asking, Lukian's used to carrying out all kinds of requests. We'll meet here tomorrow morning. Then the story will start. And you can give the wine another chance. Once you've put aside your excessive expectations, you'll find it lives up to its legend.

Was he talking about the wine or was he speaking metaphorically again? The old man gave an ambiguous smile. Suddenly, as if he'd been in the room all the time, Keferloher, his private secretary, was behind me. I nodded briefly, thanked him and followed Keferloher up the stairs. Once in my room I made it clear to myself that I had not indicated any agreement. Obviously I would spend the night there, not least because of the weather, but that of itself meant nothing. I would perhaps have liked to have exchanged a few words about the fee. Von Brücken seemed not to have given it a thought. And why was I giving it so much thought if, deep down inside, I hadn't long since agreed?

A novel. Which I could not publish until von Brücken was dead. But which I had to complete *before* he died, so he could read it. Or did I? An interesting point. I would refuse to allow myself to be put under that kind of pressure; would categorically refuse to bind myself to overly feudal conditions.

With its little windows taking up almost a third of its circumference, there was something pleasantly oriel-like about the round room to which Keferloher took me. The bed was large, a table very broad, a chair very comfortable, a fridge very full. The TV had ninety-nine channels, there were several lamps, allowing one to combine them to create a suitable ambience. I could approach him with any requests, Keferloher murmured. He pointed to a bell over the bed. The cook could make me a hot meal at any time of the day or night. The modesty that had been drummed into me automatically, if absurdly, kicked in and I assured him all my needs were already catered for.

DAY ONE

No no, you don't have to rush it. Take as long as you like, as you need, don't bother about me. I will presumably—most probably even—no longer be here to read it. Unfortunately. But I have implicit trust in you. You will receive your fee whatever happens, even if you only deliver blank pages. I imagine that under these conditions your pride will not feel too violated and, exceptionally, the expression *implicit trust* can be taken literally. Is that right?"

I nodded. What else could I do? The proposed fee exceeded my wildest dreams, would free me from financial worries for the rest of my life. Von Brücken lowered his voice.

"You're safe as long as I'm alive. After that it could be that . . . "

"That what?"

"That you'll have problems. There will be people who won't want . . . Lukian, for example. He knows what you're intending to do, what *we're* intending to do, and I don't think he approves. He would never say so out loud, but he's my heir, we have this agreement which I have to stick to, which I will stick to. So it could be that once I'm dead he won't like the idea of this book, even with the names changed, because of the role he has in it. I don't think that he will . . . you know, but he might perhaps try to buy the book off you, with all the money he'll have to throw around then. That could happen. My confidence in your vanity or, rather, in your integrity as an artist is strong enough to dispel these misgivings, more or less. Despite that, I suggest that as soon as you hear I'm dead it would be better if you went somewhere where it's not so easy for people to, let's say, *get to you*."

He knew that everything he said only served to intensify my curiosity, but I could also see genuine concern in his eyes. Not for me so much as for his book. For his story.

Outside the flurries of snow had stopped. Now and then the sun pierced the clouds, the languid, slightly yellowing shadows bringing a cosy atmosphere to the soot-grimed room.

The tape recorder started.

The Last Days of the Ice Palace

Imagine a closely mown, beautifully kept lawn. On it a pavilion in the pseudo-Chinese style with, underneath, a beautifully turned-out German family all in their Sunday best: my father, my mother, me, about thirteen, and the twins, my sisters, three years younger.

Behind it a large house, a large, white villa in the sunlight. It is bright, almost dazzlingly bright. The people are sitting around a pale green marble table. On it are six bowls of lemon ice cream. There are six of them because Keferloher has come to visit.

That was the moment when Keferloher gave our villa in Allach, our huge, white, art nouveau villa in the north of Munich, the name *Ice Palace*, as a joke, on that August afternoon when he was eating lemon ice cream with my parents in the garden pavilion and compared the color of what he was eating with the color of what he could see shining in the sun.

"Ice Palace!" I exclaimed, intoxicated by the wonderful expression, and the twin parrots took it up with their shrill little voices: "Ice Palace! Ice Palace!"

They were called Cosima and Constanze, both after composers' widows. Mostly I called them Coco One and Coco Two.

At that time Keferloher was managing director of my father's factories, factories for processing metal and constructing vulcanizing machines, which, one year after the war, had been switched to the production of various kinds of armaments. My father's visits to the works were as rare as they were reluctant; he went purely as a figurehead. He hated the expression *factory owner*; he always described himself as an *architect*, even on official documents. Without having any formal qualifications. But with justification. If anyone ever lived for architecture, it was my father; such was his passion that the question of talent is secondary. He designed churches, bridges, parks . . . All for his portfolio. Or for a distant future—after the war.

The Ice Palace contained: one cook, two cleaners, one servant, one gardener and three tutors. No chauffeur. It wasn't worth it. Papa always drove himself when he went out in the car, even though our mother thought that was dreadful. Mother suffered from occasional fainting fits. Low blood pressure. She found it embarrassing, but otherwise we were fine, a model family. A fourth child would have brought her the Mother's Cross in bronze; it was a matter of complete indifference to her.

We were such a model family that Papa had a family photograph taken every year and, framed like works of art, hung on the spiral staircase up to the second floor. I think that, for him, we were indeed a kind of work of art, laden with symbolic meaning, and if one of us children should be found wanting in our behavior, he would reproach us more for aesthetic than pedagogical reasons.

My sisters had piano lessons. I, because I had turned out not to be very musical, had to learn the trombone, an instrument which my father regarded as one that "could be mastered even if the inclination were lacking." It was, he maintained, a *sine qua non* for any person with pretensions to culture to have mastered at least *one* instrument. He also attached great importance to classical languages, as well as a solid grounding in theology. Not that he was particularly religious himself, but he regarded theology as a rich humus from which, as he put it, a determination to explore the world from a higher philosophical viewpoint would grow; not unlike present-day parents who have started sending their children to confirmation classes again to make sure they'll turn into good atheists.

My father had given much subtle thought to the organization of our family life. In this he was loyally supported by my mother, who, through obedience and devotion, was good at doing things she didn't understand. I often watched Papa stare at the floor and, frustrated by his wife's lack of understanding, seek refuge in contemplation of the carpet pattern, consoled by the knowledge that Baroness von Hohenstein, as Mama had been before marriage, would not dare to contradict any of his arrangements. Oh, I knew very well what a strain life as head of a model family was for my father, I knew what pride he laid to bed beside himself at the end of each day. This cultured man with an artistic disposition who, by ordinary standards, had achieved everything that mattered, who was a man of taste, rich and respected, had succeeded in harmonizing his duty towards the next generation with a secret life spent in higher regions. Of course I'm lying left, right and center, of course I didn't understand him the way I do now, of course I was an ungrateful brat who could put two and two together and make five, living in blissful ignorance off the fat of the land.

My sisters were lucky. They would only have been subjected to serious intellectual training if something had happened to *me*. As it was, they could remain stupid and enjoy the little things of life. My father made no secret of his low opinion of the female sex, but dismissed it as an unfortunate fact about which something ought to be done, if something *could* have been done about it.

In that respect he was perfectly happy with his wife. He showed no desire to ask or teach her to do more than was necessary. I, on the other hand, was treated like his dearest rib out of which his likeness was to be carved, was initiated into the mysteries of Teutonic Culture—which, between you and me, I found deadly boring at the time.

What my father wanted to inculcate in me above all was a form of dignity which responded to greatness with detachment, to affliction with stoicism, which was always more aware of its effect on others than of its own well-being, entirely concerned with appearances, as if a person were nothing without other people to assess them. Everything my father did, he did as if under observation by rigorous judges who gave marks for character and bearing. Individuality seemed for him to be something one could only indulge in *after* the performance, in the privacy of one's own home, so to speak, and not without constraint even then. Perhaps I'm being too harsh in the way I try to make sense of my memories, but to imagine my father exuberant, inspired by pure, boisterous joy is beyond me. I think he must have suffered from never having had to stand on his own two feet, from the fact that from the cradle he found himself part of a social order there was no sensible reason to reject. He never had to make something of himself, just had to fit in with what was already there, fill a vacant spot that was allotted him. This he did brilliantly and with great style, and it was only when his world began to fall apart that he found himself faced with decisions his mental apparatus was not equipped to cope with.

Hardly any of his architectural designs were carried out, which doesn't mean anything, since it wasn't the realization of his ideas that mattered to him. His creativity was satisfied with paper, pencil and slide rule. He would often show me, unlike the parrots, a sketch for a theater, a park, a garden bridge. I was old enough to realize that I didn't have to understand these things yet, that the only reason I was shown them was so that I would be proud of my father, not give an opinion on his creation.

My father was a classical scholar and a convinced German. In no way blindly surrendering to the Nazis, he had kept an open mind and was surprised at their successes. For him the Reich in its boundaries of 1942 compelled comparisons with Rome under Trajan. He once said something along the lines of: the Germans have given the word history back its old force and magnitude.

Yes, well . . . I practised the trombone. Very unwillingly. My mother told me that was the way it had to be. Because it was the way things were. At the time that sounded logical. The trombone does have the advantage that you can read while you're playing it.

Once while I was reading, I fainted from all the trombone playing. The parrots came running to my room and took the book away; I came to again and ran after them. At the bottom of the stairs was my father with the book in his hand. It was *Justine* by the Marquis de Sade. I'd stolen the book from his collection of *erotica*. Now, he would never have hit me—he always found physical contact rather unpleasant. He locked the book back in the cupboard and didn't speak to me for two weeks. Perhaps he was afraid of things coming out into the open. After all, I could have asked him why *he* had the book.

Mama was concerned that I might have inherited her proneness to fainting fits and from then on I didn't have to practise the trombone so much. But that was it for de Sade. All I had was an anatomical atlas with the outlines of a female body which showed the liver and the urethra in the same color. Two weeks later my father said to me:

"Remember you're a German. Dürer's looking down on you!" He pointed to a print in the hall, Dürer's self-portrait with the long hair, I think it was a surrogate, as he couldn't quite stand Jesus. *Dürer's looking down on you!* Eventually it became a catch phrase, even for my shallow sisters, that we laughed at secretly, but with a feeling of shame, of doing something forbidden. Like going out into the fields some time and shouting, *You're an old fool, God.* And you're not struck down by lightning because God happened not to be looking. Dürer, on the other hand, was always looking.

That I was educated by three private tutors was bad enough, but, to make matters worse, my father had taken it into his head, against my will and without giving any reason, to keep me out of the Hitler Youth.

"Have you any idea," he asked me, "what I had to do to spare you that?"

I rebelled in an access of patriotism, I wanted to be in the Hitler Youth, sleep in tents, bear the pennant of my platoon through Wotan's dark woods bellowing songs. And have a sheath knife. "But I want to join! Everyone else has!"

He refused even to discuss it and pushed me into my mother's arms. She strongly urged me to say nothing, it was they way things were and nothing I said or did would change my father's decision.

"Believe me," she always said, "I've known him longer than you."

His special interest was Romanesque architecture, especially that of Southern Bavaria. I think he dreamed that architecture might some day adopt a neo-Romanesque style and that he would then become the state-appointed expert, its architectural high priest. Crazy? Certainly, but given the state the country was in, nothing seemed so crazy that it didn't have a certain vague hope of realization. Perhaps that was why he tolerated the Nazis, they made almost everything seem possible, they had turned the world upside down by utilizing a simple fascination with the new which is usually underestimated in retrospect. I think that a person who, at the time, thought that fascism, though reprehensible, had such overwhelming power it would dominate the world for the next few decades, cannot simply be accused of stupidity. The course of history came very close to proving such a person right. Stupidity was the belief that good on its own was bound to emerge victorious.

To keep fit, I played tennis, three times a week, with Volker, Keferloher's first-born. He was four years older than I and therefore unsuitable as a source of information in questions of sex. He made it obvious he had to play tennis with me because *his* father was *my* father's second-in-command. We played in silence, one hour each day. In all my life I have never done anything so idiotic, at least not regularly.

Volker was later killed on the Eastern Front.

The war was coming closer. My memories become more numerous. 1944: in March the Residence Theater was completely destroyed, in April the church of St. Boniface with Friedrich Ziebland's Romanesque basilica, which my father regarded as a model of historicizing architecture. Along with the neo-Romanesque church of St. Maximilian, the chef d'oeuvre of Heinrich von Schmidt. I can even still see its details in my mind's eye. Each time Papa cried. 1944. The first year of fear. Before that the war was really great, I'd be lying if I said I felt differently. But then: phosphorus, fire, terror. The sky darkened for days on end by clouds of yellow, gray, black and brown clouds of smoke. All around us: streets littered with broken glass and rubble. The smell of burning; high, stinking piles of charred debris. In June and July the main targets of the air raids were in the north of the city, BMW was badly hit, despite the artificial fog that was supposed to protect it, The BMW and Krauss-Maffei works further west in Allach suffered less serious damage. In the middle of June the Chinese Tower in the English Garden burnt down, after that it was the turn of the zoo in Hellabrunn. A lot of animals died: zebras, antelopes, buffaloes, reindeer, camels, bears and deer. Almost all the schools in Munich were damaged. My private lessons, which had previously been been regarded with suspicion, were now out of the question. 1944 was the year of the most intense anti-aircraft fire. The shrill hum of the approaching planes swelled to a thunderous drone, the second wave, the third, the fourth. And that was when we starting having bombs with time fuses which fell into the buildings and got stuck half way down, or in the rubble, and only went off between sixty and eighty hours later. I got religion. I prayed to the Führer, "Punish them." I had never prayed to the Führer before, but the hatred I felt at the sight of the half-destroyed city drove me to worship the only one I believed possessed the power to punish such crimes. Incidentally, Krauss-Maffei survived the war almost undamaged. Unbelievable. And just imagine: though hardly anyone knows this today, during that summer, until the middle of September, a period corresponding almost exactly to the school holidays, there was not a single air raid. People relaxed a little. Then they were back, the Mustangs, Lightnings, the four-engined Stirlings, the Mosquitos, Halifaxes and Lancasters; the Brits came by night, the Yanks, with their B-17 Fortresses and B-27 Liberators, by day.

We, the pampered inhabitants of the Ice Palace, had learnt to handle gas masks, fire beaters, fire buckets, hoses and first-aid boxes, at least in theory, if not in practice. At the north-west corner of Allach there was a heavy anti-aircraft battery, with lots of Hitler Youth in action as messengers, assistants to the air-raid wardens and goodness knows what else. I was spared most of that.

And I first met Sofie.

We would hear the first detonations in the north and *only then* the sirens, that's what things had come to in Germany by that time. In our street there were a lot of people who worked in my father's factories. The street had only one air-raid shelter. My mother was unhappy with that. I wasn't. By then I had come to like the air-raid warnings.

An air-raid warning meant there was the possibility of being close to Sofie.

From that point on on everything was different. When I heard the siren—it was a wailing note, rising and falling, that lasted for a minute, followed by two rising and falling notes lasting eight seconds in all, a dreadful cacophony, but do you know something? My heart gave a shriek of delight, and if it was evening, the shriek was even louder, like the squeal of a happy pig—we would probably spend the whole night in the air-raid shelter and I would be on the top of the bunk bed, together with other children from our street, and if I managed to organize things right I would spend the whole night in bed with her, my beloved. What fourteen-year-old can say that! If a bomb exploded nearby I would have an excuse for holding Sofie's hand. She came from one of the families in our street that didn't have an awful lot to lose and so said all the more heartfelt prayers for what little they had. Every night I hoped the bombs would rain down. Oh, how I loved her! The way you love when you're not used to being in love. You've been through it, yes? Of course you have. Today it seems to me as if love suddenly appeared inside me or, rather, an openness to love did, which, once it had settled inside me, looked for a victim, the first pretty girl to turn up. That could be what it was, couldn't it? Suddenly I didn't want to join the Hitler Youth anymore, that was for children. I had a goal, a purpose, a feeling, however vague it was.

I remember those nights very clearly: my mother, who felt uncomfortable among all those ordinary people and refused to talk, my father, stoically expressionless. And us children, fully clothed with our shoes on, my heartbeat, distant detonations, Sofie asleep—she was so young and slim, her breasts already discernible and her hair, I suppose I ought to say her auburn plait, came down to her buttocks.

Her body was an enchanting vision of wonderful curves. Oh, the spell that first love casts, so immense and yet so profoundly ridiculous.

When skin starts to shine just because it's stretched over the skull of a girl with whom, on the face of it, you can find nothing wrong. That interchangeable love which fixes on some girl who happens along, but which can assume such boundless intensity and ecstasy. You think grown-ups must be brain-dead because of the silly grins they give you; they obviously have no idea what love is. When she was asleep I thought up devious ploys to be able to touch her without giving the impression of being in love. You've been through that? Who hasn't? I also thought up ploys to get us swimming in the river together, some time in the future, taking a shower together or going for walks in the woods at the new moon.

The dream of seeing her bare shoulders. But we—her shoulders and I—didn't even go out to the movies together. We quite often lay in one bed but, ridiculous though it sounds, we never came *close*. I hummed love songs, silent love songs the words of which I've forgotten, sang to myself for nights on end, never tiring of praising my love in song, it was just as it ought to be and I dreamed the whole of Germany had exploded and just we two were lying, buried alive, somewhere in the last warmth of ashes, the air was used up and I gave her my last breath in one long kiss—that kind of stuff, I take nothing of it back, it was right and it was marvellous.

I won't describe Sofie. *You* describe her, but so that everyone will feel the attraction. She wasn't anything special, at least not then. Except for me.

You'll have to find colors for Sofie such as no painter's brush ever touched, you'll have to find words the gods only bestow on poets in moments of rapt contemplation and you'll have to—no, no, that's all nonsense, presumptuous, no, just write: a beautiful, very young female, period, let the readers imagine the type they find the most beautiful, you can only convey a certain kind of magic by passing over the finer details, don't give me that condescending look, I know you'll do it very well, yes, you will.

I had two real friends. I can't remember their faces now. But I can remember their sexual organs. Alfons had a very long, bent, almost purple penis, Bodo a very short one, thick and milky white. I held the record of twenty-one seconds between first touch and ejaculation. With prior, clandestine stimulation, I could have been even quicker but to cheat in a competition was something I considered thoroughly un-German. Alfons and Bodo were my friends during two summers, then they joined the Hitler Youth. Both were killed in the war, I think, no idea really. Suddenly they weren't there anymore, out of sight, out of mind.

Can you remember what it was like? To expose your penis for the first time to the open air, at night or, what was even more arousing, in daylight in some quiet corner, made even more arousing by the possibility of someone seeing you; even more arousing: a woman; even more arousing: a young, pretty woman.

Our garden was huge, with a pavilion, a bird bath and an arbor where I pretended to be an Apache or looked at my penis. So often that I can tell you to the day (March 20, 1942) when I saw the first shimmer of pubic hair. I had already been masturbating for ages, but at the climax only a spurt of urine came. The semen arrived six months later, from one night to the next it was there, quite unannounced, wreathed in mystery. I tasted it, it was horrible, I was bitterly disappointed and gave up any hope that a girl might be prepared to swallow a flood of that juice. That girls do that at all I had learnt from the divine marquis.

Having younger sisters can have its advantages. Once I tied Coco One to a chair, pulled her dress up and had a good look at everything. She screamed and kicked, but I didn't care. I wasn't interested in her, she still had no hair and Alfons had told me that if there's no hair, their hole's only for pissing. I took my thing out and played with it, not because she turned me on, merely to show off, and jerked off on her belly. "What're you doing?" she asked and I said, "What Indians do to all white women." Then I untied her. She ran straight to Coco Two and told her all about it. Coco Two didn't believe her and asked me to do it again for her, in the garage, but when I told her she'd have to get undressed and show me her hole down there, she refused. Refused! That was asking too much! Odd, isn't it?

But to return to Sofie. At some point during the summer of 1944 she started wearing two plaits instead of one, and sometimes wore her hair loose. It was . . . indescribable. That hair, a dark firefall, a molten mass, I would have given everything—everything!—to run my fingers through it, to have a taste of that girl, nothing else was important, you could have shown me thousands of similar creatures or even brought them to me, she was the one I wanted, no one else, only her, and wholly, entirely, with everything.

And yet: my love could have lighted on any girl, on any one of all the pretty girls this side of death.

The war came just at the right time for me. It was like a dark friend you conceal from your parents, a friend you meet in secret, with secret signs.

At first my dark friend made contact over the radio. *Large bomber formations reported over such and such an area*, was our opening code, and if the alert sounded soon afterward, it meant we had to go to the air-raid shelter, and there would be the possibility of being close to Sofie.

She would sit on the bed, her arms around one of her knees—it was beyond belief that one of the old crones in the shelter didn't forbid such an obscene pose. And she used her knee as a cushion for her face, a breathtaking silhouette in the bedtime light, in the summer when it was hot and she had bare legs. I went up close to smell her, I'd have given anything to be able to kiss her thighs, and the desire to masturbate with that silhouette in front of me was equally as strong. In the crowded bunker that was impossible, at most you could put your hand in your pocket and rub your tool a bit, not enough to make you come. Perhaps I would have managed it if I'd refrained from masturbating for a few nights; I tried, I did try, but on the third night at the latest my patience always ran out and I did it three, four times in succession, wild orgies with a touch of betrayal.

Yes, betrayal, that was what I felt. I was cheating on my beloved with myself. I was sitting there, playing with myself, instead of going and conquering her, or at least confessing my love to her like a man—and failing manfully when she giggled. She never sweated. Her skin always seemed cool and smooth, her breath was slow and her eyes were the saddest eyes in the world, though I'd never seen a tear on her cheeks.

She smelled of charred wood and tallow, which sounds mustier than it in fact was. The combination of her girlish vanity on the one hand and the poverty which did not look poor, just marvellously plain and simple, on the other were an enchanting contrast, full of an eroticism which went straight to my senses. She cast a spell over me with simple means.

Sometimes, when I was sleeping next to her, I stole a strand from her loose hair and played with it, so gently that she didn't notice. I put it in my mouth and chewed on it, imagining it was her lips. I stretched out in bed then folded my body so that my head was level with her pelvis. Then I pointed my nose at her abdomen, which was no more than twenty centimeters away, and drew in the air, trying to sniff out the scent of her private parts, at the same time quivering with fear. Beneath a sky red with flames, while Germany burned. I was as far above it as the nest of an extinct bird above the clouds. It occasionally happened that someone less than ten feet away from me had a fit of hysteria because the bombs were falling close by and I took that as an excuse to grasp Sofie's hand. And do you know what she said to me? *Scaredy cat.*

She called me a scaredy cat. I said my name was Alex, to which she replied, "I know that."

For a moment I was very happy that Sofie knew my name, but then everyone in the shelter knew my name, I was the only son of the local bigwigs. Then I heard Sofie's mother saying softly, "I think our Sof's getting a bit too old to sleep in the same bed as the boss's son." And I heard my mother say to my father, "What ideas these people here get. It's no place for our children. Wouldn't it be possible—" But at that moment there was a loud detonation. I grasped Sofie's hand again, but she withdrew it, giving me a puzzled look. At the next alert my sisters were placed between us, as a buffer, and the parrots turned it into a cruel game. From the top bunk I saw my father take a pencil and notepad out of his pocket and draw something, I couldn't see exactly what, something egg-shaped. He'd had an idea, perhaps the most original idea of his life. More on that later.

There was one drawback to Sofie and it bore the name Birgit—her best friend. She lived a few streets further south, and so was never in our air-raid shelter. I got to know Birgit in the middle of October, on a wonderfully sunny autumn day. I had whittled a branch into a lance and was roaming through the woods bathed in gold to the north of Allach; it was, moreover, the first year I'd been allowed to go more than a hundred meters from my parent's house and garden. Birgit was cycling along the gravel track beside the stream while I was skewering imaginary trout with my lance, a game which I decided was silly and infantile at precisely that moment. She came riding along in her brown League-of-German-Girls uniform and stopped, a not particularly good-looking girl with light-brown hair, a prominent chin and plump calves.

"Hey, you!"

"What?"

She asked if I was Alex. I said yes and she asked, "The one who's in love with Sof?"

I went across to her and spoke quietly, as if someone could hear what we were saying.

"Rubbish." I just said: rubbish.

"Oh, right then."

"Right then what?"

"Then nothing." And with that she got back on her bike. I ran after her, shouting, "Heeey, and if I were?"

"Then I was to tell you something."

"What?"

"Why d'you want to know if you're not the one?"

God, how I hated the little minx. "No reason. You don't have to tell me," I said, and she replied, cool as you like, "No, I don't have to."

I must have looked horrified, eyes bigger than five-mark pieces.

And Birgit, who was already three or four meters away, laughed, as if she took pity on me, and stopped again. "Oh, what the hell. Sofie'll be in the gravel pit at five. If you want to meet her."

"In the gravel pit. What for?"

"To meet you, numbskull."

She rode off and I couldn't believe my good fortune. My heart was pumping away like mad, my hands were sweaty. It just sounded too good to be true. Before long it sounded like a trap to catch me. Is that a pleonasm? What d'you think? Doesn't matter. Naturally I went. Still armed with my lance, I made my way stealthily to the gravel pit. It was a huge pit for gravel and clay with three craters, just perfect for battles of the Mescalero Apaches against cowboys and bandits. Far below, at the bottom of the biggest crater, was—Sofie. She was sitting there, playing with stones in her lap. I looked all around. We'd clearly be alone down there, completely alone. I threw my lance away and ran down, taking care not to stumble. My feelings? You must find words to describe them. High-sounding words. The truth can be bombastic now and then. Sofie's skin was gleaming in the late-afternoon light. She was wearing a white League-of-German-Girls blouse and under it, visible, she already had a brassiere. She said just two letters, said them so quickly they made a word:

"Hi." Not at all bombastic.

"Hi." Then silence for quite some time. Nothing happened. She examined her stones.

"What're you doin' here?" I asked.

"What're you doin'?"

I just shrugged my shoulders. There was something horribly heavy sitting on my tongue, a lead frog perhaps, blowing out its cheeks so much that not even the slenderest little word could get past.

"I'm collectin' stones. D'you collect somethin'?"

"Nah."

"Stones're pretty. Sometimes. And cheap."

"Really?" That "Really?" was so embarrassing! My heart was pounding, thumping in my throat, pushing against my larynx until the lead frog gave a croak and that terribly embarrassing "Really?" came out.

"How much pocket money d'you get?"

To be honest, the question took me by surprise, the frog shrank and I answered, truthfully, "Two marks."

"A month?"

"A week."

"Wow! You lot really are rich. Are you savin' up for somethin'?"

"What would I save up for?" I didn't know what she was getting at. And Sofie asked, without looking at me, "Would you like a kiss?"

"From you?"

Yes, it makes you laugh, doesn't it, but that's exactly what I said. Sofie looked around and said, quite correctly, that she couldn't see anyone else there. I tilted my head to one side and nodded, as if to say that was somewhat far-fetched but one could still think about it, just for fun.

"How much is a kiss worth to you?"

I said nothing, clueless. It was beyond me. How could you

put a price on a kiss from your beloved? Any answer would have been a desecration. Sofie, however, had an answer that shocked me.

"Fifty marks?"

Something inside me, a small, hoarse voice, whispered, *She wants a token of your love.* Now tokens of one's love are expensive, I knew that, but—fifty marks! An immense sum.

"That's . . . OK." Somehow I managed to clear my throat in agreement, but in a way that left me the possible excuse that it was all an amusing game. Sofie looked at me with a smile, cool, almost businesslike, and said, "Tomorrow? Here? The same time?"

"Mhmm," I murmured and she went, left me and climbed up the steep slope without once looking back at me.

I had ended up, strangely excited and confused at the same time, in the world of commerce. During the night I crept back downstairs, to my father's study, and stole three ten-mark notes from the drawer. The other twenty I had already. I almost wanted him to notice the theft, I wanted to be beaten for my misdeed. An immense token of my love. But my father didn't notice. He was too taken up with his great idea, sitting in the conservatory, brooding over technical drawings, in a circle of candlelight.

During that night I was happy. Yes. My father too, as it happens. In the morning he called the family together and showed us a telegram. He looked bleary but euphoric.

"Family."

He only used this lapidary form of address when there was something really special.

"The minister has announced he's coming. To dinner, to discuss a project, here, in our house. In three weeks' time, on the thirteenth, in the evening."

My mother started to clap. We children joined in, hesitantly, without understanding what an honor it was for our house. I can still see my father's face, radiant with pride. The architect who was now extremely successfully organizing Hitler's armaments program, the busy man, the Führer's favorite himself was going to visit us. At the time, of course, I had no idea of the significance of this. But Papa took me on his knee, something he almost never did, ran his fingers through my hair and explained that this man was a Titan of the age, a man of ideas and deeds, visionary and pragmatic at the same time. It was a very important day for *all* of us. He expected cooperation and discipline from *everyone* in the house. "Not the slightest thing can go wrong."

I had quite different worries. The world had to keep going until five o'clock that afternoon. As for the rest, I didn't care. I cycled to the gravel pit. Sirens sounding in the distance. Air-raid imminent. I didn't care. I just cycled more quickly, reached the crater, called down, "Sofie?"

She was indeed down there, sitting waiting for me. Bombs in the distance. What excuse could I make up for my parents' benefit? I didn't care. I went down and sat next to this strange girl; she didn't seem entirely calm, no, but not really nervous either, just a little.

Airplanes, high up in the sky. The anti-aircraft barrage started.

"Your first air-raid out of doors?"

"Yes."

"Mine too." She said it as if it gave her a pleasant frisson. And for the first time I found something to say which didn't sound completely stupid.

"The aircrew have a clear view. They won't be droppin' their stuff in gravel pits."

As if on cue, a bomb landed close by. We automatically moved closer together. You might not believe it, but we were close to laughing.

Suddenly the frog on my tongue said, "I love you."

"Saphead. You don't even know me."

"Still."

"Got the money?"

I showed her the notes.

"You must be absolutely mad."

"We're rich. Make the most of it."

"OK. Let's get it over with." She placed her arms on my shoulders. I hardly moved at all, didn't want to push her into anything. I'd expected a peck on the lips, I'd have been fully satisfied with that. And then—you have to visualize it: the sky over us ablaze with a deadly firework display and Sofie kissing me the way a grown-up woman would kiss a man to whom she's decided to give herself. It was so—so overwhelming, it was one of the greatest moments of my life. Just a minute though, I don't want to tell a lie. Perhaps it doesn't matter for the story, but when we kissed the fireworks were already over, the planes had changed course. Perhaps it doesn't matter, perhaps it was significant. I leave that to you. When Sofie and I, that is our lips, just our lips, separated, the all-clear was just sounding and she said she had to get home.

"Don't you dare tell anyone."

I gave her my word of honor. And gave her the money I'd been clutching in my hand all the time. She stuck the notes down her knee-length stockings, gave me a somewhat severe but sympathetic look and said, "Get over this love. It won't get you anywhere."

"Who knows. You don't even know me."

She gave a brief smile. Slightly cruel. I have never told anyone. No, never. Not until now.

I arrived home in the darkening twilight. My mother was standing at the entrance to our villa. She rushed towards me, clasped me in her arms—and fainted. She was too heavy for me to hold her, I had to let her slip to the ground and just held her head up until some of the staff hurried over and carried her into the house.

There's something I have to tell you. A little digression. My mother suffered from bouts of depression, which she considered shameful, which is why outwardly she appeared unobtrusive, studiedly so, as if she didn't want to attract attention to herself; she was pale and gentle, though always with pursed lips, behind which a storm was raging of which we knew nothing. I think she was afraid we children might have inherited her melancholia; whenever one of us complained of a headache you could see her pupils dilate with horror. Then she prayed and the praying helped her. Anyone who didn't know her very well might have got the impression she was naive, a good mother, blindly obedient to her husband. It was only later that I learnt how heroic she must have been, what immense self-control she exerted so as not to impose on everyone around her. She never complained, not even during her worst migraines. When they came she shut herself in her sewing room upstairs and cried into a cushion.

The harangue came from my father during dinner. I can remember that at the time everything in the Ice Palace seemed rather ghostly and mysterious. There'd been a new orders that stronger light bulbs were to be painted blue, so as not to give a sign to the bomber formations. In general the order was probably ignored, but our family felt it had to set an example. The bluish gleam made for a deeply melancholy atmosphere which affected us all, especially my father, during the following weeks.

"From now on you'll not go too far from the house, understood?"

I promised and declared I wasn't hungry. I didn't want a vulgar slice of cold sausage on bread to profane the lips with which I'd kissed Sofie. Honest!

The whole night through I lay in bed, eyes open. It was pure joy. I had a secret. I put my hands under the bedclothes and pulled them straight out again. From now on I wasn't going to cheat on my beloved with myself. How long did I stick to that? you'll ask. Five whole days. Then, on the fifth day, I was punished for breaking my vow. At least that's how it appeared to me.

My sisters ran into me on the upstairs landing, looked at me and started to scream. My face was mirrored in the glass of a family photo on the spiral staircase. It was covered in red blotches.

My father was told about it by my mother as he was brooding over his strange sketches. I could eavesdrop on what was said in the conservatory through the stovepipe.

"Chicken pox? He's got chicken pox?"

"There's a lot of it about just now. It's nothing to worry about."

"You think so? I never got chicken pox. Did you?"

"Yes. When I was little—"

"Damnation. I hope he's not infected anyone."

You must note the impropriety. My father had just said *damnation*. For him that was an incredibly coarse word.

"Three weeks in bed . . . "

"Three weeks in bed! Damnation!"

I heard him get up and start pacing up and down the conservatory in desperation.

"There's too much hanging on it. I can't risk having the Minister's visit put off for a . . . children's disease. Alex'll have to go into hospital. Otherwise he'll infect everything."

"Knut, you won't get a hospital bed for a boy with chicken pox nowadays."

"You leave that to me. After all, we're not just anyone."

Thus began a truly absurd chapter in my biography. Just imagine: with his contacts and a certain amount of money my father did indeed manage to get me admitted to a hospital run by nuns on Menzingerstrasse in Nymphenburg. So there I lay, in a bare and gloomy, high-ceilinged hospital ward. A black and gold brass cross above each of the five beds. Four held wounded, mutilated grown men. One held me. I heard that Sofie, among others, had caught chicken pox. Which of us had infected the other remained unclear. But from now on Sofie would hate me, about that there was no doubt. I was in hell.

Mother and the parrots came to visit me. Twice a week. The parrots had to keep well away from me.

"Your father can't come to see you. He's very sorry, but he thinks you'll understand. It's for Germany."

Unforgettable: my dear mother by my sickbed, the twins behind her; they brought me blancmange, cookies, chocolate and a picture they'd painted themselves. A picture of a boy, his face covered in big red blotches. Around me wounded, traumatized men, who spent all the time staring at the blancmange and the cookies. Only the chocolate I kept for myself.

During that time I heard things which were definitely not suitable for a boy of my age.

Then we came to the farm. The Russkies had gone. Not one of the reconnaissance party had been left alive. They'd cut the balls off one and nailed them to the barn door.

Things like that. Some stories they probably told only to scare me. They were rough, crude men, embittered and disappointed by life or, to be more precise, by the course of the war.

There were two sisters for our ward. One, Agnes, I liked, the other, Christa, was old and fearsome. Agnes looked after us by day, while Christa's arrival meant the start of the night shift.

"Well, gentlemen? Anyone need to go? Then it's lights out. No smoking in here. And I'd be grateful if the young man would be good enough not to wet the bed again. Otherwise we'll have to put him in diapers."

The rotten old bitch! After all, I was new to hell. There were bright spots, though. Being rubbed down with a warm cloth by Sister Agnes was the high point of the day. For all the patients. Every one of us had a hard-on, apart from Lieutenant Krollmann, as his equipment had been shot away.

I'd been in for two weeks. Agnes patted me, asked me how I was, the blotches were almost gone. She was a cheerful, wiry woman with a slight Berlin accent. "Five more days, then yer'll be out."

It was even sooner. That same day, November 3, the hospital was hit. At an air-raid alert all the patients were bundled off into the cellar, but it wasn't that simple and took more time than the bombers allowed. I remember patients hobbling along for dear life, cripples shoving each other against the wall just to get to the cellar in time. I prayed. Not to Mary. Hail Sofie Full of Grace. Blessed is the fruit of Thy womb. Her radiant image hovered over me. The rumble of thunder. The new east wing of the hospital was completely destroyed. From the ground-floor window I saw what was locally known as the *Galloping Gauleiter*, a kind of wooden substitute streetcar, come screeching around the bend and stop. People leaping out, cowering against the buildings. The sighs and screams of the people in the cellar. And then, after the raid, the silent, almost apathetic procession of the patients back to their wards, assuming they were still standing. On stretchers, in the main entrance hall, lay those who'd been killed. Among them, beside each other, Sister Christa and Sister Agnes. That was the day I discovered that God doesn't exist.

The next day I was sent home *almost cured*, the beds that were left were needed for more urgent cases. The telephone network wasn't working. I walked the three kilometers home to the Ice Palace on foot.

There were charred bodies lying along the road. Some looked as if they'd been crudely carved out of coal. Just imagine: I'd never seen a dead body before. And yet I was lucky in a way. Those corpses were like the mummies of Egyptian pharaohs in a book with black-and-white photographs. There could have been worse sights.

My father had tears of joy in his eyes when he saw me. Said he loved me. But he didn't embrace me. I was banished to the luxury of my room. The following day almost a thousand planes bombed Munich. Once more we were spared.

The things von Brücken recounted were in remarkable contrast to the *way* he recounted them. His voice remained surprisingly undermodulated, almost droning on, not signaling sarcastic remarks or tragic turns of events with *ritardando* or a change of pitch. In a fascinating way, this avoidance of dramatization intensified the aura of his narrative, giving it a particularly authentic tone. At the same time my attention suffered, though not because I was bored, far from it, it was more as if I kept slipping into a trance, as if I *felt* his words rather than heard them.

An element of unreality crept into the room, a—perhaps even intentional—alienation effect; I noticed him scrutinizing me now and then, thoroughly, but with sidelong glances, like someone who doesn't want to be importunate observing you in the compartment of a train.

At times I caught myself no longer listening; instead I was thinking about the unusually *non*-accentuated sound of a word.

Von Brücken switched off the tape recorder and invited me to join him for lunch. We ate in almost monastic silence.

Only once, after the soup, did he ask a question, about the book I was working on at the moment. I replied, vaguely, that it was a kind of biographical novel, about the composer Puccini. He gave a brief smile, but didn't seem interested in details, so we waited in silence for the main course.

The Afternoon

There was a map of Europe on the kitchen wall. Old Alfred, one of our servants, recorded the current state of the Allied advance with little colored flags so that everyone in the house, including myself, could see what the situation was. At first it didn't look that dangerous for Greater Germany. We stood firm in Norway, Italy and even, thanks to the Ardennes offensive, still in parts of France. Only on the Eastern front did the flags have to be moved a little to the left almost every day.

There was a corner in the garden where you could see out into the street through a crack in the wall. Despite being confined to my room, I regularly squatted by the crack trying to catch a glimpse of Sofie among the mass of workers leaving our factory in the evening, but I never saw her. Some factory workers were busy smartening up the Ice Palace. Beds were being weeded, strings of lights hung up and gardeners were kneeling on the lawn by the entrance trimming it with scissors. That's the truth.

For almost two weeks we didn't have to go down to the cellar. The siren sounded now and then, but there were no air raids. And I didn't know whether to feel happy about that or not; whether I would be able to look Sofie in the eyes again or not. But I wanted to see her. Absolutely. And didn't see her. The great day was approaching. My mother put her hands together and prayed: "Dear Lord, please let there be no alert tonight." She confused the Brits and Yanks with God.

My father felt guilty because he hadn't been to see me in hospital, and he tried to explain the reason. We were sitting in the conservatory, the evening before the great event; for the first time he opened up his mind to me a little.

"The Minister is above all an artist. A great artist never neglects his art. On the contrary. But he can only look forward to his dreams being realized after the final victory—what could be more logical, then, than to put his creative power in the service of our armaments? As an artist he's more radical than all the rest, yes, it's fantastic, it's fanatical and German, that's what other nations envy in us."

I was impressed, I have to admit. The next evening the drive up to the Ice Palace was illuminated.

I was not considered infectious anymore, so was allowed to await the Minister's arrival at the portal with the rest of the family. In jacket and tie, of course. If my mother had had her way, I would have had to wear a jacket and tie every day, but fortunately Papa was skeptical about such upper-class extremes. Children, he always said, should be allowed to be children and not stuck in excessive clothing. A belief for which we children should have loved him, had we understood the alternative. But it was obvious to us that it was a day for solemn celebration. What a spectacle! The torches alone went so much against the demands of the blackout; I came to understand the importance of illumination for great events. Two soldiers with machine guns mounted guard. The gravel crunched under the heavy tires of a limousine.

My mother must have had a gift for praying. For two whole days there had not even been an alert. Nothing. Onlookers had gathered at the garden gate. I saw Birgit. Three men got out of the limousine, in different uniforms and long, heavy coats, brown and black.

Papa had drummed it into us that we were to bow and curtsey politely then disappear upstairs. "From then on you keep out of sight. Promise?"

And now here he was, the greatest architect after the Führer himself. He stood there, arms folded above a slight paunch, posing for us, with the repertoire of gestures for an official visit at which one must put on a show of affability, like a politician visiting a kindergarten, say. The onlookers at the gate gave the Hitler salute, but remained silent.

"Minister, this is a great honor—"

"Heil Hitler."

"Heil Hitler. Of course." Papa went pale, as if he'd made an irreparable faux pas.

"My wife, Minister . . . My children . . . "

We all shook hands. The last was Keferloher.

"Heil Hitler. Keferloher, Herr Minister. Managing director. A great honor, Herr Minister. A great honor."

Keferloher had the habit of repeating important bits in a slightly lower voice.

The Minister looked tired but we took an immediate liking to him. "Good. Shall we get in medias res right away?"

"Certainly, this way.—Children." He ushered us into the house. The parrots obeyed dutifully and ran up to their room. Soldiers busied themselves putting out the torches. I, on the other hand, took advantage of the hustle and bustle to run down to the gate. The people who had gathered there were leaving. I tugged Birgit's sleeve.

"Hello."

"Hello, carbuncle."

"Is Sofie OK? Where is she?"

"Sofie's gone."

"Where?"

"She's dead."

My heart stood still. And that's not just a manner of speaking.

Birgit looked at me and grinned. "No. She's been evacuated to the country."

I heaved a sigh of relief. "Since when?"

"Yesterday."

I looked around. Surrounded by the soldiers with the sub-machine guns, my father called out, "Alexander."

I ran back to the house. Papa sent me upstairs. "Off you go."

Half an hour later my mother took me to bed. "Keep your fingers crossed for your father. And go to sleep."

So that was how things stood. Lights out. Sofie: evacuated. That meant relative safety. Sofie was a long way away. Somewhere. Where no bombs fell. A long way away from me. I couldn't sleep that night. I got up, crept out of my bedroom and down the back stairs, a narrow, cast-iron spiral staircase, made it to the library, opened the dumb waiter, which was no longer in use, climbed in and raised the flap a little, just enough to make a peephole for me to see into the dining room.

They'd just finished dinner. My mother withdrew. That left the Minister with his adjutants, Papa and Keferloher. And Erna, our ugly serving maid, who was pouring red wine into round-bellied glasses. The blue bulbs hadn't been changed, but the large number of candles made the light feel cozier.

"Goodness me!" the Minister exclaimed. "Petrus! A nineteen-twelve Petrus! Where did you manage to get that?"

"I've taken the liberty of tapping a few sources," my father said *sotto voce*.

"You should do that more often. Especially with regard to your factories."

Many things happened that evening. Many things I didn't understand at the time. I managed to make sense of some of it with things I learnt later. My father's factories had hardly suffered any damage at all. Given that, their output was less than the Ministry expected. That much I could understand, even then. My father must have got on the Minister's nerves the whole evening. He had come to increase the company's production, not to chat about architecture. I presume my father didn't realize that. Since, in practice, it was Keferloher who ran the factories, Papa didn't know the answer to many of the questions. That irritated the Minister even more.

"Fantastic wine."

"Thank you."

"Frankly, Herr von Brücken, I'm hardly surprised you have time to concern yourself with that kind of stuff." The Minister drank in moderation but seemed unused to wine, I soon began to notice him stumbling over his words slightly.

Keferloher rushed to father's assistance. He cleared his throat: "Everything is perfectly in order here. Taking the current difficulties into account, our output is almost unchanged. Almost unchanged."

I couldn't say exactly what the Minister replied to this, it was all above my head. Today I would give it something like the following subtitles: Difficulties are challenges. Demand countermeasures. Stagnation's nothing to be proud of.

"Certainly not," my father said, "what can be done, will be done. I have to say, though, that the technical side of all that's not really my field. I should perhaps tell you that actually I'm an architect, not an economist. My special area is neo-Romanesque religious buildings, a subject in which you, as I've been told, once showed an interest."

"But that's not what we're here to discuss this evening."

"To be sure. However . . . "

Don't get me wrong. I'm not entirely sure what was going on, I was little more than a child and all I can remember is the feeling I had at the time. But that feeling was clear: my father sounded pretty superfluous. And that is putting it mildly.

He waffled on about old churches and what they meant for the tradition of the German nation. To be honest, I found it a bit embarrassing. The discussion at the table grew louder. Men gesticulating. Keferloher with plans and statistics. The Minister was here as a warmonger, a commander, not as an architect. Keferloher did his best to present facts and figures, to help my father by supplying the things he so badly lacked that evening.

"Fantastic wine. They should really be drinking it on the Western Front. So our soldiers know what they're fighting for." The Minister was getting more and more tipsy. Instead of being relieved, my father asked for a private word with him in the conservatory.

"It's important, Herr Minister. Important for the war effort."

The Minister didn't seem very keen, but if something was important for the war effort, who was he to object? So the two of them went to the conservatory and I transferred to the upper floor, to the stovepipe. Finally Papa revealed his idea.

"You perhaps have the wrong impression of me."

"Oh, yes?"

"I am very conscious of the needs of the German people, of the demands of our present situation, my designs are not solely *for peacetime*. I have something very practical in mind. Have a look at this, please. I'd very much like to hear your opinion."

"What is it?"

"The principle underlying the design is the scientifically proven fact that of all containers the ovoid has the most resistant surface. A triple system of pipes in the internal layer of the covering with a connection to the roof space ensures the air supply for several hours when the shelter has been buried beneath rubble. As long as there is not a direct hit, the bunker will withstand almost any blast wave. The oviform structure is ideal where there is falling masonry and extremely economical on space. Taking up minimum space, there is room inside for six people, say father, mother and four children. It could go into production. We could call it the *Volksbunker*."

"A private air-raid shelter?"

"Yes."

"One for every household?"

"Well, no. Not immediately. Bringing it out would cost a pretty penny. At first it would only be individuals—"

The Minister did not let my father finish. "Are you out of your mind? Do you realize what you're asking me to do?"

I heard the adjutants, their curiosity aroused, come into the room. I hurtled down the stairs in my stocking feet, went out by the back door, crept over the damp grass and looked in through the window. On my knees, well camouflaged by a bush.

My intention was to hasten to my father's aid, but once down there my courage left me.

At least in the excitement I hardly felt the cold.

"A family-sized *Volksbunker*!"

The adjutants started to hoot with laughter. Keferloher managed to control himself, but had to fight against the laughter welling up inside him. My father sat down. He never got over that laughter.

"My God, What century am I in? What war did you design this thing for, Herr von Brücken? Far be it from me to disparage your ingenuity, perhaps it'll even work, but just think: it is precisely in moments of danger that the nation must demonstrate its unity. Your aristocratic private air-raid shelter, all your neo-Romanesque delusions . . . Which war are you fighting here, actually?"

The Minister no longer seemed amused. His voice took on a threatening note.

"If this war is lost, the result will be a Germany without Romanesque, Gothic or any other kind of churches. Can't you get that into your head? A Germany without Germany! Do you realize what will happen to us then? Can you comprehend the historical consequences of defeat?"

I saw my father cry. He sat there motionless, not daring to wipe the two tears from the corner of his eyes, just sat there, sat to attention, in a way, but with trembling legs that would no longer bear him. It was so humiliating and embarrassing, above all because the Minister was probably right. The horrors of the war, which so far had left us relatively unscathed, poured into my father and took possession of him. I think that until then he'd had no idea just how bad things were. And the Minister, now clearly inebriated, showed no sign of wanting to leave him in peace.

"Do you know where we are, Herr von Brücken? Do you realize what time it is?" He hissed the words angrily, but there was a touch of desperation in his voice.

At that moment my mother, surprisingly and effectively, came through the door of the conservatory and pushed her way in between the adjutants.

"I think it's quite late, Herr Minister."

The way she said it, sharply and decisively, was extremely courageous. In that moment she was resplendent. All style and nobility. She was transformed into a woman who, if I may put it this way, gathered up her shadow and draped it over her shoulders like a Roman matron's stole. My jaw dropped. And the Minister's too. He thought for a moment and finally murmured. "Yes. Life is short, the evening long. All the best, Herr von Brücken. You will be getting new guidelines, Herr Keferloher. In writing."

"Heil Hitler," Keferloher bellowed.

The Minister turned to Mama. "My compliments, Frau von Brücken. Thank you for the wine."

"Heil Hitler," my father whispered, no, croaked, then let his arm drop and stared into space, a broken man. After that night, he hardly looked anyone in the face anymore, he looked past everyone he spoke to.

TWILIGHT

Winter arrived. On November 22 Germany's outstanding Renaissance church, St. Michael's, was almost completely destroyed, several holes were blasted in the magnificent barrel vault, the façade collapsed, the roof timbers were smashed. Papa, completely downcast, took me with him to inspect the damage. I had sworn to be a good son to him and to show interest in everything he told me. Unfortunately, with the best will in the world I couldn't drum up any enthusiasm for the church and I was ashamed of myself because of it. There's not much to tell about those months. Sometimes I sat by the pond throwing snowballs in and watching them float. A strange sight, floating snowballs when the pond was iced over and all that was left of the snowballs were little domes, like igloos in the Arctic wastes. There was a bomb crater in the middle of the tennis court. That was the nearest the bombs came to us.

Papa grew taciturn. There were even days when he forgot to shave.

In the air-raid shelter everything was as it had always been. Except no Sofie. Terrible nights. Sofie's parents looked washed out and emaciated. I asked my father to let them have the odd thing, but he refused, saying he couldn't give certain workers preferential treatment. He was right, the people weren't actually starving, there was enough bread and potatoes, sauerkraut was an excellent source of vitamins over the winter. They'd simply lost any sense of enjoyment. I tried Sofie's friend Birgit. Was Sofie OK? Had she heard anything? She'd got to the country safely, she said. That was all she knew.

Could I write to her?

"I'm not to tell you exactly where she is. You can always ask her parents. If you dare."

"Is she coming home for Christmas."

"Idiot. The ideas you get!"

In the twilight, at the end of the second shift, I hung around the factory buildings watching the workers come out of the sheds. Among them were Sofie's parents. Her father was limping, it was the first time I'd noticed, he was coughing too. I said good evening to Frau Kurtz, in passing, as if it were a chance meeting. Then I turned back and said, "By the way." Yes, that was just the expression I needed to make it sound even more casual.

"I was going to ask about your daughter. How she is."

Frau Kurtz had aged prematurely. She looked more like Dürer's mother than that of a lovely creature.

"Don't come butting in where you're not wanted, young man. Let it be."

And old Kurtz, in coarse, phlegmy Bavarian, said, "Shove off."

Frau Kurtz tried to calm her husband down. "Shh! Johann!"

Her gesture—she grabbed his arm and shook it—presumably said that I was the son of the big boss and he should restrain himself. But that didn't stop her from grabbing *my* arm immediately after and shaking it too.

"We ain't stupid. Just take a look at my man. Can't hardly walk. And now these extra shifts. Wanted to help us, did our Sofie, with your fifty marks. But once you start that kinda thing I know where it's goin' to end. At first she wouldn't tell us where she'd got it. Then you both went and got chicken pox, the whole street was talkin' about it. Just keep away from us from now on."

So that was it. Sofie had done it for her parents. I went bright red with shame. And defiance.

"But I only want to write to her."

"We're not havin' that. No."

They walked off and left me there. One of the workers gave me a shove, just like that, just for fun, into the snow. Other workers laughed. I was furious, I called out, though not in my loudest voice, "But you still took the money."

They won't have heard it. I hope not. Such ordinary people. At the time I thought, some people only exist to beget children who are different to them, altogether different.

Then Christmas came. Bluish light. The parrots played a piece for four hands, I can't remember which. A new family photograph was put up on the wall of the main staircase. We were all smiling, apart from Papa. No comparison with all the earlier, happier photos. Dürer looked down on us sadly. It wasn't that we were poorer, from the material point of view there wasn't much difference from the previous Christmas. As night fell we children were allowed to open our presents. Clothes for my sisters, an engraved wristwatch for me. The cook laid the table.

Alfred served glasses of cinnamon punch, the electric light was switched off and candles lit. Mother and the parrots sang "Silent Night, Holy Night." I accompanied them on the trombone. My father, in his favorite plush chair, hummed along quietly. I got fed up with music, started playing wrong notes.

"Come on. You can do it. Just once a year," cried Mama, but my father waved her urging aside. That was strange, as he usually set great store by doing your duty, especially when it contributed to the family idyll.

"Constanze, Cosima, will *you* play us something nice?"

The Cocos sat down at the piano again and played a Bach chaconne. They were really making an effort, and what happened? In the middle of the piece his daughters were playing, Papa began to talk to himself. My sisters tried to ignore it and plowed on.

"No Christmas trees for sale in the city."

My mother put a hand on his shoulder, but it made no impression on him.

"No bells. No church services. No Midnight Mass."

Irritated, the Cocos broke off playing. A silly, high-pitched laugh was heard, a bizarre "hee-hee-hee," which sounded almost as if it was sung. I nearly forgot. Aunt Hee-Hee-Hilde, an old, white-haired woman, had come to stay with us. Sometimes she had moments of lucidity. Fewer and fewer.

"But we never went to Midnight Mass," my mother said. "You always refused."

"The churches are all unusable. Un-us-able."

Aunt Hilde: "Hee-hee-hee."

"I was in town. I . . . " Papa paused; he looked devastated. "Darkness. Pitch-black. Windows boarded up, rubble everywhere, charred beams . . . " The things he was saying frightened us children.

"It's just the way things are. Let's be grateful for what we have." Mama ran her fingers through his hair, an unusually tender gesture which, a few months ago, would have been unthinkable in our presence. The cook announced that dinner was served. Our staff had been decimated. The gardener was working half time in the factory, as were the cleaners. I'd got rid of my tutors. Who knows where they were at that moment, what sacred duty for Germany they had to perform.

Dinner began with a simple potato soup. Aunt Hilde found a surprising number of things very funny, her shrill hee-hee-hee kept echoing around the room. What was even more eerie: my father joined in, laughing softly. Around nine Keferloher arrived with his son Lukian.

I can't remember whether at that point Volker, Keferloher's elder son, had already been killed or not. I think he had. We didn't talk about it. Long-stemmed glasses were handed around, two bottles of Sekt were opened, perhaps even genuine Champagne, at the time the difference meant nothing to me, but our wine-cellar was still full, so it could have been champagne.

"Last month our production rose by four per cent again. That's some good news for you, if you need it. Let's drink to it. And let's hope out sons can play tennis together again in the coming year." Keferloher raised his glass.

Just a minute. I'm getting my memories mixed up. That wasn't our Christmas dinner, it was the New Year. I looked at my watch. It had a second hand!

"Hee-hee-hee." Aunt Hilde stayed with us a whole week, I remember now. She was my father's sister, though only a half sister, I never found out the details, apparently there was an episode in the family history people didn't talk about. I was told my grandfather had married twice, but I think he was only married once.

"It's almost time." Mama switched on the radio. A Strauss waltz was playing.

"Twenty seconds to go!" I cried. My watch was incredibly accurate. When the two hands met, the radio announced the arrival of the new year with a long beep.

"Cheers! Happynewyear!" we wished each other. My father silently clinked glasses with everyone. It was the first time my sisters were allowed a few sips of alcohol. The newsreader's voice came over the radio. "Here is Radio Berlin—" Papa switched it off.

Aunt Hilde: "Hee-hee."

Keferloher: "Herr Direktor?"

At first Papa did not react at all. A few words were expected from him, as was usual on New Year's Eve. With visible reluctance, he got up from his plush chair. We suddenly realized he was drunk, couldn't find the words.

"Germany . . . was very great and beautiful. There are two sides to everything. Dürer is looking down on you." It was scary. He was finding it difficult not to slur his words. "Yes. The new year. Nineteen hundred and forty-five. It will bring something. Definitely. That is almost unavoidable. We will all get through it with dignity."

Embarrassed silence. But do you know what? Do you want to know what I was thinking at that moment? I'd been in love. Was still in love. That's exactly what I was thinking, with total, solemn earnestness. Let the world crumble, burn to ashes and disappear—I had been in love.

It sounds ridiculous perhaps, but in bed that night I was reconciled with life, which had granted me everything that was needful. My prayers were for Sofie: May life lavish its gifts on her, as it had on me. That was my plea to destiny. Yes. I don't mind it you put it in less high-flown words, with a touch of contemporary sarcasm, but that's the way it was.

Everyone has certain sacrificial altars in their life, dark places, patina, cobwebs, the cold of suppression, an icy hole, a vacuum, walls covered in images, where things are allowed to become unreal because they were lost. Every night I thought of Sofie and imagined her naked, bathing in a river. I saw her rise from the water, saw her budding breasts stiffen in the light breeze, her wet hair sticking to the back of her neck, and she put the little finger of her right hand in her belly button and flicked the tiny puddle away, squatted down and rubbed her thighs with a towel.

But one thing I must make clear: my dream never got much more obscene. I didn't dare incorporate myself in the picture. I was always on the outside looking in, content with quiet contemplation.

I can't remember anything special about January. Apart from a public funeral ceremony for those who had fallen in the air raids, an obligation to which my father took me for the first time, a pompous ritual, perhaps the last of its kind to go ahead undisturbed. Representatives of the Party, the state, the city and the armed forces as well as family members lined the cemetery square, decorated with pennants, where the coffins covered with the Reich flag had been set up between flames burning in tall stands. Members of the armed forces and political leaders formed the guard of honor and there was a further guard of honor composed of special units of the army, the *Luftwaffe*, the *Waffen SS* and the police. Giesler, the *gauleiter*, and Fiesler, the mayor of Munich, made speeches in memory of those who had died. Giesler and Fiesler, a rhyme that gave rise to countless jokes. After the funeral march the Führer's gigantic wreath was laid. As a matter of interest, only Germans were counted as *fallen*, foreign victims were referred to as *dead*.

In February there was only one incident worth mentioning. It wasn't something that happened to me, however, but something I was told by Lukian. Just imagine: Keferloher was sent draft papers for his one remaining son. On his sixteenth birthday.

Keferloher's horrified. He thinks about it and calls his secretary: "Schneider."—I think he was called Schneider, but I won't insist. If Schneider sounds too common, choose another name. What am I going on about? You have to use different names anyway.—Well, Schneider comes in and Keferloher asks him how many workers are absent. Twenty-five have reported sick.

Any infectious diseases going around?

No, says Schneider, as far as he knows there are no infectious diseases at the moment.

"And chicken pox?"

"Died down. No new cases since January."

"Check with BMW. And Krauss-Maffei."

Schneider looks baffled. "Ask whether there are any cases of chicken pox?"

Keferloher, as if he can't understand why Schneider needs to ask: "Yes."

To cut a long story short, they found a fat girl, eighteen years old, who was in bed with a rash, the last case of chicken pox for miles around. The important thing was to gain a few weeks. Keferloher got three for his son. He was a remarkably good father. The rest you can imagine.

"Do it!"

Lukian: "I can't."

Keferloher: "Just do it."

Lukian forced himself and gave the girl a kiss. A real one.

The girl, a fountain of wit, said, "Now you'll have to marry me."

Keferloher gave the girl's parents a parcel with ham, and schnapps. Lukian finds the whole business embarrassing, even today, but sometimes, when he's had a few, he'll tell the story. Funnier than my version. You're young, you can't realize the risk they were taking. If the worst had come to the worst all those involved could have ended up on the scaffold for something like that. And I mean *all*. But it was OK. Lukian fell ill and his draft was put off for a month.

That Schneider was a swine, though, tried to profit from the affair. He told my father what he'd observed, his suspicion that Keferloher was "undermining the national war effort." Father put him in his place—and put him in charge of a branch factory. Papa must have found it very hard to go against his principles in that way, but loyalty was a principle too, and protecting a six-teen-year-old from military service, especially one who was the son of his deputy, was a matter of course for him.

From then on Keferloher thawed and regarded my father as a kind of friend.

"May I speak openly?" I heard Keferloher ask in the conservatory. Papa nodded and the two of them went out so that they could talk without witnesses. But it was snowing and they didn't go that far into the garden so that I managed to hear a certain amount of what was said. My breath clouded the windowpane, making me invisible, and I pressed me ear against the glass.

"The war's lost." Keferloher's voice was trembling. Saying that out loud was tempting fate, it could cost him his life.

"Are you sure?"

"Yes."

"And?"

"We could get out of all this."

"Out of the war?"

"And out of what's coming afterwards."

"Where could we go?"

"Anywhere, anywhere."

There was a longish pause, then I heard my father's voice, expressionless, resigned. "You can do what you think right. We're all on our own now, every one of us."

The next thing I can remember is a conversation with my father in some ruined church. It was the middle of the day but it was hardly light at all, just leaden darkness all around. My father spoke. I recall his words as being underscored by an immense echo.

"I've brought you up as conscientiously as I was able."

"Yes, Papa."

"I don't know if everything was right. I thought it was. If we lose the war, a lot of things will probably have been wrong. I don't know if I've been a good father to you."

"Definitely."

The conversation was disturbing and at the same time slightly embarrassing. The tears were running down my father's cheeks. How could he let himself go like that?

"I love you, my son. I love our family. I loved Germany."

Do you know what I was thinking at that moment? That if only I were sixteen I could be a great hero and bring about a decisive turn in the war through one great, totally unforeseeable heroic deed.

At the end of March our factories were badly hit for the first time. The air-raid warning failed completely. Schneider was killed, along with fifteen workers, including Sofie's parents. They hadn't managed to get to the shelter in time, were burnt alive halfway there.

I had managed to get inside my beloved's mind to such an extent that I mourned them as if they had been my own parents. My future parents-in-law dead. Who would break the news to Sofie? Anyone at all? And suddenly there was a part of me that refused to believe in chance. Out of all the employees it had to be Schneider and Sofie's parents. It was crazy, certainly, but in all the madness I started to believe in a power whose fury was not so blind as at first appeared. To put it another way: from now on there was a tacit accord between me and the powers that ruled in heaven. I went into Sofie's parents' house, just like that, with all the boldness of someone who had a charmed life, saw Sofie's portrait photo on the wall of a poverty-stricken, poorly heated shack. No one stopped me. I remember a feeling of embarrassment—and something like . . . let's call it gratitude to her dead parents. I rummaged around in all the drawers. Found postcards Sofie had sent. At last I knew where she was staying. Less than a hundred and fifty kilometers away, in a village in the Allgäu.

That same evening I went to see Papa.

"I want to go to the country."

"What?"

"I want to be evacuated to the country."

My father, almost indifferent, scarcely of this world anymore, replied dully, "Why?"

"Sofie's parents are dead."

"Sofie? Who on earth is that?"

"She was with us in the air-raid shelter. The one in the same bed as me."

"Oh. Yes. I remember." Pause. "You want to go and join her?"

"Yes."

"Don't say you're in love with her?" I was encouraged by the almost cheerful tone in which he said it.

"Yes, Papa."

"Things go on. Life just continues regardless, doesn't it?"

I couldn't understand what he was getting at, so said nothing.

"Go to your room."

"Why?"

"Go to your room!" He shouted it out loud, it frightened me.

Mama brought me my supper: bread and butter with strips of pickled beetroot. Looked a bit like blood. Mama stroked my head, a gentle touch, just with her fingertips, very slow, soft, dreamy.

"Why? Why do I have to stay here? What have I done wrong?"

Mother gave me a forgiving smile. Her hair had gone gray over the winter, her complexion seemed paler than ever. With every day her vitality dwindled.

"It's the way things are. You'll see how things are when when you've children of your own. You can't understand before you do. Go to sleep now."

She gave me a kiss on the forehead and put a marzipan candy on my bedside table. Odd, since I'd already cleaned my teeth. That wasn't like her.

She left, went back downstairs and there was nothing to keep me in bed any longer. I was overcome with a very strange feeling. How shall I describe it? Goose bumps all over my body. Fear. A numbing, draining sort of fear, heavy as lead, with no apparent cause. Should I creep downstairs? Oh, I was a master at creeping, I'd perfected it, knew every place on he stairs where a carefully placed foot wouldn't make the wood creak too loud. I was an Apache. A German Mescalero.

My father was sitting in his plush chair, drinking red wine. There was something wrong. The light. Someone must have removed the blue bulbs. The Ice Palace was brightly lit, at least on the ground floor. At first I assumed Mama must have ordered it because she was worried about her husband, attributing his increasingly depressed state of mind to the blue light rather than the way the war was going. There were no servants in the house, as was usual after eight o'clock. My mother was kneeling on the floor, beside Papa, he was stroking the back of her hand, she his cheeks. The siren started its wail. Air raid imminent. The two of them hardly reacted. Mama said, with a sigh, but not really worried, "Oh dear, and the children have just got off to sleep."

"Let them be. We'll stay here tonight."

"But then I'll have to put the light out."

"No. Stay here. I've opened the last bottle of Petrus. Have a drink with me'

"But it always makes me giddy."

"Have a drink. With me. Please . . . " He poured a glass for her. Then I couldn't repress a cough. My father started, I ran quickly upstairs, threw myself on my bed. I heard steps outside the door, but no one came in, the steps receded again. I jumped out of bed, put on some clothes so I wouldn't catch cold. The siren wail changed, I rattled the doorknob. The room, my room, was locked. From the outside.

That had never happened before, never. And certainly not during an air-raid alert. I panicked. I put on some shoes, the only ones I had in my bedroom, white tennis shoes, opened the window, looked down, hesitated, hesitated for several minutes, then at last I jumped down into the snow.

Through the window into the sitting room it all looked peaceful. My parents were talking. I couldn't hear what they were saying, couldn't read it from their lips either, but the impression I had was of a quiet, affectionate conversation. Then Mama toppled over. That was nothing out of the ordinary, one of her usual fainting fits, my father gave her a kiss, then left her lying there and went up the main stairs holding the half-full bottle.

So there I am, outside the brightly lit villa, freezing cold and not knowing what's happening upstairs. Repressing a cry, I decide to run off, simply run off. Out into the country, to Sofie. But I can't. Something's calling me back, a scarcely audible voice, something inside my head. The wind's whistling, my tennis shoes are getting wet and cold, I go closer to the house, the door to the conservatory's ajar, I go in. Mama's on the floor in the sitting room next door. She doesn't move when I give her a tug, not even when I shake her and hit her. Now bombs can be heard from the north. I run up the stairs, past Dürer, past the photographs from happier times, the eyes of the people in the pictures bore into me, although viewed objectively there's no time for me to perceive that, given how fast I'm running. The doors to both the children's rooms are open. My sisters are beside each other in bed, their arms crossed over their breast. It looks unreal. I hear someone calling my name in the distance. It's my father, he's outside, in the garden. A loud, desperate cry.

"Alexander!"

I run down to the library. Hide behind the glass-fronted bookcase with the first editions. Footsteps on the main stairs. I dash out into the garden. Run from bush to bush, crouching down.

"Alexander!"

The front door's open. What a magnificent building, brightly illuminated in the darkness. My father's in the doorway, panting, looking all around, looking for me, his son that is lost. A bomb lands quite near, a fragmentation bomb, glass shatters in the conservatory. My father staggers around the ground floor, I see him staggering, from one window to the next, still clutching the bottle of red wine. He comes back to the door, yells out into the garden.

"Alexander! I love you! Alexander! Where are you?" He'd cut himself, was wiping blood off his forehead. A series of bombs go off, all in our district. The house catches fire. The horizon is lit up by severe explosions. Just a few searchlight beams wandering aimlessly around the sky. I hunker down behind my bush and pee, I feel defenceless, but I have to have a pee. Papa staggers out into the garden, plods through the snow towards me, even though he probably can't see me. When he gets too close, I run away, around the back of the house.

"Son! Stay here." It wasn't the whole house that was burning, just the library. The fire was spreading slowly from there. Not like wildfire, but slowly, strangely slowly. A strong wind was blowing that night. My mother was lying there and her face, her face was white, shining white, looking as if she had accepted what had happened. Because it was the way things were. I felt my father's breath on the back of my neck and ran away from him, up the main staircase, into my room, and jumped down into the garden for a second time, ran to the pavilion. I felt the need to have a roof over my head, even if it was only the pavilion roof. By now the whole ground floor of the Ice Palace was in flames. It took half an hour for the fire to eat its way up the stairs to the roof timbers. From time to time I heard my father calling. Calling my name. The Ice Palace was aglow and my father was standing there, tearing off his jacket and shirt, my dear father was calling my name. And I was ashamed. Ashamed because I was a miserable wretch, a creature without honor. *Here am I, your son, take me with you.*

Papa was upstairs, at one of the windows, and started to scream. Not my name, no, just single sounds. And how could I have gotten to him up there?

It was terrible—and slightly comic, too, grotesque is probably the right word, since I had to laugh. Laugh hysterically. I hope he drank the bottle in time and wasn't burnt alive. Suddenly I was overcome with a feeling of intense melancholy.

Somewhere indoors *he* was leaving me in some way or other—and he would have liked to take me with him. *Papa!* I called out and, as if in answer, a bomb exploded behind the villa, a few more meters and it would have been a direct hit. The blast hurled me into the snow, my skin was hot and damp, I thought it was blood, it was only sweat, and I ran. Ran until I was well away. Across an uncultivated field and into the woods. Looked up. The sky an inferno over the tops of the conifers. Strangely moving. The end of the world in a chaos of flashes and the thunder of guns. There—the pool with a faint reflection of the lights in the sky. I thought I was on fire, so I lay down in the snow, dipped my face in the pool with ice floating on the surface of the water. And then I cried out. Into the icy water. Into a blackness I have ever since imagined will be the blackness of death, of that moment when death will attack the light from all sides and extinguish it, until all that is left is a deep rumbling, the dying echo of the last cry. I was close to unconsciousness, it was hovering over my head, so to speak. I rolled onto my back and pulled my head out of the water, just in time to stop myself drowning. Immediately the blackness closed over my head.

I have no memory whatsoever of the next few hours. Eventually I became aware of how cold I was. First light. I was striding along a gravel path, my trousers covered in mud. Crying. Licking tears from my cheeks and shouting. Something, anything. Factory buildings. They looked familiar. A group of people in the distance. Figures in leather coats. Blurred, unreal, angels and devils in one, who had deigned to come from another world to—I've no idea what, they sang, they bobbed up and down, dark-gray spectres. I collapsed.

When I woke up I was hot. There were several heavy woollen blankets on top of me and above them Keferloher's face. Behind his face, like a distant star, a very good-natured yellow lamp.

"Calm down. It's all right. All right. Fishes don't drown."
Then everything went black again.

It wasn't sleep into which I sank, it was a rejection of every sensual stimulus, without conclusive success, the things going on around me transferred to the second floor of reality, so to speak, muffled by the ceiling, but still there. My body wanted to sleep and struggled against a demon in my brain that refused to allow it to. The things I perceived were different from a dream, yet were couched in the logic of dreams, resulting in a hybrid world which I tried to smother with my thoughts, as you would smother a fire with blankets.

There was an argument. The whispers gave way to sentences that demanded exclamation marks. Images flared up, images my eyes could not retain, they slipped away, fragments sticking to my eyelashes. The voices danced around in my head. One I recognized, it was Lukian's. He shouted:

"I don't want to stay here!"

"Shut up, Luki!"

Little by little, the scraps of perception came together in meaningful sequences. I thought I was going to suffocate, Keferloher grasped my mouth with his thumb and forefinger. I'd probably been sick and he was picking the vomit out before I choked on it.

"Alex? Can you hear me? We're taking you to safety."

The next image was quite different, more metallic, colder, although there was the glow of several kindly yellow lamps. There was a warm feeling in my stomach, I must have eaten. I was sitting there, limp and apathetic, I could feel a trembling at my back, it wasn't me, it was the side of an aircraft I was leaning against. I was inside a transport plane. Squatting beside me, or opposite me, were people, all in civilian clothes, wrapped in blankets. I can remember: curses, pleas, the roar of the engines. People looking up, heads leaning back against the side.

"But I don't want to stay here!" That was Lukian again.

"Just a few more days and it'll be all over. All over."

I suspect we were on the little runway of the Krauss-Maffei factory. The engine noise grew louder, combined with a juddering that went right through my stomach and the back of my neck, the airplane lurched from side to side, then took off. I can't remember much about it. My first flight. And I saw, or thought, that all my fellow passengers were dead, dead people, perhaps not quite dead, but almost. Eight or ten passengers, all looking pale, faceless, even the two women in their ridiculous furs. One had several chains around her neck and was crying. Then she laughed. And stuffed the knuckles of three of her fingers in her mouth. Someone calmed her down with a kiss.

One of the last of the factory planes to fly out. Keferloher must have decided I should have the free place instead of his own son. But why? And where were we going? Without any financial resources, only the things I was wearing, some of Lukian's clothes that more or less fitted. He was still almost a child and always said he couldn't remember that night, claims he never knew any precise details. The destination, he said, was northern Italy, where we could board a larger plane in relative safety, the front near Bologna being pretty quiet, or, with Vatican passes, take a ship from Genoa to South America, where everything had been prepared for a life in exile. There was something comforting about the drone of the two propellers. I didn't think about what had happened to my parents, to my sisters. As if they had never existed. Years later I learnt that the bodies in the Ice Palace were so charred that no one noticed the real cause of death. There was no slur on my family's reputation. There was no time for autopsies. It was assumed I was buried beneath the rubble, though I was at least recorded as *missing*, not as *dead*, less out of optimism than the conscientiousness of German bureaucracy.

That is what I know. What comes after is a gaping hole. Filled with dreams, with occasional lights lost in the dark. I was no longer of this world. A blinding flash. A loud, dull thud against the outside of the plane. Immediate blackness. Voices very far off—fear, pain, mechanical noises, wind—a fine, densely woven tapestry of noise, a teeming tangle of sounds and din. A field. Early morning, sunshine. Sparse woodland. My clothes singed, torn in places. Blood on my forehead. Or was that my father? No, his expression is empty, drained, rapt, mine is suffused with blood. Papa disappears into the clouds, I am alone. Over there a field, unplowed, everything in the brilliant overexposure of an Arcadian vision.

All I registered of this were the fringes, a wide river, the sun mirrored in the water so bright that it hurt, right through from my eyes to the back of my head. I was deaf, stone deaf. Inside me a chirping, a drilling and rubbing, a scraping, a rumbling, low frequencies. Different colors. The river settles for a rich reddish-brown, the water's sometimes black, sometimes purple, then light gold, the gravel silvery, the flora on the bank a bilious green. And that is the last thing I remember. I'm walking along the river. Above the glittering water is a vision of light, faint contours, a creature of kindness and love and a huge amount of hair on its head: *he* was there. Received me with a smile. Dürer was looking down on me.

POSTLUDE

There were just the two of us at dinner on the second floor, in a cozy room with a crackling stove and furnished in a pseudo-rustic, German Renaissance style. The food was not too extravagant, just asparagus soup, a light vegetable pasta, a meat course, fruit and cheese, two kinds of wine, coffee—he preferred hot milk. Neither of us spoke much. Von Brücken had been talking all day and now had no desire to open his mouth at all, except to pop in one of the few scraps of food he ate, or when a detail occurred to him that I had to note down right away. Unimportant details, that's all, there were pieces of paper for them on every table. He sometimes looked at me as if he were trying to find out how much I'd been impressed by his story, whether I was prepared to believe it all. Perhaps what he was telling me was already a touched-up version, enhanced by a few spectacular turning points. Why not? I thought that was possible, even probable, and it didn't bother me. After his death I would leave out anything I needed to so that it didn't sound made up. Perhaps I was thinking too loud, perhaps he could read that very thought in my eyes. Immediately he looked hurt and, without going into the matter, just nodded briefly and left. After a few lengths of the swimming pool and three single malts—doubles—I went to my room, escorted by a servant. I didn't sleep well that night. Around two in the morning I heard the noise of an engine, a small truck or something similar chugging up the floodlit drive. The noise came closer, cut out, the tires skidded on the snow a little. Really I was too tired to get up, but I did get up and confirmed that nothing could be seen from my window. Why was I here?

Why did the man who had commissioned me not simply have his story typed out, what did he need *me* for? Just to polish up his language a bit? Just so that his story had a different author from himself, the opposite to a ghostwriter, so to speak?

When von Brücken continued his story the following day, I thought I understood.

Through me he wanted to recover five lost years. Out of the few shreds and tatters he could still scrape together from those lost years, he wanted me to make him a carpet, a staircase woven out of ropes on which he could finally, and with dignity, stride over that gap, that abyss, victorious over chaos and darkness, with firm ground, or at least firmly invented ground beneath his feet. He couldn't give a damn whether he would ever read it or not, it appeared that the only things that existed for him were those that existed in writing at some point or other. Even with retrospective or prospective effect. ("What is written has, in a way, happened . . . ") It was some time before I could get inside his mind, even longer before I came to like it.

DAY TWO

Chaos

The stockpile of material. First-person perspective impossible for AvB. A few often recurring dreams. Only a few images branded on his mind can be retrieved, some real, others presumably left-overs from the trauma. Some things come from the unfeeling pages of medical or police files, mostly just names, places, journeys, medicines and not even much of that. Where the plane made its emergency landing and whether there were other survivors was never established. Somewhere close to the coast, probably to the north of the Po delta. A shack there. The sinister old man. Some things later brought back to the surface by hypnosis, but almost nothing from the early days. The old man going on at A. And A. not understanding. Not because he can't speak Italian. That's neither here nor there. But because A.'s deaf, deaf as a post. And dumb, rendered dumb by the severe trauma. Weeks pass, if not months, in the old fisherman's shack on the coast. Bread, water, fish. Condition: severe apathy, traumatic stupor, probably made worse by unsuitable food, lacking in vitamins. A roaring, the roar of the surf as it breaks, as a mantra. Although deaf, A. could feel the surf, not as sound, but as a light dance [*sic!*] on the skin of his shoulders and upper arms.

Despite intensive inquiries, it proved impossible to find out who the old man was (one slap, otherwise good-natured). Fleeting memories of black GIs having a barbecue on the beach. (Why no white ones?) An open-air cinema for the troops. Italian children leaning over the fence, watching. A. only sees it from a distance, as a strange luminescence when it's faintly reflected in the sea.

A shovel. A. has an intense, almost intimate relationship with a shovel. Takes it down to the beach, starts to dig a hole. Moments of conscious creativity. Horror: holes fill with water. The tragedy of every child: the collapse of the sand castle, undermined by water. Cold. The old man pulling A. up by his collar. A. staring out to sea. The pitter-patter of rain, audible on his skin. The stench of moldering fishing nets, beside which A. has to sleep, scantily covered. The old man squatting down. A dream: it's Knut, his father. Gives his cheek a little pinch. Stands up, goes out of the door towards the water, walks away on the water, heading for the horizon. A flash of lightning. The lightning turns the white horses purple. Inside the shack. Another dream: his father is sitting on coiled ropes.

Where were you? I missed you so much. His mother, very small, is lying in his father's lap. *If you only knew how great things are here. You must eat.* His sisters are sitting on a crate, in shining white clothes. Some gestures: spoon to mouth *(eat),* glass to mouth *(drink).* Day. The beach. The old man and Alex are sitting in the sand. He's smoking a cigarette, gives it to him. With a gesture tells him to take a pull on it. A. does, coughs. Two sentences, repeated over and over, that he can only hear when the old man shouts them at him from close to.

Nonseidelluogo. You don't come from here. And *nonmipuoiesserutile. I've no use for you.* Twilight. Smell of barbecued meat. Women's laughter. Black man holding out small piece of meat. A. smiles. The best mouthful of his life. The GIs laugh. A. runs off. A later memory: GI with violin, dancing and playing. A. can't hear, but he can sense vibrations in the air. The GI goes up to Alex, holds the body of the violin to his ear. A. hears the music: as a distant, deep hum that gives him goose bumps but is registered as *beautiful.*

Violent: the light of the lamp on the desk in police headquarters, behind it a carabiniere.

Funny headgear. Huge walrus mustache, gleaming black.

Carabiniere: "So?" He doesn't say it out loud, the gesture that goes with it's enough, the case is tiresome, there are so many young boys wandering around and this one's not even that young.

The old man, having established that the boy really is no use to him: "He's no use to me. Deaf and dumb."

"Can he write his name?"

"How should I know, I can't read . . . "

A presumed dialogue. The carabiniere shakes A., gives him paper and pencil. *Scrivi il tuo nome.* Write your name.

A. doesn't react. He's trembling because at that moment the plane's plummeting down for the thousandth time. He gets these attacks about twice a day, followed by a faint lasting roughly thirty seconds. The carabiniere takes off A."s watch. Holds it under the lamp.

On the back of the watch is engraved: *Von seinem Vater für Alexander.* For Alexander, from his father.

"C'è tedesco."

The old man: "He's been with me for months. I'm poor. He's no use to me."

No more memories of the old man, not even of a farewell. But a dead cormorant with no eyes in the bay. When?

A memory: yellow-red-pink-tinged mountains. One single image. Alps at sunrise? When? A truck. A. terrified because the inside of the truck reminds him of the airplane. Next memory: at the entrance to a large room, the size of a sports hall. The dormitory of a Catholic home for orphans near Bad Reichenhall in Southern Bavaria. Later on AvB will buy it up and have it pulled down.

In the beds—three-decker bunk beds—young boys of all ages. A. is taken into the dormitory. By whom? He doesn't know. Is allocated an empty bed. Memory: the great happiness of going to sleep in that bed.

Memory of a breakfast room. The children making a lot of noise, A. can't hear any of it. His deafness must have non-traumatic, physical causes. Pus in his ears. It helps briefly if he squeezes it out with the tip of his little finger, but then it hurts incredibly. Damage to the inner ear, untreated for a long time. A. at the table, tea and rusks in front of him. The boy beside him takes his rusks. Alex reacts. Squeals like a stuck pig. First sound from a supposedly mute child. The boy puts the rusks back. They all stare at him.

Later. When? Medical examination room. The doctor bending over A., listening to his heart with a stethoscope. Lets A. listen to his own heartbeat through the stethoscope. But A. doesn't react, afraid of giving himself away through the far-off heartbeat.

A slip of paper: *Deaf since your birth?*

A. doesn't react. *This watch was found on you. Are you called Alexander?*

Again the doctor writes something on the paper. No reaction from A. The middle-ear infection is given very basic treatment. Sufficient to trigger off a small, very gradual improvement. His burst eardrums heal, his chronically inflamed inner ear, that was almost destroyed, regenerates, though that does take years. Hearing is never completely restored to his left ear. Despite that, his symptoms are presumed to be purely psychological.

The doctor, an ordinary general practitioner, brought out of retirement because of the lack of personnel, has no idea what to put in the section: "Mental condition." Plumps for *mentally deficient*.

Given his condition, A. is defenceless against the rough tricks the boys play on him, up to and including attempted rape. The orphanage records mention A. being locked up in October 1946 because of an extraordinary outburst of violence: he bit the genitals of an eighteen-year-old, paid for it with three broken ribs and bruises to the head.

A memory that fits: the dormitory. Night. Three older boys looking at him, bending over his bed, one kneels on A."s chest. A. screams. They grab him, keep his mouth closed, then hold his nose to make him open it again. A furious scream from a great distance, one of the boys is roaring with pain.

"He bit me, the swine!" A. remembers the very loud words clearly and with a certain satisfaction. That same night he's put in a broom cupboard. Treated like a vicious or rabid dog. After two days and nights, in freezing temperatures and without any hot meals, A. is transferred to xxxx psychiatric clinic (name not to be given), allegedly for his own protection.

Memory: A nurse asking what A. is called. The guard answers for the new patient that he might be called Alexander. It wasn't certain.

"Personal belongings? Valuables?"

"None."

A. begins to cry, to scream, the guard hesitates, relents and pulls something out of his trouser pocket.

"Wristwatch."

"Anything else."

"Well, he bites."

"You could say that of most of them here."

After that no new memories for a long time. Treatment according to the files: medium-strength sedatives. The clinic's daily report for August 11, 1947 mentions an incident relating to the plastic cutlery from US army surplus which had been received and was put into use for the first time for patients at risk of suicide or with violent tendencies. According to the report, A. had eaten his food then bitten his plastic fork in two and swallowed the prongs; he would certainly have eaten the rest of his cutlery had staff not intervened. Subsequently, the report states, A. was given metal cutlery again, but only spoons. A. cannot remember that incident, although his memory did slowly begin to store longer sequences, and more and more still unconnected images from the past returned, unfortunately confused, with no chronological order. A. keeps this strictly to himself, doesn't tell anyone, reacts to questions with either apathy or resistance, emits growls. Until over the course of two years he comes to trust Heinrich P., a trainee nurse, who treats him in a relatively decent manner and keeps trying to get him to communicate. From then on the further progress of patient A. can be reconstructed relatively clearly from the statements of the specialists involved.

According to Heinrich P., it was a *candy*, or, rather, a single word, that triggered off Dr. Fröhlich's (name changed) exceptional interest in patient A. One morning Heinrich P. had gone to the patient's room, picked up the breakfast tray to take it away to be cleaned, and wished him his usual good morning, placing the candy (a present from his fiancée) on the patient's bed—he didn't like marzipan himself. As he closed the door, the patient had said, *Thanks, Mom.*

On that day, as Heinrich P. recalled, the doctors were discussing the Basic Law, the new constitution proposed for West Germany, in the courtyard of the clinic, while advanced patients were doing light exercises with a leather football. Dr. Schäfer and Dr. Fröhlich were deep in conversation:

Dr. Schäfer: Then at least we'll have a constitution. Not neutral, that's all I say. Otherwise no one'll feed us."

Dr. Fröhlich agrees in principle. The Basic Law, he says, was a symptom of partition, but partition wasn't all bad. "Like a cell, the country has to split in order to grow,"

"Really? That's not a very patriotic outlook."

"It isn't?"

"Well, perhaps it is in a roundabout way." (*Dialogue reconstructed.*)

You've made all this work for me, you liar . . .

Led by the nurse, who is holding his hand, patient A. comes out of the door to the main building. Nurse P. listens to the conversation, then breaks in.

"Doctor Schäfer? I asked him" —he points to A.—"if he'd like to come out into the courtyard. He said , '*Yes.*'"

Dr. Schäfer doesn't take it seriously. "Aha?"

Dr. Fröhlich: "What's wrong with him?"

Dr. Schäfer: "Feeble-minded, lethargic. Deaf into the bargain. Perhaps not completely deaf."

Dr. Fröhlich: "Hmm."

Dr. Schäfer: "Normally he never comes out into the courtyard."

Dr. Fröhlich tells the nurse to let go of the patient.

The nurse lets go of A. A. takes a few steps toward the football. Looks at it. The football players pick up the ball, stick their tongues out at him. A. keeps his eye glued to the ball.

Dr. Schäfer: "At first everything indicated a trauma caused by the war. Total amnesia. But what kind of trauma continues unchanged for four years?"

Dr. Fröhlich objects that there had been cases. Soldiers, for example . . .

Dr. Schäfer: "Soldiers, yes. Of course."

Nurse P. reports with some enthusiasm that the patient had just said *yes* and *thank you*. Perhaps even *Mom*, but he was closing the door at that point, he could have been mistaken.

Dr. Schäfer plays it down. "Nah. Sometimes it just sounds like it. Erschh." He makes a sound in his throat that could be interpreted as *yes*.

"And when they swallow: *onk.*" He makes a swallowing noise ending in a click that could be taken for *thanks*. "Let's not get carried away."

A. keeps staring at the ball. Goes over to the little strip of grass below one of the high walls. There's a daisy. It's the beginning of May 1949. A. looks at the flower with noticeable concentration.

Dr. Fröhlich: "Does he have a name?"

Dr. Schäfer: "Alexander. Perhaps."

Dr. Fröhlich calls out across the courtyard: "Alexander."

A. doesn't react, stays bent over the flower. Dr. Fröhlich squats down beside him.

"What's that, then? Do you know? It's beautiful, isn't it? A flower. It's spring. Ssspring'

"Sss . . ."

Dr. Fröhlich tries to get him to say "flower." "Fll . . ."

A.: "Sss . . ."

" . . . ower." Dr. Fröhlich stands up, pats A. on the shoulder, turns away from him.

Nurse: "Should I take him back in?"

Dr. Schäfer: "You'd better. Before it gets too much for him."

Dr. Fröhlich: "I'm interested in the case. Will you hand it over to me?"

Dr. Schäfer: "If you want. But be careful, he bites." Dr. Schäfer whispers something to his colleague.

"Ouch!"

The patient is still staring at the flower. "Sss . . ."

The nurse helps A. up, pats him, tries to lead him indoors.

"Ofie . . ."

Nurse P.: "What?"

A.: "Sss . . ."

Nurse P.: "Daissssy. That's the flower's name."

A.: "Sss . . ."

Nurse P.: "Come along then, young man."

A.: "So . . . fie . . ."

Nurse P.: "You feel so feverish, yes? We'd better get you in then."

He puts his arm around his waist, but patient A. shakes him

off. Croaks. Loud, still slurring his words, but understandable with a little good will.

A.: "I . . . want . . . to . . . stay . . .

Dr. Schäfer, witnessing this scene, expresses his surprise in rather drastic fashion.

"Great shit!"

Dr. Fröhlich can't resist ribbing his colleague. "Abracadabra—only been my patient for ten minutes and he's chatting away already."

Dr. Schäfer grits his teeth and hisses softly.

During the weeks that follow patient A. still speaks rather hesitantly, he has to relearn how to articulate fluently. Dr. Fröhlich now spends several hours each day on the case, eventually taking Alexander home with him where his rehabilitation continues apace. His remaining memories can soon be ordered chronologically. And they're constantly increasing.

A few years later Nurse P. is given a villa by his former patient. A great career opens up for Dr. Fröhlich. But that's still in the future. Five weeks later Alexander and Dr. Fröhlich are riding in a streetcar in Munich. The doctor has undertaken the excursion on his own responsibility and at his own risk. The boy is interested and eager to learn.

"Is the Führer really dead?"

"As far as we know. Yes, I think he is. Let's assume so."

"Did the Americans . . . eat . . . him?"

Dr. Fröhlich doesn't know what to answer. Perhaps the boy is mentally disturbed after all. Some of the things he says suggest that.

The two of them are standing on overgrown land. Midday. July 1949. They are looking at the remains of the gravel drive leading up to the Ice Palace. All that is left of the main building are charred walls, of the garden pavilion just the foundations, the wood was presumably chopped up for firewood. Alex is wearing old clothes that are much too big for him, lent him by the doctor from his wardrobe.

"This is where you lived, you say?"

Alex nods.

"Let's try again. Your sisters were called?"

"Coco."

"What? Both of them?"

Alex tries to concentrate, says yes, hesitantly, almost apologetically, can't really believe himself that's what it was, puts on a sullen expression. They stop again a few streets further on.

"And what was here?"

"Sofie . . . "

"Sofie. Sofie who?"

Alex can't remember. Sighs.

"Was she perhaps your—girl friend?"

"No . . . We had . . . this illness. Chickenpox . . . "

"Hmm. Where did you go to school?"

"Teachers . . . came . . . "

"Oh. Mhmm. Posh. And you can't remember . . . any relatives?"

Alex thinks. Then his expression relaxes, he smiles.

"Aunt . . . She was . . . Teeheehee."

Dr. Fröhlich gives an equivocal nod and notes it down. *Patient makes a gesture. Two fingers rotating at the side of his head.*

"You think . . . do you?"

Dr. Fröhlich refuses to commit himself.

"Well, the Brückens lived back there and there was an Alexander v. Brücken who was reported missing. That much is certain. That's why we've come here."

They go along a narrow street, past a row of narrow two-story houses with only a few very small windows. Dr. Fröhlich rings the bell at the door Alexander is gesturing towards with his hand. A woman opens the door; she's about fifty. He introduces himself.

"Yes?" The woman wipes her fingers on her grubby apron.

"Did a girl called Sofie perhaps once live here?"

"I don't know. What is it you want?"

Alex suddenly does a kind of dance. "KURTZ!"

"Courts? What do you mean, courts?"

"She was *called* Kurtz! She . . . had a friend . . . nasty . . . " He slaps his forehead, he can't remember the name. "Friend! Bitch! Asshole!"

Dr. Fröhlich apologizes, the young man, he tells her, is unfortunately very worked up. With a snort of irritation the woman closes the door.

When they reach the factory Alexander goes quiet. He looks proud and his eyes shine. The buildings are still imposing.

"All this belonged to your family?"

Alex nods. "Ours! Mine!"

"But no one here recognizes you?"

"The watch!" Alexander points to his wristwatch. New memories are arriving by the minute.

Something about: K for . . . . Connie and Cosie. Hohenstein. Dürer. Photos.

"Perhaps we should wait until you can remember more and then come back?"

"Keferloher!"

"Who's that?"

"Fishes." Alex bites his fingernails.

"What is it? Are you getting worked up?"

"I . . . know. Keferloher. There."

They go into the factory entrance hall. A bare office building with immensely high ceilings. Everything looks familiar, just like it was before the war. The receptionist in her glass box is puzzled by the strange couple, the greying man with the thick glasses and the boy in the too-long trousers.

"Excuse me, my name is Dr. Fröhlich. We would like to speak to Herr . . . Keferloher."

The receptionist with the dyed blond hair regrets: they've come at the wrong time. The managing director is in a board meeting. No one can see him today.

Dr. Fröhlich lowers his voice, speaks in confidential tones. It is, he says, pretty important.

"Impossible. I'm sorry. I can put you through to his office, for an appointment. What shall I say it's about?"

At this point Alexander joins in and stares at the woman, he, yes, there's no other way of putting it, he's sniffing at her.

"Hair always long, you, not so yellow . . . always . . . looked so good."

"Oh."

Dr. Fröhlich pushes his way between them, places his hands on Alex's shoulders, apologizes. "He probably means you didn't use to be blond. Is that correct?"

"What's that to do . . . Oh, what the . . . Yes, that's right. If you must know."

"Do you know this boy perhaps?"

The receptionist is fairly sure about it. She does have the feeling she knows the face from somewhere or other. Even if it's not familiar.

"Errm." She can't bring herself to give a definite answer. She's beginning to feel there's something uncanny about the whole business.

Alex is trembling. For a moment it looks as if he's going to have a fit, he plucks at his clothes until he recovers himself, then he cries, in a low voice, as if it's afraid of its own echo, "I . . . Alexander von Brücken—let me go in there! Please!"

The receptionist shows no reaction. But she is impressed.

She says nothing, just chews a pencil. It could be true. She mustn't make a mistake. She's seen the boss's little boy a few times. The vague resemblance is undeniable. It's all too much for her and she's worried about her job.

"I don't think he's lying. Help us."

"Blond's better," says Alexander.

"Less of your cheek, young man." But she only says that just to say something. Then she gets up and waves to them, with four fingers, as if she's playing the castanets.

"OK then. Follow me." Alex and Dr. Fröhlich, hand in hand, go up a flight of stairs and to the end of a long, empty corridor. To a wide door, made of mahogany.

The receptionist, close to a nervous breakdown, goes off. Leaves the two of them alone, she wants to keep out of it. "Please tell them you managed to slip past me somehow or other, yes?"

Dr. Fröhlich nods his thanks then turns to his protégé. Gives his cheek a little pinch.

"Shall we?"

"Knut. Father, Connie. Cosima. Mama. Felice."

"Off we go, then." He opens the door to the conference room. The doctor is as worked up as his patient; he soothes himself with the thought that the worst that can happen would be prosecution for trespass.

A large, brightly lit room. Board meeting. Keferloher at the head of the long table, beside him his son, Lukian. Opposite him, in a wheelchair by the window, Aunt Hilde. As the—thus far—sole survivor of the v. Brücken family she attends the annual general meeting as guest of honor and principal heiress. The proceedings to have her certified incapable of managing her own affairs had been running for a year. For some reason or other the authorities seem to be dragging their feet, probably because Aunt Hilde does have occasional moments of clarity.

Seven board members in all, dignified middle-aged gentlemen. They stare at the intruders.

Keferloher puts on an astonished look, amused rather than outraged.

"What do we—what's all this about?" His eye falls on the boy who's looking at him.

"Can someone tell me . . . " Keferloher's jaw drops, he has a suspicion who has just come in but immediately regains control of himself.

Alexander steps forward, places his wristwatch on the table.

"Good afternoon, Keferloher Herr."

"What—What's all this?"

"Heeheehee."

"Lukian. Hi."

"Alexander?" Lukian, who is only in the room to admire his father, who is only there to sniff the aroma of power, speaks the magic word that puts all those present in a flurry. Whispering. Muttering.

Keferloher appears nervous, but aggressive.

"Alexander? Nonsense. Utter nonsense. There's no resemblance whatsoever . . . Who's that person over there?" Keferloher aims his forefinger at Dr. Fröhlich, who clears his throat and introduces himself.

Aunt Hilde cries out, "Alexander? Is it you? Come here. Yes, you just come over here."

All those around the table stare at Aunt Hilde. It is presumably the first ray of light in her life for a long time.

"Oh, haven't you *grown*. Oh, isn't this *wonderful*. Could I have a glass of champagne, please? You really are *tall* now!" Aunt Hilde holds out her bony hand to Alexander, who touches it briefly, he feels revulsion at all the brown spots.

Keferloher doesn't know how to react, what strategy to adopt. Can't make up his mind. Aunt Hilde is given a glass of champagne, she's cheered up no end and asks her nephew if he's brought his little sisters along too.

"No, Aunt Heehee. The Cocos are dead."

Alex turns to Lukian. Holds out his hand stiffly across the table.

It was an important moment. Loaded with repercussions. For a while nothing happened, nothing at all. Lukian was being torn. He did stand up, but he was thinking things over, he could feel his father's eyes on him, his father right beside him, and it was making him sweat. And then . . . then he looked me in the eye and took my hand, he decided our future lives, *mine* and *his*, in that second he decided in favor of *me* and against his father. Who knows what would have happened if he had acted otherwise.

"It's him . . . it really is. It's Alexander."

His father, furious, was waving his head from side to side, but said nothing. He seemed to realize that they couldn't simply ignore me, that at the very least there would be an investigation.

More and more memories poured back into me now that I saw these faces. It was like a second birth. Like breaking out of an egg and seeing the light. And language came back too, a thousand more words every second.

"How are you, Luki?" To me it seemed as if only a few months had passed and I turned to old Keferloher and said, in a friendly voice:

"Fishes don't drown . . . "

That knocked him flat. Confused, horrified, he stared at me. Until I quoted his words he'd presumably hoped I was a swindler who could be unmasked in time.

"Alexander?"

In his eyes I could see something between disbelief and fear.

"The plane . . . " I said. He probably thought I was hinting at something. Wrong. It simply occurred to me at that point that there was something about a plane and it was only after a few seconds that other words joined the word "plane," forming a chain, a story.

"My God!" Keferloher stood up, pale, came over to me quickly and embraced me, held me tight, as if he wanted to stifle my memory.

"Jesus! Alex! Alexander! We could never have foreseen this, after all this time. Could never have foreseen it."

"Heeheehee."

The other members of the board started to clap, to shout *bravo.* Like everything loud, it hurt my ears. I asked them to stop, but they went on clapping and cheering, visibly moved. I grasped Dr. Fröhlich's hand and he accepted Keferloher's suggestion that first and foremost I should get treatment in a really good hospital, above all psychological treatment. Fröhlich feared a relapse brought on by overstimulation. He promised me he would keep an eye on me while I was there and he's never broken his promise. I have much, so much, for which to be grateful to that good, good man. I was treated in the ENT department of Schwabing Hospital; the press had been informed and was hungry for information, for details. The son that was lost, returned from a desert of the mind, a fantastic story. My identity was established beyond doubt with the aid of the records of our former family dentist. My head healed within a few weeks, thanks to new and expensive medicines from the States that we procured via Switzerland. Of course there are those who maintain I've never been completely healed; that may well be true, but very soon I could remember everything, almost everything.

"Do you mean the time *before* the plane crash, or after as well?"

"It was an unsuccessful forced landing. Though not entirely unsuccessful, of course."

"If you insist. You had this folder with the notes put in my room. But—there are a few things I'd like to ask. How am I to fill out all those years with five or six pages of garbled ramblings. Who were the other passengers on the plane? What happened to them? Were you the only survivor? And that old man, was he really a *fisherman*? It sounds so, well, a bit like, I don't know, romantic notions of the sea. Almost unbelievable. And your time in the orphanage! The tortures! The attempted rape! That's important, I could make something of that. But you say almost nothing about it. Why?"

Von Brücken nodded, looked down at himself and raised his hands in a gesture of apology. "Firstly, the business with the airplane's a delicate matter. I wasn't the only survivor, not at all. The passengers had various reasons for fleeing, some were presumably trying to get away from the Nazis, some were perhaps Nazis themselves, it's not my place to speculate. Secondly, you're going to write a *novel*, not my biography. If you find the fisherman too picturesque, make him a potter, it doesn't matter.

"Thirdly: there's a lot that I still can't remember, even today, or that I've repressed. Disgusting things happened during those years. I know that in your books you like to play with disgusting material. I've no objection to that. But those years were above all a time without Sofie. That's why they're *not* important. Lost years."

There followed a long silence. *He* was the one commissioning the work, that was made quite clear. So what, I thought, he'll die and I'll write. I will decide what's important and what's not. Later, however, I came to understand many things better. And refrained from adding more than was absolutely necessary to the material.

Von Brücken suggested we have a coffee break, adding that, unfortunately, coffee didn't agree with him anymore but he was sure it would do me good.

"You're wrong if you think I'm trying to keep you on a short leash. There are lots of blind spots to come where you can let your imagination run riot, indeed, you'll have to . . . "

1949/50

Winter in Wuppertal. Afternoon, overcast, thin splashes of light in the sky. That almost otherworldly, late-December atmosphere, cold and jaundiced, purple and yellowing at the edges of the horizon, which certain minds nevertheless find congenial, inducing a pleasant melancholy. A long row of bare poplars stands guard on the rise above the valley, along which a coal train passes, its whistle wailing. Preschool kids are making a snowman, all jagged edges, from the frozen snow. Others are rampaging by the fence. The teacher, hair blowing in the wind, is smoking a cigarette.

"Can we have a snowball fight, Fräul'n Kramer?"

"No too rough now, OK?"

They choose teams. A considerably older teacher with a headscarf appears behind young Fräulein Kramer. "You should only let them have a snowball fight when the snow's fresh and soft. Not when it's frozen and there's ice. Understood?"

Fräulein Kramer nods. Now she has to forbid the children to do something she's just allowed. How does that make her look?

In the evening she'll go to the café to spend some of her first paycheck, read the newspaper, meet her best friend and drink tea, with as much sugar as she likes, there's no extra charge for it anymore.

Her friend will hand her a newspaper cutting, months old, with a bright-red headline: HEIR TO FIRM PRESUMED DEAD RETURNS.

Sofie will take the cutting, glance at it, put it down and ask Birgit, "Why're you showing me this?"

Birgit will say he looks quite good, in the picture. Sofie will reply that it's all so far, far away, but she's glad for him, of course.

Birgit won't give up that easily. "C'm on now! Your first kiss. You never forget that."

"Doesn't count. It was only for money."

Sofie will put lots of sugar in her tea. Then one more spoonful. Birgit will tell her how she's getting on at university. She's gradually getting to know where she has to go and when. And the Nazi profs are all there again. Like weeds, they keep coming back. In-cre-dible.

Being at university must be great, Sofie will sigh, immediately adding, as if to anticipate a question Birgit hasn't put, "I couldn't live off your parents any longer." As she says that she pulls such a face Birgit gets worried and pats her on the shoulder.

"What's up, girl? I thought you liked the kindergarten?"

"Have I any choice?"

"Just a minute—that's the first I've heard of this. You like children, don't you. You're a *born* kindergarten teacher, if ever there was one."

Sofie will light a cigarette and ask, "I am? Really? Is that in my passport? What I was born for?"

Birgit will snort and lean back, this time she won't feel like pandering to Sofie's moods. All in all, Sofie's been lucky, very lucky given the difficult times. Birgit won't actually say that out loud, she won't say it at all, but it'll be clear enough for Sofie to pick up and she'll immediately apologize for spoiling the post-work atmosphere. "Will you take me with you one evening?"

"To the Circle?"

"Won't I fit in?"

"Of course you will. If you'd like."

"Birgit?"

"What now? I'll take you along, if you want, just don't ask me whether you'll fit in again."

The waitress will serve two fresh pots of tea, each with a shot of Stroh rum. The strong alcohol will put Sofie in the mood to come out with everything she thought through during the afternoon and packaged up in sentences.

"I have to make something of my life. I don't want to have to keep saying to myself, you were lucky Birgit was there, and her parents, her kind parents, be glad, it could have been much worse. There's no point in thinking like that—not in the long term. Am I being ungrateful? I'm in good health, OK, and I'm not content with that. Do you think that's being ungrateful?" And Sofie will pour out everything once again, chew it over again. The business with the American lieutenant who was in love with her and would definitely have married her. The American who—this must be mentioned every time, it doesn't get any less incredible with repetition—wanted to keep sex until they were married and never touched her below the belly button, only kissed her above it.

"Just imagine. I'd be in the States now, would be an American. Could I go to university there? I asked him. Of course, he said, you'll learn English, then go to college. Whatever you want.—And what about children? Later, he said, there's plenty of time for that. God, I went through it all with him, point by point, like a draft contract."

"We lost the war, darling. Remember?"

"Really? I didn't lose the war. I just happened to be there. When you showed me the picture of Alexander just now, it all came back to me. Everything."

Before the two of them decide to go dancing, Sofie Kramer will ask her stepsister not to mention anything she reads about Alexander von Brücken in future, whatever newspaper it's in. She'll even make Birgit promise.

LOOKING FOR LODGINGS

At the time I was living in a two-room suite in the Bayrischer Hof, which had only recently been restored. I regarded this as a waste of money, but was told it was necessary for my security. There would certainly have been cheaper alternatives, even though the hotel was not half as chic and smart as it had been before the war. During the 1949/50 season some rooms were still divided up among two or three guests. The building had been badly hit by bombs, but one room, and that the most splendid one, had been found almost undamaged beneath the rubble and a new hotel had been built around it. The Bayrischer Hof immediately attained the status of a metaphor, a symbol of reconstruction. And I, without being aware of it, was part of that metaphor. In the summer of 1949 the first restaurant to be reopened in Munich after the war was in that room; life returned tentatively to the city. Being a symbol meant nothing to me, I was simply lonely. Keferloher could have taken me into his house in Allach, for example, but the idea didn't seem to occur to him for one minute. You must remember: I was a kind of Kaspar Hauser who was missing five years of his development. And even if the memories did return, by the hundred every day, I remained an adolescent boy in a strange waking dream and many things were beyond me. Keferloher realized this and presumably thought he could mold me to his purposes. What he hadn't counted on, however, was my energy. Perhaps a person has to spend years in a semi-stupor to generate energy like that.

I got them to swap the slim secretaire for a large desk and soon it was covered with balance sheets, files, supply lists, account books, bank statements. Keferloher sent me everything I asked for, probably on the assumption I wouldn't be able to make anything of these dossiers of power. And indeed, studying our firm's accounts was like trying to translate Sumerian cuneiform script into comprehensible German at sight. There were liabilities and assets and unfortunately you sometimes couldn't tell which were which. Occasionally I managed to drive Keferloher into a corner with my questions so that he was forced to answer in words understandable to the layman. For example the question of how much cash I had at my disposal. He answered evasively, slippery as a fish, so it wasn't easy to put a figure on it, especially then, after the currency reform, lots of it was tied to this and that and couldn't be realized just at the moment. Rubbish. I kept on at him until finally, with much clearing of the throat and waving of both hands, he named a figure, a sum which seemed mightily impressive. And the rogue was keeping quiet about all the funds salted away in Swiss bank accounts. During the war, and for this I have to be grateful to him, he had managed to get a lot to a safe place, some through outrageously illegal transactions. He naturally took a different view, to me he presented himself as a kind of resistance fighter.

"But that's incredible!"

"Isn't it . . . We must gives thanks to God . . . thanks to God."

"And it's all mine?"

"Well, most of it."

"And I can do what I want with it?"

"In theory. When you're twenty-one."

Keferloher made great efforts to downplay the significance of his role.

"Until them I'm your guardian. Which doesn't mean I won't involve you in important decisions on the firm's affairs. Assuming you want to be involved."

"That's great. I don't want to live in this hotel anymore. Will you buy somewhere for me? Not in the city. Somewhere outside, in the country."

Keferloher hesitated. Then nodded. Real estate, he said, was always a good investment and at the moment there were properties going very cheap.

"What's our chief accountant called?"

"Dr. Fichtner."

"Ask him to come and see me tomorrow. I want to learn everything about the company. He's to give me three hours instruction every day."

"Hmmm . . . Three hours? Three? He won't be in the office during that time . . . "

"Keferloher?" For the first time I called him *Keferloher*, without the *Herr* in front.

"Yes?"

"I can remember the night with the airplane."

"Oh yes? It must have been a terrible night. I had hoped . . . "

"You were doing what you thought was best for me, weren't you?"

"Alexander . . . I don't know quite how to take your question. My own son was meant to go on that plane. My own son! For your sake I kept him here. I just wanted to get *you* to safety. To safety."

"Thanks."

That was my entire response. Just, "Thanks." The fact that he then gave me a searching look, as if to see whether and how far it was meant sarcastically, convinced me he felt guilty. It may well be true that the plane was meant to take me somewhere, anywhere far away from the war. But also far away from his wheelings and dealings. At the time that must have been much more important to him than the safety of his son.

Dr. Fichtner taught me economics for three months. I represented better future prospects for him than Keferloher, so he didn't put up much resistance. Power and what you can do with it! The intoxication of power, an erotic substitute. I tasted it. But Fichtner was just a puppet on a string with no ambition, no class.

Lukian was the key figure in my plans. Keferloher bought this little castle where we are now, dirt cheap, for 70,000 new German marks. I presume he imagined that here, in the country, well away from Munich, my sphere of activity would be restricted. But I tell you, it doesn't matter where you are as long as people come to you.

Lukian came when I called him. He was surprisingly intelligent and became my friend.

At that time the castle was half in ruins, the estate had neither a park nor a surrounding wall and the asphalt on the drive had a thousand potholes. It wasn't particularly impressive, needed a certain amount of investment, so basically the price was fair. I was given control over a small part of the fortune that was to come to me, enough at least to allow me to make my first excursions into the world of finance. I believed all kinds of dangers were possible, so got an emergency rucksack full of cash ready in case I needed to flee. I cooked my own meals. Took my driving license in the local town and bought a second-hand sports car, which I parked in the nearby woods so I could escape in it if necessary. That may all sound paranoid, at the time it seemed sensible, like the cunning of an Apache. I was still thinking like a little boy who'd read too many adventure stories. But I kept everything strictly to myself, how I was thinking, what when and where. At least for the time being. I lived in fear of my life, especially after Dr. Fichtner told me how much old Keferloher had cheated my family out of over the years, though there was perhaps not sufficient proof to take legal action against him. Nor would I have dared to do so, I was neither old enough nor experienced enough. Still, time was on my side. At last I could concentrate on the things that were important to me.

As far as Sofie was concerned, Lukian became my, what shall I call it? My assistant? Agent? Spy? Once a week he came out from Munich on his motorbike to see me. Usually without his father's knowledge. And I always asked him the same question. *Had he found out anything about Sofie?*

Every time he shook his head. Perhaps she'd got married, he said, a Sofie Kurtz was nowhere to be found. Her name wasn't recorded in any municipal registry office, he'd sent out hundreds of enquiries, all responses had been in the negative. Perhaps she was dead or had left the country. Nor had he been able to find any living relatives.

Sofie had disappeared without trace. You'll be wondering why it bothered me, how and why the madness began. There's no satisfactory answer to that.

The nearest I can get to one is that there had been nothing beautiful in my life apart from Sofie, she had been more than just some girl, she was a higher beauty made flesh. Something I could have, enjoy, but would never—this much is clear from my present perspective—profane by anything as crass as possession. Although . . . That's all rubbish. At that time I certainly wanted to—yes, possess, caress, use her, you can call it whatever you like, but please do me the favor and avoid the word *fuck*. Not because I'm a prude, good Lord, no, in places it would even be the *mot juste*, but it wouldn't be right for the phenomenon as a whole, it would be too profane. Agreed?

I wanted Lukian to go through the municipal registers again, every single one in every damn corner of the Republic. I told him to employ a few people to do it; there were plenty out there who'd be grateful for the chance, who couldn't manage heavy labor but knew how to operate a typewriter and a telephone. If that didn't produce a result, he was to start on the marriage records.

Nowadays, thanks to computers, a search like that would present no great problem, at the time it was a labor of Hercules. But I was lucky. Lukian came to enjoy the search and demonstrated certain qualities—tenacity, industriousness, conscientiousness—and a talent for organization. I came to like him, and soon I couldn't do without him, he was my, how shall I put it, my brother-in-arms. If Sofie had indeed got married, I wanted to know. If she was dead, it was possible I would never find out. That perturbed me more than even the absolute certainty of her death would have.

We asked some of those who'd been evacuated with her. They all remembered Sofie. None of them had any idea where she was. At the end of the war, they said, she'd left the Allgäu village on her own initiative. Still, that meant she'd survived the war. There was one girl, she was only seventeen, perhaps she just enjoyed the attention, but this girl claimed she'd seen her once, from a distance, on the platform at Munich station by a train bound for Frankfurt, in the company of an American soldier. She couldn't be a hundred percent sure, the girl said, which is why I took her statement seriously. And it really churned me up. Was Sofie a GI bride? Would I ever find her again in the States? Could the girl at least remember the soldier's rank? But despite two hundred marks in cash, she couldn't. That spoke for her honesty.

February 1951

I'll never forget this, Luki. Your choosing me."

He was embarrassed and stared at the ground. What did he want to do with his life, I asked.

Lukian just shrugged his shoulders. We were taking a walk in the snow, a long walk right around the woods, it was February 1951. The time had come to tell him everything and get him on my side. It involved a certain risk, but I had to find someone to share the burden that was weighing me down before I collapsed under it. I felt physically sick at the thought of the imminent power struggle. There were still enough corrupt members left on the board who would stick to old Keferloher. And for the press I was yesterday's news. No one would miss me. Even Aunt Hilde had passed away peacefully three weeks previously.

"Next month, when I'm twenty-one, I'm going to chuck your father out."

Lukian said nothing, just stared at the snow, lips pressed together.

"I've already got Fichtner on my side. He'd be prepared to testify against him. Conradi too. And Melchior. They'll throw in the towel. All of them." At least two thirds of that was a brazen lie, I'd had no more contact with Conradi than with Melchior.

"I don't want him to go to prison."

"He won't have to. What good would that be to anyone?"

"OK."

As Lukian was never one to waste words, the simple OK from his lips was as good as a full declaration of consent. Still, I insisted on hearing it again.

"OK?"
"OK."
"OK."

Lukian and Fichtner provided me with evidence, which we deposited with a lawyer. The documents were so damning that even if I were suddenly to catch cold and die, he was bound to be seen as the one who'd brought on my cough. Then Conradi turned up of his own accord and pledged loyalty to me. He did the same to Keferloher, but so what? Suddenly everything was simple. You can dramatize it a bit in your novel, but not too much, eh? I was overcome with a feeling of jubilation, such as the old Roman emperors must have felt when the last obstacle on the road to the throne had been removed. You've not asked me what I did about women at that time. Answer: there weren't any. Apart from Sofie. As an idea. More an idea than a person. At the same time there was the existential eroticism of survival which became the eroticism of power.

I now had full access to my accounts. The possibilities were endless. And I had learnt—just in time, at the very last minute—everything I needed to operate this machinery. Part of me was still a child, part grown up and devious. Transmuted into an idea, my longing for Sofie watched over my awakening desires, neutralizing them. God knows, there were temptations enough, girls, women, offering themselves to me more shamelessly than bitches in heat. Very attractive ones among them too, pretty ones, even a few who would have been lovable. With one or the other I could perhaps have been happy, could have lived a privileged but banal life.

Sofie did not permit that. She was so strong within me, so powerful and bright. If I thought of another woman when masturbating, I was ashamed afterwards of my unfaithful thoughts, as if I were still fifteen.

Yes, yes, I know. It sounds . . . That's the reason I chose you.

You're welcome to present it in your usual irreverent manner, with a touch of sarcasm if you like, but nothing nasty, please, that would be inappropriate. What was going on inside me was a kind of crusade and however much devastation it causes, you can't judge a crusade like an ordinary crime.

I blamed the fact that Sofie could not be found on my own lack of imagination, rubbing salt into the wound. I had considered almost every possibility imaginable. That she was dead or married or had gone abroad. There was just one, basically obvious, possibility I had not considered. That she had been adopted. Birgit Kramer's parents had adopted her and taken her with them to Wuppertal when they moved there. It was years before the penny dropped. They weren't wasted years. The *search* for Sofie was the *way* to Sofie and—I won't bother with the cliché. And I had plenty of other things to do as well.

I bought people. I entered people on my lists the way others collect coins or stamps. Some were paid in cash, others with checks, or the payment was dressed up as a present; there were others who were paid in the currency of promises, or simply the vague prospect of my favor. I bought women, clever and beautiful ones, I bought men, unscrupulous and tight-lipped ones, I kept a register of my growing army, noting the good qualities and bad qualities, risks and services of each, predicting their rise or fall in value, as if they were stocks and shares. Many of them didn't know their names were filed away in my books, others were not aware of the point at which they had been recruited, but suspected that was the case. Why are you pulling a face like that? As if it applied to you. Your case is quite different. I'm being open with you, the business between the two of us is clear and above board, there's nothing dishonorable about it.

"I wasn't pulling a face."

"Yes. Perhaps that's it."

Birgit has finally taken Sofie to the Circle, the notorious left-wing Wuppertal debating club. Officially designated the *Center for Political Education*, it is, in fact, a beer cellar in a working-class district where, on Saturday afternoons, political education is provided for those students who are unhappy with what the university has to offer. Who finances this is not entirely clear, presumably the German Communist Party, which doesn't bother the capitalistically minded landlord, as long as enough drink is consumed.

Sofie sits in the back row with Birgit, feeling very much a visitor in an alien world, intimidated; every question she would like to ask seems so stupid that she prefers not to ask it. In dogmatic tones the speaker at the front is giving a lecture on late capitalism and the imminent collapse of the world economy. The Communist Party, which at the time has seats in the German parliament, invokes the threat of German remilitarization in the Federal Republic and advocates close links with the East. There is a strangely disciplined, propagandistic atmosphere, more akin to political instruction than free debate. The expression "world peace" crops up so often it offers all the participants a sense of importance which some greedily appropriate to themselves. Sometimes instructional films are shown about model firms or, rather, collectives with happy workers and fulfilled graduates, brain and brawn allied in the struggle. Sofie, a trainee kindergarten teacher, can't really understand why she would be more useful at a kindergarten in the East than here. On the contrary. The West urgently needs kindergarten teachers who will give the children a socialist view of the world. That is always assuming, of course, that Sofie would want to remain a kindergarten teacher. She wants to get on in the world, she'd like to be as well-educated as Birgit, to go to university, except the war has left her with a non-academic school-leaving certificate which doesn't do justice to her intelligence, or her ambition. It seems unlikely that the GDR will offer talented kindergarten teachers the chance to qualify for university entrance; replies to inquiries on the subject receive extremely vague answers from the local Party association.

The speaker ends her lecture expressing the hope that all those present will regard attendance at the mass demonstration in Cologne on May 1 as a duty. At that moment Rolf Schnitgerhans who, because the seventy present fill the hall, has had to stand at the back, tears a sheet off his sketch pad and passes it forward. It shows a rear view of Birgit and Sofie, very competently done. Birgit picks up the drawing and turns around.

Rolf has black horn-rimmed spectacles which do nothing to spoil his good looks. An athletic man of around twenty-two with brown wavy hair, his white turtleneck sweater under a beige cord jacket suggests a comfortably-off, middle-class background. He has a friendly, saucy grin and since—a deliberate ploy—he's approaching both women at once, neither feels it's her job to rebuff him straight away. They get to know each other. Light cigarettes, shake hands, introduce themselves.

"Hi, I'm Rolf. Rolf Schnitgerhans."

"Brigit Kramer."

"Sofie. Kramer too."

"Sisters then?"

"In a way. Sof was adopted by my parents."

Sofie snorts quietly. She simply cannot stand being called Sof. She's already got rid of her Bavarian accent, which was never very strong anyway. Rolf leans forward and has a good look at one woman, then the other, as one might assess two precious stones one after the other, coming so close it's decidedly impertinent, but funny as well.

"I did wonder. You don't look at all alike."

Birgit asks flirtatiously whether that's aimed at her. She's only vaguely aware that her question is a kind of snub to Sofie, creating a competitive situation. Rolf, much more sensitive to these things, gets out of it with a laugh.

"Not at all. No one's aiming anything at anyone here. Should we go somewhere else? D'you fancy some music?"

Half an hour later the three of them are sitting in Wuppertal's most popular jazz bar, the Four Bar Blues, drinking beer. Up on the stage a trio's playing, double bass, saxophone and piano.

"You aiming to be a judge or an attorney?" Birgit's asked.

"Don't know yet. My first year."

"And you?"

"I'm a kindergarten teacher."

"Aha?" Rolf doesn't seem completely put off. Not particularly fascinated either. Unfortunately.

"I'm a trombonist. Honest. I'm studying the trombone. Organ construction as a subsidiary. I've a combo of my own. Clatrombassacco."

Birgit would like an explanation.

"Clarinet, trombone, bass, accordion. Bit of an odd combination. Had to take what was there. We're playing here. Tomorrow evening. Coming?"

The two women don't reply, but they smile, take a drag at their cigarettes, look to one side with becoming modesty. They will go, but for the moment they keep that to themselves, they don't want to appear too keen. When, after several glasses of beer, they say goodbye out in the street, Birgit, this time fully aware of what she's doing, tries to get Rolf to declare a preference. She waves the sheet of paper she's holding and asks, "And who gets to keep the drawing?"

She says it with a coyness that's explicit. She could just as well have demanded that Rolf be so good as to declare which of the two of them he has his eye on. Rolf is taken aback for a moment, wonders how he can get out of the situation diplomatically and says, over his shoulder, as he turns to leave, "Give it to your parents."

Birgit and Sofie look at each other with a grin, both aware that they are attracted to Rolf, that, if necessary, they will fight over him. Birgit puts the drawing in her handbag. On the way home nothing is said, the silence gets more and more tense, even though both of them spend the whole time wondering how to break it. Eventually it becomes such a pregnant silence that one of them could only speak if she had decided to yield, to show weakness. In Birgit's parents' little house on the hill above the southern end of the town the two friends go to their rooms wordlessly, with just a nodded good night.

Next morning, while they're all having breakfast together, Birgit tries put things right, to defuse the situation, and actually does give the drawing to their parents. A sporting gesture. The "sisters" embrace.

That afternoon it seems to Sofie as though the sun is standing still in the sky, and with it time down on earth. Around her the children are playing in the snow. Arms folded, she stares out into the grayness as if she's looking at a wall separating her from the evening. At home she puts on make-up, drawing caustic remarks from her foster parents. Underneath her worn coat, (it's the only one she has) she's wearing a nice dress, her prettiest, light blue with a silver belt and a broad collar. She enters the bar fifteen minutes before the arranged time. Too late.

Rolf is standing at the bar with Birgit, holding her hand, running his fingers through her hair. Birgit sees Sofie and waves to her, a wave in which there is both pride of possession and a certain gloating relish; at the same time it's an invitation to come over, accept the result like a good sport and congratulate the well-turned-out young couple.

"We ran into each other at the university," Birgit explains in order to stall any accusations of unfair competition. Sofie says nothing, she's wondering whether to turn on her heel and leave but can't quite bring herself to do so, that would be admitting defeat. The poky little bar's full, the atmosphere relaxed. Rolf, all in black, gives Sofie a peck on either cheek then excuses himself, he has to go on stage. His combo plays. And not badly either. Rather weird, slightly eerie stuff, avant-garde jazz with truncated melodic elements, tonal confetti scattered over the swirl of noise. The audience likes it, or think they ought to like it. Rolf's a talented trombonist. He's the one with the flow, the swing, the rest of the group charge around the rhythmic prison, now more, now less furiously. A fury designed to mask untidy playing, overcrude modulations. The landlord at least is sending clear signals to the stage, he wants something people can dance to. Sofie gets drunk on beer. Birgit, not taking her eye off Rolf for one moment, puts her right arm around her.

"Don't go into a huff."

"I'm not."

"Yes you are. Come on . . . You hardly know him."

"And you?"

"There's something inside me says he's Mr. Right. When that happens you just have to grab your chance. I'm not trying to do you down. You must see that. No hard feelings, eh?"

Sofie doesn't see. She pushes Birgit's arm away. Sulks. Still. She would never have gone so far as to call Rolf *Mr. Right*. To say it straight out like that, no, she wouldn't have been so bold, so ready to take a risk, so in that sense Birgit has the right of the stronger, more determined love on her side. The slut. One more beer and Sofie's wishing her all the best. It's her tipsy reason speaking, not her wounded heart.

THE MOBILIZATION

Old Keferloher was getting more and more suspicious of my activities, my financial transactions. Summoned Lukian. What was it all about? These people weren't on any staff list. "What's he doing, setting up a bodyguard?"

"It's not what you think. He's looking for his first love. She's called Sofie. Sofie Kurtz. Her parents worked here. They died in the air raid."

"Oh, really?" Keferloher claimed he vaguely remembered, which was definitely a lie.

"Now he's looking for Sofie all over the country. *That's* what he needs these people for."

"That's what he *told* you."

"You've nothing to fear, Papa."

"What should I have to *fear*, for God's sake?"

"Exactly. Just as I said."

Lukian and I had set up an office in Moosach, a couple of kilometers from Allach, where the factories were. A large room full of telephones and filing cabinets. The office of the Sofie research team, who were paid weekly. Five or six people of my age, grateful for the unusual work. I was a generous boss. Firstly I could afford it, secondly it made me feel good and thirdly it raised staff morale. Every Monday I went there for the weekly meeting.

"We've got a Sofie Kurtz, Boss."

"Where?"

"Hamburg. Problem is, she's twenty-three."

"Check it out. She could have lied about her age. Go there, take a photo."

"We've another Sofie—Kurz without the t. In Sigmaringen. Twenty. Married name Schwarzenbeck."

"Ditto. Nothing from the small ads?"

"Piles of false alarms," Sylvia reported. She was the only woman on the team and worked harder than all the rest. She found the whole business incredibly romantic and simply worshipped me.

"Nevertheless we'll do another series. This time half page. If that doesn't get us anywhere, we'll try posters. All over the country, in every town."

It was a wonderful time. I had power—and a goal. I could do these people some good, offer them employment which wasn't as banal as what they would otherwise have had to do. And I was on my way to *Sofie*. Yes, I did enjoy those months. God, it was an extraordinary time, still directed by an innocent compulsion taking me to her, to my beloved.

MAY 1951

Rolf and Birgit are having breakfast in bed. Birgit is reading the newspaper, he's pouring another cup of coffee. She turns the page. Discovers a half-page advertisement. Bold type.

Missing: Sofie Kurtz, about 20, formerly resident in Munich-Allach, evacuated November '44. War orphan. Anyone who knows this person is asked to call the number below. All responses treated confidentially.

For the times the ad is not unusual.

"What's that you're reading?"

"Nothing." Birgit closes the newspaper. Rolf announces he's not going to the Circle any longer. There's no future in it. Says it's just radical rubbish. Birgit doesn't agree. A certain amount of radical action's needed to make things happen. Following ideas through. Otherwise, she says, they'll reintroduce military service.

"There'll be icebergs in the Mediterranean first."

"I can see you being drafted, my lad."

"You'd like that," Rolf mutters, rolling on top of her. He wants to fuck, Birgit pushes him off.

"Stop it."

"What's up? 'M I the class enemy?"

Birgit doesn't reply, but to describe rational thinking as *radical rubbish* strikes her as puerile, worries her, she takes it as a personal insult.

During the summer the two sisters have rented rooms of their own and greatly reduced their contact with each other. Rolf's increasing lethargy regarding political developments is equally increasingly getting on Birgit's nerves. More and more he simply demands satisfaction—without discussion—thus losing some of his attractiveness, and Birgit decides to go and see Sofie at the kindergarten.

How is she, she asks, while children are running around and around them, has she been reading the papers?

"The papers? Why?"

Birgit is close to telling her about the missing-person ad, but shrinks back from it when the instructress comes between them, weighing in with angry words of authority. A tragedy is in progress.

Little Emil is sitting on the john vomiting. Perhaps if little Emil had not eaten the sandwich with the old meat loaf . . . But he did and he's vomiting. Sofie runs off. The instructress says, very sarcastically, that she hopes she hasn't interrupted anything important. Birgit, equally sarcastically: "Is there anything on earth more important than a puking infant?"

The instructress, irritated, counters with: "No, but it'll take a few more years for you to learn that."

"More than a few, I hope."

"God forbid."

While this is going on, Sofie's wiping little Emil's mouth and crying. Little Emil feels guilty and cries too.

Birgit goes over to a wastepaper basket and almost throws the newspaper in. Almost. Puts it back in her handbag. Why she doesn't do what she could do, namely give Sofie the paper and let *her* make the decision, whether Birgit is being considerate or envious—she doesn't know, she really doesn't.

SEPTEMBER '51

In the late summer of '51 I decided to stop looking for Sofie. Instead I looked for her friend Birgit. It seemed unlikely that she would know anything or even still be in contact with Sofie, but since nothing else had produced results, I put my hope in the few traces that remained.

"She was called Birgit Somethingorother and lived at number ten Hormayrstrasse. Find her surname, use an old register of inhabitants. What are you waiting for?"

My research team, above all Sylvia, made huge efforts, even though success would mean unemployment for them. I wasn't conscious of that and, believe me, I'd grown fond of the gang, I'd never have put any of them out on the street. But the lack of success was driving me crazy and I was already paranoid anyway. Consequently I quite often threatened the young people, or even swore at them, accusing them of not being conscientious enough. Money changes people, that's a cliché, sometimes true, sometimes not; in my case it was true and I'm ashamed of it. But the fact was that I *couldn't help* being afraid; there were hundreds of dubious characters out there who wanted something from me. They all claimed they wanted what was best for me, by which most of them meant my money. My rise from deaf-mute, war-damaged lunatic to millionaire brought me a lot of disagreeable business which I found tiresome above all because I wasn't much interested in the money itself, only in the opportunities it afforded.

If it hadn't been for Sofie or, rather, the quiet hope of finding Sofie, I would have come to a different arrangement with Keferloher. I'd have let him carry on plundering the firm as long as I was granted a nice pad somewhere with two hot meals a day and peace and quiet for the rest of my life. I'm sure you won't believe me, but it's the truth. At least I think so. You can't be sure of the truth after so much time. Unfortunately.

A few days later Sylvia brought me the information. Birgit's surname was Kramer, they had been bombed out in March '45 and her parents had told the authorities they intended to go and live with relatives in Wuppertal. In the Wuppertal register of inhabitants there was a Birgit Kramer of the right age who was enrolled at the university and studying law. Her parents were called Klaus and something I can't remember, but in the official papers an *adoption* was mentioned. Ye gods! There was my beloved's new name: Sofie Kramer, née Kurtz. Suddenly things were moving at breakneck speed, I had no time to get rid of Keferloher, instead I went to Wuppertal, in a rush and by myself. I could have been more sensible, could have prepared everything, but, well . . .

OCTOBER '51

An autumn day. Birgit, Rolf and Sofie, arm in arm, Rolf in the middle, are crossing a square, singing, "Brothers, the sun calls to freedom." Passersby give them angry looks. One old man, whom you wouldn't have thought still capable of such fury, brandishes his stick at them. They run, laughing, and lean against an advertising pillar. The trio has rearranged itself, Rolf and Birgit are still together, but there's hardly any talk of marriage now. And Sofie, glad to have the two of them because they offer her the possibility of something different from the hated kindergarten, suppresses any passion or jealousy she feels and goes along with them, picking up this and that. Birgit wants to know why the text of the socialist song is so patriarchal. "Why does it say *brothers?* Why not *sisters?* Or *Brothers and sisters the sun calls/ To freedom . . . er . . . To freedom er . . . tum tiddly tum?* Something like that?"

Sofie leans back against the pillar, panting. "Exactly. Why not?"

Rolf points out that *Brothers and sisters the sun calls to freedom* sounds like incest in the nudist camp. The women laugh.

"Or, as someone said at one of the meetings recently: *The struggle for human rights is inextricably bound up with the struggle for women's rights.*"

They all giggle, even more uncontrollably. Rolf puts his arms around the two sisters. "Come here."

He gives both of them a smacking kiss, first Birgit, then Sofie. With a snort of pique, Birgit pulls away. Sofie's disturbed by the kiss. It could have been—could have been—intended quite innocently; it was right on the borderline between friendly and intimate.

"Hey! What's up with you?" Rolf feels Birgit's contempt is an unjust punishment.

"OK, OK. It's nothing." Birgit calms things down, but in such a way that makes it clear there is something, quite a lot in fact.

"Then don't be like that."

Birgit suddenly turns to Sofie and hisses at her. "Why don't you finally find yourself a guy?"

"Whaat?"

"It's true. I'm only asking."

"What business is it of yours?"

Birgit doesn't reveal what business of hers it is, instead she turns to Rolf. "If we hadn't chanced to run into each other at the university, you'd be going around with *her* now, wouldn't you?"

Rolf, just in the mood to toy with her feelings, replies, "Wasn't chance at all. You came *looking* for me. You were *lying in wait* for me."

"Oh, thank you very much!" Birgit is furious, feels exposed, threatens to slap Rolf. He tries to defuse the situation.

"Don't be so petty. It was just a joke?"

"No, it's true. And you tell her, just to make me look bad."

Sofie's fed up with the quarreling. "Hey, you two sort this out between yourselves, OK? Not in front of me."

Rolf apologizes for spoiling the outing.

"You don't need to apologize for me," Birgit declares acidly.

"I'm not."

"Ciao," says Sofie, wanting to get away from the scene. Her conscience is clear.

"Don't go." Rolf calls out. "It'll be over in a minute."

Birgit blows her top. "You're talking about me as if I was weak in the head. Do you realize that?" Birgit has grabbed Rolf's arm.

"Sometimes I do think you're one note short of a bar."

Birgit gives him one of the threatened slaps, on account, and stalks off in high dudgeon and high heels. Sofie, to avoid getting into an even more delicate situation, stalks off too, in not quite so high dudgeon. Rolf ends up by himself, leaning against the pillar and blinking in disbelief. Is his conscience clear? If he looks deep inside himself, then no, his conscience isn't entirely clear. He'd quite like to sleep with Sofie. Definitely. It's quite natural. That he wouldn't mind doesn't mean he's going to go ahead and do it. Though if Birgit insists on carrying on like this, why not? He's starting to get fed up with the moody cow.

Afternoon. A tenement block. Sofie arrives and opens the door. Alexander's sitting beside it dressed in very ordinary, almost shabby clothes. She doesn't recognize him. He looks at her. *He* recognizes her. She walks past him, runs up the stairs, to her one-room flat. Beside the bed there's a bicycle. She throws her coat and handbag on the bed. Cries. Washes her face in the basin. There's a ring at the door. She goes and opens it. Alexander's standing outside.

Face to face. His expectant, hers tearstained.

"Yes? What do you want?"

"Oh. Is it . . . inconvenient?"

She's seen the guy somewhere before. But where? And when?

"What is it?" The tears well up. Without waiting for an answer, she closes the door.

Alexander makes a helpless gesture, the situation's beyond him, he goes to knock, doesn't. Stands at the door, irresolute. He waits. Sits on the doormat.

The door opens again, slowly. Sofie has herself under control once more.

"Sorry. What is it?"

Alexander springs to his feet, the effect is elastic but not athletic since he ends up off-balance and has to steady himself.

"We know each other . . . from way back . . . "

I don't know how to describe it so you can understand, it really needs mythical hyperbole. It's the way Orpheus must have felt when he saw Eurydice again in Hades, when the prince of the underworld hesitantly granted him a sight of his lost beloved and the prospect of a return to the upper world; that's the way I felt then, at the end of a long journey, endless fireworks going off inside my head, the meaning of my life made flesh there before me, and before us was life, mine, hers, unbelievable possibilities, as if I had been born again and could remember how tremendous life had seemed in my cradle, something like that, euphoria, ecstasy. Reconciled with all the pain, endowed with the most profound understanding of the cosmos, you'll find words for it that are believable and not too bombastic, although the effect on the reader must *be* bombastic, something like that can't be put across bit by bit, it has to remain a whole and only accessible to the elect. To put it in plain prose: I was on a high.

"Alexander?"

She remembered my name! O sweetest of joys!

"Not the best time?"

"Shit. Come in."

Yes, her lips had pronounced my name directly preceeded by the word *shit*. At the time the word was only rarely used, and definitely not in front of strangers. Just picture it: we go into her room and she starts telling me about her problems, Rolf and life in general. Just because she needed someone to talk to, anyone. So there I was, listening.

"I think I'm still in love with him. Birgit senses that. She's smart and I'm stupid."

"Hmm." I offered her my handkerchief.

"It's not my fault."

"What's he like, this Rolf?"

"He plays the trombone."

She'd touched a sore point. "I used to play the trombone myself. A long time ago."

"What are you doing here anyway?" At last she asked a question.

"Oh . . . "

"It's not chance, is it? You didn't just happen to be passing?"

What should I say? What should I think? It had certainly been a mistake simply to burst into her life like this. And things got even worse. I asked, "Have you anything on this evening?"

"This evening? No."

She handed back my damp handkerchief. I still have it today.

"It wasn't easy to find you. With your different name."

"You've been looking for me, have you?" The question sounded like a reproach, as if I'd forced myself on her.

"Should I leave?"

She couldn't say, she thought about it, this way and that. Then, shaking her head, she said I might as well stay, it made no difference now. I took her in my arms. At first she accepted it, then she gently pushed me away.

"I'm OK now. We hardly know each other."

"Would you like to come to my place for a meal this evening?"

"What're you having?"

"I don't know. Something good. Whatever you want."

"Why not. This shitty day's ruined anyway."

"If we're going to eat at my place we're going to have to . . . have to fly."

"How d'you mean?"

The expression on her face—wonderful, so far she hadn't really cottoned on to who I was, presumably just saw me as some stupid boy from the past.

"I live some way away. We wouldn't get there by train for this evening."

Her jaw dropped, but I think she didn't want to appear naive, nowadays they'd say *uncool*.

"Sure."

You must realize that I was completely crazy. In my boldest dreams I had certainly reckoned with getting Sofie out of there, with taking her with me. I'd commandeered one of the firm's planes, it was at nearby Düsseldorf airport. A six-seater Junkers 150, fifteen years old. Nothing special, but enough to make quite an impression. The kind of thing one does at that age: show off, swagger, try to look big. There was meant to be a swanky limousine with a chauffeur waiting for us outside her tenement, but it didn't work. In 1951 it was difficult to organize a big limousine, but not *that* difficult, only unfortunately the driver got the address wrong so I was left standing there looking stupid. A cliff hanger with no denouement.—"What're we waiting for?"—"You'll see, it'll be here in a moment."—"Is something going to come soon?"

Embarrassing. Nothing came and we went, after having waited for twenty minutes, to the taxi rank. Incredible though it may sound, we hardly spoke a word to each other, not until we reached the airport and I took her to the hangar, the plane was coming out onto the runway and I was quivering with fear, a fear I wanted to conquer together with her, with Sofie, my first flight since that very first, terrible one, I was sweating and taciturn, agitated, trembling, and Sofie asked, "Are you really serious about this?"

"It's the way things are." The sentence slipped out, my mother's favorite comment.

"OK."

Looking back I could kick myself for hours on end for the way I behaved. With her I seemed shy, awkward, boring, apart from when I had a trembling fit, which I tried to cover up with arrogance and big talk. I must have seemed insufferable and it was only Sofie's marked curiosity that got her to actually board the plane. Perhaps she wanted to see what I had to offer, to get a clear idea of the opportunities. That's always been my problem, the people I met always saw the opportunities my wealth offered before they saw me as a person, I was a being with tentacles made of opportunity, a kind of wish tree, a facilitator of wish fulfillment. Sofie was never calculating, she was greedy for new experiences, but never simply *greedy*. Otherwise everything would have been easy. But on that day she was curious to know what she had in me, I'm quite sure of that, and if I'd been better, more charming, more elegant, more witty, if a lovable person had appeared from behind the tentacles, then—perhaps!—everything would have been different.

Von Brücken slumped, as if trying to withdraw into his chair, pressed his upper body against the leather and groaned.

God, I was lovable, generous, good-natured, willing to learn, I wasn't even too bad-looking! But unfortunately I was also young and stupid and lacking in self-control. And—let's not forget—beside myself, completely beside myself because my divine beloved was there in the flesh, sitting beside me, beautiful and desired like no other woman on earth. And I made the mistake of assuming that she was meant for me, for me alone, that I just had to find Sofie and bring her to me and all would be right with the world, with the whole universe. Anything else was completely inconceivable, we'd love each other, be there for each other, it all seemed so obvious. A car picked us up from the tiny airfield in Durach and took barely half an hour to reach the Owl's Nest. Even then it wasn't a ruin anymore, though the furnishings still left something to be desired as far as taste and style were concerned, a barn of a place but all in all nice enough. Architecture out of a fairy tale, a bit romantic with something of an enchanted castle and definitely—if you lived in a one-room box in a Wuppertal tenement—impressive. The sight of it made Sofie squirm, as if it was something unreal. I misinterpreted her expression as shyness or embarrassment, in fact she felt uncomfortable and didn't know how she was going to get out again. She felt frightened and I, not registering her fear as fear, but as amazement, was even pleased at her amazement, her fear.

"That's where I live now," I stated, nonchalantly, as if I were pointing to an empty barrel by the roadside. All the lights were on in the castle, it was already getting dark and I wanted the first impression to be of warmth, of a blaze of light. What can have been going on inside Sofie during those minutes? Possibly she was even becoming aware that she might have followed a monster to his lair. The loneliness of the Owl's Nest in a landscape empty of other human habitation—Sofie's attitude suddenly changed, she became recalcitrant, as if she had acted thoughtlessly and had to resist, as if she'd ended up in the stronghold of a condottiere where she would be at his mercy, for good or ill.

"Good Lord!"

What my stupid ears heard in those two words was appreciation instead of bewilderment. I had had the dining room lit by dozens of candelabras, even though there was no problem with the electricity supply. My staff have never had to observe any fussy rules about dress, apart from that evening, when I'd ordered that they should all wear dark suits to make it more of a solemn occasion. In fact, the effect was eerie. I was immature, full of the bombast of historical paintings, I conjured up the repertoire of a ceremonial that had long become mannered, wanting to make it a grandiose moment. And unintentionally set up something terrifying. We sat opposite each other, at a monstrous table, at least facing each other across the middle, not at either end of the twelve-foot-long surface. I had asked Sofie to tell me what her favorite dishes were; she'd said chicken and fruit tart *à l'alsacienne*, which is what we had. In all seriousness, I considered myself the perfect host.

She'd never drunk champagne in her life before, so I had some brought up, and not any old champagne, but the very best, although it probably didn't make any difference as she wouldn't have been able to distinguish the subtle differences in quality anyway. In retrospect I feel as if I'd been spoiling an animal, with the best of intentions, but with no understanding of its limitations. Just a minute, that sounds too dismissive, I'll put it another way: instead of creating an atmosphere of intimacy, a feeling of security, I transported Sofie into an alien, sumptuous fairy-tale world and fairly tales are not only homely, they have their dark, surreal side as well.

"That's . . . You're crazy!" She said it straight out and still I didn't understand.

"D'you like it? Good, isn't it?" We were eating chicken with fantastic spices. Or so I thought. Sofie, with every mouthful, was eating fear.

"D'you live here by yourself?"

"Apart from the staff, yes."

"But that's . . . " She shook her head, she was trying to keep her spirits up.

"It was more cramped where I lived before," I said vaguely. God knows, If I'd told her, if I'd let out everything that had happened to me I might have salvaged something from the evening. Idiot that I was, I didn't want to bore her with tales of woe.

"What have you been doing all this time?" She was quite prepared to help me out; she was fighting tooth and nail against the portentous atmosphere to which I was subjecting her.

"Not much. I've been thinking of you." Why didn't I tell her the story of my life? Why?

"You waste your time doing that? What do you want from me? It's crazy. This hall! You can't have a conversation in here."

"You get used to it."

"It sounds more like a crypt in here."

I slapped my forehead and apologized. Like an idiot, I'd forgotten the music. When I rang, a violinist in white tie and tails came in and played gypsy music by Liszt and Brahms. I'd imagined it as very romantic, but it must have sounded like a parody of a dance of death.

Sofie couldn't eat another mouthful. She hunched her shoulders and shivered, as if she were chilly.

"So this's how you think it'll be?"

"What?"

"Us."

"I've . . . no experience." Suddenly I felt embarrassed by the whole business. I'd just wanted to make it nice for her. For a moment, a brief moment, I was angry with Sofie, but that wasn't possible, it went against the whole way I saw things, so I became angry with myself. I'd wanted to play the great lover and all I'd managed was a grotesque caricature.

"Tell me, Alex, are you serious? You're in love with me? Still? Just because I kissed you once back then?"

"You shouldn't say things like that . . . as if it was nothing."

"But it was nothing!" She drank some champagne, perhaps too much and too quickly. "Why are you showing me all this?"

"I haven't shown you everything. I've a swimming pool. And a film projector. We could watch something. The paddock's empty. I don't like horses. But if *you* like them, we'll put some back in."

"Alex, you can't do this. I'm not in love with you. You're trying to buy me, like a packet of butter."

"I . . . I'm not trying to buy you."

"Goddammit!" She was almost getting hysterical. I felt sick. "Of course it's a temptation. Do you realize what you're doing to me?"

"*What I*—what I'm doing to you?"

It was strange, but my voice sounded more drunk than hers.

Definitely. Her voice sounded so brutal and when she changed to a whisper, I was ready to hate her.

"Look, I'm sure you think you . . . But . . . There was this American lieutenant. He brought me flowers, for a whole week. I could have gone with him. I wasn't in love with him, and yet I let him give me flowers—and much more useful things, things you couldn't get like butter, coffee, cigarettes—and I let him kiss me and we talked about what it would be like. Over there. I was seventeen."

"Why are you telling me this now? I was desperately looking for a switch to turn off her story.

"I behaved like a whore. And I'm never going to do that again. I almost let myself be bought. I almost went to America, started a new life. It would have been so simple. So *logical*. He would have done everything for me. He was good-looking into the bargain, and great in bed . . . "

Now she was tormenting me. Later I discovered things with the lieutenant had gone no farther than a few kisses. Nothing else.

"Why are you telling me this?"

"You don't like hearing it, do you? Something like that would be quite alien to *you*. Have you ever gone *hungry*, just for one day even?"

Then I knew there was a God and that he must be a cruel God. What could I say? Everything, but everything, I could tell her would sound made up. Sofie was unstoppable. And she really laid into me.

"I almost *sold* myself. And now you come along and—Oh, damn, damn and damn! Do you realize how much I wish I were just a little bit in love with you? Do you realize what it's like to be nothing, to have nothing? All this shit here's a kind of rape."

I was too baffled to say anything at all.

"The simple fact is, you weren't there when I could have used your help . . . I don't know where you've been all this time.

I did think of you sometimes, wondered what had become of you, imagined what it would be like if you came along to take me away from my shitty life. But now I've come to terms with my shitty life and I'm in love with my stepsister's boyfriend—and then I get on a plane to dine in a funny haunted castle . . . "

She burst into tears, wept over her Alsatian fruit tart, I waved the violinist out of the room, the hall, rather.

"Forgive me." Actually the way I was being treated seemed so unjust I felt more like hitting or raping her.

"I drank the champagne too quickly, I'm a bit drunk. Are you going to take advantage of that?"

Was that perhaps what Sofie wanted? Even today I'm not sure. Did she have what you might call a corrupt part that wanted to be taken by force that evening? But that's wisdom, if wisdom it is, that came after the fact. At the time I said softly, "I love you."

She climbed over the table and gave me a kiss. I realized it was the kiss from the gravel pit all those years ago, repeated. A kind of payment in arrears.

"Thanks for the meal. Can they take me to Munich. To the train?"

"I'll always love you, Sofie."

"Then keep it to yourself!" It came out as a scream.

Keep a stiff upper lip in the moment of defeat. Our father's maxims lie deep beneath our skin, only to surface at the most unsuitable moments. Keeping a stiff upper lip—there are different ways of looking at it. Perhaps my father *did* keep a stiff upper lip, in his eyes. I called for the car and asked the driver if he could manage to drive Sofie to Wuppertal that night.

He said yes. Perhaps it was the answer he thought he had to give his lord and master. Sofie, however, insisted on being taken to Munich; she was sure there'd be a night train. It'd be better if you left this discussion out of the novel, it'd sound too much like petty haggling. We were standing outside. The driver asked what he should do if there was no night train. I said he should leave that to the lady. God, I wanted to give Sofie money, for the train or for a night in a hotel, it was the least I could do, don't you think? But I couldn't bring myself to offer her money, what would it have looked like? But when you're in love, you worry about your loved one—what things look like should be a matter of complete indifference. I wish I had something more romantic to tell you. It was a bitter, decisive moment and I was wondering whether I could give her some money and how to go about it, or why I shouldn't. Money, money, money.

That was the minute Time had chosen to make it clear to me that I could only see myself in association with money.

Finally I heard myself stammer, "Listen, if you should need help, in whatever way, then . . . "

"You're probably a nice guy, Alexander, and I'm crazy. Perhaps I'll feel stupid for the way I've behaved, perhaps that's the way the world is, but I have to find that out for myself. You live in your world—and I live in one you don't need." She hesitated. What came next was a touch too hysterical, too over-the-top, even for her.

"I'm dead to you—all the best. And thanks again."

I lit a cigarette, felt the urge to get drunk. Sofie got in the car, the car drove off and suddenly the scene, *our* scene, was over. The tears were running down my cheeks, I was filled with the awareness that Sofie was no longer there anymore, simply wasn't there. I could have run after the car, could have shouted out, ordered the driver to stop so that the future could start again, the opportunity was there for three or four seconds, then it was too late.

That night I sent all the staff away on leave. I wanted to be alone in my haunted castle, all alone with my fury, my disappointment. Oh, if only I could have worked up a hatred of Sofie, a purifying, cathartic hatred, what prospects that would have opened up for my future life! But the hatred that did come, as it had to, as if in accordance with some law of chemistry, was directed purely against myself. And it was justified. I'd made so many mistakes, I'd treated my beloved as if she were just any girl. If there'd been a firearm lying around in the castle that night, we two wouldn't be here talking to each other now. Remarkable, really, that there wasn't one, not even a hunting rifle or something like that.

I felt slightly sorry for von Brücken. I was surprised to register this response inside myself and resisted it, as if I'd been emotionally duped. I felt I ought to say something to skim off some of the sentiment from the mood that had arisen and, in my smart-aleck way, remarked that Sofie came over as a bit uptight. Principles were fine in a woman, but to go all hysterical like that . . .

"Uptight? No! you mustn't talk about her like that. Resolute, yes. Hysterical? What's that supposed to mean? Of course she reacted hysterically, it was inevitable after being confronted with so much in such a short time. She felt she'd got into the wrong film—and her reaction was quite correct, not to let things get too intimate. After all, she must have felt afraid as well."

"I'm sorry, you may well be right, but if you don't mind my asking, there's one thing . . . "

"Yes?"

"I simply can't understand *why* you were in love with her, what the attraction was."

Von Brücken opened his eyes wide. "Why I was in love with her? How on earth should *I* know? That was what I wanted to ask *you*."

"Oh, right."

"Why do you fall in love with someone you hardly know? That kind of thing's supposed to happen, isn't it?"

An angry sharpness had crept into his voice, still under control, but clearly audible. He noticed it himself, took a deep breath and relaxed.

The kindergarten in Wuppertal, the next morning. Sofie, suffering from a lack of sleep, hangs her jacket on one of the little hooks screwed into a strip of wood at waist height. From the kitchenette comes the grating voice of the instructress. "You're late."

"Sorry." She doesn't say it as much as breathe it.

"Don't you feel well?"

"'S OK. Thanks."

Emil comes running up to her, clasps her around the knees. Sofie has to put her hand against the wall for support. She won't admit it to herself, but she can't stand Emil, she almost finds the little fellow repulsive. Then she cries.

December '51

Later that year, at the beginning of December, when Dr. Fröhlich had managed to get me back on my feet again and I had regained the will to live, to survive Sofie, we had the first big party at the castle. The whole of the board were invited, with wives; my research team was there too, it hadn't been easy to find them new positions in the firm in which their talents weren't entirely wasted. Sylvia became my secretary. To have a female about you who adores you, isn't bad-looking, and is honest and hardworking into the bargain, isn't something you cast aside, especially not when you've just decided to try and lead a *normal* life—"normal" in quotation marks. The official reason for the party was the completion of the renovation of the Owl's Nest. The room we're sitting in looked magnificent, quite different from the way it looks now, I've had all the decorative bits removed. I can show you photos, if you're interested, but you mustn't describe it too precisely, please remember that. Oh yes, there was another, unofficial reason for calling the board together. I was taking over the running of the von Brücken firm. So far I'd remained passive, had let Keferloher get on with it, but now, if only to take my mind off my self-hatred, I'd decided to assume my father's role, with all the duties that entailed. Most of the members of the board knew all about it and arrangements had been made to persuade them to approve it. Arrangements, financial arrangements, to be more precise, they were unnecessary actually, but they allowed me to sleep more soundly. I made a speech with a euphoric vision of the future, prepared by Dr. Fichtner and larded with sensible comments, to demonstrate my competence. My rallying cry was *investment*. Money in the bank was lazy money, your money had to work for you to bring in more money. By pure chance it happened to be the right strategy for the 1950s. Keferloher didn't seem particularly surprised, he had his informants, of course, and he accepted the inevitable, probably because he was simply too much of a coward to take extreme measures against me.

"Congratulations, Alexander. In the name of the whole board heartiest congratulations."

He gave me a present, some ancient statue with no head, wrapped up in paper. An allegory of wisdom, if I remember rightly. Sapientia with no head. Definitely an insinuation, but so what? I thanked him and handed Keferloher a letter.

"And that's for you." I turned around. "Lukian, can I have a quick word with you?" Lukian followed me into what at the time was my study. As we closed the door I could see Keferloher open the letter and read it on the spot, with growing horror. It seemed a good idea to lock the door.

"Luki, any moment now your father's going to go berserk. Can you forgive me? Truly and honestly? I have to know."

Lukian said that was OK, his father had had his time and plenty of fun, we needn't worry about him.

"That's true. And I've plans for you."

"Plans?"

"We're expanding the firm. We're setting up a new branch. In Wuppertal."

"Wuppertal? Why Wuppertal, if you don't mind my asking?"

"We're expanding."

"In *Wuppertal*."

"I want Sofie to be happy."

"Sorry?"

There was a violent rattling of the doorknob. Then knocking on the door. First with the flat of the hand, then with fists. Keferloher's voice could be heard, at full volume. The loss of face seemed to concern him much less than the loss of power.

"Alexander! You can't do this! We've got to talk!"

"But I don't want to go to Wuppertal. What's all this about, Alex?"

"You'll be very important for me. In Wuppertal. I'll explain everything."

Old Keferloher was thumping the door even harder. We both had to laugh.

"You're mad," Luki muttered.

"I am? Probably."

"Alexander! You ungrateful little —! Open this door!"

"Tell me one thing. Why Sofie? After all this time? Why don't you take Sylvia? What's wrong with her?"

"Luki? Are you in there?"

"Look, Luki, there's a door there—to your father. And one here—to Wuppertal. Choose."

It sounded more vehement than it was meant to. We sat down together and after I'd given Luki a rough outline of my plans he no longer thought I was quite so crazy. I wanted Sofie to have a decent life and if she refused to let me help her, she'd just have to be helped *secretly*. I'd given up trying to get her for myself, but that was no reason to leave her living in poverty without protection. Lukian was to keep an eye on Sofie, quietly, staying in the background, that was all, a fulfilling task with a high degree of fun. We came to an arrangement. In future he would be my sole number two, with a princely salary; in return he had to agree to a somewhat unconventional lifestyle for a few years.

"Right then, which door is it to be? Daddy or Wuppertal?"

"Wuppertal."

"Well done! Let's celebrate." From outside Keferloher's voice could be heard, gradually getting fainter. *"Alexander? Hey! Keep your hands off me. Hey!"* Security were showing him the way out.

"You'll regret this, asshole! You and your delusions of grandeur!"

With his bawling Keferloher even managed to bring a smile to my face, the first in weeks.

The eroticism of power has seldom been adequately celebrated by writers for the plain and simple reason that hardly any writers have ever possessed power in the trivial sense and felt its thrill for themselves. Power or, rather, the exercise of power, gave me new life, that's true, I sublimated, repressed the love I felt, grew into adulthood, and into a fantastic businessman. With skill and a large amount of luck I took the firm of von Brücken to new heights, in the years that followed I laid the foundations for an empire. Alexander the Great was my nickname, even to my competitors. But all that's not particularly interesting. It should be mentioned that during that night I slept with Sylvia, on the rebound, so to speak and . . . for whatever reason; I was pretty drunk but, believe me, I managed to fake an orgasm for her and for myself. It was the first time I'd slept with a woman, be it noted. Slept is the *mot juste*.

JUNE 1953

Rolf has had seven very angry scenes with Birgit. Six times they made up, but after the seventh he's finally left her and maintains he's always been latently in love with Sofie. And after his separation from Birgit's been made official, he can come out. For a week now Sofie's no longer been a virgin, which does wonders for her self-confidence. She's not quite sure whether she's really in love with Rolf, or just enjoys the belated victory over her stepsister, but she needs Rolf around her, his warmth, his desire, apart from that there's little motivation in her life. On the wall over her bed is a poster of Lenin which Rolf complains doesn't exactly do anything for his libido. Sofie ignores that, she has different problems.

"Birgit'll probably never speak to me again."

"And if she doesn't? Does that bother you?"

"Yes. Of course."

"Then go and see her. Have a heart-to-heart."

The two women meet the following day, in the street, by chance, though one could also say there's a small-town inevitability about it. Contrary to everything Sofie fears, Birgit's happy to talk, even to make up, though she does warn her stingily against Rolf. He's bourgeois and stuck in his ways, she says, he believes in astrology, he's a typical Cancer. On the other hand she doesn't deny his qualities as a sensitive lover and even expresses relief that Sofie's finally been made into a proper woman, no matter who did it. Birgit doesn't say so, but she's always assumed the cause of a certain tendency to hysteria in Sofie lay in the fact that she was still a virgin. Twenty-two's leaving it a bit late, even in the fifties. It's the time when people start seeing a sexual as well as a political cause behind all sorts of effect. Perhaps not in the newspapers yet, but certainly in books for the highbrow reader. Birgit's on a Sartre trip at the moment and finds Henry Miller, whom she reads in the English original, repulsive but interesting. Sofie herself never consciously put off her defloration and refuses to attach much importance to the matter. Birgit's constant digs were tedious but basically irrelevant.

In the window of the radio shop a television is showing the coronation of Elizabeth the Second. The two women join the cluster of people watching. Mock the rapt sighs.

"Look at them. Servile lot. Monarchists every one of them. Apart from the Nazis, of course."

"I've made up my mind. I'm handing in my notice."

"What? Now you're qualified? Are you crazy?"

"I'm going to night school. I'll do the school-leaving certificate. Then I'll go to university."

"Really? And what will you live on?"

"If I have to I'll work as a cleaner."

"Are you sure? Are you strong enough?"

"If not, I'll just string myself up."

Birgit puts her arm around her stepsister. She's not used to hearing her talk like this.

"I'll ask my parents—our parents. Perhaps they'll chip in something."

"I'd rather you didn't. Thanks."

Elizabeth the Second receives the crown.

That summer, after a delay of fourteen years, *Gone with the Wind* reaches the German cinemas. Sofie sees the film three times and cries her eyes out. She gets a new nickname: *Scarlett*. Despite the fact that she identifies much more closely with Rhett Butler.

Rolf's combo's playing in the Four Bar Blues. For the last time. The last encore. Rolf has decided to leave music-making to more talented players. Not that he lacks talent. Just courage. In future he wants to concentrate on what's important. For him what's important is what is safe. Sofie and Birgit are in the audience. Applause. The band leaves the little stage. Rolf, somewhat depressed, sits down beside Sofie and gives her a kiss. Birgit accepts it, no reaction. The Communist Party's become irrelevant, the systems have become fixed. The popular uprising in the GDR leads to a vehement argument between Birgit and Sofie. Birgit thinks it wasn't a popular uprising at all, just a series of concerted operations by saboteurs who've infiltrated the country. Sofie refuses to be told what to think anymore. Not by Brigit nor by anyone else.

Sofie's developing. She'll call her instructress a nasty slave-driver and a *Nazi cow*, she'll throw a cup of hot tea—124 degrees—in her face, which will have no lasting physical effects on the *Nazi cow* since the liquid will cool down as it flies through the air by a decisive ten (!) degrees. Lacking visible wounds, the *Nazi cow* will refrain from reporting it to the police and leave it at instant dismissal. As she said she would, Sofie will go out to work as a cleaner. Go to night school. Her adoptive parents will chip in, Rolf as well, who completes his studies with top grades and now teaches what he's learned, namely organ construction, a profession with a future, for the moment, so many bombed-out churches are being rebuilt and armed with music. Everyone's busy. Rolf and Sofie live quite happily together for a few years, both too fully occupied to harbor any doubts.

In 1956 Sofie decides on a short hairstyle, which means her hair just comes down to her shoulders now. Speaking of shoulders, over the bed, with a rifle across his shoulders, James Dean is now hanging beside Lenin. Rolf's not too keen on that either. He suspects Sofie's thinking about James Dean when they have sex. On the other hand, that seems healthier than if she were to think of Lenin during sex. Anyway, Jimmy's not a danger any-more, being already dead.

Politically the country's shifting to the right, say some, get-ting back to normal, say others. Rearmament, scarcely thought possible, becomes a reality. Sofie's protests make no difference whatsoever. In the middle of 1956 the German parliament votes in favor of compulsory military service. Birgit has always said they would. And keeps pointing that out, at every possible op-portunity.

Sofie's working at a supermarket checkout. "Supermarket" is a new word. Sofie is handed the night-school leaving certifi-cate, which qualifies her to go to university, grade average A–. Rolf's pretty proud of Sofie for getting through night school so smoothly, he didn't think she was that clever. The idea that un-known influences might be at work never occurred to him, never occurred to anyone. Which is not to belittle Sofie's achievement.

July '56

Sofie is twenty-five, has an outstanding school-leaving certificate and a faithful, rather boring boyfriend. For the last time she comes home with her old schoolbag. Birgit's given her a pigskin briefcase with a lock for her birthday, that's what she's going to use in future. As Sofie's unlocking the door to her apartment, a young man with thin, light brown hair and a narrow face comes out of the apartment opposite. She's seen him fairly often, he seems to live a quiet life there, across the landing. Probably a student— and soon she'll be proud to be a student too. So she just has to get to know her future fellow student, even though he looks pasty-faced and tries to avoid eye contact.

"Good evening," she calls out loud across the landing.

"Good evening," the man replies softly, trying to slip past her. It doesn't work.

"I've just graduated from night school!"

"Oh. Congratulations." Pasty-face, in collar and tie, stops, turns around, raises his beret. How can anyone wear such an awful hat if they're not French.

"Thanks. I feel I could embrace the whole world. We've never been introduced. I'm Sofie."

"I'm Lukian." They shake hands.

"I was going to come and see you anyway."

"Why?" Pasty-face clutches his briefcase.

"It might get a bit noisy. We're having a party tonight."

"Of course. Go ahead, don't worry about me."

"Do drop in and have a beer."

The man thinks about it, still clutching his briefcase tight, suddenly produces an unexpected smile. "I might just do that."

"See you." On a high, Sofie stumbles into her apartment, throws open all the windows, dances to swing music from the radio. She's forgotten to ask Pasty-face what he does.

Lukian reports there's been an *encounter*. He's been *invited*. How should he behave?

First reply: *With reserve.* Second reply, ten minutes after the first: in whatever way he considers right. Whatever comes most naturally. He has *carte blanche*.

It's the evening, which means the graduation party. In the eight-by-five room are Rolf, Sofie, Birgit, Birgit's new lover, the members of Rolf's former combo, five of Sofie's fellow students from night school, her math teacher and a few of her other acquaintances. There's hardly any room for dancing, but that's made up for by the barrel of beer in the bathtub. And the jazz played loud on the radio. Music that's just waiting to be called rock-'n'-roll. Each guest has had to bring their own glass for the beer. Thanks to Birgit, who, after her final exam, can put "lawyer" on her door-plate, the discussion quickly degenerates into a political argument.

"And? What's happened? We've got military service, that's what. You just refused to believe it."

"It had to come. We're just a buffer. Rearmed cannon fodder for when the Reds invade." Rolf talks as if he'd foreseen everything and Birgit blows her top. As intended.

"Are you seriously suggesting the Soviet Union has aggressive intentions?"

From one moment to the next Rolf feels isolated and publicly denounced. Excluded, as if he'd been robbed of his youth. "You just wait and see," he says quietly, so as not to say too much but still show firmness in his own eyes.

Three months later, when the popular uprising in Hungary's crushed by Russian tanks, the argument flares up again, but on this evening it ends abruptly with Brigit's exclamation, "God, am I glad I got rid of you. You're horrible!"

"Hey, hey. This is *my* party, right, Mrs. Attorney?" Sofie tries to exercise her authority, without success. Birgit insists on retaining the intellectual high ground. "Khrushchev's nothing but a lump of jelly with no backbone. Stalin had his faults, true, but Hitler would have just laughed at a Khrushchev."

"Stalin was a monster," says Rolf, a practising Catholic. "Socialism—fine, but on a Christian basis."

"You—*organ maker*!" Suddenly it sounds like an obscene insult.

The clarinettist from Rolf's combo mumbles drunkenly, "Y'can't break an omelet without . . . making eggs." Everyone knows what he's getting at.

"Go to the bathroom if you're going to be sick," Sofie tells him. There's a ring at the door, Rolf snarls, "Get over there, then!"

"Over there everything's fine. It's *here* that we have to fight."

"Ridiculous."

Sofie goes to the door. Lukian's there, with a bouquet.

"Congratulations again. I thought I'd just bring these around."

"Wow! Come in. What was your name now? Lukian? My God, flowers—they take up so much room. Something to drink would've been OK, too." Sofie makes no bones about the fact that she has an aversion to cut flowers, but in such a way that it sounds like a lack of refinement no one could take amiss. Lukian stands at the door, a smile on his face, not moving an inch, like a pillar of salt.

"Sorry but I can't come in . . . I've things to do, that is, my boss rang and I have to go somewhere . . . unfortunately."

"And you still bring me a bouquet? That's sweet of you."

"A pity. Honestly. We'll . . . see each other?"

"Well, if you can't, you can't. Thanks. So long." Sofie closes the door. Odd, she thinks, to bring a bouquet like that, must've cost five marks, then chicken out . . . Very mysterious. Only— she doesn't want to think about it just now.

Birgit asks who it was.

What business is it of hers who it was? "Only my next-door neighbor," Sofie mutters and takes the flowers to the bathroom.

"And what does he do?" Now it's Rolf who's asking as he contemplates the bouquet, which in his opinion must have cost *seven* marks.

"No idea. I've only exchanged half a dozen words at most with him."

Rolf stares at the bouquet in the washbasin. "Half a dozen words? And then a whole flower arrangement?"

"Rolf!" Eyes blazing, Sofie cuts him short. She sometimes wishes he would show a bit of jealousy, but not just now. Because there's not the slightest reason for it and the stupid bouquet is getting on her nerves. The discussion in the background gets on to whether Germany can retain the soccer world championship, at which the women in the room turn up the radio even louder. The clarinettist from Rolf's combo's stretched out in Sofie's bed, it's the only one, and is fast asleep, snoring. The party continues until half past five in the morning, ending up with discussions about the sexes, about the differences in sexual desire between men and women and the social constraints resulting from them. Under the pretext of a sociological argument experiences of orgasms are exchanged. Just the way parties ought to be around half past five in the morning: honest, touching and instructive.

Because the supply of alcohol runs out towards the end, Rolf is despatched to the gas station. He comes back with beer and brandy. Sofie's math teacher is completely drunk and babbles on, no one's listening to him, about a good star watching over her, then falls asleep.

The Good Times

During those years we hardly had to intervene at all. Sofie was happy. Impecunious, but happy. Fairly happy. We saw no reason to change anything. Except once, at the certificate exam, in math, we gave a little help there . . . And the instructress who was going to take Sofie to court, because of the tea, we pacified her, that was all."

"I understand. And what were you doing all this time?"

"Trivial stuff. I had to have something to pass the time. The v. Brücken firm was growing. It was fun. I bought more and more people. Above all young, ambitious scientists with new ideas. My appointment schedule was full, I was always seeing people, bribing people, receiving honors, launching ships, laying foundation stones, attending weddings, award ceremonies, patent suits, etcetera, etcetera. It was a hell of a lot of work. Sometimes, when the loneliness became too much for me, there were temptations. My agents were everywhere, Lukian was only one of them. Here, I'll show you something."

He handed me a photo (black-and-white) of Sofie asleep. It was the first and only picture of her I saw. Quite pretty. Her nose a bit more pointed than I'd imagined. How had I imagined her? How had the photo come to be taken? Would it be indiscreet to ask? Rubbish. So I asked, but von Brücken simply replied that it had presumably been taken in the night of that party, when they were all drunk, or, rather, the morning after, when there was some daylight, Lukian had taken it. How? Secretly. Of course. It wasn't important, he said, dismissively.

"I'd been deceiving myself, you know. I never managed to

get Sofie out of my head. At most with medication. Let's stop for today, I'm tired and I'm sure you're hungry . . . Please excuse me if I've been inconsiderate."

I liked the story. It seemed capable of development, however far-fetched and made-up it sounded. It'd need a few changes, I thought, to make the whole thing more believable, more organic. Von Brücken had found the right man in me. The whole complex, the construct, the skeleton needed a bit of flesh slapped on the bones, and then a skin. Finally the bloom on the skin.

During that night I heard noises outside again. Like the noise of construction work some way off. During the day I saw very few staff in the castle, a servant now and then, sometimes the cook, by chance, if he happened to be in the drive smoking a cigarillo. Why would they be building at night? And what? I opened the window to the north that looked out over the park, saw occasional flashes of light, heard the noise of machines, the rare sound of a human voice in the stillness issuing a curt order. The snow had stopped and it was clear as far as the tall firs surrounding the park like a screen.

I rang, as was my right, I thought, even if the noise hardly disturbed me when the windows were closed. Lukian Keferloher came himself, in a dressing gown that looked more like an old admiral's uniform, royal blue with a gold belt and high collar.

"What can I do for you?

"There's work going on in the park, isn't there? I can hear it."

"I'm sorry about that. You must have good hearing. Which I haven't anymore, unfortunately."

"What's going on out there? Why's the work being done at night?"

"The reason's simple. The work is out in the open. By day there are always helicopters flying over, newspapers, other firms, the The Federal Intelligence Agency. They might film what's being built and the boss doesn't want that. That's all."

"Aha. The FIA? Sounds dangerous."

"It's a long story. I'm sure the boss'll tell you, I wouldn't like to anticipate."

I invited Lukian Keferloher to have a glass of wine with me. After a brief demur, he accepted and sat down opposite me on the chaise longue under the middle window. I raised my glass to him. "You don't like me, do you? You're *against* the project."

In a quiet voice he replied that that was true, but his antipathy was directed solely against the project, not me personally. "I don't think it's right to write all that down. But I won't attempt to stop it. Perhaps it has to be done. It's difficult to judge."

"By the way," I tried to make it as casual, as nonchalant as possible, "what is it that's being built out there?"

"A tomb."

I was taken aback by his openness. "A tomb?"

"The boss hasn't long to live and he wants to be buried in his park."

Was that possible? I asked. "I mean legally. Isn't burial in a cemetery compulsory here in Germany?"

"If you're Alexander von Brücken, even if one day you *were* Alexander von Brücken, you enjoy certain privileges. If necessary, the park will be declared a cemetery by the authorities."

"Aha. Cunning."

"Most things in life are just a question of what you call them. I know the boss would be unhappy if the construction work were halted. Should I give the order all the same? You can get me to arrange it, your welfare is my number one priority."

I said no, it wasn't that bad, I was sorry I'd woken him.

He hadn't been sleeping, he replied, and wished me a quiet, peaceful night.

DAY THREE

1961, May

The great hall of Wuppertal University is the scene of a momentous argument between Rolf and Sofie. There is a transcript of the discussion, which both parties conducted at full volume, in von Brücken's files.

"I want to start a family at last! We're old enough!"

"Rolf, I've got my finals soon."

"So what? Just the right time."

"And if I fail? I'd have to repeat the year saddled with a brat. It's too risky."

"Please don't say brat. It would be a *child*, our child. Not a brat!"

"I don't want children. Not now."

"At least we could finally get married. For my parents' sake, if for nothing else. We could be happy."

"Could be—but aren't."

"You're telling me that—to my face?"

"Where else? To your arse?"

I gave von Brücken the transcript back.

"Errm. I don't quite understand. Was there someone hiding behind a column taking it all down in shorthand?"

"I've no idea if they were behind a column. The pair of them were really *loud* apparently."

Von Brücken looked away, looked at the ceiling, then his head dropped and he said he'd collected what he could get. He'd been a collector. A passionate collector. And would I please stop giving him those reproachful looks.

In 1961 Sofie gets her master's degree in Political Studies and *doesn't* get pregnant. Rolf makes one further, final effort to persuade her, but without success. After that he breaks off the relationship pretty abruptly. Sofie, who had been toying with the idea of moving to the East after completing her studies, is thrown into doubt just in time by the building of the Berlin Wall. Should one force people, even very stupid ones, to accept what is good for them? Even wall them in alive? Slowly and painfully she comes to comprehend that her idea of a just socialism is not something that will abolish oppression as a matter of course, as a logical step forward longed for by mankind. What should she do now? Continue to work at the supermarket checkout? Now that she no longer has any financial support from Rolf and Birgit's parents have died, fairly soon one after the other and without leaving a pfennig, the demands of the real world become more and more pressing. The Communist Party has finally been banned and Sofie accepts an interest-free loan from Birgit in order to give herself time to think about her future. Decides to do a doctorate. She's involved, in a voluntary capacity, in the organization of the Easter marches against nuclear weapons in Germany. The right-wing CDU's election posters have the portrait of Adenauer and the slogan: *No experiments!* Sofie sheds a few tears for the dead space-dog Laika. Adolf Eichmann is tried and executed. Sofie writes to Hannah Arendt. The letter is lost in the post so that she never gets a reply; ever since she's had a thing about philosophers, she sees them as arrogant and herself as inferior, not worthy of a reply. Elvis is serving in the US army in Germany, Castro takes over in Cuba, Kennedy becomes US president, Gargarin conquers space, Pele weaves his magic spells with the ball. Sofie falls in love with Camus, with his books as well, but above all with his face. Unfortunately Camus's just as dead as James Dean.

"What did the letter to Hannah Arendt say?"

"No idea. There is such a thing as the inviolability of postal correspondence. Do you think I stole Sofie's mail? I only learnt about the letter later, from her diary. No, my activities were discreet and showed respect. Though I did have to get that damn wall built just so as not to lose sight of Sofie."

Von Brücken gave me a grin. "Sorry. Joke. But a few basics: the Second World War had not been as devastating for Germany as is often maintained. Only about one in ten German soldiers had been killed. The Russians had suffered much heavier losses. And you must bear in mind that only around 15 per cent of Germany's huge industrial capacity had been destroyed. To put the supposed economic *miracle* in its proper perspective. And if, so far, you've allowed me a certain power, then please multiply it by ten or twenty to get at least some idea of the real situation. I was thirty years old and a god, or at least as close to being a god as is possible for a mortal man. Which was a matter of such complete indifference to me, it makes you want to weep. I had anesthetized myself with work, but yearning can't be . . . Oh, *you* find the words to express it.

Lukian, by the way, didn't live *right next door* to Sofie all the time. To ask that would have been unreasonable. The apartment was his official residence, yes, but he only slept there at weekends. After all, I couldn't stop him getting married, starting a family, having a life of his own, all that kind of thing. There had to be limits to the madness. That he should lose his family in such a tragic way—his young wife and his six-month-old son died in a car crash. It was a tragedy that made him question fate; he broke with his God and for a while couldn't stand me because of my "success." I had, as I said, several other informants in Wuppertal, apart from him, and Lukian didn't know about them all, not by a long chalk, so it was difficult for him to do anything unbeknown to me. Still, he was cunning—he still is and I wouldn't put it past him to have seen himself even then as a rival to me and have had a little affair with Sofie without my knowing. Nothing wrong with that. Sofie slept with some pretty repulsive characters. Lukian's not repulsive. You must definite-ly ask him about it—after I'm dead. After I'm dead he might even tell the truth. And if *you* learn the truth, it will be as if *I* had. Do you understand?"

"No. Well . . . yes."

MARCH 1963

Three months after the terrible accident, Lukian returns to his Wuppertal apartment. There's nothing here to remind him of Lore and Ben; at 34, he thinks, one ought to be able to start again, to let the dead rest in peace. He loved Lore, and he loved his six-month-old son even more, although—he finds it difficult to put this into words—although it's odd to love a little boy, who can't speak a single word, more than his wife, who is charming and educated, witty and kind-hearted. A love triggered off by chemistry, dictated by physical instincts and hormones. If you're really honest, he thinks, one six-month-old child is very like another, they don't have much in the way of personality. And the helplessness of infants has always struck Lukian as frightening. He feels as if his family was under threat from the very beginning, as if the tragedy was in the air. His anger fuels terrible thoughts, he imagines that deep down inside Alexander must be glad about what's happened, after all it means his closest associate and friend, who was slipping away from him, has returned to the fold. During his nighttime tears and railing against God, Lukian even imagines Alexander might be responsible for the accident, which is absolute nonsense, the drunk driver who has Lore and Ben on his conscience was a seventy-year-old Dutch pensioner who mixed up the brake pedal and the accelerator. Everyone finds it hard to accept the banality of such a tragic blow and looks for a meaning behind it all so as not to end up facing life feeling impotent and violated. How fragile everything is—and how pigheadedly most people carry on as if that weren't the case. It's remarkable, he thinks, how much mankind manages to achieve, despite the awareness of death we're saddled with. Or precisely because of it? At Alexander's request he's been reading Camus and found it not very convincing. He sees a happy Sisyphus as a complete idiot.

At that moment the doorbell rings, for the first time that year. He opens the door. It's Sofie, Sofie whom he's hardly registered as a person, just as an obsessive product of his boss's overheated imagination. She's wearing a white dress, neatly taken in at the waist and with a turned-up collar, and dangling her handbag in front of her knees.

"Good afternoon. Errm, I—you do remember who I am?"

"Of course. The girl next door."

"We hardly ever run into each other. Pity really, I keep thinking of that lovely bouquet—and I've never really thanked you for it."

"Don't mention it."

"I never hear anything from your apartment . . . That's why I kept forgetting."

"I'm afraid I can't ask you in just at the moment. It's in such a state . . . "

"There's no need. I just came to say goodbye."

"Goodbye?"

"I'm going away. To Berlin. The look on your face! You don't think it's a good idea?"

Lukian's face lights up, he's always hated Wuppertal. "Oh . . . no, that's . . . fantastic."

Sofie gives him a questioning look: *Was I such a lousy neighbor?*

Lukian forces his lips into a smile. " I mean—I've been . . . thinking myself of . . . "

"Going to *Berlin?* What a coincidence! What is it you do? Oh God, there's me being inquisitive again."

"Don't worry, it doesn't matter, er, I'm an . . . editor." It's so many years since Lukian prepared this answer, together with a credible life-story, that he has to rack his brains for a moment before he remembers it.

"Oh! How interesting! Which publishers do you work for? Sorry, I really am being *too* inquisitive." Sofie simpers, strokes her chin coquettishly with her thumb and forefinger.

"I work er . . . freelance. Here and there."

"That's incredibly interesting."

"Not really . . . And your friend? Is he going to Berlin too?

"We've separated. He's married now."

"Married? That was quick."

"Quick? S'pose so. He was in a hurry. Children and all that. Hopped on board the first woman to come along. Fancy going for a little walk?"

"Errm." She's suddenly addressed him by the familiar *du*, which Lukian finds disconcerting. What would his boss think? But he says Yes, just: Yes. And then repeats it, energetically, resolutely and quite unnecessarily: YES.

"Fine. Great! I'll just get my coat."

It's March 22, a Friday. Sofie and Lukian are chatting at a snack bar by the station, drinking mulled wine with too much cinnamon.

"D'you edit fiction or non-fiction?"

"Mostly. Err . . . the first."

"I get the feeling you don't like talking about yourself or your work."

"Well . . . *Belle et triste.* Some things are beautiful, most are sad."

"Would you really like to be a writer yourself? Or is that just a silly cliché about publishers' editors?"

"Perhaps. Perhaps that's . . . "

"I sometimes write poems. They're certainly not beautiful, but they're very, very sad."

"Hmm." he can't bring himself to address her directly, it would mean using the *du* himself.

"Don't worry. No one's ever going to see the stuff. Apart from me."

"Oh . . . Who knows?" He says it in a mildly sarcastic tone, which he immediately regrets. To cover up he asks her what she's studying.

"Political studies. But I've already graduated."

"What can one do with that?"

Sofie smiles. "Start a revolution? No, I don't really know myself. At the moment I'm working on my thesis. It's on the specifically political aspects of Camus' philosophy."

"Oh, really?" Fortunately it's a topic on which Lukian can pretend to be well-read with a clear conscience. He really loves Camus, he says, especially the *Myth of Sisyphus.*

"Oh yes? I don't particularly like that book."

After the mulled wine they're both a bit more relaxed. Lukian suggests they go to a nearby gallery which was reviewed in the local newspaper.

"What is there to see there?"

"I don't know. Something with TVs. The artist calls it Video Art."

"What could that be?"

Lukian says they could always go and see, perhaps it'd be a nice surprise. The artist was Asian. Sofie says it sounds exciting.

In the little Parnassus Gallery the two of them look at installations by a certain Nam June Paik. They're bizarre-looking works, ahead of their time. Basically just a number of TVs with the pictures distorted by electromagnetic interference. Lukian can't see much in it. Sofie suspects his opinion comes from conservative, bourgeois prejudice and says *she* likes it. She likes almost everything that's *new.* The important thing is to experiment.

"Then I like it too."

"What kind of attitude's that?"

"They call it opportunism."

Sofie has to laugh. Lukian turns away, suddenly he's uncomfortable with the situation. He's already getting on with Sofie so well he can make her laugh. Where's it all going to end?

"Why are you going to Berlin?" He's addressed her directly and he's used the formal *Sie*, afraid of where the *du* might lead. But then he finds that's going too far and repeats the question, with the more intimate *du*.

"Birgit's set up her chambers there with a couple of colleagues. Birgit's my stepsister, she's a lawyer."

"Oh, yes?"

"Things're happening in Berlin. I'll get some sort of work there. And here—here everything reminds me of Rolf. It's stifling."

"I can understand that. Sometimes it's advisable to change towns."

What a load of shit I'm talking, he thinks. And what do I say if she asks me where I grew up, where was it I thought of? I can hardly say Munich-Allach.

It's better if *he* asks the questions.

"You—you—" He keeps inadvertently using *Sie*, has to correct himself. "Excuse me saying so, but you don't sound entirely happy . . . "

"You know, Luc—I may call you Luc, mayn't I? Doesn't sound so old-fashioned."

"Please do, everyone calls me Luc."

"I'm afraid I'm the kind of woman who's never going to be completely happy. There's something inside me preventing it, my blood's probably too high octane. Or it's the way the world is that's to blame. I can't quite say. Perhaps I'll pack the thesis in. Too much like hard work. If I'm going to do that, it might as well be well paid."

"That would be . . . " Lukian doesn't complete the sentence, looks at his watch. "There's something I have to do. I have to go. Pity."

"Yes . . . " Sofie doesn't quite know why she thinks it's a pity too. This guy seems awkward, inhibited, not quite on the ball most of the time. And yet there's something about him, something mysterious.

Lukian gives her his visiting card. "Perhaps you'll get in touch—when you're in Berlin."

"Sure. I thought you were going to go there too?"

"Er, yes, perhaps not straight away, I mean, that remains to be seen, that is, probably. Then I'm sure we'll run into each other."

"Sure. It's just a big village, really. I'd like that." It's dark outside and cold. Sofie shivers, despite the smart white lambskin coat she won in a competition. Lukian could take advantage of the opportunity and put his arm around her.

"I have . . . " He lowers his voice, obligations

"Of course."

"I've really enjoyed talking with you. All the best for Berlin. Never say die. Always remember: the world's a crazier place than you'd think possible." He shakes her hand.

"Is it really?"

"Believe me, it is." He takes her hand in both of his, gives it a squeeze and turns away, hurries off. The tears are welling up in his eyes and he just manages to conceal them from her. Sofie's baffled. The guy spoke to her as if she had a tumor or something.

Lukian immediately came to the Owl's Nest. He was quite agitated. Churned up inside. We talked out there, in the park. He wasn't enjoying the life he was leading any longer, that was plain to see. He didn't actually say so in words, he was probably looking for a viable alternative. I was going through a crisis myself at the time, was dependent on pills. To be able to sleep now and then I needed veronal, later morphine injections that

Dr. Fröhlich gave me. I looked bleary and unkempt, had let my beard grow and hardly attended any meetings outside the castle. I was slowly becoming a phantom, a gray legend. It turned out that a businessman in my league could cut all the fancy stuff and deal with everything just as well by telephone. My behavior toward others became somewhat uncouth which, in retrospect, I very much regret. Lukian made great efforts to conceal his restlessness, which he didn't need to; after all, he'd lost his family and with them his life had presumably lost its meaning. He had every right to feel restless. I sensed or, rather, I thought I sensed why he was acting in such a controlled manner. He'd fallen head over heels in love with Sofie.

"She's going to Berlin! Next week! I hinted that I was about to go to Berlin too. She swallowed it."

"No. No . . . "

"I'd be quite happy to go to Berlin, Alex. I've never liked it in Wuppertal."

"No. You're staying here with me. Look at my face. I'm ill. I can't sleep anymore. That's all madness."

Lukian gave me a startled look, maybe I was shouting. Then he changed his tactics, threw off all restraint.

"Alex, I think I could get close to Sofie. Pretty close. I think she likes me. And she'll need us in Berlin."

"You'd do that for me?"

"Yes. It's my job."

"It's got to stop!"

"What?"

"THIS!" Again I was shouting.

Lukian squatted down beside me, like a grown-up with a child. And do you know what he said? Something terribly funny, funny in a twisted way and terrible.

"We can't leave Sofie on her own now."

"Why not?"

"She's not happy. She's writing poems!"

I laughed so much the tears ran down my cheeks. At some point or other I stopped laughing and just cried. Tears of self-pity. Why was I incapable of making something sensible of my life, why? Could I squander all the possibilities that were open to me on a person who felt nothing for me? What had so far been justified as a charming quirk, a piece of whimsy, was developing more and more into the waste of a whole life. And now Luki was starting to lose control.

During that night I had all the photographs my people had secretly taken of Sofie burnt in the meadow behind the castle. I watched from the library as one of the servants thrust the blazing torch into the pile. Watched, through my binoculars, Luki bend down and take one of the photos. The one of Sofie asleep that I showed you. A beautiful picture. Today I'm grateful that he did.

I sent for Dr. Fröhlich. Begged him to help me. To help me properly, not just give me morphine or that kind of thing. On the contrary, I needed a cure for my addiction. To get back on my own two feet.

Dr. Fröhlich was fantastic because he always managed to give you the feeling that anything that could happen in life was normal and could be put right with a few simple measures. He advised me to have a bath, shave and put on some clean, freshly ironed clothes. That was half the battle, so to speak. Then he gave me a sedative, not an authorized one, something very strong they use to calm down cows when they're calving.

"My life's burning away down there!"

"Let it burn. Make a new one."

I slept for three days and nights.

A Minor Skirmish

Lukian's psychiatrist claims he suffers from a guilty conscience because of the way he allowed his father to be ousted. Lukian thinks that's plausible, though it would never have occurred to him. While Alexander's sleeping, Lukian goes to see his parents. They live on Lake Tegern, in a renovated farmhouse with a huge garden and access to the water, they have everything to let them make the most of their remaining years. The idiots can't see that.

"You've been away so long. He's never forgiven you. If at least you'd written."

"But I did."

"Only to me. *He* doesn't want to see you." Mother Keferloher pours coffee. Father Keferloher's voice immediately echoes through the house. "Of course I want to see him."

Keferloher, considerably aged, is standing in the doorway to the living room.

"Son?"

"Dad?"

"Well? What is it?" Keferloher shuffles towards his son in cavernous felt slippers, then turns aside, scratches his stomach and collapses onto the sofa.

"How are you, Father?"

"That's neither here nor there. How is he?"

"Who?"

"Your lord and master. Has he gone mad?"

"What makes you say that?"

"He is mad. I know."

"Is that so?" Lukian would prefer not to pursue the matter any farther.

"We know the score. We know which way the wind's blowing. Is he far enough gone yet?

"Far enough for what?"

"You think I don't know? The way he goes around? I know everything. Everything!"

"Dad . . ."

"We can have him certified. You're Deputy Director now. We'll take over the business. Me and you, my son. That's why you've come, isn't it?"

Lukian says nothing, eats a piece of hazelnut cake. Father Keferloher giggles to himself.

"Are you surprised at all the things I know? You didn't expect that, did you? We've been watching you two, for a long time now. I knew that one day you'd come."

"And now, unfortunately, I have to go again." Suddenly it all comes back to Lukian. Why he broke with his father, why it was so very necessary.

"Tell that swine we're keeping an eye on him. Lots of eyes."

Lukian doesn't reply, gives his mother a kiss on the cheek and leaves, gasping for breath. It's a crucial experience for him. That people who have everything, but everything, they need to enjoy their old age to the full, apart from the ridiculous, transitory bit of power they once possessed, that such people find it impossible to return to a simple state of grace, of grateful enjoyment—Lukian vows he will never end up like that. Suddenly he realizes what an advantage it can be to live in the shadow of another, without the tedious obligation to represent something in the eyes of the world. His abortive visit to his parents has done nothing to reconcile him with his father, but at least it has made him a little more reconciled with himself.

CHEMISTRY AND CAPERS

When I woke from my deep sleep, Lukian and Doctor Fröhlich were by my bed. My friends. Lukian had decided to ignore his psychiatrist and to stick by me. He hadn't found it easy and I thanked him with a Mediterranean cruise, yacht and crew included. I asked Dr. Fröhlich for advice beyond the purely medicinal, he was the only person who was fully aware of the extent of my physical degeneration.

"Even if it sounds stupid," he said, "fall in love."

"Who with?"

"Who do you like?"

"Even if I did know someone, how can you fall in love with someone you only *like?*"

"Quite simple: you fool yourself. Autosuggestion. It has nothing to do with deceiving yourself, it's a natural defence mechanism of the brain against loneliness and emotional deprivation. You don't need to be ashamed of it and it's remarkable what this defence mechanism can often lead to."

"For you everything's just chemistry, isn't it, Doctor?"

"What else? Do you like Sylvia?"

I have mentioned that she had been my secretary. What I haven't mentioned is that she wasn't up to the demands made on her and pretty quickly had asked for a transfer back to Munich. It wasn't her work that was to blame, that wasn't bad at all, but my craziness was too much for her, my fixation with Sofie, the photos all over the place, my addiction, my caprices, the way I kept my distance—we had really only slept together that one time, a dozen years ago. And she was in love with me.

"Yes, she's very nice."

"Well, then. Does she like you?"

"More than just like."

"Good. Excellent. Would she be available?"

"Probably."

"There you are. Send for her. What you need at the moment is affection, genuine affection. Female warmth. Something to get your hands on." He made the appropriate gesture.

Fröhlich insisted we use the formal *Sie* to each other, it would help me, he said, to regard him as an authority figure. He had become a kind of fatherly friend to me and before I had come of age he addressed me by the familiar *du*; after that, however, whenever I suggested we stick to *du*, he said no, because otherwise he could not remain my doctor.

Perhaps he was a charlatan?

"But that's sick!" I cried. "Only someone with a warped mind could summon a person just so they . . . "

"Alexander, don't delude yourself. Don't try to be a person you're not. You're right, *someone* can't. *You* can. *You* are ill. And there are means open to *you* that are not open to others. That's why you fell ill in the first place. Use *your* means to combat your means. Only *then* will it be an equal fight." He lowered his voice a little. "You won't have to lie to Sylvia or pretend you're madly in love with her, she'll be content with less than that. Now that the Sofie business's over she'll be happy to come back to you."

"That all sounds as if you'd already sounded Sylvia out?"

"Put out feelers. Just put out a few feelers." He laughed and scratched his gray beard.

There's something important I must mention, even if it might seem irrelevant at the moment. But this is the place for it, even though no serious film director would have brought it in here. My chauffeur at the time, a young lad—no, the details aren't really important. So, to cut a long story short: it was around that time that the Beatles' first long-playing record came out in England.

To be honest, I'd never been very keen on music. You will despise me for that, but I want to be honest about my lack of culture.

But that music, the Beatles' music, had an immensely therapeutic effect on me. It was with that—perhaps, in the political sphere, with the assassination of Kennedy—that the sixties became a separate era for me. And the business with Sylvia went more or less the way Dr. Fröhlich had proposed and prophesied.

She had a contract as my *personal assistant*—Jesus, now this all sounds so bizarre, but I swear I really liked the woman and persuaded myself, no, I was certain that our arrangement was the best she could hope to get out of life. See, now you're grinning!

But the summer of '63 was really pleasant. We went about it quietly, gave each other shy kisses, drank wine—Dr. Fröhlich had directed me to drink good red wine. In the long run, he said, a person like me couldn't live without some addiction or other and good red wine was better than anything else I might get into. And a wave machine was installed in the swimming pool, one of the first in Germany. Swimming was my sport and when it was hot enough Sylvia and I went down to the river to bathe, in the rapids, it was a bit dangerous, but exciting. And I had all the huge daubs and ostentatious tapestries, which I'd let myself be persuaded were tasteful, cleared out of the great hall. Instead it was made into a kind of cinema; I had a large screen installed where films were shown every evening. I liked *La Dolce Vita* or *Zorba the Greek*, films which drew me, as part of the audience, into them. In the winter we made snowmen, bought cross-country skis and, beside the fire in the large tiled stove I could spend hours staring into, hours, I kissed Sylvia's stomach, out of gratitude because she really was good to me. She undressed, completely, just imagine, and she could have an orgasm if you simply stroked her breasts. That kind of thing can go to a man's head. But I don't want to tell you too much, just enough to indicate that what went on between us had its own distinctive quality and was not particularly dominated by sex. It would be easy to describe it in a nasty way and make Sylvia into a kind of sex doll, but that was not the case. Sometimes I left Lukian in charge of the business for months on end, our profit margins remained almost as high as ever. In places where we weren't working ourselves, our money was working for us, and if thoughts of Sofie crept into my brain, I drank the red wine prescribed by my physician. I won't lie, I still knew where Sofie was and what she was doing, but not in detail, more like glancing through a newspaper that belongs to a competitor, just to keep your eye in. Things looked good for me, there was hope. A bit of hope. And then, the years had flown by, *Revolver* came out, the Beatles' best album, it simply blew my mind. In that year, 1966, Dr. Fröhlich died. It affected me deeply and I'm not exaggerating when I say it meant a break in my life. But it was just Fröhlich as a *person* I missed, not his character, his advice, his intelligence.

At that time we, Sylvia and I, felt we were a couple; once we borrowed Lukian's yacht and sailed incognito around Sicily, with a little detour to Malta. Back in Germany we occasionally appeared in public together, went to the opera in Munich, or to the races in Baden-Baden. When the Beatles appeared at Circus Krone in 1966 I was in the audience, hidden behind a thick pair of sunglasses. I had the suite next to theirs in the Bayrischer Hof and I got all their autographs. Since I didn't speak much English, an interpreter was brought in specially. I exchanged a few words with John Lennon when I caught him one night adding extra figures to an oil painting in the hotel corridor; and he did it so skillfully, no one noticed the difference between before and after.

What we said to each other was trivial. *What are you doing? Painting? Great!*—that kind of thing. But it really gave me a high, talking to someone I admired. Something completely new for me. And for Sylvia? She could make nothing of the Beatles, the music did nothing for her. She didn't even try to pretend otherwise. You'll laugh or cry or think me a spoilt child, but that was probably the reason the construct started to crack and finally came crashing down. Sylvia was incapable of sharing my one musical euphoria and my reaction was to feel offended. Of course, it wasn't a spoilt child rearing its ugly head but the lie contained in our relationship. Still, you're welcome to portray me as a bastard in this chapter, I didn't deserve any better.

As if there were relationships *without* lies. As if *good* relationships were even *possible* without lies. I'd bought rings for us, only silver ones, plain but beautiful rings as an emblem of our liaison. While we were watching a film in the castle cinema—it was *Goldfinger*, though I don't think the title had anything to do with it—I suddenly felt fed up with it all and grasped Sylvia's hand, pulled the ring off her finger, took off mine and swallowed both of them. It was a gesture in place of all the words I couldn't be bothered to say; it gave me a night of severe stomach cramps until I got rid of the rings in the morning—and that was it.

This basically bearable phase of my life simply came to an end, like a summer holiday. Sylvia was provided for, of course, and she came back to the castle from time to time, it wasn't like that, we remained friends, but as far as—how shall I put it? As far as what Dr. Fröhlich called "female warmth' was concerned, I was alone once more. And the madness returned, naturally, the madness had been quietly waiting, twiddling its thumbs behind my back, until its turn came again. I sent Lukian to Berlin. He had no objections, he immediately looked delighted. I'm almost sure he'd been there already now and then, without my knowledge, without my permission, and seen Sofie. I would even be disappointed if that hadn't been the case.

1967

Birgit, together with two other ambitious, profit-oriented women lawyers, runs a moderately successful practice in Berlin-Schöneberg that specializes in commercial law. Sofie works for them and, despite her (unfortunately uncompleted) doctoral thesis, is little more than an overpaid secretary who's allowed to draft a document now and then, deals with the mail and makes coffee. She tries hard to feel grateful for the thirty-hour week, but that doesn't stop the work being dull and non-creative, doesn't stop it being a favor her stepsister's done her, nothing more. But the city makes up for a lot; Sofie's content with life.

She has a cheap (it's in need of renovation), three-room apartment on the more middle-class edge of the working-class district of Kreuzberg. It's a very neighborly area, lots of barbecues in the yard in summer, in winter they help carry up coal for elderly ladies living on the upper floors. It's more or less a matter of course.

Sofie has joined the GSSU, the German Socialist Students' Union. From her point of view, the main parties are almost indistinguishable from each other and the setting-up of the Grand Coalition between the Social Democrats and the Christian Democrats at the end of the previous year was the logical consequence. More and more often people are saying an extraparliamentary opposition is necessary. Sofie, who by this time has really short hair, a kind of crewcut, and loves wearing jeans, has joined the fight for university reform or, to put it another way, against antiquated social structures. A wave of youthful protest, set off by the Vietnam War, spills over from America to Europe. Many individual groups, who've fallen out with each other, are swept along by the current of the times and thrown together in a large-scale movement, before disintegrating back into minuscule cliques in a few years time. The campaign against Axel Springer's right-wing newspaper empire is being prepared and tactics discussed in Berlin. In view of the powerful position of the Springer Press, the annual conference of the Socialist University Association demands a law against the concentration of ownership of the press. The Socialist University Association is too soft for the GSSU, there are more and more demonstrations, some of them violent, directed against the Springer Building in Kreuzberg. For Birgit, thirty-five's too old to take part in this kind of demonstration in person. Sofie, one year older, is committed to them body and soul. Within a few months young people's attitudes, music and fashions undergo such a far-reaching change as has hardly ever occured before in the history of mankind. It's an exciting time, with revolutions preached and longed for. For Sofie, right in the middle of it, at the heart of events, so to speak, life suddenly becomes meaningful and significant, she feels she has found a road leading to a foreseeable goal. Like many other young graduates, she gives classes in politics in the evening, on a voluntary basis. Anyone can take advantage of them and they're followed by discussion groups where everyone gets high and which increasingly tend toward orgies of freedom, noise and hedonistic love. What dreary stodge was served up at the Circle in Wuppertal by comparison! This is the metropolis, bursting with life, everything's bright, thrusting, in a whirl. Mostly anyway.

At the moment, the end of February, the city's in the grip of the cold. It's going to be some summer, but no one knows that just now. Among the two dozen who have come to hear Sofie in a poorly heated shack in the east end of the city is Henry. It's clear to him, even before a single word has crossed her lips, that he'd like to take advantage of the pretty speaker.

Alongside all the young girls who've suddenly become interested in politics, Sofie feels she's close to saying farewell to her youth. But Henry's twenty-seven and his lust's written all over his face, which she finds pleasantly disconcerting. He goes around in leather and plays the hard man with a soft center. Sofie quickly feels drawn to him, not least because of the no-nonsense, no-beating-about-the-bush way he approaches her.

Perhaps it's her deep-seated inferiority complex which makes the muscular, intellectually somewhat basic, but clearly very honest ("I want you.") guy seem attractive to her.

The beginning of March. Having made it to Sofie's bedroom, Henry displays his new tattoos. Marx on the left shoulder, Engels on the right. Sofie thinks it's, well . . . but why not? She subordinates her aesthetic response to the purely ideological. Then she is fucked until it feels like she's never been fucked before, at least to a certain extent she feels as if she has only had an indication, an earnest hint of things to come, of things still on the program. Henry comes down on her like a storm on exposed countryside. It can't really be compared to Rolf. And certainly not to the three brief little affairs she's had since. Sofie experiences the ecstasy of a (regular!) multiple orgasm. It's difficult to find arguments to counter that, neither the fact that Henry doesn't possess a toothbrush of his own, nor that he drinks the cheapest canned beer, burps out loud and has only heard of Beethoven from a Chuck Berry song. He has a tendency toward violence, which at first only vents itself at demonstrations. He's desperate for escalation, is always the one to throw the first cobblestone. He persuades Sofie to throw one as well, tells her it would help to liberate her from her petty-bourgeois inhibitions. Not wanting to be called petty bourgeois and inhibited, she finally tries it out, like the first time she took a deep drag on a joint. The stone hardly travels twenty meters, doesn't injure anyone—yet from that moment on there's a police photo showing Sofie throwing a stone, a shy grimace on her face, the open-mouthed expression of someone who's not quite sure about themselves. Through Henry she discovers a facet of her personality that would probably otherwise never have surfaced. That spring is an exception to the rule, a boundary crossed, a feast of fun and very, very good sex.

Which Henry doesn't just have with her alone. He screws anything floating around that he can pick up. Laughs off reproaches as bourgeois attempts at repression. The time comes when communes are set up in which everyone sleeps with everyone else according to a schedule. Sofie finds that revolting but never says so out loud for fear of being thought conventional. And old.

However, her jealousy turns out to be negligible compared with Henry's jealousy the moment he suspects she's looked another man in the eyes for a tenth of a second too long. Then he tends to go wild with rage, bawling and shouting, which Sofie is graciously prepared to interpret as a sign of his love. Spring of '67 excuses many things.

You have to imagine what it was like— the world was going wild, was buzzing, everything seemed to be changing. And me? I stayed in my castle, a depressed escapist, listening to reports that my beloved had fallen for a tattooed beer drinker and was uttering alarming cries of pleasure during the night. The sense of being excluded—you know, whatever my own personal attitude to this revolution, I would never have been allowed to take part in it simply because I had too much money and power. OK, I could have given up my money and power, but I would never have been believed, just as, deep down inside, I didn't believe in the revolution. But did I envy them! You know, I was sure this drunken phase wouldn't last long, but for the moment it was there, was present in all its intoxication and it made some people indubitably happy. God, was I fed up with myself! What was my wealth worth if it barred me from all the orgies and ecstasies these young people got more or less for free on a daily basis? Everything Lukian told me about *Henry* led to fear. Fear and concern for my beloved, who was clearly sexually in thrall to this *creature*.

THE OPERA

The Shah's coming to Berlin." Henry's seen it in the newspaper and tells Sofie over breakfast. She doesn't immediately realize why it's important and for whom.

"So what?"

"Things'll be happening."

Sofie still doesn't understand what things will be happening.

Lukian was on the telephone. "The Shah's coming to Berlin. We've an invitation to the Opera."

"Fine. We accept." Anything would have suited me. I had to get out of my lethargy, back into the world.

"We accept?"

"I'm fed up of sitting around here."

May 31, 1967. Mehringdamm. The doorbell rings. Henry goes—for the last time without concern—to open the door. Police storm the apartment, take him and Sofie away in handcuffs. Without giving any explanation.

Lukian met Sylvia and me at the airport. We'd heard about the arrest around eleven and arrived at Berlin-Tegel towards four, two days earlier than planned. Sylvia had immediately said she was happy to accompany me.

"Is she OK?"

"As well as can be expected." Lukian didn't really reassure me. "Her sister's looking after her."

"That's not enough," I said, but in fact it was enough for the moment. Birgit got Sofie released. She must have really put herself out, she'd made them show her the evidence, had talked to the prosecutor, not taken "no' for an answer, made a big impression.

A warder beckons Sofie out of her cell. "You're getting out. Pack your stuff." Sofie is outraged that this person should insult her by using the familiar *du*, but she says nothing and follows him, there's no stuff for her to pack, out into the corridor, full of anger at the police state, of which she is now a victim. Birgit's waiting for her outside, embraces her and drives her to the office, waiting for a word of thanks during the whole journey. Instead:

"What about Henry?"

"He stays."

"How did you get me out and not Henry?"

"He's got a record."

"I didn't know that."

"Car theft. Grievous bodily harm. Vandalism. Does that turn you on?"

"What's that supposed to mean?" They fall silent. Birgit has made a resolution never to have an argument in the car. It could easily lead to an accident.

In the office, from which Sofie has been absent without explanation for four weeks, they have a cup of coffee. During those four weeks the rooms have been completely renovated, Sofie hardly recognizes the place. It's all so swish. Birgit must be making a mint. War profiteer.

"Now listen. Because of the Persian pasha the police have their sights on all demonstrators who've been involved in violence. I've talked to the prosecutor and managed to convince her you're harmless. Or, to put it another way, she's recognized they can't prove you've caused any damage. So for the moment the matter's regarded as too trifling to take any further. But please—don't let yourself be photographed with a stone in your hand again. That's stupid. Not worthy of you. Proceedings have been initiated against your boyfriend for not paying a bar tab and theft. They'll keep him inside for a few days, then let him go. He'll survive."

"OK, is that it?" Sofie is irritated by the superior, condescending tone Birgit has deliberately adopted.

"You're welcome. If you want to come back to work here you can start next week."

Sofie doesn't reply. A few hours later she's a bit sorry about that, but just at the moment she couldn't care less. Without a word she leaves the office and bursts into tears out in the street.

The main thing was that Sofie was free. And Henry was inside. In fact I was enjoying the situation. While in holding, Henry was beaten up—some fellow prisoners from a proletarian background took offence at his flowing locks. I swear I had nothing to do with it. Why have him beaten up when I could just as well have had him killed? You must remember: I hadn't seen Sofie for a good fifteen years, except for photos. And I wanted to see her again at last, face to face. That she would be out on the street, taking part in the demonstration against the Shah, was obvious. In my suite in the Bristol-Kempinski Hotel I saw one of the people who were to keep an eye on Sofie during the demonstration. One of seven very fit, trained men. Some had no idea who they were working for.

"Will you be able to let me see her?" We were talking about seeing Sofie from a distance, through my opera glasses, no more than that.

"No problem, Boss. I'll have a placard, painted green. I'll stand beside her."

"Good."

Don't shake your head like that. It was just a bit of innocent fun.

What we hadn't reckoned with, of course, was the violence of the over a hundred Persian secret agents. By midday on June

2 they had already started laying into the demonstrators outside Schöneberg Town Hall, just imagine, the police did nothing, nothing at all, to stop the state visitor's thugs. They'd gone completely over the top and were laying into the crowd with sticks and truncheons, a crowd whose protests up to that point had been merely verbal and nonviolent. Unbelievable. Later on, the police even assisted the Shah's thugs. Makes you ashamed to be German. Toward evening the situation deteriorated. You know, to my shame I have to confess politics never meant much to me. Shah Reza Pahlavi was said to be a murderer, a torturer, but the women's magazines treated him and the charming Farah Diba like a fairy-tale king and his queen. Large sections of the population regarded the rowdy students as spoilsports, the press said the kind of things ordinary people wanted to hear and almost without exception stirred things up against the critical voices, talked about gangs of badly brought-up savages. I had no clear opinion on all this, I was politically illiterate. As a businessman I was naturally suspicious of socialism, and there was nothing that happened later to make me change that. But on that day. . . Let's take things as they happened:

The *crème de la crème* turned up at the entrance to Berlin's opera house, to enjoy Mozart's *Magic Flute*. The Shah was driven up to be greeted by a furious uproar of boos and whistles. Some of the people had put paper bags over their heads with the Shah's face painted on them. They wanted the murderous prince, the tyrant, to be, well, staring into his own face. The practical side-effect was that the demonstrators were masked. A few paint bombs were thrown, some bricks already. And I, with my opera glasses, was scanning the crowd for Sofie. Or for a man carrying a green placard. Do stop laughing.

I had no idea the crowd would be so big. Now the odd egg and smoke bomb was being thrown, nothing too bad, a wide area of the square in front of the opera had been cordoned off by police and Persian secret service. I was desperately looking for the green placard. Mayor Albertz was standing right next to me. I heard him say to Duensing, the chief of police, "When I go out, I want everything cleared, right?" "*Jawohl, Herr Bürgermeister!*" Duensing barked. And passed the order on to one of his subordinates: "Truncheons out, clear the square."

Sylvia tugged my sleeve, "What's up? Are we going in or not?"

"You two go on ahead." I gave Lukian two of the three invitations. You must understand that I had no idea what was happening out there. I watched through my opera glasses as some Eastern-looking characters, armed with steel rods, started laying into the crowd. My concern for Sofie was so great, I was quite happy to forgo the pleasure of the *Magic Flute*. I ran down the street alongside the opera toward Ernst-Reuter-Platz until I was past the cordon and could cross over. Without even one bodyguard, I was standing on the edge of a scene of chaos and panic, in my formal dress. I took off my dinner jacket, so I wouldn't stand out too much.

Sofie is shocked at the unbridled violence that is unleashed on the demonstrators. One man, his face distorted with fury, is hitting out in all directions with a steel rod, blood is flowing, people screaming as they fall to the ground. Sofie bends down over an injured student and presses her handkerchief to his nose, which is streaming with blood. All the while the rod-man's spinning around and around, like a dervish in a trance, slashing to the right and to the left. Suddenly the protecting crowd has receded, there's just Sofie and the dazed student on the ground—and the rod-man's not dancing anymore, he's running toward the pair. It's the end, Sofie thinks, but from behind her two men, no longer young, both *hulking great brutes*, appear, hurl themselves at the rod-man, smash into him and knock him to the ground.

One of the two bends over Sofie, lifts her up, drags her over to the side of a building. "Come along. Things are getting too hot here."

Sofie has just managed to gasp her thanks, when several hundred police storm the square. After brief resistance the two *hulks* are overcome and handcuffed. Sofie manages to escape from the attack, runs down a little sidestreet heading south.

I stayed on the edge of the fracas. Not because I'm particularly cowardly, but because it was only from there that one had any chance of getting some kind of overall view. I tore off my bow tie and pulled my shirt out of my trousers to fit in better with the surroundings. Buttons flew off and rolled down the street. I found the man with the green anti-Vietnam placard, he was leaning against an advertising pillar by the edge of the sidewalk, he'd been pretty badly beaten up. His placard was torn, the handle broken in two. Not fifty meters away from me the police were arresting everyone they could catch. Some demonstrators were trapped.

"You OK?"

"Hey, boss, what're you doin' here?" He sounded slightly delirious. His upper lip was burst.

"Lean on me. Off we go." We staggered along for a few steps, but the man was all in, he needed medical assistance, his legs gave way, and I left him lying in a doorway. Sofie was more important. Nor could I imagine, to be honest, that the police would attack a man who was already injured. And then, out of the corner of my eye, I saw her. My beloved was sitting in the open gateway leading to a courtyard, hammering a letterbox with her fists in rage. The police were driving some of those who were trying to get away from them down the little sidestreet, it looked like those pictures you see of Pamplona where people get chased through the streets—though of their own free will, of course—by bulls.

I ran over to my beloved, crying, "We've got to get away from here." I was quite happy to accept the risk that Sofie might recognize me, I was disguised by my beard and sunglasses, my face had got a bit puffy with the years. A fat woman in a blue apron and a black wart by her nose the size of fifty-pfennig pieces came down the stairs, shouted at us, what did we think we were doing, scum like us had no business there. Wailing sirens passed. We staggered across the yard and the noise from the street was scarcely audible, it was almost a haven of peace. A big guy came running up to me, it was one of my mine, perhaps the only one who'd not yet been caught. "Everything OK, Boss?" I nodded and placed my finger on my lips to tell him to keep quiet, fortunately Sofie hadn't noticed what he'd called me, her eyes were swollen, she was presumably suffering from shock. The three of us went up the stairs at the farther end of the rectangular block, old wooden stairs up to the second floor where we rested, squatting against the cool wall between the doors to two apartments; I turned my face away from Sofie, though it was entirely unnecessary, it was almost dark in the corridor. We smoked and I disguised my voice if I had to say something. Sofie wanted to know who we were, the man, *my* man, said he was called Martin. Perhaps he really was. Or perhaps not. I called myself *Boris*, the first name that came into my head. Why? Because that was the name of the current world chess champion. A shot was heard in one of the courtyards outside. Sofie wanted to go and see what had happened, we held her back. Down below some people were running from A to B. My heart was beating so hard I was afraid all the time I might faint. The last time I'd been so close to my beloved was during the night bombing raids, over twenty years ago. We didn't talk much, our fear of being discovered was too great. What we said—banal stuff, an attempt to come to terms with what we'd just experienced, so more sighs, gasps and wheezes than words. We smoked the whole time. I held Sofie's hand for several minutes. Please don't describe how I felt, I don't know and I don't believe anyone could describe how it was. We sang, very softly, more humming than singing. It was almost funny, not because it sounded wrong, but we sang anything that occurred to us, and Sofie's "We Shall Overcome" modulated into Martin's "We'll Meet Again" and I hummed "It's Been a Hard Day's Night," but in the tempo of a slow blues, it had a touch of something droll but mystical. A strange melancholy, so intense it made you feel good.

I got to my feet shortly before ten. I didn't say goodbye, just patted Martin on the shoulder, patted Sofie on the shoulder and went down the stairs, out into the street, past people rushing around frantically, and headed for Kurfürstendamm. I had to make several detours, in many places people were still being chased and beaten up. An ambulance screeched around the corner, siren wailing. Later I learnt that it was taking away the body of Benno Ohnesorg, a defenceless 27-year-old student who had been shot or, to put it more precisely, executed by Police Sergeant Kurass. While the next day the press twisted the events scandalously, with inflammatory attacks on the students, who they claimed were responsible for the disastrous way things had developed, many others regarded the night of June 2 as the beginning of a just revolution. Sylvia and Lukian were waiting for me at the hotel. The opera, they said, had been very nice, but they had been worried about me. What had been happening outside? Inside they hadn't heard anything, just music. We went to the grill bar next to the Kempinski to have a late supper. I couldn't eat a thing. Opposite the grill bar, with a good view from the window, was the Bank for Commerce and Industry. Two middle-aged gentlemen in expensive suits came out of the building, laughing, with markedly rapid steps, like in a silent movie, and I decided to change my life for good. A life dictated by money is just high-class slavery, not worth a damn. That was the way I was thinking at that moment. Childishly simpleminded. You don't need to gloss it over. Let's finish early today. I don't feel well.

It was evening when von Brücken dismissed me. His voice was hoarse and the painkillers affected his memory, which was why he preferred to suffer during the day and only have injections in the evening. That day I had to eat by myself; he had never had a particularly good appetite, up to now he had dined with me more out of politeness. A politeness which, as the pain increased, he was no longer willing nor able to maintain.

During that cold, clear night, I decided to have a look at the tomb in the park. That was impolite on my part, it had nothing to do with me, it was like looking into someone else's bedroom. On the other hand, I hadn't been forbidden to go there. And in the typical way you can justify anything to yourself, I told myself my curiosity could just as well be seen as sympathetic interest. I went out by the front entrance. There was a guard not far from the drive who whispered something into his Microport, but made no attempt to stop me going for a walk. There was snow-covered grass to cross to get to the edge of the park and the crunch of my steps sounded incredibly loud to me. There was white, very white light from some waist-high lamps, placed here and there according to some unfathomable geometrical design. Once I'd reached the fir trees, I looked around to see if anyone was following me. No one. The usual quiet building noise could be heard from the middle of the big water meadow. After the conifers came rings of various deciduous trees, among the islands of birches, all bare, of course, but during the summer they must have made it at least very difficult, if not impossible, to see the big meadow. Bright lights were being used, I could make out the hazy outlines of a building with a rounded top, shaped like an igloo only a little more cylindrical, recalling a helmet from the Spanish Armada or the head of the alien from the film of the same name. In front some men were at work, on either side were vehicles parked in the snow, delivery vans, tractors, diggers. My appearance did not go unnoticed, but no one seemed to have any objection to my being there, occasionally a worker would put two fingers to his right temple in greeting. A figure came toward me, in a long, dark coat. Hands in pockets, it gradually emerged from the darkness and approached me.

"Can you not sleep?" It was Lukian. Either he was there by chance, or he'd been told I'd gone out and had taken a short cut.

"I could sleep." There was no reason to lie. "I was simply curious."

"Great. Alexander will appreciate that. But you've come too soon."

"Can't I have a look?"

"Of course you can." Lukian took my arm, a surprisingly familiar gesture from him, which therefore had a slight suggestion of force. "Only not now. It's not finished yet. We beg you to exercise a little patience. Please. No one will ever learn so much about all this as you, Alexander has selected you, he trusts your abilities, let things take their course."

He asked me to return to the house. As far as was possible to judge in the light, the igloo—the mausoleum, the Spanish helmet—appeared to be built of black porphyry.

I asked Lukian if he would tell me a bit more about Berlin 1967, the Boss had only hinted briefly at his role in a way that suggested he had been in the city already. It struck me—for the first time I'd referred to von Brücken as the *Boss*. I immediately felt unhappy with it.

Lukian said nothing as he gently urged me back toward the house, he remained silent for a long time, then he said that even I couldn't hope to portray life in all its complexity, no one could ever hope to do that, but that didn't matter, it was Alexander von Brücken who was employing me, not Life, I simply just had to try to put what had been described to me into words. No easy task. Beyond that there would always be speculation, no story ever had an end, it could continue endlessly in its fractals. Or to use a literary image—I was, after all, a writer: Great fleas have little fleas upon their backs to bite 'em. And little fleas have lesser fleas, and so on ad infinitum.

"I'm sorry, but that sounds unsatisfactory."

"Unsatisfactory?" Lukian repeated the word, slight distaste in his voice.

"Not very cooperative."

"Alexander's a great flea; whether or not I'm a lesser flea who's gotten lost somewhere in his story can be of no possible interest to you." Modifying his severe tone slightly, he turned around in a circle once, both hands in his coat pockets. There was only room for *everything* once, he said. In that specific moment when that *everything* happened. Every moment was unrepeatable and even the most competent art could only reproduce it in fragments. Moreover it happened to be a fact of life that life was mostly unsatisfactory. Apart from moments.

I couldn't quite make him out. On the one hand it sounded as if he just wanted to be pressed a little more, on the other his words suggested a fatalistic acceptance of his lot which had long since come to terms with transience and was unwilling to stir up anything unless it was absolutely necessary. But then why was he talking to me at all? He accompanied me to my room and waited until he was sure I'd locked it from inside. I felt I'd been treated like a child, reprimanded, and yet this was outweighed by the feeling that Lukian was no longer indifferent or totally opposed to my project, that he had accepted me in a way as the last piece needed to complete the jigsaw.

DAY FOUR

AD INFINITUM.
THE PARALLELS BEGIN TO CONVERGE

That night, after a quarter bottle of whiskey and a hot bath, I couldn't stand it in the hotel. I needed to know whether Sofie had managed to get home. The people I had on the spot had almost all been locked up, replacements were on their way, but mobile communication hardly existed in those days, only bulky walkie-talkies, moreover I was certain Sofie hadn't recognized me, wouldn't recognize me, so what was wrong with going to her place? I didn't want to do her any harm, didn't want to force my way into her life, just give her a little help here and there, protect her, look after her. Surely that's not reprehensible? Is it? Say something. Why don't you reply? Is there an ethics of love? Wildlife photographers perhaps have unwritten rules about not intervening in the natural course of events, not taking sides, and in physics it's well known that the observation of an experiment always influences it —

"Doesn't that only apply to quantum physics?"

"Maybe. Doesn't matter. It's not that I'm trying to justify myself simply because, according to the stupid adage, all's fair in love and war. And that the way to hell is paved with good intentions is a false pearl of wisdom I've already heard. What I want you to tell me is: was what I did *reprehensible*?

What did he want me to say? I caught myself looking for an answer that would strike him as honest. For example that, whatever the intention, passing oneself off as someone else remained a deception and therefore showed disrespect for others. However, a large part of human life was based on deliberate disrespect and deception. One couldn't get on one's high horse and talk of guilt, at most of the first link in a chain of cause and effect leading to unforeseeable consequences. Living meant initiating chains of cause and effect. Even the most strict Buddhists had not managed to escape that. Was that how I should put it?

"It's not my place to judge you."

"What?! Why do you think you're here? *In order* to judge me, that's why!" He sounded furious. "Your novel will be the verdict on my life, I want you to be harsh but just, and please don't spare me, I'll be dead, but—" He paused and pressed the palms of his hands on his face. "I don't *want* to be dead." Von Brücken laughed. "Sorry. We mustn't get too personal."

Where was I? Oh yes, that July night I was standing on Mehringdamm looking up at the three windows of Sofie's apartment, all brightly lit. It certainly *looked* reassuring. But it wasn't enough for me. At three in the morning I rang the bell. Someone opened. The place was full, you can't imagine how full, so full that hardly anyone noticed me.

Practically the whole of her class was there. It wasn't clear to me whether they were having a party or whether they'd declared a state of emergency and were meeting to discuss the situation. That may sound rather cynical, but in fact it wasn't that easy to ascertain. The people, more men than women, were in all the rooms, sitting down, beer was being drunk, two radios were on, one with jazz, the other was being used to listen in to the police radio. No one wondered who I was until somebody noticed my Italian shoes.

"Who the hell's that?" Suddenly the room went quiet, then Sofie looked up.

"He helped me."

Immediately the discussions and debates continued. The only thing that annoyed me was that I appeared to be of no further interest to Sofie either. She neither said hello nor asked how I came to know her address. I must have prepared an explanation, in case she did, but I honestly can't say what it was, it won't have been very convincing. And by the way, since my Italian shoes have come up, I should perhaps also mention that almost all the men were in collar and tie, I don't want you to start imagining a band of robbers with unkempt beards, that only came later. White shirt, narrow black tie, that's what a lot of these so-called red revolutionaries looked like, that is those who felt it important to emphasize their intellectual pretensions. In the farthest room I saw *Martin*, if that was his name— all at once I realized Sofie must have assumed *he* had given me the address, mystery solved. Martin was snoring on the sofa, seemed to have had a fair amount to drink. Should I be angry with him? After all, the guy was on duty, in a way. Still, let him enjoy his well-earned rest.

A certain Holger, late twenties, full beard and check shirt, no white shirt, no tie, was sitting listening to the police radio and announced that all hell was still let loose out there.

"And how do we know we can trust him?" The question flew past me, it was only after a while that I realized it was about me. A sinewy young blond guy, his hair already thinning, was staring at me. He was called Olaf and even the lefties considered him slightly paranoid, as I later learnt. It was only now that I picked up a can of beer from the bath, as a kind of proletarian emblem.

"Hey, I asked a question, is no one here listening to me?" Olaf refused to let it go. At that moment Martin woke up, looked around, started and croaked, his mouth dry, "I know him. He's OK."

We briefly made eye contact. I thought and decided I must give my new name, in case Martin had forgotten it."

"I'm Boris."

"And you know him?" Olaf insisted.

"We're in the same business." Martin's color changed several times as he said that. He frowned, made an effort to function precisely, not to talk nonsense, but those few apparently innocent words dropped me in it. Sofie turned to me. "You're a taxi driver?"

"Err . . . yes. For the moment."

Holger interrupted us. "There's a report of a dead pig."

They all crowded around the radio. It was a false report, but that didn't become clear until the next day.

"That's the start of the revolution!" Olaf applauded, clapping loudly. "Off we go! We must fight!"

Sofie said she'd had enough of violence. She was talking like a kindergarten teacher, Olaf snapped. That touched a raw spot. Furious, she pursed her lips. It looked as if she was going respond with something just as cheap, but she restrained herself and muttered, with a touch of self-irony, "Sometimes I feel like that," adding, "when I look at you lot."

"I'm not going to grow old gracefully! You can bet your life on that."

You bastard, I thought. My hatred of Olaf was settled and irreversible. How could he say something that horrible about my Sofie? But when I looked around, I realized Sofie and I were in fact the oldest there. It was something I'd never previously been brought face to face with: that generations after mine had managed to see the light of day. An industrialist in my position is still a stripling at thirty-seven, a belated *wunderkind*. Here, among all these people who were scarcely more than children, I was dangerously close to forty, the age beyond which, as the slogan of the time said, no one was to be trusted.

Holger who, despite his check shirt, clearly felt he was an intellectual alpha male, raised both arms in an almost priestly gesture of calming.

"We'll do nothing at all without instructions. Escalation demands coordination. Otherwise the pigs'll simply walk all over us. I'll get on the phone."

"Henry'd go out! Lead the way! Blaze a trail! With fire! You have to take a night like this by the scruff of the neck and throw

it to the ground like a brute beast and brand your mark on it!"
There was a glint, a flicker in Olaf's eyes, a sign of the desire for
action that was simmering, boiling inside him with no outlet.

"Who's Henry?" I asked in a whisper of feigned curiosity.

"My boyfriend. He's in the slammer." At last Sofie shook my
hand.

"Oh. I'm sorry."

"My uncle has a gun store." This, uttered *allegro moderato*,
came from Karin, a very pretty nineteen-year-old flower child.
I say *flower child*, because then you can immediately picture
what she was actually like, even though the term *flower child*
hadn't been coined then. She wore some kind of Far-Eastern
gear, a gilet with fantastic embroidery over sack-like purple
trousers and she was smoking a fat, misshapen self-rolled cigarette with a strange odor. It was all exciting and unreal. I didn't
belong there, but it was fun, like an excursion to another planet.
I just couldn't tear myself away. I became aware of how much I
was missing out on. OK, I could drink the most expensive wine
every evening, I'd visited the Elysian fields of morphine, could
have films delivered before they were on general release, had
cruised the Mediterranean with a Sylvia who . . . No matter: I
could afford anything that had a price. But this here, this kind
of thing, was something I'd never had, this mix of energy and
rage and optimism—don't give me that look, I know what it
sounds like, it sounds disingenuous for me to claim I envied
these have-nots.

What I'm trying to say is that on *that night*, that's what I'm
talking about, on that night I'd have given anything to be able
to cast off my old skin and choose a new way of life. You're
probably thinking that ought to have been easy for *me*. Who
else could if I couldn't? But that's not the way things are. My
unsatisfying life offered a number of possibilities. You don't
swap that for a life with only *one* possibility, which just *might* be
satisfying. Let's not beat about the bush. We're slaves to our

comfort, to our power. Life's too short and our willpower too weak to rebel against it.

"Are these all friends of yours?" I asked my beloved.

"Friends? I'm more like a mother to them."

"You help 'em learn things?"

"I try. But as far as the decisive factor's concerned, each individual has to learn what that is for themselves."

"What is the decisive factor?"

"It depends. On the person. Usually it's connected with a decision."

"I don't follow."

Sofie seemed weary. What she now said must have been a subject about which she'd argued with herself for years and years.

"I mean, who's right? Gandhi or Che Guevara? Gandhi's not as sexy as Che, that's for sure. Something's happening, out there, it's become a police state. You get a slap, you can turn the other cheek, then the cheeks of your ass, but that's it, after that you run out of cheeks. What should I say to the guys who want to go and get guns now? I don't know and I don't want to be responsible for what they do, for the decision they arrive at. D'you follow me?"

"What an exciting life you lead."

"You don't?"

"Well, you know. Today was exciting, but normally . . . "

"You must come across all sorts of things in your job."

"You think so? It's a way of making a living." I really had to be careful what I said, I'd only been a cabdriver for fifteen minutes and I couldn't even drive. I'd passed my driver's test seventeen years before, but I'm sure I'd forgotten everything by then.

We chatted a little about Seneca and the Stoics and politics and I can't remember what else.

"So what d'you do when you're not driving a taxi—"

I broke in. "I like this song, d'you fancy a dance?"

"Here? In the kitchen?"

"Why not?"

"Here, There and Everywhere" was on the radio. Sofie nodded.

Now I remember. Earlier that evening, on the stairs in the darkness of the tenement, we talked briefly about the Beatles. I'd called their music revolutionary, said it had enriched, changed my life. Sofie's reply had been that to use the word *revolutionary* in connection with music was rubbish. And if you did, then perhaps the Stones were doing something for the revolution, in a roundabout way, but certainly not those nice Beatles. But even she thought "Here, There and Everywhere" was *beautiful*. That at least.

At that time beauty wasn't a term used seriously in political discourse, beauty was considered a forbidden word, devoid of significance. Writers couldn't use it without laying themselves open to the accusation of producing kitsch. At most it would crop up in discussions about the oppression of women by patriarchal, sexist aesthetics, but even then the word used wasn't *beautiful*, but *attractive*. I was delighted to hear the word *beautiful* from Sofie's lips, even though, were it queried, she would certainly have replaced it with another.

We danced, but not too close. It was the atmosphere that brought us together, that was all, the aura of a hazy early morning when most of the guests have already taken their leave, at least in spirit, and weariness ends up in a phase of rapt melancholy. The song lasted three minutes. I was floating in infinite space and wished the blade of some heavenly guillotine would descend to bring a swift end to this indescribable bliss so that it could not be threatened again. The indescribable bliss lasted three minutes.

Instead Holger came in, bawling that they'd killed *Benno*. He—like many others after him—talked of *Benno* as if he were a close friend. So the body I'd seen being driven away with my own eyes was called Benno. Benno Ohnesorg. Just imagine he'd not been called Benno, "Carefree," but, I don't know, Peter Müller—OK, OK, that's irrelevant. Word suddenly went around that there was to be a kind of picket, a silent protest, perhaps also a demonstration, we were all to go to the *scene of the crime*. Some, however, were completely incapable and others thought it could be a trap set up by the police, who just wanted to get the demonstrators on record.

Sofie put on a clean shirt. She stood there for a moment, granting me a sight of her bra, then went to the washbasin and gave her face a good scrub.

"Can you take us there in your taxi?" She was asking *me*. I stammered something along the lines of er, well, no . . . I'd left my taxi near the Opera and the tires had been slashed. Sounded not impossible. Instead Martin, who had more or less sobered up, offered to drive us there. Perfect camouflage—he was working as a taxi driver. Seven of us crammed into his Mercedes, Sofie and me, Holger, Olaf, Karin, a curly-headed lad I didn't know, and Martin driving. Olaf was sitting in the front passenger seat, with Karin in his lap. I had Sofie in my lap, it meant nothing, lack of space meant it had to be like that. I kept wondering whether Sofie could feel my erection, I realized I'd ventured too far and was in danger of getting stuck in an awkward situation; what had started as a little adventure was becoming serious, I had to get away, had to make a break.

Here, There and Everywhere. Wouldn't that be a good title? Just a suggestion. No?

THERE

The rear courtyard around five in the morning—closed off. It's almost light already and strangely quiet. A considerable crowd has gathered at the barrier, through which only *residents* are allowed to pass. Flowers are placed there, candles lit. Sofie, Karin and the five men have to mourn in the third row.

"We heard the shot," Sofie whispers, "but we didn't know it was a shot, it sounded like a bang, like when you burst a paper bag you've blown up, there was no way we could have known what had happened."

"Who's *we*?" Karin finds it terribly exciting, she'd have loved to have heard the shot herself.

"Martin, Boris and me. That was when I met the two of them. Without them it might have been *me* on the receiving end." She looks around, would like the others to confirm her story. Neither Boris nor Martin are behind her.

"Aren't they here? Didn't they say goodbye?"

"There's something not quite kosher about that Boris. I knew right from the start. Did you see the shoes he was wearing?" Olaf's upper lip twists in a sneer of contempt. He's getting on everyone's nerves.

"He probably has to see about his taxi."

"Probably!" Olaf grins scornfully.

On that day a lot of people in Germany start to revise their ideas. For the first time ordinary people, who so far have looked down on the students, feel sympathy for them, share their feelings. A splinter group of theory-laden political agitators makes the GSSU the driving force behind the student movement.

Diary 6.3.67

Early evening, big demo against the Shah outside the Opera. Massive police presence. Persian thugs, others as well, unknown origin. Two somewhat older m., Boris and Martin, latter very nice looking, pulled me up some tenement stairs. Fighting down below. We smoked and talked. Boris thinks the Beatles revolutionary. Silly. While we're talking a bang/shot. Went home once dark. Flat full. Feel like a mother without courage. Radio: report of death of student Benno Ohnesorg. (Prob. THE bang/shot.) Martin turned up later, Boris later still. Discussion, highbrow stuff, the Stoics, Nero. He reminds me of someone, can't say who, must ask him sometime. Holger shooting off his mouth again. Olaf calls me a kindergarten teacher. Spiteful little devil, bombastic ramblings. Karin thinks I'm old. Martin and Boris both vanished. Breakfast at Holger's. Fell asleep.

EVERYWHERE

Two days later Sofie's taking her class again, the shack's full to bursting. A lot are listening, some just come to start the evening off, meet friends. Martin listens attentively, as usual, writes some things down in his notebook. Boris hasn't turned up. After the class someone tugs Martin's sleeve out in the street. Where did he disappear to that day without even saying goodbye? Him and his pal?

"Work to do."

He strikes Sofie as unnaturally taciturn. "Can you pass on a message?"

"Who to?"

"Boris."

"Sure. If I see him."

"But you know him well. You said so."

"Yeah, yeah . . . More or less. 'S a big city."

"Don't you work for the same firm?"

"Nah. Boris has his own taxi. Works for himself. What's the message?"

"Nothing." Sofie's unsure. Didn't Boris say he was driving a taxi *for the moment*? Does someone like that drive their own Merc? The phony. They're all phonies.

"I'm all mixed up. You going to take me home?"

"Who? Me?"

Sofie takes Martin's arm. "Of course you."

HERE

When I got back to the hotel suite at half past five in the morning, Lukian and Sylvia were in bed, naked, snuggled up to each other, it brought a smile to my face. More than that, a grin. It seemed the ideal, natural solution, I was happy for both of them. Although it was probably nothing serious, just the the two of them making the best of the situation. Enviable creatures. Lukian woke up, covered his nakedness with the sheet and asked what had happened.

"I can't drive a car at all."

"Sorry?"

"I'm a taxi driver now—and I can't drive."

"Jesus. What d'you mean, you can't drive? You used to have that sports car . . . "

"I'm sure I'll have forgotten everything."

"It's something you don't forget. Once at the wheel it'll all come back to you."

Lukian always knew how to say the right thing.

Demonstrations were banned throughout the whole of Berlin. It was the big moment for the GSSU, which countered with an information campaign, distributing leaflets which were finally read instead of being thrown away unread—and I was in a huge, empty parking lot, learning to drive again in Martin's taxi.

"So she asked about me?" The car juddered, the engine spluttered, the gears clashed.

"You could say," said Martin.

"Did she ask about me or didn't she?"

"Yes, Boss."

"So what did she say?"

"Nothing . . . "

"What exactly?"

"If I could pass on a message to my *pal Boris*."

"And?"

"That was it. Except that she was all mixed up."

"In what way mixed up?"

"She didn't go into it."

"Did you go to her flat?"

"Er, no, Boss . . . Should I have?"

He was a charmingly clumsy liar. For ages now new people had been keeping the Mehringdamm apartment under surveillance. Martin had been there. I'm sure I could have found out details, but I didn't want to. Even the bug in the apartment— there, you look horrified, yes, there was a bug in her apartment, three in fact, but only for emergencies, no one eavesdropped on Sofie, you have to believe me, my people were forbidden to listen in without specific orders from me. I was afraid because Henry would be released soon, I'd dreamed he might use violence toward Sofie, that was the only reason. When you're afraid, every dream seems to come from Cassandra's Information Bureau. You do understand? Henry was insisting on his right to be picked up by taxi from the prison. I was tempted. Yes, OK, the bugs were in operation that day. You'll hear everything.

"Sofie Kramer. I need a taxi at 67 Mehringdamm. In a quarter of an hour."

You should have seen how smoothly everything went. The taxi she'd ordered got stuck on the way, involved in a slight collision. Instead *I* turned up at 67 Mehringdamm. Why? I don't know why. What a crazy time it was when everything didn't just seem possible, it was possible.

Sofie came out of the building, got in, said *Good afternoon. We have to go to Tegel, to the pri—* "Boris?"

"Hi."

"It can't be true."

"What can't? How are you?"

"Oh, shit. No, I'm fine. Such a coincidence."

"Where exactly are you going?"

"Look, I'm sorry, but . . . "

"Sorry? Why?"

She looked at her watch, presumably wondering whether to order another taxi. But why? And time was getting short already.

"Boris? Will you do me a favor? A big favor?"

"What?"

"Pretend you don't know me. Don't ask why. Please."

We set off. And then she did tell me why I wasn't to know her. I had to swear on it. Seriously.

Henry was waiting outside the prison gates with a kind of bulging sailor's kitbag beside him. Sofie got out of the taxi, threw herself at him, kissed him, looking nervous, as if she had something else on her mind; I felt sorry for her and amused at the same time, no, not at the same time, one after the other, that's more what it was. Electric shocks and flashes of light in quick succession.

"I was startin' to think you weren't coming."

"There was the congestion in the city."

"I've got congestion too. Hormone congestion." He pawed her greedily. I felt sick.

"Come on, Henry. Later! At home."

I drove off. My divine beloved and the filthy swine were sitting in the back, smooching. Two thirds of the time I was just looking at the rear-view mirror.

"What's that on your forehead?"

"It's OK," Henry grunted, almost proud of the scab on his forehead.

"Who beat you up? The fuzz?"

"Yeah."

The liar. I knew everything. Can you imagine what that's like? Knowing everything.

Sofie kissed the scar, I missed a yield sign and almost caused an accident.

"Hey! You watch out!" Henry was talking to me.

"Sorry." Oh, damn. A mistake. I could feel the tingle in the back of my neck. A real Berlin taxi driver would never have apologized for making a mistake.

"They hand out taxi licenses to just about anyone these days."

"These things happen," Sofie said. Did she look delightful!

"And you? Been havin' a great time, eh?" He sounded angry.

"What d'you mean, a great time?"

"One hell of a party, I heard. Wish I'd been there."

"I found it all rather sad."

"Can't wait to get active again. That tart Birgit only came to see me twice. Couldn't do anything. So she said. She doesn't like me, I'll tell you that for nothing."

"Rubbish. She did what she could."

"Just that she can't do anything. You been screwin' anyone?"

"Course not. What's all this about?"

"I'll find out. Better if you tell me now."

"Don't talk crap."

"Hey, girl, am I hot! You could fry eggs on me." He tried to force her head down onto his lap.

"Stoppit! Not here."

"Hey, driver. It woulda been quicker to Mehringdamm across the canal."

"There's a traffic jam there. You in a hurry?"

"You could say that." The swine turned back to my divine beloved. "You miss me?"

"Course."

"Feel."

I couldn't see, but I'm sure he was putting her hand in his crotch.

"Stop it. Please."

"Keep your eyes on the traffic." The swine was talking to me. I pulled over, braked.

"What's all this?"

In the rear-view mirror I could see the expression on Sofie's face, mutely pleading. I lit a cigarette. Despite all the pain, I felt alive.

"What's up? Is he out of his mind?"

I got out, left the door open and walked off with measured steps, just managing to keep the vomit in my throat down.

"He's just walked off!" Henry couldn't believe it.

"Then we'll walk off. Come on." Sofie pulled the swine out of the car. There was a bug in it so that later on I could complete the dialogue between them.

"I've never seen anythin' like that before."

"Come on. He's just a head case."

"I've a good mind to beat the shit out of him."

"You want to end up back in prison?"

"He can't treat us like that."

"But it means we don't have to pay, that's not to be sniffed at. Come on, it's only three blocks."

"D'you know him?"

"No. What makes you say that?"

"What's going on here?"

"No idea. Honest. Come on, we'll walk."

They walked.

Transcript of tape recording June 16 1967, afternoon. Mehringdamm apartment.

— Henry: You danced with some guy. Here in the kitchen! Holger told me.

— Sofie: OK, so I danced with him. That was all.

— Henry: You taking the piss out of me?

(slapping noise)

— Sofie: You won't hit me again!

(slapping noise)

— Henry: Got it wrong, sweetie.

— Sofie: You shit!

(clattering noises)

"How could you bear it?"

"What would you have done in my place?" With a faint sigh the old man shrugged his shoulders. I wasn't sure what to answer. However, in order to lure my employer out of his reserve, to assure him I understood, I was on his side, I put on a grim look. "I'd have bumped the guy off."

"You see! You see! What a temptation! A lot of men would have come to the same decision and most probably ended up in prison. I, on the other hand, could most likely have got away with it. Although—you mustn't think I had murderers and cut-throats in my squad. They were all decent men who got enough money from me to stay decent. I did *play* with the idea, that I will admit. Now you're thinking that if I actually had done it I'd keep it from you. No. Why? I don't want weave a nimbus round me, but I do insist that to tell the story properly you must assume I had the best of intentions. Please don't portray me as the deranged commander of a private army; that would be to tart up the story with the crudely romantic image of a robber chief. I was a businessman who was in love, perhaps pathologically in love, but who never took anything as far as he could have. Perhaps—perhaps that was a mistake?"

Excursus

Von Brücken had neither time, patience nor memory enough to recount everything in detail. To make up for it there was the store of materials. A mountain of material. The first version of this book was twelve hundred pages long, until I forced myself to do the obvious and condense it drastically. Some things I could only reconstruct after I'd listened to the tapes, including the conversation between him and Sofie during the night of June 2, 1967 in the kitchen of Sofie's Mehringdamm apartment. It seems to me in a certain way symptomatic, therefore illuminating, which is why I've reproduced it here—contrary to the demands of fictional plot structure—in its entire length, word for word.

Sofie: What should I say to the guys who want to go and get guns now? I don't know and I don't want to be responsible for what they do, for the decision they come to. D'you follow me?

Alexander: What an exciting life you lead.

Sofie: You don't?

Alexander: Well, you know. Today was exciting, but normally . . .

Sofie: You must come across all sorts of things in your job.

Alexander: You think so? It's a way of making a living. The way is the goal. Nothing more.

Sofie: The way is the goal—I presume that adage's meant to encourage people, but it makes me feel sad. Doesn't it mean you'll never arrive anywhere? You carry on along the way, seeking, and eventually death shuts off all the roads. I don't believe there's anything after that. If there were, it would reduce life to the status of a kind of childhood, a kind of puberty full of questions and anguish and pain. I want to arrive somewhere eventually and live, even if its only for a short while, live happily, with a happiness you can touch, hug tight. It doesn't have to last long, just long enough for me to become aware of it, so I can shout out to the sun, today I feel great, today I've found what I've been seeking for so long, everything's wonderful and I would like, very humbly, to say thank you. Perhaps happiness like that is possible—and if I should ever find it, I would never taint it with the fear of losing it again. It's there, it's a gift. It *will* be lost again and I suppose that knowing that is meant to deaden the pain. I think Seneca said that.

Alexander: Sounds like him. I never could stand Seneca. He waffled on about confronting fear with dignity, accepting what could not be avoided with a tranquil mind, but it was easy for him, he was the richest man in Rome, with an estimated fortune of three billion marks in modern currency, what a man like that says comes from too privileged a position to . . .

Sofie: But he died bravely and in style when Nero ordered him to commit suicide. He got into the bath, cut open his arteries . . .

Alexander: Well, what else could he do? He chose the gentlest way of dying in which the senses slowly fade. Moreover he was well aware that posterity would watch and judge how he died very closely. Moreover he was old and had a life full of pleasure behind him. Would it not have been more glorious by far if he had tried to kill the tyrant?

Sofie: Philosophers don't kill, that would have been beneath Seneca's dignity. Anyway, Nero had been his pupil. If he killed him wouldn't that be tantamount to admitting he'd been a poor teacher?

Alexander: Which he obviously had been. So you think he refrained from tyrannicide out of vanity?

Sofie: I think that someone like Seneca simply felt that intervening in mundane affairs was beneath him, his life was lived on a spiritual plane. Unfortunately I can't do that, I'm too stupid.

Alexander: But his death wasn't freely chosen, he wasn't on a spiritual plane then, but on the very earthly plane dictated by the madness of his emperor.

Sofie: Perhaps it wasn't madness and Seneca was indeed planning to overthrow him?

Alexander: Whatever. For me that kind of thing doesn't represent a successful life. Simply submitting to it doesn't lessen the tragedy. That's all eyewash to retain a touch of dignity and make the crime out to be a minor irritation you just have to put up with, like a bee sting. No thanks. Shall we play Rousseau and Voltaire?

Sofie: Haven't read either of them. Do we have to?

Alexander: Err . . .

Sofie: Mankind would have been spared a lot of misery if he'd killed Nero, that's for sure. But then someone else would have had to make themselves available. Thinkers are there for thinking, you can't expect them to do everything.

Alexander: So you think there are some situations we can't master without using violence?

Sofie: Yes, I do. But the question is whether a situation can be assessed objectively, so objectively that it gives a person the right to intervene with violence.

Alexander: And now? Who is to be killed now so that things change?

Sofie: That's the problem. There's no emperor anymore, just a hydra with a million heads. Robespierre was the last to try to chop them all off. Today it's systems we're fighting against, and systems only change when the majority of their population is dissatisfied with them, or when they're defeated in war by another system.

Alexander: But can one reason with the majority? That's something that's always bothered me about democracy. I find majorities threatening. For me, many so-called moral people act out of fear and vanity in such a way that they get the fewest reproaches and as much praise as possible.

Sofie: Hmmm.

(At this point several people come into the kitchen, there's the chink of bottles and someone can clearly be heard saying, Isn't there any more beer? *Roughly seven seconds of Sofie's text are inaudible.)*

Alexander: If you take action against something, I mean, can you take action in any way against anything without having to take some criticism from someone or other as well? Tit for tat? Give and take? A trade-off? A deal? It's the way of the world.

Sofie: I think you're too cynical—and just playing with words. I believe there are heroes who act without thinking of themselves.

Alexander: It's certainly possible, but impossible to prove.

Sofie: You know, Boris, I really enjoy having a philosophical argument with you here, but it's not getting me anywhere.

Alexander: You don't see really enjoying it as getting you anywhere?

Sofie: No. Just now there are a number of ways of enjoying life, if you follow the herd. It might help me, but it helps no one else.

Alexander: I see. True satisfaction only comes from interfering in other people's affairs?

Sofie: What sort of crap is that? Helping people isn't interfering.

Alexander: Err—why not? It can be both. Always is both.

Sofie: Now that's getting too abstract for me. I suspect the problem is that there's an infinite number of planes on which you can argue about mankind and what is necessary, only you mustn't mix them up. To get rid of oppression, to want to help, you have to think like a doctor or a soldier. To get something done, a doctor or a soldier must hang on to a simple truth, a basic but valid and effective system of values from which they can derive pragmatic conclusions.

Alexander: But there's never just the one truth.

Sofie: Yes there is. There must be. One fundamental truth, the basic truth, the lowest common denominator of humanity.

Alexander: And you want to find it and formulate it then take action on it

Sofie: Action. For the moment you've spoilt the word for me by linking it up with trade-offs and deals. Sounds too much like big business. I feel I have to make a decision, sooner rather than later, a decision one way or another. A decision whether I'm going to smash someone's face in or not, so to speak.

(*Once more someone—male—comes into the kitchen. This person, very drunk, appears to start molesting Sofie, who can be heard saying,* Behave yourself. *The person, wheezing, almost grunting, apparently loses his balance and stumbles against the edge of the table, makes a whimpering sound and leaves the kitchen.*)

Alexander: Why is mankind so important to you?

Sofie: What kind of a question is *that*? I'm part of it, aren't I? Aren't you?

Alexander: You can be part of the universe or the solar system or the earth or a nation or a tribe, of a family or a couple. Or just live your own life.

Sofie: That would be narcissism. Egoism. Weren't you arguing five minutes ago that Seneca should have killed Nero? What are you suggesting now? Escapism? Withdrawal into the private sphere?

Alexander: Five minutes ago's five minutes ago, now is now. Sometimes I feel that trying to combat stupidity's a symptom of an even greater stupidity. I want to remain free to argue sometimes this way, sometimes that, because my mind doesn't think along set patterns, because it changes direction every minute and because every minute I become a different person. Which I find pretty exciting.

Sofie: I'd call it drifting aimlessly, stumbling haphazardly, swaying this way and that, with no principles whatsoever. Fickle. Unpolitical.

Alexander: I've no objection to that. We should be sparing with principles.

Sofie: Individualistic hubris gets us nowhere. You take yourself far too seriously, that's your problem.

Alexander: I don't see why I shouldn't be as important as anyone else on the planet. OK, artists give the world much more than I do, I can respect that. The Beatles . . .

Sofie: Not them again! I'm not saying that you, as a taxi driver, are less important than anyone else, but the obverse of that is that every person's as important as you and there's a duty to help those who are suffering.

Alexander: I do that.

Sofie: You? How?

Alexander: Donations.

Sofie: Oh, great. I suppose it makes you feel very generous.

Alexander: I donate quite a lot. If everyone was to donate as much as I do—

Sofie: Sorry, but we're just not on the same wavelength. You drag everything down to the same level, the level of the collection box.

Alexander: So? It's not sexy, I suppose? Money always helps. Politics rarely. Anyone who's got enough money can give some away. Anyone who has power clings on to it. Give good people power and—

Sofie: What's all this crap you're talking? Do you think it makes any difference to the world if you give away a tenth of your wages as a taxi driver? Do you really think that? But it lets you sleep easy at nights.

Alexander: Now listen—

Sofie: So what d'you do when you're not driving a taxi—
Alexander: I like this song, d'you fancy a dance?
Sofie: Here? In the kitchen?
Alexander: Why not?

End of excursus.

ACTION

July 1967. Near Hermannplatz. Dark. A flashlight beam. A shrill alarm bell goes off. Karin and Olaf are robbing a gun store. Wearing stocking masks, in twenty-five seconds they've filled a Santa Claus sack with guns and ammunition, plus an *Excalibur*, a sword with a slightly sharpened double blade, no real use for the revolution, but it fulfils one of Olaf's childhood dreams. They leave by the window they've smashed in, throw the booty in their Peugeot, drive off in the direction of Columbiadamm, turn off at some garden plots and park the car by the wall of the cemeteries along Bergmannstrasse. They wait, listen for police sirens, which don't come, no one's followed them. They pull the stockings off their heads and let out exultant whoops. Olaf brandishes the sword. It looks childish, only Karin's so turned on by it she demands instant satisfaction.

Wannsee, by the lakeside, high summer. Martin, Olaf, Karin, Holger, Birgit, Henry and Sofie in bathing costumes. Sofie's wearing sunglasses, which scarcely conceal her black eye.

Olaf, Holger and Henry are playing skat. Karin's sunbathing, a portable radio beside her. Mahler's *Lieder eines fahrenden Gesellen* is on. Karin doesn't like it, turns the knob, gets Rudi Dutschke's voice: *It is very clear to us that there are many comrades in the Association who are no longer prepared to accept abstract socialism, which has nothing to do with their lives as they live them, as a political position . . . Refusal to cooperate in the environment of one's own institution demands a guerilla mentality if integration and cynicism are not to be the next stop.*

That doesn't keep her amused for long either, finally she finds some rock music by Iron Butterfly.

Birgit's taken the day off to have a chat with her stepsister. Which means she asks prying questions. How she's getting by financially, what she sees as her future, whether that black eye was Henry. Sofie's not very forthcoming. She finds her sister's presence downright embarrassing. Only the fact that she's a lawyer they might need sometime stops her making a permanent break with her.

"I don't understand you."

"You don't have to understand everything."

"What're you living on?"

At that point Henry's voice comes bellowing over the lakeside. "Eighty and 'n ace. With two, play three, schneider declared—that makes forty pfennigs from each of you."

"You're keeping him?"

"He's good at cards."

"That can't be true."

Henry's heard the last remark. "At our intrigues again, are we, Madame Lawyer?"

"You just shut up."

"Bad time o' the month? Or's it the menopause?"

"Stop it, Henry." Sofie's finding it all more and more embarrassing.

"Get us a few beers from the kiosk, eh?"

"Get them yourself."

Martin intervenes. "I'll get the beer."

"Ah, the knight in shining armor," Henry mocks as Martin goes off. Then he turns back to Birgit. "What're you doin' here, anyway?"

"Your breath reeks of alcohol."

"Fancy a sniff, do you?" He leans over, his mouth close to hers. "But you're not getting it." Henry laughs at his own joke, then announces he's going for a swim. His behavior's brought the two stepsisters a little closer together. Birgit confesses she's left the GSSU. She's more credible as a lawyer, she says, if she doesn't belong to the lot she might have to defend some day.

"You never were more than a name on a file, were you? Just along for the ride?"

Sofie regrets it as soon as the words are out of her mouth. To be fair, she's no reason to criticize Birgit, certainly not on the personal level. She's regularly offered Sofie money, without being asked. Once Sofie even accepted it, reluctantly, but it was necessary. The two women walk along the shore. Can she tell her something, Sofie asks, as a lawyer, under the seal of confidentiality?

"What d'you think? Of course you can?"

Sofie whispers. Two friends of hers have robbed a gun store.

"Karin's uncle's?"

"Which store's irrelevant. Twenty working pistols, Walthers, with ammo."

"And?"

"The stuff's in my apartment."

"What! Are you stupid?"

"Don't call me *stupid*." Sofie's inferiority complex toward Birgit almost brings the conversation to an end. Birgit apologizes, out of curiosity, if nothing else.

"Olaf didn't have the guts to offer the guns for sale. So he went to Henry, offered him fifty-fifty. He deposited the sack in my cellar. Since then he's been selling them. Three hundred marks apiece. Seven or eight've gone already."

"Sofie!"

"He didn't even ask me. I discovered the sack by chance and told him what I thought. Take your stuff, I said, and get out of my apartment. To which he replied: Where should I go? In three weeks I'll've got rid of it and we can take a vacation, in Spain."

"Sofie!"

"I know what I'm called, thank you. Instead tell me what I should do."

Birgit thinks it over, and not just to make a show. It really isn't that simple.

"If you go to the fuzz and tell them what happened, you've a very good chance of a suspended sentence."

"I can't do that."

No better solution can be found. Evening comes, they go back into town.

ON TAPE

V on Brücken was operating the tape recorder beside his desk. I felt uncomfortable hearing these recordings, they made Sofie too much of a physical presence. I had not imagined her voice so soft and deep. It gave the whole business a touch of the obscene; it had probably been like that for some time already, but I had never been really aware of it until now. Perhaps the idea that the material I was working on would be turned into a *novel* had soothed too many of my scruples as I overstepped several ethical marks. Until now I had been able to play with the possibility that what I was being presented with was a fiction. The addition of an acoustic element brought reality, if only ostensible reality, threateningly close, and I felt a bit queasy—which helped me understand why at one time people had located the soul in the stomach.

"Listen. It was an exciting moment. We heard Sofie and Henry arguing."

He started the tape.

Tape recording September 10, 1967, Mehringdamm apartment.
— Sofie: Can't we at least store the guns somewhere else?
— Henry: Where? Under some bushes in the zoo or what?

"As you can hear, the reception was weak and very distorted. I asked the technician why. At first he couldn't think of a reason. Then something occurred to him.

"Frequency modulation from another source? Perhaps the telephone's being tapped."

"Well, yes, but—"

"I mean *by someone else*. Apart from us. That would explain the interference." '

Alexander fell into a fit of giggling which sounded oddly uninhibited, exaggerated. "Do you understand? Do you at least begin to understand how exciting it was and how depressing? And once more I ask you: what would you have done in my place?"

He'd felt, he said, like the hunchback of Notre Dame having to watch the noose being tied around the neck of his beloved Esmeralda down below.

"I had to make it possible for her to get out of all this. I felt like the wildlife photographer I mentioned before—this isn't meant to sound dismissive or elitist—the wildlife photographer who had decided he absolutely refused to interfere with the natural course of events at any point. Just observe. Let everything take its course. Now I had to decide. What would you have done in my place? The affair was starting to develop its own momentum. Henry was selling the stolen guns, just like that, to anyone who happened to hear about them. Like a greedy little idiot. Naturally he very quickly had the wrong man knocking at the door. I mean, if you *think* you live in a police state, you should at least behave accordingly. Not a bit of it. The very next evening a young man came to Sofie's apartment. Henry asked him if he had the dough. They went down to the cellar. Henry rummaged around for the sack with the guns behind a few old suitcases. Couldn't find it."

Von Brücken fast forwarded a few feet and pressed the 'play' button again.

Tape recording September 11, evening, Mehringdamm apartment – cellar
– Henry: Damn!

– Young man: What's wrong? Where're the goods?
– Henry: Just a mo. I'll sort this out.

Sofie was having a bath. No, just a minute, she was having a shower. Henry rushed in and must have pulled her out from under the jet. She screamed at him, furious. Hey, just a minute!

Tape recording September 11, 1967, evening, Mehringdamm apartment – bathroom
– Sofie: What the hell d'you think you're doing. Are you off your rocker?
– Henry: What've you done with the sack?
– Sofie: What?
– Henry: You've put the stuff away someplace.
– Sofie: No I haven't.
– Henry: Who else, then?
– Sofie: I've not put anything away. You must be crazy.
– Henry: If you think you can muck around with me, you've another think coming. I've a customer down there.

"For the first time we could prove we did some good by keeping Sofie out of prison. Naturally it was *us* who'd moved the sack, just in time. The task of the police plant was obviously to get Henry at least to say 'gun'."

Tape recording September 11, 1967, evening, Mehringdamm apartment – cellar
– Henry: I'm really sorry. The stuff's gone. Vanished.
– Young man: You mean I'm not going to get a gun?

"The last sentence was such a crude trap even a clown like Henry finally smelt a rat."

– Henry: I can give you a glass of water.

– Young man: But you promised me a Walther 65, with ammo. I came here specially and now I've got to go away empty-handed.

– Henry: What are you going on about? There you are.

"Presumably Henry was giving him his money back. If you listen carefully, you can hear the rustle of paper."

– Young man: Will I get the gun later?

– Henry: The what? Come on, Let's go up. Perhaps I'll manage to get some of the Bordeaux '65 again some time.

– Young man: Bordeaux? Eh? Are you takin' the piss?

– Henry: So long. Now just fuck off.

"Henry pushed the undercover policeman out onto the landing, slammed the apartment door and whistled cheerfully to himself. The cop realized there was nothing doing for the moment and cleared off. Unfortunately, for Sofie that wasn't the end of the matter."

Tape recording September 11, 1967, evening, Mehringdamm apartment – kitchen

– Henry: Listen, I'm not angry with you, on the contrary, that was a pig, I sussed him out. So I'm really grateful – or I will be when you tell me where the goods are.

– Sofie: But I haven't done anything with them.

– Henry: Honest?

– Sofie: Honest.

– Henry: So was it that shitty sister of yours? Does she have a key to the cellar?

– Sofie: No.

– Henry: Who has one then?

– Sofie: I don't know.

(Slapping noise)

– Henry: No one does that to me.
– Sofie: It wasn't me!
– Henry: Stop your screaming!

"Henry started to hit her. He didn't stop at the slaps that had become routine, he really laid into her. I heard my beloved screaming and crying. I'm asking you again: what would you have done?"

Von Brücken paused. He seemed to be going through the whole situation again; moisture appeared in the corner of his eyes. He was so moved he couldn't carry on speaking and, contrary to his usual habit, took a pill in my presence. Outside it had started to snow again and I suggested we call it a day.

"No, no," he whispered, visibly affected. "I'm OK now." He apologized for his loss of control. Naturally he'd dashed out, straight across the street, had run up the stairs and rung the bell. Since no one answered he'd used his duplicate key.

"You had a duplicate key? Where did you get that?"

"My dear young friend, there's nothing to it. A tenement! I went in. The two of them were in the bedroom, Sofie, bleeding from her nose, was kneeling on the floor. Henry was grabbing her hair so tight his fingers were clenched in a fist. Listen."

Tape recording September 11, 1967, evening, Mehringdamm apartment – bedroom
– Henry: And who's this? How did he get in?
– Alexander: Let go of her, you swine.
– Sofie: Boris?
– Henry: I know him. Hey, just a minute, it's . . . it's that *taxi driver!*

Henry was so taken aback he actually did let go of Sofie and stamped on the floor twice before he ran at me. What a powerhouse he was! I turned around and ran back down the three flights of stairs. He'd seen the key in my hand. Presumably he thought I wasn't just the guy who'd stolen his guns but his girlfriend's secret admirer as well. And he was right about that, of course. Despite all my fear for my physical wellbeing, I've seldom felt so euphoric. That mixture of fear and euphoria, strange. I ran out and, not looking either way, straight across Mehringdamm, with all its traffic. Henry was only ten feet behind me and suddenly the bus was on him. Even today I can still here the dull thud and the sound of breaking bones, the dragging sound, the sound of clothes tearing and of flesh rubbing against Tarmac, the horrified cries of pedestrians. Suddenly it was as if everything around me was in slow motion and weightless, but cruel, I don't know, right beside me was an advertising pillar and it was laughing. Has anything like that ever happened to you? No? The people in the sidewalk café with its orange lighting had all stood up, were staring, goggle-eyed, I saw Sofie come running out of the building, fling herself on Henry's dead body, kneel down beside him and take his head in her arm.

Two tears ran down Alexander's cheeks.

"What should I do? What would you have done? I ran away."

"It was an accident?"

"Yes. Unless God moonlights as a bus driver now and then."

"And then? You just ran off?"

"Should I have waited for the police to come? Take my particulars? Although – looked at objectively – it was an accident, I blamed myself. Perhaps rightly."

Von Brücken seemed exhausted, his slack eyelid quivered; he poured himself a glass of port and tossed it down greedily.

"That night we trashed the taxi; the guns were dumped in the canal. Martin went to Morocco for a year, it was something he'd always wanted to do. I withdrew to the castle here to do some serious thinking. Sylvia dealt with the formal side of things.

Von Brücken was slumped down in his chair. Outside, twilight was creeping over the countryside. We could hardly see each other, yet neither of us lifted a finger to operate the light switch. Only when I thought von Brücken had fallen asleep did I venture to ask quietly, who, then, had looked after Sofie. As soon as I'd asked it, the question struck me as absurd. He, however, seemed to like it. He smiled. As if, in a kind of way, he was moved.

"Just Lukian stayed in Berlin. He insisted. We couldn't leave Sofie on her own now, he said."

FRACTALS

That night I asked Lukian to tell me something about those days. Again he stalled, saying his story wasn't relevant, this wasn't about him. But perhaps, I suggested, it was about Sofie. He gave me a penetrating stare, which rested on me for quite a while, an almost amused look in his eye.

"Alexander knew very well why he selected *you* of all people."

"How d'you mean?"

The two of us, Alexander and me, he said, were of a similar type. Basically, in my novels I did the same as Alexander had done, I on paper, he in the wildlife enclosure that was society. Every person eventually became a character and the power I, as author, had over my fictional world was comparable to that Alexander had over the real world.

"With your help he's turning it all into a – let's give you the benefit of the doubt – *work of art*. It's his way of justifying the whole business, retrospectively. I'm not going to stop him, but I don't see why I should support him."

I countered that transformation into a work of art wasn't the worst thing that could happen to someone's life. He shook his head. Works of art were lies, he said. Perhaps it would best if the story were to stay a fragment, only fragments retained an option on the truth.

With that, and quite logically, he left the room with little more than a nod.

DAY FIVE

FRIENDS AND HELPERS

In May 1970 two officials from the Federal Bureau of Criminal Investigation came to see me at the Owl's Nest. The background to this was rather odd. Believe it or not, during the previous three years I'd tried once and for all to leave my beloved to fend for herself. True, there was a certain amount of secret support here and there. She struggled through with various temporary jobs, but I didn't want to hear the details. It was enough for me to know that in an emergency, a real emergency, help would be forthcoming.

During those three years I felt as if I'd gone to prison of my own free will. A beautiful, spacious prison where I'd locked myself up to do penance. I devoted myself to philosophy, music and fine art. In a way I was trying, by cultural refinement, to sublimate my existence, to live it on an abstract, metaphysical level. My last connection with Sofie was Lukian. I was living vicariously through him. And he was enjoying it. What I know, I know from him and it's possible there was a lot he didn't tell me. Or made up.

But let's get back to the two FBCI officers. One introduced himself as Friedrich Steinmetz, the other was called Höfer. They wanted to know something about my relationship with a Fraulein Kramer, née Kurtz, currently resident in Berlin.

I was uncommunicative, probably *too* uncommunicative, in my agitation I forgot to ask what had brought them here. Sofie Kramer, I mumbled, Sofie Kramer, oh yes, no, you couldn't really call that a *relationship*. I'd once tried to make contact with her through the classified ads, nationwide.

Steinmetz said he'd call that a kind of relationship. Höfer remained silent the whole time.

I didn't deny that I'd known her. During the dark days of the war.

"Do you know what she's doing?"

"It's so long ago. Wasn't she a kindergarten teacher at one time?"

"She took up a rather different career after that. But we needn't talk about that. It's nothing to do with you."

"No."

"You're not married?"

I replied that I was wedded to my work.

"What is it you do?"

I told him I was working on a project my father had bequeathed me. I held up a sketch.

"Look, the so-called *ovibunker*, an egg-shaped family shelter. We're about to go into production. It's going to be a big hit. In it you'll survive a nuclear war. At least for a few days."

Steinmetz realized I was *probably* having him on, but he wasn't entirely sure. Was there anything more I could tell them about Sofie Kramer, he asked.

In all those years, I sighed, she'd never sent me a single postcard. The mean thing. Women!

Steinmetz asked about *Lukian Keferloher*. He worked for me, didn't he?

I nodded. Used to, that was.

Officially Lukian was not on any salary list, hadn't been for years.

Why? I asked.

This Keferloher had an intimate relationship with Fräulein Kramer.

I assured him I knew nothing about that. Lukian had left the firm and was working as a publisher's editor, freelance, that was the last I'd heard.

Steinmetz had nothing he could use, nothing at all. Bearing that in mind, his behavior toward me was pretty outrageous.

Was there any other way in which I could be of assistance?

Steinmetz pressed his lips together in rage. Was I aware, he asked, that Sofie Kramer was suspected of having committed serious offences?

"Oh dear! Really?"

"Listen, Herr von Brücken, you are, as I well know, a man of enormous influence, a man who has served his country well. But there are limits and you would do well to avoid upsetting certain people."

"But surely *any* citizen, my dear Herr Steinmetz, should make that a matter of principle, no matter what his influence and services. Am I not right?"

I was keen to see what would come next, but nothing did. The two detectives left, plainly dissatisfied. But let me tell you – this is the reason why I've brought in that scene in advance of its place in the chronology – that was the first I heard of *serious offences* my beloved was supposed to have committed. It was like a cloud of lead falling on me. I'd had no idea, no idea at all.

PRINZENSTRASSE

In 1968, at the end of October, Lukian makes contact with Sofie. Without instructions, off his own bat. He speaks to her in a cafe in Kreuzberg, later he claims it was spontaneous, an impulse he couldn't resist.

"Excuse me?"

"YES?" she almost screams the syllable, audibly startled.

"We've met before, I think. Wuppertal? Some years ago. Lukian, your former neighbor. Do you remember?"

"Oh, yes . . . " Sofie's lips are slightly parted, she's thinking. Lukian. She remembers. The opportunistic literary gent. Luc. The bouquet, mulled wine and Video Art.

"You recognized me? I thought people wouldn't . . . " Sofie's wearing dark glasses and has her bleached hair very full and long, with a fringe hanging down over her eyebrows.

"Why? Is that important to you? Not being recognized?"

Sofie doesn't seem to have understood his question, appears preoccupied. "What?"

"I've been watching you a bit. You keep looking around."

"I did have the feeling I was being . . . watched. But not by you."

"Hmm. How's things? Not so good?"

"Not so good, no. Are you still working as an editor?"

"Now and then. I get by. How about you?"

"Welfare,"

"Oh."

"Could be worse. Will you show me your apartment?"

"My apartment?" Lukian raises his eyebrows.

"D'you want to talk to me? Or rather not?"

"Sure. Love to. Of course."

"Give me your address." She hands him a beer mat. "I'll come around. This evening."

Lukian's baffled, says they could just as well talk there. Sofie whispers that she doesn't want to get him mixed up in anything, she'll explain everything. That evening.

Lukian phoned to tell me about making contact with Sofie. I made no objections. I told him to do as he thought fit, I didn't care. Inwardly I was cursing him for acting without authorization, but that was only at the beginning. Later on I genuinely couldn't care less. Though that's not quite the right way of putting it. What do you say when something appears acceptable because anything else would be even worse? To be honest I had suspected the contact had happened even earlier and in a way I was relieved that he was including me in.

That same evening Sofie Kramer goes to Lukian's apartment in Prinzenstrasse.

"It's nice that we ran into each other again," says Lukian, helping his guest out of her somewhat mangy lambskin coat. It's an act of male courtesy Sofie can't bear. She pushes his hand away, then apologizes.

"Sorry. I must make a strange impression on you."

"You always have done. In the best possible way,"

"Thanks. Have you anything to drink?"

"What would you like?"

"Wine."

"Italian red?" Lukian uncorks a bottle of top-class Primitivo Puglia. He thinks it won't arouse Sofie's suspicions as it says *Primitivo* on the label.

Sofie collapses onto the sofa. She ruffles her hair with her fingers, as if it's too heavy. "For some reason I have the feeling

I can tell you something. Luc? You're not working for the fuzz, are you?"

"No."

"The Springer Press?"

"Not for them either."

Reassured for the moment, Sofie puts her glass to her lips and downs it in one. No response to its quality, not even a gesture or look.

"Holger's forced me out. Holger lives at my place, that's why I don't like going home. It's difficult. Holger gets a monthly check from the East. I found that out. Inadvertently, because I was looking through his things, I didn't mean any harm."

"Who's Holger."

"A kind of . . . superior. In the Marxist-Leninist group. My boyfriend died last year, but the GSSU still uses my apartment."

"Ermmm." Lukian indicates it's all Greek to him.

"They treat me like a dimwit. The GSSU's close to splitting, Holger's on the other wing, the one that's prepared to use violence. Since the assassination of Rudi Dutschke the pacifists among us don't have much of a say. Holger squats in my pad, nice and cozy. And I'm stuck with it. My home's more or less a guest house, it's used for planning operations."

"By whom?"

"You don't need to know. You can imagine."

Lukian nods. Half understanding, half concerned.

"I'm so fed up with everything. At one point I even wanted to go back to my old job, but no one'll employ a kindergarten teacher who's been a political activist. I think my phone's being bugged. I can't stand it in my apartment any longer. They picked up Olaf because he insisted on swiping some stupid sword, an *Excalibur*."

"Excalibur? Who's Olaf?"

"Naturally he squealed, blamed everything on Henry."

"Henry?"

"My boyfriend who's dead. Run over by a bus. He had his faults, but I wouldn't wish that on anyone—his blood all over me—I really shouldn't be drinking red wine. Well, it's OK now. At least . . . Since then the fuzz've been keeping tabs on me. I just don't know what to do. If I kick up a fuss, they threaten to fit me up for something."

"The fuzz?"

"No, my comrades."

"Nice comrades."

Sofie tells him about the trench warfare in the GSSU, the arguments between Castroists, anarcho-syndicalists, Trotskyists, Leninists, and supporters of Marcuse. About debates on emancipation, about her work in the Council of the Campaign for Women's Liberation ("Liberate our socialist jocks from their bourgeois cocks"), about all the mcp's among the revolutionaries, semi-savages, sex-mad boozers, hardly any better than fraternity students. Women who argue against violence weren't taken seriously and ridiculed as "kindergarten teachers." She tells him about women who went underground just to get the men to show some respect. About all those who use the revolution to fuel their ego trips. About the spring when the revolution seemed to near in Paris and then vanished into the distance because they hesitated and argued at the decisive moment, now the bourgeoisie was fighting back, they'd already lost the workers, though nobody but her would admit it. The Russians' stupid invasion of Prague had sobered a lot of them up, wakened them out of an easy dream. And another problem was that she was too old for this generation, too burdened with experience. Sometimes, she says, she dreams of simply taking off, going far, far away. At the end of this review the bottle's empty.

"Is that what you really want? To get away?"

"I don't know. Sometimes I think I'll manage somehow, there's still hope, and there's a guardian angel watching over me."

A guardian angel? How did she mean?

"For example six months ago – I was right on the edge, the next day I'd've had to go and find a job on a checkout, some-where, anywhere. There was this man selling lottery tickets right outside the door. You know, a man with a tray with lottery tickets hanging around his neck, you hardly see them anymore. He saw me and gave me a grin. Don't turn your back on your luck, lovely lady. Just one mark a ticket. I hardly had enough for my breakfast. But the way he *looked at* me . . . Almost begging me. I bought a ticket. You're not going to believe this, but I won ten thousand marks. Can you imagine? Because I didn't have a bank account, the man from the lottery came the next day with a little briefcase full of cash. Fortunately Holger was out . . . "

Lukian decides it wouldn't be too bold to touch Sofie on the shoulder with two fingers.

"Why didn't you just take off with the money?"

"But I did! To Paris! Only – suddenly there were lots of peo-ple who wanted to go to Paris, I just had to help them—and for that many ten thousand doesn't go far. Especially in Paris. Paris was *fantastic*. Have you got any more of that red wine, it's not bad. Listen—I feel like getting drunk, is that OK?"

"Of course. I understand."

"You think you understand? You understand nothing. Sorry. You're a nice guy. *Nice.* Can I doss down on your sofa? I'll tell you straight: I'd like to drink your wine, but I don't want to sleep with you. Is that OK? I'll pay you back for the wine later on. Just in case you're thinking I'm being too brazen."

"That's fine. Stay here. The wine's . . . fairly primitive."

"Sometimes I see my guardian angel in my dreams."

"Really? What does he look like?"

"You know, basically I'm convinced everyone gets one op-portunity during their lifetime, or even two or three. For ex-ample I could have been a grand lady. You've no idea. 'S odd, me telling you all this. Somehow I have the feeling I can tell you everything. You just sit there thinking, God, surely the silly cow's going to shut up sometime. Must be the time of the month and the rest of the time all she gets is lousy sex."

"That's certainly not what I'm thinking."

"Why not? Might be the truth."

"It's none of my business."

"Don't put on airs like that! It is your business because I'm sitting here in your apartment. If it's none of your business, I'll go."

"I didn't mean it like that, I was just . . . "

"You know, Holger wants to do banks. I've nothing against that, but you need guns to do banks and if you use guns, eventually you're going to *use* them."

"*Do* banks? You mean *hold up* banks? Rob them?"

"Should I set one up? Can you lend me the capital for that?"

Lukian says nothing, although he does actually consider the possibility. Sofie's movements are gradually getting less coordinated.

"Now I remember what you said to me, all those years ago in Wuppertal. The world's a crazier place than you think— something like that. I liked that. It stuck, somehow. Even though it's trite. Really. I think that basic'ly the world's quite simple. Simply a pile o' shit. And you're stuck right in it—with a tiny shovel. You start shovellin' and clear a little patch. Just big enough for you to stretch out on—end of story." Sofie falls asleep sitting on the sofa, her glass still in her hand.

The next day Lukian called me. Described what had happened. Sofie was sleeping it off. On his sofa. She was drinking, he said, that much was clear. We had to do something.

"We've done far too much already."

"Alex? What if I can make her happy? What then?"

It came out of the blue. Luki must have summoned up all his courage, I could hear him holding his breath. The bastard.

What could I say? What would *you* have said? I said the only thing I could say, unless I wanted to see myself as a total shit.

"If *she's* happy, then I'll be happy too."

"So I've a free hand?" A long pause. "Alex?"

"Yes."

After that *yes*, I felt quite good about myself, almost noble, no, more like: absolutely noble. Not long after, I still felt noble, but I didn't feel good, oh no. I realized that everything was about to start from the beginning. Lukian was powerful—not as powerful as me, but still, he could and would use his power. On the other hand, where does power start? Perhaps Lukian would manage to live a more or less normal life with her, I thought, always assuming she got involved with him, that was. To be honest, I didn't really imagine that was likely to happen, I thought the whole thing would simply go away.

What I had overlooked, of course, was that in Sofie's wretched situation any man who was kind to her, treated her in a reasonably decent, helpful and sensitive fashion, was a godsend she wasn't going to refuse out of hand. The result was Sofie and Lukian's brief period of happiness. She had a drinking problem, but for his sake she kept it within limits. Lukian got publishers to send him manuscripts which they'd rejected as hopeless and on which he scribbled various comments in order to feign employment as a copy editor; he even had books printed with the imprint of fictional small publishers and *Editor: Lukian Keferloher* facing the title page. He didn't even have to change his name, oh, how I envied him. Sofie showed her gratitude by doing housework even though her mind told her it was beneath her. When Lukian's cleaning woman turned up one morning, he avoided the potential embarrassment quite elegantly. And if you think I kept the two of them under surveillance, you're wrong, there was nothing like that, I kept out of it. They slept in the same bed, but didn't have sex, or at most just a bit of cuddling. That was what Lukian reported to me. Yes, OK, I did insist on *that*, he was to tell me what the situation was now and then, to confirm that Sofie was fine. I had promised to withdraw completely if the two of them ever became what we now call an item.

Most of the time von Brücken whispered and avoided eye contact with me. I could see the episode had affected him deeply and he found it difficult to talk about it. He apologized, then slid off his chair and sat down on the floor. I had no option but to slide off my stool as well and we continued the conversation hunkered down on the floor. I didn't make an issue of it, so far he'd not shown much in the way of eccentricities. Perhaps there was a simple reason for his change of position; he may have found the pain he suffered easier to bear like that.

I'm sure you'll have noticed: Lukian's not exactly good-looking; at the time he was even less so. He's never had much of a sense of humor, either, but somehow he managed to appear honest and steady, virtues which must have made a deep impression on Sofie. He could be gallant, he was a good cook and a good listener. Naturally he was well-educated, he liked to read Dostoyevsky to Sofie and wasn't a bad pianist either. He really made an effort and he must have seen Sofie's affection for him as a kind of triumph over me.

Sometimes you get the feeling you could leave everything that's been at the checkroom. Throw it off and start from scratch. As though a door's opened and if you go through it, everything will be different.

Lukian wrote down these words of Sofie's and read them to me over the phone, moving me to tears. She had come to trust him so much he was even allowed to read a few of her poems. Unfortunately it was trivial stuff, however at times he seemed determined to use a front man to set up a publisher where the stuff could appear in print, it wasn't much worse than lots of other trash. Despite the torment, I enjoyed following the more and more single-minded way he went about twisting reality until it was pure theater. I was even proud of him and relieved to see that he didn't seem to be very different from me. His behavior was a yardstick against which I could measure mine. Was he doing something bad? Initially I was concerned that he didn't genuinely love Sofie, that in reality all he wanted was to outdo or humiliate me, that he was having a good time in my role—the shadow who supplants his master and finally starts to live his own life. Then he said the ominous three words.

Lukian: I love you.

Sofie: Oh, yes?

Lukian: I loved you way back in Wuppertal. But first, you were living with that Rolf, then you'd gone.

Sofie: You've a fantastic memory for names. *Rolf.* Was there really a Rolf? It seems millions of light years away.

Lukian: I didn't know him. But I hated him.

Sofie: Oh, he was OK. In retrospect. My mother was such a practical person. If something wasn't *totally* bad, she clung onto it. As hard as she could. And she always used to say to me: there'll come a time, child, when you'll understand—I can't remember exactly how she put it, nor have I ever understood . . . At least . . . If you loved me back then, you'd have said so. You can't love someone and not tell them.

Lukian: That's rather a sweeping statement. There are . . .

Sofie: Kiss me. There's something about you, a smell, a feeling, a radiance I only get in my dreams when I'm dreaming of my guardian angel.

Later he told me he didn't sleep with her, he couldn't get it up out of fear of *me*. I'm sure that was just a load of claptrap to placate me and at the same time make me feel guilty. Why bother? That was the time of the first free love communes. *Bildzeitung* had reported on them, full of sham outrage; in fact it was grateful to them as a neverending source of pornographic fantasies for its readers. The idea that Sofie might join a commune—oh, yes, that would really have hit me hard. But why should I begrudge my friend Lukian something Sofie had already engaged in with an animal like Henry?

Presumably Sofie was close to returning Lukian's love. It seemed to be merely a matter of letting the body's chemical processes take their course. Then suddenly the idyll came to an end. If you ask Lukian about Sofie now, he won't be very forthcoming, understandably so, since you'll be touching the one place in his life where he was human enough to feel the hurt. Apart, of course, from the death of his family or his father's dementia—he died insane. By the way, I feel much better now, shall we sit in chairs like civilized human beings again.

He staggered to his feet and collapsed into his chair with a groan; I stuck the stool under my butt.

"You've never complained about sitting on that stool."

"The stool's OK."

"I can get them to bring a more comfortable chair. You only have to say. The stool was important for me. As long as you stayed sitting on it, I was sure I could tell you my story to the very end."

"Aha."

"Now I feel a little more confident about you. It's important for me. I simply don't have the time to go over things again. Would you like a chair?"

"No, I find the stool very comfortable. Otherwise I would have complained."

Von Brücken smiled, but it was a good-natured smile. The look in his eyes was a plea for forgiveness. I nodded. "Please go on."

"Lukian called me from a phone booth, one morning in December. He sounded very worked up, like someone trying to change the direction of his life."

I feel horrible talking about it. And we won't talk about her anymore. I love this woman. Throw me out, if you like. Let her go. Let me have her.

Well. What can a man say to that? To the only friend he has?

If you tell me she's OK now and then. If you promise to look after her.

While Lukian was in the phone booth talking to—or, rather, *negotiating with* me, Sofie went to the bathroom. Opened a wall cupboard. Looked at the range of pills. Lots of stimulants and tranquilizers. They didn't fit in with the image she had of her *Luc.* God only knows what made her do it, a fit of curiosity or paranoia maybe, but she searched the bedroom. Ended up with the photo in her hand. It was really well hidden, you can't say Lukian had been careless. As he came back into the apartment, Sofie ran past him and out, clutching just a small suitcase.

The photo was in the bedroom cupboard, underneath all the carefully folded bedlinen. No, that's where it *had* been. Now it was lying on the bed, a silent reproach. You remember? The photo Lukian had rescued from the auto-da-fé and kept. Sofie asleep in her Wuppertal apartment. What can the poor woman have thought when she saw it?

Groaning, von Brücken massaged his stomach, then rang for some tea, fennel tea, from the smell. He added a tiny drop of cognac.

"You too?"

"No thanks."

"It wasn't until a few days later, after he'd searched the whole city for her, that Luki told me about the disaster."

— *I've lost her.*
— *What d'you mean, lost her?*
— *I've messed things up, Alex, really messed them up.*
— *What do you want me to do?*
— *Help me.*
— *No.*

"You didn't help him?"

"Why? He'd taken my place and now he came crawling to me because he didn't know what to do. I was furious. My poor beloved. Why couldn't he be happy with Sofie, why did he have to keep her *photo*? She must have been out of her mind with fear. The most harmless version she could think up to explain the existence of that photo was bad enough to shake her faith in reality."

The End of Availability

After spending three days with Birgit, which end in a spectacular row, Sofie returns to her apartment on Mehringdamm. She expresses contrition to Holger, goes through the obligatory self-criticism and is graciously accepted back into the fold after she has declared her readiness to participate in the active struggle. A few days later she leaves Berlin and goes underground, becoming part of a revolutionary cell.

In February 1969 she takes part in her first bank robbery. The revolution needs money. The hold-up of the Krefeld West branch of a savings bank is successful. None of the robbers is recognized. The haul is about 30,000 marks. It's more than a year before Sofie's name appears on the wanted list. Delving into her earlier personal life, the FBCI comes across Lukian Keferloher or, rather, his double life as a publisher's editor and former board member of the Von Brücken Company. Although they cannot prove any actual illegality, he's regarded as suspicious and worth keeping under constant surveillance. Just as other people retire to spend more time with their family, Lukian retires to spend more time with the firm's senior management, this time officially as private secretary to Alexander von Brücken and vice president with no specific area of responsibility. In March 1972 he marries Sylvia Tanner.

"Lukian's never forgiven himself his mistake. What's worse, he didn't regard the mistake as simply a mistake but as the hand of fate. Naturally he was still in love with Sofie, but he couldn't do anything for her anymore. The only person who could—at least theoretically—do something for her was me. But that would have demanded a huge investment both in terms of finance and of logistics. So far Sofie had been, if you'll excuse the word, *available*. Keeping her under surveillance had been ungentlemanly, true, but easy and above all not forbidden. We had to pay a few people, a few technicians, bribe a few low-grade officials, it wasn't particularly expensive. Now it was different. To find her we'd've had to compete with the police, send in undercover agents who might possibly—just possibly—have eventually been able to make contact with her, at great personal risk to themselves. But getting people to join the underground is a quite different kettle of fish. I mean, I'm sure we'd have found volunteers, people will do anything if there's enough money in it, but even for me that was sticking my neck out too far. It would have left me open to blackmail, too many people would have asked questions or had to be let in on the secret, there would have been resistance in the firm, the police would have got wind of it, in short, it just wasn't doable. What was doable, we did. For example we got into contact with Birgit Kramer, who was now called Birgit Felsentein, having married into an upper-class Charlottenburg family and completely succumbed to the charm of the bourgeoisie.

"She assumed the man I sent to see her was a police spy, despite the fact that he pretended to be a private detective. Even if Sofie had got in touch with her, Birgit would have had no reason to tell us. Anyway, the relationship between the two stepsisters seemed to have suffered a terminal breakdown.

"Sofie remained invisible. I listened to Wagner, whom until then I had never liked, with different ears. We weren't gods any longer, at most Titans, but castrated ones. The police state the demonstrators had protested against was nothing compared with the police state that now developed, with greatly improved technical facilities. The world was becoming interlinked, the network more and more tightly knit. Investigative techniques became more sophisticated as the revolutionaries became more radical, evolving from stone-throwers into terrorists.

"Lukian married Sylvia because he thought it meant he would at least be doing good to one person. Perhaps that sounds rather simplistic, but it was true, Sylvia was really happy with him. The reverse wasn't quite the case, but Lukian concealed it. His attitude was that of a good loser who, having lost one thing, goes for the next best. He was enviable for the pragmatism which had been deeply ingrained in him.

"The great movement broke up, dispersed, was absorbed into the underground, leaving behind the comfortable part-time occupation of armchair sympathizer, the leading terrorists were caught, we had the Olympic Games in Munich and two years later, also in Munich, became world's champions at soccer. Munich sort of became the city of the anti-movement. You wrote in an essay once that you could remember as an eight-year-old seeing the newspaper boys distributing a special edition outside the Hertie building in Schwabing. Do you remember? It was about the arrest of Gudrun Ensslin."

"I remember. Even my mother, who was completely apolitical, bought one. There was the atmosphere of a street party."

"That's what brought you to my notice. Did you know that that was the very last special edition of a newspaper here in Germany?"

"No, to be honest I didn't. Was it really?"

"Nowadays you can hardly imagine the fear a few armed individuals, including a slim, pretty woman like Gudrun Ensslin, managed to arouse.

"Sofie never had anything to do with the Red Army Faction; if anything—all this is pretty unclear—she was associated with the June 2 Movement. You remember, the date of the demonstration when Benno Ohnesorg was shot. For the timorous citizens they were all part of the same *mishpoche*. Oh, I was worried stiff about my beloved, sometimes I even hoped she would get caught so that I could do something for her. But somehow she managed to avoid arrest and that filled me with a kind of pride. Perhaps she'd slipped away to some distant country. She appeared not to have been involved in the known terrorist attacks, certainly her name never appeared in connection with them. Basically she was being sought in connection with a few bank robberies, that was all. I can well imagine that, given the way she was, she would quickly become an outsider among her comrades-in-arms. Perhaps she was already dead? After the murder of Schmücker, whom they claimed was a traitor to the cause, almost anything seemed possible. When rumors appeared that some terrorists were being trained in armed combat in the Yemen I used front men to make contact with government agencies there. Of course, officially they were looking into the possibility of arms exports, even though weapons were never produced in my factories; I'd had to push that through against the will of the board of directors. But we did produce this or that which opened various doors for us. Incidentally, don't ask me why, but I made my father's dream, the ovoid private air-raid shelter, a reality. We produced a hundred, at a unit price of 364,000 marks; within two years they were sold out. It wasn't a profitable piece of business, more a piece of grotesque sentimentality.

"I would like to ask you why you did that."

"I was afraid you would. Well, perhaps it sounds completely *meshugge*, but if my father was watching me from somewhere it might get him to take back the curse, which I'm sure he never actually uttered but which was clearly hanging over my life. That crazy enough? Anyway, I needed something to keep me occupied."

"You wouldn't be taking the piss, would you?"

"No, that would be stupid. You have to be nice to people who're going to outlive you."

"Machiavelli?"

"No, home grown. Holger was picked up pretty quickly, got three years, renounced his convictions, like so many others, shaved off his beard and became a therapist. Despite that, we contacted him, he needed money to set himself up; there were masses of boxes with documents, minutes of meetings, bills, old leaflets, all packed in plastic bags when the Mehringdamm apartment was abandoned and kept out of the hands of the police. That's how we came into possession of Sofie's diary. It covers the years from May 1965 to January 1968. I hesitated a long time before reading it. It's not a very intimate account, thank God, she only kept it sporadically and it's almost dispassionate in tone, more a reminder than a confession, many of the entries are strangely terse or even banal. Even now I hesitate to make it available to you, that is, after a struggle I've decided to hand it over to you on the express condition that you don't use any details from it that go beyond what you might call historical interest in Sofie."

"Thank you."

Alexander handed me a sewn notebook with about seventy pages of entries, in purple ink, recording the state of Sofie's psyche over two and a half years. With one exception—the entry for June 3 1967—I have not used it. What it contained was either too banal or too personal. Useful information has been incorporated into the text in a different form.

BLUEBERRY JUICE WITH HONEY

The years passed: 1971, 1972, 1973, 1974, 1975. To list each one separately. I ought to list each month, each day, each minute, each second to show how much meaningless time I had to get through. The Beatles had broken up. I made them fantastic offers for a reunion tour, but without success. George Harrison sent me a signed copy of his solo album, *All Things Must Pass.* During those years I hardly ever appeared in my official capacity, never, really, my reputation as an eccentric recluse, a dark *éminence grise* hidden away from the world, grew from rumor to legend. My wealth grew as well, doubled every three years without my having to do much about it. My name was widely hated as the epitome of the capitalist dictator. And that despite the fact that I didn't sit on my money like Dagobert Duck, but my excesses of philanthropy were never truly recognized. Quite rightly so, in a way, I donated money dispassionately, threw away huge sums as if I needed to relieve myself, rarely drawing attention to it. It meant nothing to me. I killed time with long novels and Mahler's symphonies. Lukian was the only person I could bear to have around me, a kind of fellow prisoner. Sylvia Keferloher, née Tanner, died from cancer of the pancreas. We had her flown to the States, to the best doctors, but to no avail. As she was dying, she started to ramble, talked gibberish, cursed the world, saw angels which were half sea-snails and asked for blueberry juice with honey. We took turns holding her hand, there were embarrassing scenes when she accused us of just doing it for show, of not really meaning it, of wishing we were far away, away from her, oh, how I love you, my children. To the very end she kept telling us how much she loved us.

It affected me deeply, but still, when her death was inevitable I thought of making a bargain with God—or the gods, I had long been flexible in that respect: take Sylvia and let Sofie live. Shake on it. It's a deal.

On the face of it Luki took her death calmly, but he had become very accustomed to her. His mourning was genuine. As was mine, even if my mourning was only half for Sylvia, the other half for the tragic impossibility of being happy with Sylvia. I decided to talk myself into believing things a lot more in future. I realized that happiness is not unconnected with self-deception. Dr. Fröhlich had been right. Deception is not purely negative, there are always winners and losers, and if you go about self-deception cleverly enough you can siphon off the loser and grant the winner his moment of triumph. I persuaded myself I had an interest, a passionate interest in oil paintings, and soon I really did. It was a good way of occupying my time, poring over catalogues of auctions from all over the world, bidding by telephone, seeking and collecting and also, given the crazy way old masters were increasing in value, making a profit out of it too. Well, the fun lasted a few weeks, then came another "interest" and another. I wasn't living, I was vegetating my life away, even if it was a sumptuous life. And then something happened which was as incomprehensible as . . . I can't think of a suitable simile but I'm sure one'll occur to you. The telephone rang, I lifted the receiver and that nice switchboard operator from the Munich factory, I can't remember her name, said she was sorry to disturb me, but there was someone on the line who ab-so-lute-ly had to speak to me. Her name was Sofie Kurtz and she'd refused to take no for an answer. Should she put her through?

THE REALLY HIGH NOTES

A rented two-room flat somewhere on the outskirts of Herne, January 1976. Sofie's drinking white Baden wine straight from the bottle, sitting all by herself in a corner on a bare mattress. The curtains are drawn. Apart from her there are two men and another woman in the room, watching *Crime Watch* on their tiny black-and-white television. Every few minutes the woman gives her a sharp warning glance. It doesn't bother Sofie. She's off the hard stuff, fulfilling the condition of the group's ultimatum. This's just white wine and her first bottle today. She'll stop at one and a half, that's a reasonable, generally acceptable ration. The program finishes without the bank robbery in Recklinghausen being mentioned, probably the haul was too little, not even nine thousand marks. They're all shit scared of *Crime Watch*, the favorite Friday evening viewing for the West German amateur informer; thousands pass on information after the program, some of it useful, those people have eyes everywhere.

Sofie staggers to the bathroom, looks at her haggard face in the mirror. Soon she'll be forty-five, fifteen years older than anyone else in the group. The banks don't keep as much on the premises as they used to, they have to go out to collect their housekeeping money at shorter and shorter intervals. And a fair amount from that has to be passed on to the front-line fighters. Sofie's group is solely concerned with replenishing the money supply, apart from her none of them is on the wanted list. The others thought her alcoholism made her a security risk, so she had to promise to give up spirits, otherwise she was threatened with *expulsion*.

"My nerves aren't up to any more bank robberies," she says to the mirror, which repeats it, word by word, only silently and with a pained expression.

"You do it well. As long as you haven't had one too many." The man right at the back of the mirror's called Jacob, twenty-eight. If he was flabbier he'd look like the film director Rainer Werner Fassbinder.

Jacob has connections which provide the group with new ID cards twice a year that are so perfectly forged no police check has ever found anything wrong with them.

"We ought to do something creative," Sofie says. Not this chickenshit. The risk was getting bigger and bigger, the yield less and less. It couldn't go on for much longer.

Jacob agrees and smiles, placing a thin file beside the wash-basin. A proposal from above. She should have a look at it. It concerned *her* personally.

"Me?" Sofie's suspicious of anything that concerns her personally. Always expects the worst. Doesn't trust any of them. She picks up the file hesitantly, leafs through it.

Jacob watches her closely. "You used to know him, didn't you?"

Sofie seems nervous, has a frog in her throat, blinks rapidly.

"That's years and years ago. I'm sure he won't remember me anymore."

"Just imagine how much that'd bring in. At almost no risk. If he goes along with it. We ought to try it. One really big operation. Then you can retire."

"I'm sure he'll have hundreds of guards keeping watch. The whole group'd get bust. He lives in the backwoods of Bavaria."

"Come on. You'll meet him by yourself. If he doesn't come alone we drop it."

Sofie continues to protest for a while, but Jacob refuses to give up the idea and lets the others in on it.

"I picked up the phone. You can't imagine what was going on inside me, but you'll have to pretend you can, you'll have to describe it in a way that's both credible and full of passion, hit the really high notes.

— Yes?
— Alexander?
— Yes.
— This is Sofie. D'you remember? We used to know each other . . . years ago. Twenty-five years?

I couldn't believe it. The sweat was pouring off me. My beloved, whom I'd almost thought was dead, was talking to me. My knees gave way. Eventually I said:

— I know who you are.
— Is your telephone bugged?
— No.

The idea had never occurred to me. Was my telephone bugged? It wasn't entirely out of the question.

— Listen. Are you still there?
— I'm here. Where are you?
— I can't tell you that.
— You sound so close. As if you're just around the corner.
— Just listen for a moment! 'S important. Are you listening?
— Yes.
— One of our people's found a file on you which says we used to know each other.
— Hmmm. What kind of file? The FBCI?
— Rubbish. Listen, it's not a joke. We intend to kidnap you. Two million ransom.
— Aha.

— I'm supposed to ring you up and lure you to a rendezvous. That's where you'll be grabbed. I couldn't really refuse.
— Sure, I understand.

I found the conversation so amusing I had to get a grip on myself to stop myself crying.

— That's why I called.
— Where am I to go?
— What?
— Where am I to go?
— Nowhere, idiot. I don't want it to happen.
— Why not?
— You do ask some stupid questions.
— But it's a great idea. I'd love to see you again.
— Hey, it's not funny, not funny at all. Don't be so goddam stupid. I mean it seriously.

I was so excited I was scrabbling around the floor on my knees, trembling with joy. She meant it seriously!

— But I don't want you to get into trouble because of me, Sofie.
— What?
— If I don't turn up at the rendezvous, your people'll get suspicious.
— Are you out of your mind? I'm the woman on the wanted posters, remember? You'd never come to a rendezvous with me. I told them that, but they still forced me to call you. OK, that's it. Stay put in your bunker for the next few days and nothing'll happen to you.
— But . . . nothing would happen to me anyway. I'd pay up.
— Are you sick, or what?
— I just want to cooperate. Two million, that's neither here

nor there, I want to see you again. Come here. I'll give you twice the amount. Bring your friends with you.

We seemed to be on different wavelengths. Everything went quiet at the other end of the line, very quiet, for almost thirty seconds, I was already fearing the worst. Then I heard her breathing, irregularly. My beloved seemed somewhat taken aback by the situation.

— I call you to warn you and you make fun of me
— Yes, I wasn't thinking, you can't come here, that's nonsense, you can't trust me. I'll come to you. I could bring the money with me. Tell them you're meeting me alone. Where should we meet?
— Forget it, numskull!

She sounded as if she was getting increasingly angry. Why wasn't it clear to me.

— Please, tell me. Where were we to have met? Tell me.
— A pub not far from you. Called the White Stag, for all that's worth.
— I know it. When?
— Tomorrow evening at ten. What's the point? I suppose you think you're being big . . .
— I'll be there. You can have the money. In small bills, if you like. It's a bit tight, timewise, but it's doable. Are you still there?

She hung up. Perhaps someone had interrupted her. I immediately gave orders for the money to be ready by the next afternoon, in 100-mark bills, packed in an attaché case. Twenty thousand 100-mark bills. It wasn't that small an amount, purely from the question of size. Perhaps I'd need two or three attaché cases.

Von Brücken made an effort to reproduce for me the euphoria he'd felt on that day. The result was a fascinatingly multilayered piece of ham acting that kept on breaking down and turning tragic, slapstick turning into self-reproach, self-mockery.

Sofie comes out of the phone booth. Jacob's waiting in the car. The tank's almost empty and he's switched the engine off so he's shivering with cold, his arms crossed over his chest and rocking back and forward.

"So? What did he say?"

"That he'll bring his ransom with him." Sofie adopts an icily sarcastic tone.

"Don't talk crap."

"He saw through it right away."

"Oh well, it was worth a try."

"Waste of time."

By nine the next evening I was sitting in the White Stag. Waiting. So worked up I needed a brandy. And another. The White Stag was an ordinary bar where the local farmers played skat at five pfennigs a point. I waited, gripped with excitement. Any moment now they were going to kidnap me, threaten to kill me. And if I was going to die, I thought, at least I would be able to look Sofie in the eye as I did so.

Don't groan like that. OK, OK . . . At some point the barman tapped me on the shoulder, took away my glass and pointed at the clock on the wall. It was midnight. Lights out. You're welcome to portray me as a fool. Don't hold back on the comedy. At least I'd spoken to her. And I could tell myself she'd refused to take the money *for my sake*. Out of concern for me."

"If I write that, no one's going to believe it."

"Why not? I'm sorry, but why not? Some novelists would exploit the opportunity, would describe a dramatic kidnapping, a dramatic death-threat, an even more dramatic rescue and an absolutely dramatic escape through the ice-cold night. THAT would be beyond belief. Don't you understand? It was only for a short while that I was disappointed. Then I was happy. Sofie had warned me! Had betrayed her own comrades just to warn me! She was *not entirely without feelings* for me. Can you imagine what that meant to me?"

The memory was too much for Alexander, he sobbed and leant right back in his chair. We ended the session. As soon as I'd left the room, embarrassed, he rang for the doctor.

During that night for the first time there was no building noise to be heard, nor floodlight beams to be seen wandering around the park.

Was the mausoleum finished, I asked. The word *mausoleum* was a bit too grand, Lukian said, for a plain stone grave eight foot high. Geometrically the construction corresponded to a quail's egg with the top half sticking out of the ground. He couldn't repress a grin at von Brücken's morbid self-irony.

Incidentally, he told me, he'd had a rethink. I was going to write my novel anyway, he could tell that from looking at me. At me and my shabby clothes. If it was to be his fate to end up as a character in a work of art, then he might as well influence it as far as possible.

We were sitting on stools at the bar of the swimming pool, helping ourselves to whiskey from the inverted bottles. Lukian quickly became almost confiding, without, however, divesting himself of his characteristic didactic, slightly embittered style.

The June 2 movement as such, he said, was not in contact with East Germany, apart from individuals. Only at the end of the seventies, when the remaining members of the RAF were absorbed, were there official, if highly secret, records of meetings with the Stasi. He could let me have earlier, unofficial files which contained some things about Sofie's time in the underground. They might fill in a few blank spots on Sofie's biographical map. It was with great difficulty that he had managed to obtain these notes, often handwritten, after the Wall had come down, to stop them falling into the wrong hands. He had to remind me, however, that these documents did not always contain the *truth*. They had been written by *officials*, if one could call them that, who were not impartial, never mind *fair*. This material had to be treated with care, by someone with the ability to read between the lines and to interpret it. A few dates and places named in them might, however, be of use to me.

I declined his offer. I was suspicious of this sudden change of mind. Did Alexander know about this material?

Of course, only he didn't think much of it, maintaining that in it Sofie was observed through ideological spectacles and, one might say, caricatured. At midnight he placed a large file on my bed. I declined once more.

"May I ask another question?"

"Ask away."

"Is Sofie still alive?"

Lukian Keferloher gave me a slightly quizzical look, shrugged his shoulders and smiled.

"I've been wondering all along when you'd ask that?"

"And?"

"I can't give you an answer."

"Because you don't know or because you don't want to?"

"I don't want to give a final answer to that."

"Are you afraid I might misrepresent Sofie?

"No one who didn't know her can describe her adequately. Not even Alexander can."

"But *you* could?"

Lukian ignored the question, it was like water off a duck's back; he seemed to look down on it as if it were a puddle in the gutter. That, he said, was not the main point. What I had to write down was *Alexander's* story, not his, he'd tried to make that clear to me the previous day. He had to keep completely out of it. Was there anything else I wished?

"Peace on earth."

He promised to do his best.

DAY SIX

HELL FOR LEATHER

Early in the morning of October 24 1976 an Opel Commodore with four members of Sofie's group is called over for a routine check by the traffic police at the East-West German border near Helmstedt. Sofie, at the wheel, pulls over to the right and takes the vehicle documents out of the glove compartment. Jacob's not there, at the moment he's on business in Berlin. Two relatively young policemen approach the car. The agreed strategy for this situation is as follows. Firstly: avoid violence against traffic police for as long as possible. Secondly: only open fire when the opposing side is unmistakably proceeding to an arrest. Thirdly: if the situation then escalates, show no mercy. All means available must be employed to avoid arrest.

"Documents please. Driver's and vehicle license."

Sofie hands over both. The second policeman inspects the car.

As arranged for this scenario, one of the men in the back asks if he can go out to have a pee. It disperses the target area.

"If you must."

The man, whose identity has not been established to this day, stands by the edge of the road.

"Put the lights on."

They check that the lights are working. There's nothing wrong with them.

"Open the trunk, please." The woman in the front passenger seat, her name is Friederike (*all names have been changed*), gets out and goes around the car. The trunk's empty, there's no reason not to open it. Despite that, as if at some secret signal, Friederike X and the man, Y, standing by the edge of the road fiddling with his trousers, pull out their guns and open fire. The two policemen, Holger M. and Hans-Peter P. fall, seriously wounded with shots to the chest and stomach. Friederike X takes their service revolvers and gets back in the car with them.

"Off we go."

Sofie doesn't react.

"Put your foot down, for God's sake!"

Again Sofie shows no reaction. Friederike X gets out, runs around the car, roughly shoves Sofie into the passenger seat and takes the wheel herself.

Twenty minutes later, after driving like hell for leather over autumnally greasy country roads, the quartet reaches a shack on the edge of the forest near Salzgitter. The Opel's put in a garage knocked together out of fiberboard. The shack in the foothills of the Harz mountains belongs to a former forester who doesn't use it any longer and has given it to his son, a left-wing sympathizer and ex-bedmate of Friederike X. It's high season for mushrooms. And a Sunday. If the weather wasn't so lousy there'd be dozens of people about in the woods. Inside the shack a big row erupts, starting with an almost surreal silence. There are antlers on the wall and no electricity, just a hand-operated pump and an earth closet. The portable radio runs on batteries. They won't be able to spend more than one night here, the group'll have to disperse, find hideouts in the city and form new cells. That's the standard procedure. Blondie is on the radio. The news reports the shooting, the two wounded policemen are in hospital, fighting for their lives.

"What?! They're not dead?" Y. can't believe it. Sofie gets up, looks at him, slaps him, goes out of the shack and sits down in the drizzle.

Inside a lively discussion starts.

"So far she's been OK."

"So far it's never come to the crunch."

"She failed! She's not going to put me in danger like that again!"

"And how do you think you're going to arrange that? Set her down at a service area? Or deliver her to an animal home?"

"If she'd at least come and say—Listen, I fucked up, I'm sorry . . . " Z, a man who so far has said nothing, tries to steer the discussion into a more conciliatory channel. "She's only been like that since Ulrike was murdered."

Ulrike Meinhof's death in her prison cell had indeed hit Sofie hard. How could such a strong, intelligent woman despair of the way the world was going, when there were endless possibilities, more than anyone could envisage. How could a mother, a mother who was an example to many, hang herself on Mother's Day of all days? Commit suicide in such demeaning fashion? Many on the left believed it was murder, but not Sofie. No state, however stupid, would provide its enemies with a ready-made martyr. Not in that way. You could just as well poison someone with pills and make it look like illness. Why hang them? It was more than just an idol that died with Ulrike Meinhof, with her a large part of Sofie's courage and determination died, too.

"That's no excuse."

"My feelings too. She's a risk."

"It worked out all right again."

Sofie suddenly appears in the doorway. They all immediately fall silent.

"It worked out well again, did it? Go on then, celebrate."

"In your place I'd keep my trap shut."

"The papers were fine. They'd have let us drive on. Why? Why did you do that?"

"You couldn't see. You were in the car. The pigs noticed something."

"What?"

"Doesn't matter. They noticed something, and if they didn't they were too stupid. What's the point? It happened. But you—you put us in danger. All of us. You failed completely and that's a fact."

"I did, did I? And are you going to shoot me now?" She says it very calmly, her voice slightly hoarse, almost as if she's in a trance, serene, beyond fear and hysteria. She takes out one of the police pistols.

"Isn't it strange? There's only a piece of metal in there. But depending on where that piece of metal ends up, there, or there, or here—" She points the barrel at the heads of everyone in the shack, including her own, one after the other. She doesn't complete the sentence. Her thoughts are all in a tangle, she suddenly thinks it's outrageous the effects a piece of metal can have, never mind the state of the thoughts it bursts into. She puts the pistol down on the windowledge. No one says a word. Friederike X makes tea on the camping stove.

OVER THE WALL

T he next day in a building in Strausberg to the north-east of Berlin, Jacob, an "unofficial collaborator," meets a Stasi colonel with special powers. The officer, who's around fifty, is annoyed by the most recent events.

"You can't afford to do that kind of thing. You're not part of the Central Council of Vagrant Hash Rebels anymore. Traffic police! That means bad press."

Jacob nods submissively. Without the forged ID cards from the Ministry they're not going to last more than a few weeks, or even days. Friederike X described Sofie's failure to him over the telephone, ruthlessly exaggerating. In her version Sofie was drunk and drew suspicion on herself, so they'd been forced to take action. And that, with a little added exaggeration, is how he describes the affair to the Stasi colonel. He listens, then taps his desk with his pencil, like Fate knocking at the door.

"Get rid of her."

Jacob nods, then points out that *that* would get them an even worse press. The colonel thinks for a moment. "Bad press doesn't last forever."

To Jacob that sounds pretty cynical. You couldn't criticize her for anything, he tells the colonel, apart from her drink problem. And her soft heart and weak nerves. She'd been active for ages, apart from which—

"What?"

"She has an appealing face. Still has. Looks good on posters. We shouldn't underestimate its effectiveness among the general population."

"True." The colonel considers the case again, runs it through his mind, slowly, back and forward, from ear to ear. The picture on the wanted poster shows a pretty woman with big dark eyes.

"Immense visual potential," the colonel declares. "But perhaps we could use it in reverse. An accident, perhaps. Ideally, of course, you'd get her shot by the class enemy."

His unofficial collaborator suggests that might be difficult to arrange. He suspects that Sofie K. would not resist the state forces if they tried to grab her. He has, he says, a different proposal.

It's the moment of conception of a model that's going to become standard practice.

A Way Out Rather than a Goal

uki gave you the Stasi stuff?"

"Yes."

"Good. OK, I suppose we have to approach it like an historian. Any information, even falsified, is better than none. Naturally I did a bit of research. By a miracle the two seriously wounded policemen survived. They didn't need to work for the rest of their lives, I saw to that."

The next day the Opel Commodore is abandoned. Jacob's back with the group listening to harsh complaints about Sofie: she aimed a pistol at her comrades, jabbering incoherently. The only reason she seemed relatively clear-headed now, apart from the trembling, was an enforced night without alcohol. Jacob's brought a BMW. He's going to drive the group to Hamburg, for reorientation. He sets Sofie down at a country station, hands her a small sum for travel and demands her gun.

"I don't have a gun."

Jacob believes her but uses it as an excuse to frisk her all over. He's always wanted to do that.

"You go to Braunschweig."

"Why?"

"Orders." He hands her an envelope. "I don't know anything more myself. Take the train. You'll be reassigned in Braunschweig."

"Is this farewell forever?"

"No idea." Jacob ignores the ambiguity in her question. "Tell me, are you sad?"

Sofie doesn't reply. She takes the envelope and doesn't look back. The BMW drives off with a screech of rubber. In the envelope is a new ID card, the details of which she has to learn off by heart. There's also the key to the hideaway in Braunschweig. She gets on the train, buys a ticket from the conductor and stares out of the window. The first snow has fallen.

The Braunschweig Base consists of a single large, almost empty room plus kitchen on the sixth floor of a rundown tenement building. The blinds are closed. Sofie opens them, letting in light and air. In the bathtub there's a coprolite of human origin. Old mattresses are propped up against the wall. The kitchen cupboard contains three cans of ravioli, a pepper pot and a packet of teabags. Underneath the sink Sofie finds a square package about the size of a hatbox. She holds it in her hands. Puts it back. The telephone rings. She goes over to it.

"Yes?"

"Did you find the package?" It's Jacob's voice.

"I did."

"Open it."

"I have done so."

"Open it."

"How do you know I haven't opened it?"

"That's an order." Jacob hangs up.

Night falls. Sofie and the package look at each other.

She makes a will, a personal one that's very short because she's nothing to leave and a political one she tears up. Political testaments are for the big fish, people like Hitler or Goebbels. *I'm just Sofie, a footnote to the history of the class war.* Sounds stupid. No person's a footnote. She opens a can of ravioli, heats it up and spews it out again. It's not entirely the fault of the ravioli.

She discovers what Socrates must have felt when he was faced with the bowl of hemlock. She can imagine the

Bildzeitung headlines: **TERRORIST BLOWS HERSELF UP MAKING A BOMB**. And underneath, in smaller letters: **THE RIGHT VICTIM FOR ONCE**.

So that's it as far as life's concerned. At least she's going out with a bang.

Sofie writes several letters, one to Birgit, one to Rolf, one to Lukian as well. And tears them all up. Once every hour she decides to flee. All she's left with is two hundred marks, but she could easily improve that, she thinks, she could do a bank, with a toy revolver, and if the worst should come to the worst, she's still—a woman. She's devastated to find how little of her there's left. Is that it?

The package. It comes to everyone sometime or other. The full package. No one can escape it.

Today or tomorrow, what difference does it make? Perhaps her comrades are right? There are voices in the room, whispering, telling her that's the way it is, that's the best, she must make the best of it, not write pretentious testaments and letters, that won't help the cause. They'll say she died in the execution of her convictions. A tragic figure with big, dark eyes. She goes to the filling station and buys some alcohol. Enough to poison herself. But she doesn't want to die drunk. Not dead drunk.

Around midnight, after a bottle of wine, she takes the first layer of wrapping paper off the package. Pieces of fine wire are tied around the cardboard box inside. Perhaps she should regard them as lifelines, tracks leading to the void, perhaps it has to be, perhaps it's for the best, part of a higher order. Perhaps it's appropriate for a life like hers to die drunk. As a protest. To be out of her mind when her brains are blown out. At that moment she has an idea which doesn't seem entirely absurd. Alexander. He could help her get out of this life, to get a better one. How about it? No, impossible, it would declare her whole life a farce. Most people's death is banal, without the bowl of hemlock, they lose everything they don't want to give up, die some way or other, some time or other. At least she'll be going out in a *flash*.

Around three in the morning Sofie picks up the kitchen knife and cuts the wires. Nothing happens. Now there's just a length of sticky tape around the package.

Thirty seconds later the phone rings.

"Yes?"

"Have you opened the package?"

"Yes."

"And? What d'you think?"

"I don't really know."

Silence at the other end of the line. For minutes.

"Jacob? Are you still there?"

"Any moment there'll be a ring at the door. Two short, one long. Open it."

Sofie gets her coat. Thinks of going out, stares at the package, no idea where to go, what to do.

The doorbell rings. Two short, one long. She hesitates, freezes, leans against the refrigerator. Hears the sound of a key turning in the lock. The door to the apartment opens, very slowly. Sofie can see the shadow of the door moving across the wall. She switches off the light.

A man's voice she doesn't recognize says, "Sofie?"

She'd hiding in the kitchen, squatting under the sink, her coat covering her.

The man crosses the apartment with quiet steps, finds the light switch, comes into the kitchen.

"Sofie?"

"Stay where you are! Whoever you are."

"I've come to take care of you."

"I don't know you."

"What are you afraid of?"

He comes closer. For the first time she regrets not being

armed. She's clasping a butter knife, but you couldn't call that being *armed*. The man's middle aged, a bony face, going gray at the temples, slightly pudgy, but that's concealed by a loose-fitting black trenchcoat.

"Listen. We've had discussions about you. Long discussions. We argued and argued. You can't imagine how concerned about you we are . . . People like you a lot. Only—you're no use to the movement any longer. You know that yourself."

"Where should I go, then?"

"We've decided that the most effective thing you have to offer is your face on the wanted posters. So let it stay there. As long as possible. With as little change as possible. You can start a new life. You've been very lucky. In your place I'd smile. Honestly." The pale man smiles, as if he needs to show her how. He has large, fleshy hands with lots of hair on the back of his fingers.

"A new life? I don't know you."

"New name, new profession, new everything. That's what you want, isn't it? That's your dream?"

Under his coat the man's wearing a plain gray suit; he shows her his big empty hands. "Come with me, everything's going to be OK."

Sofie, drunk, puts down the butter knife, cowers. The man holds out his hand to her.

"What's in the package?" She gives a short cry when he touches her shoulder.

"If you'd opened it, you'd know. Take my hand."

She refuses. She wants to know, instead of taking his hand she picks up the package, fumbles with the sticky tape, sticks her fingers through it. Perhaps she is *armed* after all and just didn't know it. A gigantic explosion. At the end of her life. Why not? It means nothing to her.

The man sighs out loud. "Come on, stop taking yourself so seriously."

Sofie tears at the packaging, rips off the lid. Releasing a compressed spring. A jack-in-the-box shoots out, a black-and-red jack-in-the-box with a hook nose and a silent laugh.

"Satisfied?" the man asks, condescension mixed with understanding, before finally taking Sofie by the hand. She's only semiconscious, it's been the longest night of her life.

"If you'd trusted us, you'd still be operational. But we'll look after you all the same. That's the way we are."

FIRSTLY TO THIRDLY: THE GREAT GAME

I can't believe you just let all this happen."
"Now just a minute. Hasn't your attitude changed! You're not underestimating my power anymore, now you're *over-estimating* it. Firstly: I didn't know where Sofie was, what she was doing, whether she was in danger or not and if she was, what kind of danger. Secondly: I would perhaps have been able to help her, but at a high price; I'd have had to intervene in her life from above again, perhaps even making things worse than they already were. Thirdly: of course I tried to help her—how could you imagine otherwise? All the time. Though at the top level. I'd made a kind of truce with the of FBCI, not actually with the Bureau itself, of course, but with certain the big guns in it, but that was sufficient, and if they'd caught Sofie, alive, there was the possibility of forged medical reports and a lenient sentence followed by custody in a secure psychiatric unit—I'd already prepared for that by setting up a special clinic, with doctors who were on my payroll—oh yes, I can see the little monkey of doubt scampering to and fro across your face again. Can you imagine what all that cost me? But that was nothing, it could be entered under *charitable donations* without arousing suspicion. The Von Brücken Clinic even made a profit and became part of my welfare program; it's not unusual for industrial magnates to lend their name to hospitals. A very extravagant, eccentric plan, but OK. Unfortunately something unanticipated intervened. Sofie was granted exile in the other part of Germany. It was years before I heard about it, before that I'd been looking for her in the Near East, it sounds funny now—I should have been looking for her in the *nearest* East. But at the time I

was naïve enough to base my calculations on what was probable. I'd even included her death in them and intended, if that were the case, to find her body and bring it back in order to set up a memorial for it here in the Owl's Nest. At least to be with her in mourning. And then! What a wonderful, moving day when it came to my ears that she was probably still alive, a protégé of the Stasi!

I felt old, far too soon. If I can give you a piece of advice: you're old at seventy, at fifty you're nowhere near it. Lots of people waste the best years of their life just because they think silly young girls won't take up with them anymore. Stuff your silly young girls! Sofie was alive. Perhaps. Naturally I did everything permissible for a man in my position. Only I had to go about it incredibly carefully, it wasn't a children's game any longer, it had become part of the great game. And before you ask, yes, I enjoyed it, it gave meaning to my life. Only—you must imagine how laborious it was, how painstaking, how circumspect we had to be. Months passed, years, before our work produced a tiny scrap of new information. What a political bombshell if it had come out, perhaps the best kept secret of the GDR! It wasn't just Sofie, soon much harder types were provided with new identities, the most wanted terrorists of the RAF! Every movement I made threatened to knock over a domino, with catastrophic effect. I put myself in danger personally, I'm sure the Stasi would not have shown any special consideration for me, even the few cautious contacts were only possible because I had so much money. That was the good thing about the German Democratic Republic, it always needed money. I found money for it, invested in completely nonsensical projects, right to the limit of what was permissible, there were mutterings on the board. What you must understand is that a consortium of that size never belongs to one person alone, even if that's what it looks like on paper. It was during that period that Lukian really came into his own. He created a network of intermediaries, who had intermediaries, who had intermediaries. The only trouble was that it was never clear which intermediaries were to be taken seriously and their palms greased, which not. The GDR was a paranoid state, with a high rate of fluctuation among its dignitaries.

It took almost eight years before the network was firmly enough established for me to become part of it myself. Even at that point, Sofie's new identity was not much more than a conjecture, a rumor. Later on we could more or less reconstruct a lot of things from the Stasi files, understand what it must have felt like. It must have been purgatory for Sofie. She'd wanted to change the world and there she was, stuck in a banal, useless existence inside the walled-in ruin of what she'd once seen as a socialist utopia. But I didn't know that. To my shame I have to confess that I even reckoned it was possible she might have settled for domestic, conjugal bliss over there. Otherwise I might perhaps have been more venturesome, might have staked everything on one or other of the opportunities that arose. The reproaches I've heaped on myself! But can you blame anyone who's in the dark for feeling his way forward, keeping low and whispering, instead of running and yelling and lashing out wildly?

Von Brücken groaned. At first I assumed it was an exaggerated aural illustration of the emotional torments he had been through, but then I realized the torment was of a more mundane nature. He pressed the concealed bell on his desk and less than twenty seconds later I had my first sight of the doctor who looked after him, a bald, middle-aged man with a chin like the prow of a ship and delicate slim-fingered hands. Taking no notice of me, he unbuttoned Alexander's shirtsleeve.

The lord of the castle, whose employees had once respectfully referred to him as the *Imperator*, now no more than an old man, a patient writhing in agony, whispered that I should spend the rest of the day studying the files, he had to ask me to excuse him. He waved me out of the room with a fluttering gesture. He seemed extremely uncomfortable about letting himself be seen like that by me, even though his suffering made me feel more sympathetic toward him, of which he must have been aware. It was more important for him to conceal it from me, not, I think, from vanity, but from his profound sense of his duty as host.

Intense Desire

This meant that for the first time I had the opportunity to explore the park by daylight. It was a clear, windy day, the temperature relatively mild, a few degrees above freezing. There was no one to be seen anywhere in the park. The work on the tomb appeared to be finished. It stood there, gleaming blackly in the middle of the big water meadow, surrounded by gigantic fairy rings of oaks and poplars and birches. Paths of white marble slabs radiated in four directions from the tomb, ending abruptly when they reached the first ring of trees. Hidden under the snow, I had not noticed them before; now that it had thawed, the paths formed a stark contrast to the black of the tomb. I would have preferred a closely mown lawn of green all around, but they presumably had to take into account the fact that the meadow would occasionally be under water and turn into a quagmire. I didn't know and had never dared ask what stage Alexander's illness had reached. That day was the first time I considered the possibility that I might never hear the end of his story. A terrible prospect—what would I do then?

That evening I was overcome with an intense desire for female company. I couldn't concentrate on the files, drank a lot and paced up and down my room. There was a numb, tingling sensation in my arms and shoulders, they no longer seemed to belong to me and I felt like whirling them around, flinging them up in the air the way a rock guitarist does and dancing at the same time. But I couldn't quite bring myself to do it and my body began to feel heavier and heavier, more and more cumbersome.

I asked Lukian to show me the village inn where Alexander had waited for Sofie. He said it had disappeared years ago; it sounded like an excuse.

Then any inn, any bar, just to get out of this castle, please. He pulled out his mobile and took me down the stairs to the main entrance where a car was waiting with a chauffeur, the same one who'd brought me from the station.

"If you need drugs, you only have to say so. You look as if you do. We can cater to anything here."

I didn't know what I needed. I told the driver to take me someplace with bright lights, even if it was just a cheap dive with a juke box. The chauffeur shrugged his shoulders when Lukian instructed him to do anything I wanted. We drove to the village. It was just before nine and there wasn't much on offer. A Greek restaurant, a bistro, a disco with an adjoining bar, though without a red-light license. I realized I didn't have much cash on me, enough for a couple of drinks. Around me, lounging provocatively against the bar, were locals, farm workers who regarded me suspiciously, sensing the outsider and promptly planning ways of putting one over on me. The woman behind the bar was full-bosomed and uncouth, cheap music, produced for idiots, was booming out of the loudspeakers. The chauffeur preferred to wait in the car. Feeling exposed and unsatisfied, I downed two gin and tonics, paid and left.

The locals looked disappointed, losing out on the chance of playing some cruel trick. On the way back to the castle the chauffeur started telling me about the nearest brothel. It was only thirty kilometers away and they could charge it to the castle's account. If I wanted I only had to say.

"We have an account with them?" I asked, using the first person plural. "How come?"

They used to send for girls to be brought to the castle, the chauffeur said. Not anymore.

"Really? Who sent for girls?" I wanted all the details.

The chauffeur, opening up a bit as he wallowed in memories, said that in the old days everything had been different, he'd often driven a few girls to the castle in the evening and back again in the morning.

"Who for?"

That, the chauffeur said, was beyond his knowledge, he was the chauffeur, that was all.

He seemed to be summing up his limited existence in that one sentence, without making it into a complaint. What he said seemed intended more as a justification.

But what business was it of mine? Was I really bothered by the idea that Alexander had not lived the life of an ascetic, an anchorite? He would certainly have often had members of the board staying for whom he would have provided a companion for the night, as would have been usual when the means were available. I had to smile at the way I was already beginning to develop the future hero of my novel. Or, possibly, the way Alexander had got me to do precisely that.

DAY SEVEN

The No One's Rose

When I entered the grand chamber at ten the next morning he was waiting for me lying in a bed that had been put in the middle of the huge room. Oddly enough, Alexander was wearing a blue jacket over his pajamas; perhaps he thought it made me feel it was less intimate. The doctors, he told me, had ordered him to stay in bed and rest. He'd never believed in staying in bed and resting, but if they insisted, he was prepared to compromise. Had I read the files?

I'd only had a quick look, I replied. I'd felt more like going out.

"I understand. I heard about it. A sudden need for some life, I suppose."

"You could put it that way."

"Now you know what it's like for me, every day, every hour, every minute."

During that night does Sofie think she's gong to start new life from scratch? She decides to accept the offer and disappear for a few weeks until she's got her drink problem under control and the furore about her has died down. It's only later that she realizes what she's let herself in for, everything takes her by surprise, almost like a surprise attack. In her diary the drive through the night is compared to a ghost train, but it goes past good ghosts who are, admittedly, full of their own importance but who form a protective canopy over her. *Decision: to trust. Then sleep.* It's in there. At the Helmstedt border she crosses into the territory of the German Democratic Republic. In a black Mercedes with diplomatic license plates. Once across the border, they immediately change cars and get into an inconspicuous Wartburg. They're heading for Grünau, a housing estate made from prefabricated slabs on the western outskirts of Leipzig. They arrive there early in the morning, the first workers are leaving the estate and heading for the streetcar stop. An empty two-room apartment has been prepared for Sofie on the sixth and last floor. She mustn't leave it under any circumstances during the next few days. In her own interest (who else's?) a new identity has to be worked out first. The order is still made as a request, but a forceful one. Sofie sees that the apartment is not dissimilar to the one in Braunschweig, almost as bare, apart from a radio, a narrow bed, a refrigerator and non-absorbent toilet paper she's not used to. Among the groceries are two crates of Pilsner and at least there's heating from a plant that serves the whole district, so there's no need to lug coal up the stairs. Nothing happens during the next few days, Sofie lies in bed or stands at the window, feeling safe—which surprisingly isn't a good feeling, it's hard to explain, she couldn't do so herself. It's in her diary. She doesn't venture out of the apartment and sticks a beer mat over the spy hole in the door so no one can tell from outside that the light's on. The radio's old, reception weak, it can only get Western stations with a lot of crackling and background noise. Finally a removal firm delivers some furniture, secondhand furniture in various disgusting shades of brown. According to the driver's log it's supposed to come from a village near to Rostock. She doesn't have to sign for it. The neighbors don't seem interested in the new arrival, assuming they've even noticed. A plump, energetic looking woman, a little over fifty, comes to see Sofie. She's wearing a headscarf and leather boots, has a key to the apartment. She is, she says, reception committee and instructor in one. "Cedcadin."

"Kramer."

The woman, whose complexion resembles a russet apple,

gives a broad grin. "*Ce*ntral *De*partment for *Cad*res and *In*struction. For the moment you can just call me Major." She makes an effort to speak standard German, though her Thuringian accent comes through now and then. "We've worked out a biography for you. Get it off by heart. I'm the only one that knows here. And that's how it's going to stay. Any problems, you bring 'em to me. Your new documents. Hundred percent genuine. Certificate of citizenship. Congratulations. Some books, work your way through 'em. You know absolutely nothing about Rostock, I s'pose? That'll have to change. For the moment don't go outside, you're ill and if the neighbors ask, cough a lot." The woman, one of the very few female officers in the Ministry of State Security and therefore someone who knows how to assert herself, makes a not unsympathetic impression. That comes from her soft features which actually aren't soft, just fat, but her dark voice has a soothing, severe-but-good-natured quality.

Sofie studies her new ID.

"*Inge Schulz?* 'S that what I'm called now?" The question has a certain note of dissatisfaction which the Major cannot understand. After all, she's called Schulz, only with a *t* before the *z* and an *e* at the end.

But why, Sofie moans, change her first name? Why couldn't they let her keep her old one?

"What are names anyway? You were a qualified goldsmith in Rostock, unable to work since last year because of an impairment of the motor functions. Weren't you?"

"A qualified goldsmith?"

"You don't like it? A goldsmith's good. They sit around in back rooms, no one sees them much."

"But I know nothing at all about a goldsmith's work."

"Exactly. Who does? Oh, by the way, here's the address of a clinic. All the latest equipment. You report there next week."

"What for?"

Frau Schultze of the Central Department for Cadres and Instruction, a major in the Ministry of State Security, gives an exasperated groan. All these questions, it's just not done. "Treatment for alcoholism. Paid for by the State."

"But I've got it under control. I'm off the hard stuff."

"Remains to be seen. Two in five's going it a bit."

"Sorry?"

"Two crates of beer in five days. Averages out at six pints a day. You call that normal?"

But, Sofie protests, there wasn't anything else to do in the empty flat. The Major laughs, at a pitch that's uncomfortable on the ear. From now on she comes for a few hours each day, plays the private tutor. Freshly acquired knowledge of daily life under socialism is revised and tested. Initiation ceremony when? Training where? What merit awards? For what? Gained where? There's even a list of all the films she could have seen in the GDR, the others she'd better forget. What does a bus ticket cost, what a pound of butter? What products can be bought in Konsum, what's only available in Intershops? Sofie doesn't want to appear ungrateful and cooperates, reads up on her new background. She's given a telephone with an individual connection, she's not to talk on it, that would arouse suspicion if people thought she'd had a telephone installed in her apartment that quickly. It's a special telephone: she can be called on it, but can only dial the numbers one to eight. That's enough for her to call Major Schultze in an emergency or, if she's doesn't happen to be available, an unnamed superior.

"No contact with relatives or acquaintances. Not with anyone. And definitely not with former comrades. No political activity. No guns. Six hundred marks early retirement pension will be paid into your account every month, the rent for the apartment's thirty-nine marks so you should be able to manage comfortably on that. And so that there's no misunderstanding: as of now you're subject to the laws of the German Democratic Republic. You've to report personal contact with anyone at all to me."

"I'd like to work again."

Frau Schultze leans back on the narrow sofa, subjects Fräulein Schulz to a disgruntled scrutiny, then shakes her head before raising the left corner of her mouth. "What can you do?"

"I was a kindergarten teacher."

"Forget it. Anything else?"

"But you know. I ran instruction courses. Subject area Marxism-Leninism."

Now Major Schultze's all sympathy. "And what use d'you think that is over here?"

A few days later Inge Schulz obediently checks into St. George's Clinic where she's allocated one of the few single rooms and is given several injections. Her question as to what they contain fades away unanswered. The friendly, still young doctor tells her they're making things as easy as possible for her. Physical withdrawal's nothing much, it only takes a few days. Inge Schulz asks not to be strapped down under any circumstances.

"Of course not. Don't you worry." Patient Schulz loses consciousness for several days. When she comes around she has a headache and stomachache, stays in the clinic for observation and is discharged a week after entering. She's happy to follow her doctor's advice to drink large amounts of water. The thirst is almost unbearable, but it finally disappears, giving way to a feeling of physical wellbeing, she feels years younger and is determined that physical withdrawal will be followed by psychological withdrawal. Little by little she's allowed to go out of the apartment, at first for one hour a day, then two and even three. While at first Major Schultze did the shopping, now Frau Schulz's allowed more and more to provide for herself. The first six hundred marks appear in her bank account, to be spent as she thinks fit. Inge Schulz enjoys the new world around her, it feels like playing at shopping as she used to as a child. To fill in her leisure time, she's issued with a library card. She can go to the cinema or to concerts as well, with the proviso that she's back home by 10.30, a nighttime curfew, in fact, but Inge Schulz has no cause to complain, what would she do, out after 10.30? Hang around in bars? Even if she wanted to, she'd feel unsure of herself, couldn't survive fifteen minutes chatting with the regulars without being unmasked as a westerner. First of all she has to familiarize herself with all the little details of everyday life under socialism until they're part of her. She seems to have more and more time to fill in. A hard, gray winter. Tickets for the buses and streetcars are dirt cheap. Inge, always with a scarf over her mouth, spends a lot of time traveling around Leipzig eavesdropping on people, back home she imitates the accent, assimilates the tone of certain words. Her wardrobe's been completely replaced, she was given some clothes to be going on with, all of them one size too big, they all hang a bit loose. She'd like to do some sport, but can't decide what. For the moment she's not allowed to join a club, she's not sufficiently adapted yet. Physical exercises are soon abandoned, that kind of discipline's beyond Inge, so she tries writing poetry again, even prose. Nothing comes of it. She needs some kind of drug. If not alcohol, then hope and if not hope, then work. Her mind needs one or the other, anesthetizing or uplifting. Some meaning. A purpose. The neighbors continue to leave her in peace. No one rings the bell and asks how she is. The neighbors aren't stupid, they realize there's something special going on, something to do with the Stasi, they only have to admire Major Schultze's exquisite leather boots for that. Neighbors in East Germany have a nose for these things, moreover by targeting certain individuals with one-to-one interviews Major Schultze has made sure the neighbors keep out of anything to do with Inge Schulz.

In the middle of March Inge/Sofie feels like a prisoner for the first time. In a fit of rage she demolishes her wardrobe. That's not on. The Major makes that quite clear. Inge/Sofie, strangely unintimidated, has no difficulty in expressing herself in even clearer terms. Uninhibitedly, with a total lack of respect, she spews out needs at the top of her voice.

"I can't just sit around here!"

"We'll see. You are a difficult person!"

While the GDR usually operates on the principle of collective supervision, of strict social control, in the case of Sofie Kramer the Ministry of State Security has gone for isolation. Some senior officers are uneasy about the whole business.

For a few months Inge Schulz is strung along with the prospect of a suitable job, she just has to wait until it becomes vacant. Now and then she's slipped an envelope with some Western money so that she can buy herself the odd item in the Intershop.

"Any complaints?" Major Schultze asks on such occasions in harsh tones and Inge Schulz answers with an obedient but quiet *no*.

Her poems and prose writing are the first things to arouse interest in her, she's to show them to her liaison officer, as the term now is, to be checked. Inge doesn't refuse, though she suspects her writing's long since been looked over. A few simple tricks have told her that the apartment's regularly searched. Her writings meet with no criticism, they're returned without comment. It is, however, indicated that it would be better if she didn't keep a diary.

She agrees, but still keeps a diary. At first without particularly trying to conceal the fact, but after the first notebooks simply disappear, she finds more and more cunning hiding places.

Almost all of these diaries are extant, which means that at

some point they were all discovered. And the records tell us precisely *when* they were discovered, some after weeks, others only months later.

Somehow or other Inge manages to get through the spring and summer. She goes out in the fresh air a lot and develops a tentative interest in nature. She spends hours walking in the park and feeds the birds with oatflakes and chopped-up hazelnuts.

In the fall of '77, later to be called the "German Autumn" in the West, when the industrialist Hans Martin Schleyer and the RAF members Andreas Baader, Gudrun Ensslin and Jan-Carl Raspe die and the hostages are freed from the plane in Mogadishu by a German GSG9 task force, Inge Schulz falls ill with severe depression. She asks for and is given sedatives, to which she proves allergic.

She can't deal with the political developments, from that distance she can't evaluate them, feels she's been condemned to impotence. This time, unlike the case of Ulrike Meinhof, she doesn't believe the terrorists in Stammheim Prison committed suicide, she believes they were executed by the state. At the same time she feels that what she sees as the hysterical, pointless and childish terrorism of the RAF is just as bad.

Entries in her diary indicate psychotic phases.

10. 19.77
Life's short, isn't it? It can seem very long. When you have to wait. There's no reason for it? You're the reason. For everything. You ought to smile. Our first child would be grown up now we'd be grandparents I'd construct organs and great organists would play them you'd be proud of me. You're not really to blame at all she's too old for us—and she was such a timid little thing. As of now you're subject to the laws of the Jejune Democratic Republic. That's not a dream. Children always start off at zero. No mat-

ter what people say. That's not a dream! She's still too alive some
never get enough I can't get enough air enough air

During those weeks of violence there's a date and a sentence
that changes her life for good.

10. 21.77
after forty-three days we have ended the miserable existence
of hanns martin schleyer.

This is the sentence that compels me finally to distance myself
completely from the armed struggle, even if there should ever
come a time when I could take part in it. Such a sentence dis-
qualifies a cause forever.

The result is a dramatic collapse. Her medical files have presumably been deliberately lost, but what is certain is that
Inge/Sofie comes close to dying. After a circulatory collapse
she's discovered by chance and given emergency treatment. She
is saved by the kiss of life from Major Schultze.

During the four weeks in hospital her body recovers from her
allergic symptoms, she's left with periodic signs of paralysis in the
hands and feet. Which makes her early retirement on grounds of
impairment of the motor functions seem even more plausible.

She's forty-seven and she weighs fifty kilos. Her doctor urges
her to eat food with more vitamins. She needs to put on weight
and eat more meat.

"And please be careful with any kind of sedative. Avoid
sleeping pills and don't bother with injections at the dentist's.
Even if it hurts."

As it happens, most dentists in the GDR don't bother with
injections anyway.

Further depression is the result. Inge/Sofie feels old and
worn out. Useless.

*

There is evidence that Major Schultze has been trying to get her superiors to arrange a job for Sofie since the late summer at least. She's started drinking again, though only in moderation. Her daily intake almost never exceeds a bottle of Grey Monk, a sweet and sickly white wine. The surveillance is noticeably reduced. Her apartment is now only subject to sporadic searches, the main aim of them being to give the subject the feeling she's still important. Major Schultze has her protégée's best interests at heart.

In the winter of 1977/78 Inge/Sofie starts work at the Georgi Dimitrov Museum, formerly the Reich Law Courts, in which Leipzig's art collections are temporarily housed. She now wears her hair very short and she hasn't put on that much weight. Work starts at 9:00 P.M., finishes at six in the morning. She's on duty there four days a week, in a post that's usually reserved for old men and is, strictly speaking, hardly necessary. Who would think of breaking into the museum at night and stealing pictures? And even if the heating should break down during the night, or a window be left open, the damage to the pictures would be minimal. Inge/Sofie longs for people, colleagues, but it's made clear to her that she is to accept the position and stop moaning. Her income rises to 800 marks, which really isn't bad for lower-grade employees.

An ancient night porter shows Sofie what his old, her new job involves, shows her the vast halls. ("Lucas Cranach, Caspar David Friedrich, Rubens, Frans Hals, Tintoretto. Take y'r pick. Over 2,000 paintings, 800 sculptures and 55,000 drawings!")

And a little table in the lodge by the entrance. With a reading lamp, a telephone, a tray for files.

"Bring a lotta readin' along. 'S great job, nuthin' to do, more or less."

That's not what Inge/Sofie wants to hear.

"Do the rounds, twice a night. No one'll notice if you only do one. Nuthin's ever happened here. Y' set up the mousetraps in the evenin' and take 'em away in the mornin'." He shows her the report book.

"You're not security here, there's others do that, the guards're outside. All y're doin's sittin' around. Check the thermometer, that's all. In the mornin' you write: *Nothing to report* in the book and that's another night over 'n done with. 'Nless somethin' *does* happen, then you write somethin' else. 'S only happened to me twice in seven years. Once a bulb went 'n the other time a pipe burst in the john."

"Am I alone in the building?"

"Of course. You afraid? No smoking. Spoils the pictures. If you must, then in the entrance or in the john."

He hands over the keys for the front door and the offices.

"Only local calls, obviously. An' ev'ry one noted down, with the reason. Zero's blocked. The cleaners come at six and the day janitor takes over. OK?"

Inge/Sofie feels stupid taking this job. But, she tells herself, it can't be the end of the road. She'll go along with it, gain the trust of those above her and get allocated to something more responsible later on. Major Schultze has long become a kind of friend, at least she's a human being and neither over-strict nor hostile, there'll be room for negotiation. Hope likes the sound of its own voice and prattles on eternally.

At first the work's not unexciting. Going around the museum, an imposing building that used to house the law courts, with a torch at night can set off fits of panic, you have to fight against them. Two hundred of the over four hundred rooms are used for the fine arts. It keeps you occupied. Not for long, but it's a few weeks before everything's routine. Inge Schulz listens to a lot of music on her portable radio, classical music she's not had much time for previously. She specially likes the violin solo from Dvorak's 9th symphony, *From the New World*. It's striking how often it's played in the late-night radio concert. In contrast to former times, Sofie now wears high heels, they make a nice loud clacking noise in the nocturnal silence. She smokes more than she used to, sitting on the john with the door open. Looking at herself in the mirror over the washbasin. She never imagined her life would be like this. The mousetraps are leftovers from earlier times, thank God. No mouse ever finds its way in here.

Sometimes, when there's suitably elegiac music, she dances in front of the mirror, slowly, swaying, both feet on the floor, eyes closed, plowing with her shoulders through an imaginary viscous sea, half dancing, half swimming. It reminds her of Boris humming *A Hard Day's Night* in blues rhythm. Oddball. All in all the oddest person she's come across in her whole life, apart from Alexander, of course. Wonder what they're doing now? At times, when she feels like it, Sofie takes her clothes off and goes through the rooms naked, only blind pictures to look at her. Pictures—uninterested, self-sufficient, framed and hung. There's a huge parking lot outside the museum, illuminated by a few lamps. Smoking, contrary to regulations, she looks at it from a window on the second floor, it has a feel of openness, of a landing strip, a stage, the fog collects there toward morning, sometimes two magpies are quarreling. Or crows. And the fog, and the smoke, her breath in winter clouding the glass, astonishing, the fog, her breath, the smoke, astonishing. She can't read for long in these vast halls, it's as if the silence were pressing down too hard on the back of her neck.

Inge/Sofie does her shopping in the early morning, too tired to get to know a man. She's slim and still quite pretty, the mirrors tell her. It shouldn't be that difficult. She acquires an aquarium and spends her savings on a little Grundig color television from the Intershop. The first television that's her own property. She notes: *Watched Crime Watch—with enjoyment instead of fear. A bit. Enjoyed the fear. Paradoxical.*

For Christmas she's given presents in the form of a bottle of Rumanian red wine and some English biscuits from the State-owned delicatessen, presented to her in the name of socialist solidarity by Major Schultze. A nice gesture which proves they're happy with her.

Sometimes I'd like to be dead, but up there looking down on everything, without me in it.

During the annual bookfair, when thousands of visitors stream into the city, Sofie's to take leave and spend it in her apartment. Better safe than sorry.

Says Major Schultze.

The Dark Wood

I had dozens of lawyers under contract, top lawyers, but also less well-known ones, just very good, hardworking attorneys with left-wing backgrounds who, apparently for selfless, idealistic reasons, looked after terrorists who'd been arrested. A relatively straightforward way of worming information out of grateful clients. But it wasn't until 1981, when others had chosen the same escape route, that the whisper came that she might possibly be living *over the border*, in the GDR, only—under what name? It turned out to be very difficult to discover that and if you're going to object that money speeds everything up, I will point out that first of all you have to find the right person to approach, otherwise it's like shouting at the top of your voice into a dark wood. I started the long and tedious process of feeling my way forward. Anywhere else on the planet would have been an easier place to search for her. I needed people I could rely on one hundred percent. Apart from Lukian there was no one. Perhaps you can never rely on someone else one hundred percent, who knows? At least my life wasn't so dull anymore, I had things to do, intrigues to plot, people to bribe, contacts to establish and to keep up. Just a minute, delete that last sentence, please. It sounds obscene if I talk of my *dull life* in connection with that of my beloved. And all the time I was wondering if I was perhaps on the wrong track after all, especially when there were reports in the media that this or that terrorist had been sighted in Yemen, in a Palestinian training camp. At least I could talk to the Palestinians. They demanded a hefty fee for the information that they knew nothing of a Sofie Kramer, but at least the information came in a form that left no reason to doubt its genuineness. They liked me because I was German, they assumed I had lots of murdered Jews to my name.

Inge/Sofie doesn't go to pieces. On the contrary. In order to survive, she sets off on an orgy of autosuggestion in the course of which she heroically persuades herself that things aren't that bad. Improvements should start with small things. In January 1981 she fixes a spice rack to the kitchen wall. A week later she paints the walls pale yellow. She's lucky, she finds someone—official antiques dealers are extremely rare—who sells her a nice, comfortable *Biedermeier* sofa; in the Intershop she acquires relatively stylish clothes and underwear. She realizes how beautiful Leipzig is if she stares at it long enough. For the afternoons she prescribes a regime of walks for herself, in Rosental and the Auenwald, a park running through the middle of the city. That becomes the key to survival: uncultivated nature which is unconcerned which political system happens to be in power. Inge/Sofie reads *Walden*, develops an interest in botany, joins the Gardens Association and applies for a plot, spends her weekends in the woods, go swimming in the open-air pool (*the rivers are too polluted*) collects mushrooms in the fall, goes skating to keep fit in winter.

After the Berlin Reichstag, the Dimitrov Museum is the second largest non-industrial building in Germany from the time of the Empire, a contrast with Sofie who's five foot four. The huge edifice with its huge cupola and its huge pillars has always frightened her, but there are other ways of looking at it. She's been given the task of making sure this stone monster doesn't run off. So she has to sit in it at night with all her weight. How could someone who bears such a responsibility feel tiny?

She continues her self-education by reading books which don't fit into any ideological pigeonhole: Kant, Montesquieu and Tacitus, the novels of Fallada, the poems in Celan's *No*

One's Rose. If you make the effort and suppress the side of you that's a politically aware human being, life in the GDR's certainly livable. The one thing that doesn't respond to autosuggestion is loneliness. By this time Inge Schulz is venturing out, to dances, to bars with music, there are contacts, occasionally sex, without them ever developing into a relationship. The men, such as there are, whom she finds interesting and who reciprocate, soon notice that she's a woman with a secret, that she's tensed up, acting out a part, she can't let herself go, no more than men can let themselves go with her. She suspects every man who behaves in an open and friendly manner toward her of sleeping with her *on higher orders*. When the conversation gets around to her background or her former profession she becomes unsure of herself, reels off a lifeless, learnt-off-by-heart biography and falls silent. She's no longer so beautiful that men pursue her for her beauty alone. Although she's never been aware of it before, she now realizes belatedly how often her outward appearance must have been of decisive use.

Or could have been. That doesn't make her proud or sad, it's more disillusioning. It diminishes all her proud dreams, setting them against a downright animal foundation, as if the world functioned solely on the basis of either monetary or sexual contacts and contracts. Something inside her resists this insight, rejects it as cynicism to which one mustn't succumb.

The only relationship which lasts for a few weeks is a strange one. Ludwig, twenty-two, a student of Russian literature, speaks to her in the Auenwald park. He sometimes saw her taking a walk there, he said, and he loved the way she would stop where paths crossed or flowers had been watered, dreaming and dancing a few steps. Was she a dancer, would he have the opportunity of admiring her on the stage? It's an undoubtedly original and charming pick-up technique which, since it's delivered with a slight stutter, doesn't sound in the least bombastic or prepared in advance. The young man's tall and gaunt, with black hair and clothed in existentialist black, not a pretty boy, but his narrow, pale face has a consumptively aristocratic look, perhaps caused by his velvet scarf, a creature of sentimental decadence with a sparse mustache. Sofie notices his fingers with their well-groomed nails. All in all his appearance is idiosyncratic enough to dispel the suspicion that he might be an agent of the state. Sofie remains silent, but the young man simply stands there, waiting for an answer. Without being importunate or imploring. He just stands there, polite, hands clasped over his breast, not trying to force himself on her, awaiting a response. It's a warm summer's evening.

You must resist cynicism. Isolation encourages cynicism. Sofie, who hasn't said a word, takes a scrap of paper out of her shirt pocket, then a pencil and writes:

We could love each other. Without talking. The young man seems pleased with that. He writes his reply:

Where?

Sofie takes his hand. For three wonderful weeks he goes to see her regularly. He thinks she's dumb and doesn't speak himself—out of solidarity, as it were. Sometimes they exchange scraps of paper. He proves clumsy and inexperienced in bed, always comes too soon, but afterwards he's prepared to caress Sofie at length, to kiss her all over her body. There's something to it until he reveals—by letter—that he's a reincarnation of Dostoyevsky. Her dumbness, he writes, has touched him profoundly, made a great impression on him. She has been a beacon, a *passionate flame,* a *torch shining through the storm.* But the great, fitting companion he wishes, longs to have at his side, which he needs for his life as an artist, must be capable of communicating with him in a more fluent manner than on laborious scraps of paper. Unfortunately. It breaks his heart, but— this is the consolation Ludwig offers—the day will come when her role will receive due recognition in his biography.

The guy definitely wasn't on the Stasi payroll. Perhaps not even on the same planet. On the other hand he had learnt to employ his tongue to good effect without using it to form words. Sofie grins. No harm done, she wasn't in love with him. She just used him, the way men use women instead of loving them. Now she can understand men better. And after all, she thinks, if Ludwig is the reincarnation of Dostoyevsky, then my life will have had some meaning. As a torch shining through the storm. Perhaps Ludwig truly *is* Fyodor, who can tell? She never hears anything of Ludwig again and catches herself thinking a dangerous thought: nothing's certain, every person can die in the hope that their potential might find its true expression posthumously in a radical revision of the actual facts of their life. Was that a form of final consolation, she asks herself, or a variant of the ultimate piss-taking? The idea that she can't here and now have the last word on her own self, can't shed her own self as a success or failure, that she must remain at the mercy of others' opinion beyond death, is a stinging blow to her pride. Life was meant to be immense, certainly, but manageable, that too. Something common sense ought to be able to cope with. Or was sense not common among the human race?

Sometimes I'd like to be alive, but up there looking down on everything, with me in it.

Major Schultze, the only person to whom Sofie can pour out her troubles now and then, is transferred to Magdeburg and breaks off contact without warning. Her successor, Captain Horst Endewitt, plays the narrow-minded bureaucrat who finds the Inge Schulz case awkward and dubious. Endewitt only puts in the occasional appearance. He's always businesslike in his dealings with her and if, with his hoarse voice, he often sounds malicious, at least he doesn't make any attempt even to pretend he's looking after her on a personal level. Moreover, one of his most striking features is that he sticks strictly to the letter of the law with the result that Sofie's apartment is only searched when there are reasonable grounds to suspect her of anti-state propaganda, that is basically never. That's the reason why her diaries after May '83 have been lost. Inge Schulz is dead and buried and sometimes that's how Sofie feels.

She doesn't get much pleasure out of her aquarium anymore, but she feels an obligation towards her fish and starts talking to them. They accept it without comment.

Inge's well liked by the Museum administration since she volunteers for all holiday duty. Sometimes, perhaps three or four times in the year, she receives a nocturnal visit from her predecessor. One of those is New Year's Eve 1982. The old man, who looks much older than his seventy years, lives alone, as she does, and feels the pull of his former workplace. He goes around the rooms with her, providing the odd nugget of interesting information about the pictures, which they look at in the light of two torches. That night he gets fresh, demands a kiss from Inge. "C'm on, enjoy yourself. What's the harm? A kiss between colleagues." Inge puts him in his place and the old-age pensioner gets his own back by saying, "Oh, c'm on, I'm not *that* much older than you."

His nasty little remark hits Inge harder than he intended. She realizes there's a danger life's going to pass her by. Irreversibly and with nothing to show for it. The self-deception she's put so much effort into constructing starts to wobble. She throws the old man out, though she's sorry she has to do it, most of the time he was nice and she could easily have granted him a kiss.

A few days later she phones Endewitt.

"I want to *do* something. I'm buried alive here. The pictures can manage very well without me."

"They're very pleased with you in the Museum. Happy New Year." Endewitt doesn't sound very interested, and that's putting it mildly.

"But I could learn to do something. Anything. Something useful."

"Have you started drinking again?"

"No . . . Why d'you ask? Only the odd drop, the same as everyone . . . "

"'S not a problem. Drink as much as you like. For all I care."

End of conversation. Inge's hung up.

Dead fish are floating in the aquarium. They're given a kind of variation on a burial at sea in the lavatory. Inge Schulz logically follows this up by getting drunk in a bar where after ten o'clock, apart from spirits, only *gentlemen's sets* are served, that is a glass of champagne plus a Pilsner. Perhaps they're trying to ensure a certain standard of clientele. Or perhaps the intention's to get them to form couples, the man drinking the beer, the woman the champagne. But then shouldn't they be called *his'n hers sets*? Sofie resolves to let the first desperate male to proposition her drag her off to his lair, just to give her the feeling of being needed. She even imagines it'll turn her on. But what's on offer in the Stagecoach that evening's either out of the question or not interested in her.

As she's making her way home around three in the morning (no taxi anywhere to be seen, of course, that would be pure luck, she would have had to order a taxi hours ago. Why is that the case? What has socialism got to do with taxis? There are some things she just doesn't understand. During all her years there she never realizes there are the very popular *bandit cabs*), plastered and sticking our her thumb whenever a car passes her on the long way out to the suburb (on the other hand a hitcher soon gets a lift and travels free. Perhaps that's why there are so few taxis and you get a lift quickly, because there aren't any taxis—how close to its own neck can a snake eating its own tail get? Mathematical problems at three in the morning, drunk, on the edge of the highway), a Lada stops, the man waves her to get in. Doesn't ask where she's going. That should make her uneasy, and it does, but the car's already set off.

"Where am I going? You've no idea, have you?"

Without taking his eyes off the road, the man, around thirty, wearing a leather jacket and a Cossack hat, sticks a cigarette between her lips. He has a neatly trimmed beard, a broad nose and thick lips, she can't make out more than a silhouette. "I'll take you where you want to go."

"So why don't you ask me where I want to go?"

"You only have to tell me."

"I'm going to Grünau."

"Then that's where we'll go," the man says.

"But we're already going there. We're going to Grünau. Directly to Grünau."

"Then it's OK."

And nothing more is said. The Lada stops outside her block. She probably ought to say *thanks*. It's just that she can't bring herself to.

"Can you manage the stairs? Shall I see you up them?"

She's probably just imagining it, but the man smiles, as he makes the offer, a repulsive smile.

"No, thanks." There, she's managed to get the word out, without compromising herself.

The man mumbles something, she doesn't quite catch it, what was it he said? *Go on sheep, fuck off.* Is that what he said? Her right heel already in the snow on the sidewalk, Sofie turns her upper body back toward him, a remarkable physical effort.

"*What* did you say?"

"Go 'n sleep it off."

During the day Sofie likes to stand on a bridge watching the water slowly drifting past. She particularly likes it when there are thin ice floes which, split up into a thousand pieces, have some ruler-straight edges making them look like shattered windowpanes, shimmering, now light gray, now silver, occasionally bluish, turquoise or almost black, the spectrum of imploding screens.

Spring comes and, as with so many depressives, the new growth bursting out all over doesn't cheer her up, on the contrary, she feels she can't keep up with the cycle of the seasons any longer, she's an ugly relic of winter which sensitive people must find repulsive.

What am I? A failure who's retired early, using a few memories to delude herself that she has a past worth bothering about. Still. It did have its moments. If there were only someone around she could tell about it. There comes a point when living in the present gives way to talking about the past. But what if there's no one to listen to you?

Wouldn't it be nice if she could say to someone, "D'you remember?"

My God, I'm thinking like an old woman.

Just at that moment, which invites, indeed impels her to consider suicide, she recognizes a man sitting reading the newspaper at the streetcar stop outside the main railway station. Is it *him?* It looks like it. Yes, it is. Seven years older, more mature, stiff and fat. *Can* it be him? She never really liked him, but a familiar face from the distant past is more than she can resist. Flouting all directives, she addresses him.

"Jacob?"

The man looks up at her. Raises his reading glasses, squints. Whispers:

"Sofie?"

How good it is to hear her name, her true name.

"Jacob. What're you doing here?"

Jacob doesn't really know what to say. He looks around,

first this way, then that, clears his throat, folds up his news-paper.

"Listen . . . There shouldn't be any contact between us."

"Between us two?"

"Between all of us who're over here."

"*All?* How many are there?"

"A few. Followed your example. I'm called Moritz now, Moritz Müller."

"Inge Schulz. Can you spare a few minutes?"

"What for?"

"I just have to talk to someone who knows who I am. So I don't forget it myself."

"Not a good idea, here. How's things?"

"Shit awful. Where d'you live? What're you doing?"

"Hmm." Jacob takes out his wallet, proudly shows her a photo. "My wife. Met her through the combine. I'm a repro-graphic photographer. Not a bad job. That's our son. The sec-ond's due next month. I can't take you home with me, you un-derstand that, don't you?"

"I live on the outskirts, Grünau. Will you come and see me?"

"Listen . . . let the past be. 'S a waste of time."

"I haven't got anything else."

"You should've made better use of your time."

"Arsehole!"

"What's this? You never liked me anyway. What d'you want?" He's talking to himself, Sofie's already gone.

"Now you come running to me! Stupid bitch!"

MAIL

A t the end of 1983 she was given, surprisingly quickly, the
garden plot she'd applied for; it helped disperse the
thoughts of suicide a little. It was only a temporary
lightening of her mood. Unfortunately her fingers were definitely not green. Everything she planted either drowned or
shriveled. The following year she tried to persuade Endewitt to
allow her to leave the country, not to go to West Germany, no,
but to Yemen, she'd like to look after children there or be useful in some other way. Endewitt rejects her request, forbids her
absolutely to make an official application for an exit visa. At
least he doesn't try to delude her, but makes it crystal clear that
there's no way she can leave the country, official reaction to any
such attempts would be *uncompromising*. Sofie knows what
that means and accepts her fate. But then . . .

Von Brücken sat up in bed. Shoved a hand under his pillow.
And smiled.

"In 1985, March 11, she wrote me a postcard. It was fantastic! Just imagine, she was looking for *help*—and from me! Naturally that was of enormous help to *me* in my search. Perhaps it
sounds like a joke, but it isn't. She hadn't written her address
on the card. But she did tell me her name! To be precise, she
didn't write the postcard to me, but to Birgit Kramer, who by
that time had a double-barreled name. Birgit Kramer-Felsen-
stein. I'd never quite lost sight of her. She didn't need to show
me the card, I'd have found out about it by another route, but
she did. The cry for help was unambiguous. Here, read it."

Von Brücken handed me a picture postcard of Leipzig. It

showed, in black and white, the voluminous bulk of the Dimitrov Museum. The message, in almost childish handwriting, read:

Dear Birgit, I'm fine.
I often think back to the time with Rolf and you.
My vacation here's making me a different person.
Greetings to Alexander the Great. If you should see him.
Inge Schulz, your sister.

Neat, wasn't it? Suddenly everything was changed, as if a dark blanket of cloud over me had parted. There was her name, her new name, and the building on the other side of the card also seemed to be a clue. At last we had some facts, something to work on. There had to be no mistakes, there was always the possibility the Stasi knew something about the postcard. But that little risk—to hell with it. It was clear to me that Sofie was imprisoned, was forced to be a different person and her so-called *vacation*, her duress, was so bad that she was appealing to *Alexander the Great*. Who once cut through the Gordian knot. I discussed it with Lukian. At first he tried to get me to sober up. Someone was trying to pull my leg, he said. I should forget the whole thing. No one of my standing could enter the GDR without being observed. Nor could he either.

We were sitting here, just the way you and I are now. And I didn't agree with him. No one had taken a photo of me for seventeen years, I said. No one knew what I looked like. I wanted a passport, a well made one that would pass muster, it couldn't be that difficult. What's the point of having contacts.

In September '85 there was the *Brötzmann* incident. They were Inge Schulz's new neighbors on the sixth floor of the tenement block. Like everyone here, Herr and Frau Brötzmann like watching television from the West, though only light entertainment programs, preferably hosted by Thomas Gottschalk, they've no problem reconciling him with their socialist consciences. But it quite often happens that Herr Brötzmann falls asleep while watching TV and only wakes up after the channel closes down. Sometimes, however, pictures of terrorists on the run are shown before the national anthem with which the evening's viewing ends. Not that Frau Margit Brötzmann ever shows particular interest in them when she comes to fetch her snoring husband to bed after midnight. But something sticks, even if it's only a sketchy resemblance. Since then Frau Schulz from next door seems somehow familiar.

"Don't worry your head about that, Margit," her husband, half asleep, insists.

"I tell you, I've seen her someplace."

"Leave it. Frau Schulz takes out the garbage and washes the stairs. That's all we're bothered about."

Unfortunately Frau Brötzmann doesn't heed her husband's sensible advice, she wants to push herself forward. First problem: by now the photo of Sofie Kramer bears only a remote similarity to the Inge Schulz of today. Second problem: Frau Brötzmann doesn't want to admit that she watches West German TV. Everybody does, but to say so publicly?

So how can she push herself forward without committing herself? An anonymous note to the district police station to the effect that they should run a check on Frau Schulz, her similarity to the wanted Sofie K. was striking if not alarming.

The whole business gets badly snarled up among the various hierarchies of the GDR, departments that know something come up against departments that know less, or nothing at all, and there are departments none of the others know about, it's all very complex and complicated. It causes a big stir and someone from very high up has to crack the whip. Frau Brötzmann (a comparison of handwriting quickly establishes her identity as

the letter-writer) receives a visitor, a clear (actually pretty unclear) explanation and—part appeasement, part gag—the lowest civilian decoration. She will never report anyone to the police again, not even anonymously. Inge Schulz has to move, but
not far and the simple one-room apartment that's just become
vacant on the edge of the wonderful zoo in Leipzig is an improvement. She's given notice; her job in the Museum stops at
the end of the year. She's told that they think she's worked for
long enough now, she's earned the right to a quiet retirement.
Inge Schulz, severely paranoid, wonders whether an untimely
end is being prepared for her, every night she's afraid they're going to come for her, she can hardly sleep and at times treats her
few social contacts in an offhand manner.

One of them who thinks he knows her quite well is Fritz
Langenscheidt, her liquor merchant, who sometimes puts a
case of French wine on one side for regular customers when he
gets some in every six months. D! O! C! as he emphasizes, letter by letter. Inge glances briefly at the label before rejecting the
dishwater. The Grey Monk has considerably weakened her
physical and mental constitution, she's on Polish vodka now,
more or less the only imported alcohol of real quality.

"You're a hard one to please," says Fritz Langenscheidt,
"I've kept a case specially for you. Take it. It's not every day you
can get your hands on that. You can barter it for anything. If
you don't want it for yourself, it makes a great present for your
friends."

"I haven't any friends. I'm more likely to be shot tomorrow."

"'OK, so it's a no, then. I just can't make you out. Why d'y-
ou think you're goin' to be shot?"

Inge Schulz, already at the door, turns around and gives
Herr Langenscheidt—45, greying, bags under his eyes, pasty
faced and greasy—a piercing, almost brazen look, and asks,
"Are you in love with me?"

"Am I what?" The liquor merchant, two children and, most recently, a grandchild, thinks he must have misheard. Inge Schulz gives him a sassy grin.

"If my liquor merchant doesn't love me, who will?"

"Well if you put it like that . . . "

He likes this woman with her strange sense of humor. He could tell her so, but she's already left the store. And she knows anyway.

In the morning a giraffe bellows. That's nice.

During the night in the museum Inge writes a simple little poem she quite likes but forgets as soon as she's drunk.

I can
go on
no longer
no
go on
you can
go on
longer

Like so many poems, it ends up in the trash can and later with Endewitt. By now he's been promoted to lieutenant colonel. He thinks: If the worst should come to the worst, after all, he has to bear that in mind, if the worst should come to the worst, it's a great farewell letter. If you cut off the last four lines. At this point there are no concrete plans to get rid of Inge, just a vague directive. If the worst should turn out to be an emergency.

Inge Schulz suffers from hallucinations. At night, when she does her rounds with the heavy torch (more a kind of miner's lamp) she hears soft music, which only exists inside her head.

(Or? Remote parts of the building are used as a synchronization studio by the state film company.) Paintings she shines her torch on seemed changed, faces are twisted in mockery and malice. Her life's turned into a museum. Somewhere here, she thinks to herself, in one of these vast, dark chambers, she'll probably hang as well one day, perhaps she's just in one of the archives, hidden in a drawer, forgotten, of no special value. Oh dear. No, it's not that bad. There's her picture. The painter has done an unflattering picture of her. Pure photorealism. Socialist Realist sadness. Old, amazed, holding a torch. It's not a painting at all. It's a mirror.

The next morning, after she's finished work, Inge Schulz wanders around town. She doesn't want to go home, wants to clear her mind in the fresh air. Feels she's being observed. She poured the vodka down the john and now she scoops up cold water from a fountain over her head. She goes into a church, sits in one of the pews right at the back and falls asleep. No one wakes her, no one pesters her. Until a young pastor, not yet thirty, tugs at her sleeve.

"We're closing."

"What? What time is it?"

"Almost six. You've slept right through the whole day."

"I . . . I'd like to talk to someone."

"What about?"

"I don't believe in God. Just to make that clear."

"Would you like to?"

"No . . . No."

"You could pretend. That often helps." The pastor seems really nice, relatively relaxed, almost endowed with a sense of humor.

"And if he's a brutal God, what then?"

"Talk to him about it. Rebuke him. Start a dialogue."

Inge shakes her head. She doesn't want a conversation with God. It'd be too one-sided. She wants to talk to a human being.

"OK then. Go ahead. I'm at your disposal." The pastor sits down beside her.

Inge Schulz starts to say something several times, but new things keep occurring to her, she's trembling slightly. Then she gets up and leaves the church, without saying goodbye. Once home she resolves to phone in to say she's ill, but then forgets. Her desire for alcohol's so great she's ashamed. But the fact that she's ashamed gives her ground for hope. She won't get drunk. A little at most, to get rid of the pain. Just enough to dull the throbbing, burning sensation at her temples.

THE INVASION

I got my passport. It was as good as genuine. No, as far the technical aspects were concerned, it *was* genuine. As genuine as a forged passport can be. I'm not allowed to go into more detail about it, anyway it's irrelevant. I intended to travel to the GDR by car, a not too conspicuous but powerful middle of the range car. An Opel Admiral was souped up a bit. It looked old and shabby but the engine had 180 horsepower. Windows of bulletproof glass. Strengthened bodywork. And a concealed compartment in the trunk with just about enough room for a thin person. Yes, I know, it sounds like a spy thriller, but why not? I wanted to bring Sofie out. Now you tell me: what can't you understand about that?

"I didn't say anything."

"But you pulled one of those faces."

"I didn't pull a face."

"Good morning. I thought you might come back. Or, rather, I hoped you would."

"Hope is the fantasy world of impotence. Is this here a Catholic church?"

"No."

"Would you hear my confession? Despite that?"

"But you don't believe in God. Or so I thought."

"That's got damn all to do with confession. Can't you be a bit flexible for once?"

The pastor of St. Nicholas, Wolfgang Westermüller, is a man who can definitely be flexible, has to be. In this particular case he's reached one of the limits of his pliability. However, he does promise to listen, although he suspects the woman will be putting herself in danger if she talks to him. He feels obliged to indicate that. She must realize, he says, that he's under constant surveillance by the Stasi and that this meeting will certainly be reported.

"Huh," says Inge Schulz, "you don't say." She can't stop herself laughing out loud. The pastor, unhappy with the way she's behaving, makes a fluttering gesture to tell her to control herself. "What's your problem?"

"I need to change something and I can't change anything. I'm stuck in a trap."

"You can always change things. Everywhere."

"You mean the wallpaper. Or the flowers in the vase? Or what?"

Before they can even start a discussion, two powerfully built men come into the church, take Inge by the arms and hustle her to the exit. Come with us. And please don't make a fuss.

Endewitt sees her after she's been kept waiting in his outer office for two hours.

"What's a woman like you doing in a church? In that church?"

"I was cold."

Endewitt's not entirely satisfied with this explanation. That church, he says, is a breeding ground for subversive forces. A rathole. "Are you a rat? What about your self-respect? We're worried about you. You don't appear to be very grateful. The others in your group are dead, past history, in jail or on the run. And you? Here you have a clean bed, a carefree life—aren't you ashamed of yourself? After everything the state's done for you, you just let yourself go like that. Just look at yourself. You have obligations."

What a feeling that was, crossing the border! My passport

was checked. The name on it was *Alexander Kurtz*. They didn't even search the car.

"The reason for your visit to the German Democratic Republic?"

"Study."

"Report to the local office tomorrow."

"Will do. Thanks."

"Drive on."

"I don't know that goddamned priest at all. And never talk to me about my *self-respect* again. Or tell me I ought *to be ashamed* of myself. Or that I have a carefree life. I haven't *any* kind of life . . . "

Endewitt's expecting his second child to be born any hour. That's probably the reason why on that particular day Inge Schulz's not his number one priority. He leaves it at a strong warning, a concrete threat, and afterward he feels he's been too softhearted.

That night Inge Schulz says farewell to the museum. In two senses. Why wait until the end of the year? It's the middle of November. Why spend a further six weeks going round these rooms, sitting there in solitude? She must start a new life, a daylight life. That's a good start, no one can forbid her from doing that. She'll stop drinking. Live on her small pension and perhaps somehow, eventually, there'll be a chance to *escape*.

After his first daughter's born and there are no complications, Endewitt spends just an hour with his wife before going back to his office, to catch up on work. He summarizes the events of the day and reports to his immediate superior in East Berlin.

He mentions the double contact between Inge Schulz and Pastor Westermüller at the end of his report, without making a big thing of it, merely noting the incident.

Contact terminated he writes, Inge Schulz was given a *severe warning*, which she *more or less* accepted.

I drove on to Leipzig without stopping and rented a room in a modest bed and breakfast. My first walk, at around ten o'-clock at night, took me to the Dimitrov Museum. The bulbous building was dark. Only one light was on, inside, in a room beside the entrance porch, with the blinds down.

I didn't want to go closer and look suspicious. Naturally I'd done some research in the months after the postcard and found out that there was an Inge Schulz on the museum's payroll, but the address given there, in the modern estate in Grünau, turned out to be an old one and her new address was kept secret. What kind of work she did, and when, wasn't clear, I'd had to take extreme care; I thought it would be easy to sort it all out on the spot.

As I said, I was going under the name of Alexander *Kurtz*, the name Sofie had as a girl; if necessary I could claim to be related to her, a brother from her father's first marriage, something like that. Why not? A man who wanted to see his half sister, some such kind of sentimental find-a-long-lost-relative bullshit. Anyway, at the time—I feel I must add this since you're pulling one of those faces again—at the time—

"I'm not pulling a face."

"Oh yes you are. So, at the time—you'll have to mention this for younger readers who don't know—the GDR didn't have such a bad reputation. People had no idea what kind of state it was, what it was capable of in individual cases. The left wing dismissed all the rumors that filtered through as right-wing propaganda. *Smart thinking = left-wing thinking* was what they said. I thought I was reasonably smart myself, but that doesn't mean I was left-wing, I was neither left-wing nor right-wing, I was an industrialist, pragmatic, but sometimes my thinking was of necessity left-wing, without my really realizing. That was why

I approached my excursion in a rather naive manner. What could happen to me? They're not going to torture me, I thought, I was a respectable citizen of the Federal Republic—now you are pulling a face again, but now it's OK, you're quite right to laugh at my naiveté.

Von Brücken smiled, then he felt a violent pain, curled up in the foetal position and, although he tried to hide it from me, bit his pillow to stop himself crying out loud.

After a few minutes he attempted to continue with his story, but he soon had to give up, He rang for the doctor and, with weary gestures of apology, waved me out of the room.

During the night several ambulances came up the drive. I asked Lukian how Alexander was. He said he should have been taken to hospital ages ago, but the Boss had refused, so now the hospital was coming to him, they were setting up an intensive care unit in the great chamber.

"I have to speak to you," he whispered, drawing with him me out of the house.

Why all the fuss?

You could never be sure, he said, not even out there. He asked me to speak in a whisper too.

"The pain's getting worse. In future he won't be able to endure being conscious for one second without morphine. Please bear that in mind."

"In what way is that important?"

"Well—" Lukian Keferloher started to say something, then decided not to. Presumably he was going to tell me that people on morphine occasionally tended to take a glorified view of things. Perhaps he was close to finally revealing his own perspective on the whole business. But he broke off, just broke off, his chin slumped on his chest. He raised his clenched hands to his mouth and bit on them.

DAY EIGHT

POSSIBLE CONSEQUENCES

Lieutenant Colonel Endewitt is astonished when he receives orders over the telephone to respond to any further Schulz-Westermüller contact by arresting his charge, Frau Schulz. It was to be done *discreetly and without delay*. For particular combinations of circumstances he had a *free hand*. Top priority was *not* the person involved but maintaining the secrecy of her identity. Horst Endewitt goes pale. From a purely personal point of view he quite likes Inge Schulz and what is hinted at, the *free hand*—that sounds as if they want to get rid of the problem in the most definitive way, without saying so clearly. He thinks that's going over the top, even questionable, but as a soldier he has to obey the order. He decides to give Inge Schulz a severe warning, a good rap on the knuckles, he has to be cruel to be kind, so that she understands what's at stake. The possible consequences. A shiver goes down his spine at the thought of having to drive to the woods with Inge Schulz at some point. He's not going to let it come to that. And he curses himself for having been so lenient toward this obstinate woman up to now. Then he thinks of his newborn child and smiles. You have to be able to keep things in different compartments. Life's just not possible otherwise.

When I went to von Brücken next morning he was very much down in the mouth. That's the right expression. Like a host who feels he has to apologize for an embarrassing situation. His voice was weak and cracked. He was breathing rapidly.

He was sorry to die, he said, he'd never done it before and therefore had no experience of it. But we were getting toward the end, not only his personal end, but that of his story. If he could hold out long enough.

The next evening—Endewitt's put it off until then—he doesn't find Inge Schulz at her place of work. They've had to persuade the old ex-porter to stand in temporarily, since Frau Schulz hasn't turned up, without giving any reason or calling in sick. That makes her situation even worse, much worse, for, according to the latest directives, that has to be reported to Berlin. Has to be. Ought to be. Perhaps not straight away. A free hand. If the higher-ups can use woolly expressions then there can't be anything wrong with a woolly interpretation.

Endewitt goes to see if Inge's in her apartment, which she isn't, and goes to see if she's in the church in the morning, which she isn't either, fortunately. Inge Schulz is starting to get on his nerves. He has more important things to do now.

The second day passed with me wandering around the city on my amateur search for Sofie. My visa would run out the next day, it looked as if I was going to fail in the finishing straight. On the other hand, I was talking to myself night and day. How would I *address* Sofie? How would I introduce myself? As *Boris?* As the Alexander von Brücken to whom she had sent a cry for help? Would she recognize *both of them* in me? How could I explain that? How much would I confess to her? Should I just ask her to slip into the trunk of my car?

But then someone suddenly addressed *me*, right there in the street. He introduced himself as Horst Endewitt and asked me, without mentioning his military rank, to accompany him to his office. Was he sure, I asked, that it was *me* he wanted to speak to? He was, he said, sure. I didn't resist and followed the man to a building on the Dittrichring. We went into an office where Endewitt, very polite and respectful all the time, offered me a chair and a coffee.

"There's just the two of us here, Herr von Brücken. Please speak openly and sensibly and I'll do the same."

I was so flabbergasted that for the moment I said nothing at all. Like a child caught masturbating, I looked around a non-existent corner.

Endewitt was enjoying his big moment. But he seemed calm and collected and certainly not cruel by nature. He attempted to relax the tension, held out his cigarette case to me, asked for my passport, examined it and said it was *excellently done*. He even handed it back.

"What gave me away?"

Endewitt smiled to himself, as if that was something grown-ups just knew, only children couldn't understand. He was massaging the corners of his mouth with two fingers.

"Since your commendable intensification of relations with our state, we have learnt a certain amount about you, including some things which gave us pause for thought. We have to admit that you have proceeded cautiously and discreetly. But, as it happens, not quite cautiously and discreetly enough. We have been aware of your remarkable obsession with this woman since 1967. Since your comic turn with the taxi. The postcard was a trial balloon we sent out. We were just interested to see what would happen."

"Sofie wasn't asking me for help?"

"No. I wrote the card myself."

It was like a blow to the solar plexus. Perhaps he was lying.

"But until then I didn't know what Sofie was called now—why did you tell me that?"

"You'd have found out soon enough, it was only a matter of time. I just speeded things up a little." With a self-congratulatory grin, he said there were times when his job could be fun, could be creative, oh yes.

"Has someone betrayed me?"

"Please. You know very well that's a question that can never be answered." He took a long pull at his cigarette and I, paralyzed with horror, did the same in an effort to relax. We looked at each other and smoked. My knees were trembling and I crossed my legs to conceal the fact.

"So what happens now?"

"That's a problem, no question. Mine, among others. Yours even more, of course." Very carefully he stubbed out his cigarette, only two-thirds finished, in the ashtray. He clasped his hands behind his head, stretched his head back until some finger joints cracked then adopted the posture of Rodin's Thinker.

"You have, there's no argument about that, committed several crimes. Forgery, entering the GDR under a false name; we could add attempted incitement to illegal emigration. It mounts up to quite a bit." He made a dramatic pause before going on, "On the other hand—"

"Yes?"

"On the other hand, what can we do with you? Your people know where you are, some of them, at least, and you're a friend of our country, a benefactor, we'd be pretty stupid to hold you here. So—what would *you* suggest?"

How do you answer a question like that? What answer would you have given? Put yourself in my position—what would be your answer? And remember that this here's just a game, like doing it on the simulator, so to speak. Come on then, off you go.

I thought for a bit, then said that kind of game was childish but that I could well imagine how he felt, he really had been up shit creek and desperate for a paddle. That was exactly what he wanted to hear.

I said, "It's obvious, Herr Endewitt, that what I have to suggest is what is best for Sofie and for me. Let us leave, without any fuss. Sofie goes in my trunk and afterward she'll live in the Owl's Nest with me and I will personally guarantee that nothing about Inge Schulz and her time in Leipzig is ever made public."

"But what if she should talk, eventually?"

"Then she's lying. Even now she could approach the media in the West by sending a letter with her story—if she wanted, but why *should* she want to? Just let Sofie and me leave."

"Yes, I suppose that would be best." He paused, presumably, I imagined, to gloat over the ray of hope he had allowed me. "However, there are difficulties."

"Such as?"

"There are differing attitudes to the Inge Schulz case over here. Recently she has become a kind of problem child that some people would like to get rid of. Get rid of for good, I mean."

"If it's a question of a ransom—"

"No no, you can't bribe me. You can try, but—I'm not insane. I'm too small a cog to accept money from you, it would be the end of me."

That wasn't my opinion. I told him that his country's economy was in such a bad way that we just had to wait for it to collapse, it would only be a matter of a few years, and he could retire with a golden handshake at absolutely no risk. After that he looked at me as if *I* were insane. He couldn't repress a grin.

"With all due respect, I don't think such dreams will get us anywhere. My powers in this case are limited. There is no question of me being able to let the two of you leave, that would have to be okayed from the very top and I don't think—" He hesitated. "But that's none of your business."

Clearly the Politburo hadn't been kept up to date about Inge Schulz. I assumed that the news of my entry to the GDR had not gone beyond Horst Endewitt's desk or, possibly, that the connection between me and Sofie had never been made clear to the *very top*. But what did he want from me? He could have had anything. I shifted my chair a little closer to his desk.

"So what do *you* suggest?" It was a momentary relief to give Endewitt a dose of his own medicine.

"Inge Schulz must die."

"Sorry?"

"Inge Schulz is there, in the files. She's lived here and she must die, so that the file on her can be closed. And in case Sofie Kramer ever claims she was once Inge Schulz, we need to have a body to point to."

Aha. It sounded reasonable. Sounded like a plan that needed fine tuning. I leant forward to create a kind of conspiratorial atmosphere. It was all so absurd.

While I was negotiating with Endewitt about Sofie's future, his people were looking for Inge Schulz, trying to get to her before she could do something stupid. A macabre situation. And Endewitt, intoxicated with power, relaxed more and more, offered me a brandy and showed me a polaroid of his newly born daughter.

"Do you know what a frozen roast is?"

"No. I mean—presumably not as I understand it."

Inge Schulz spends that day with her liquor merchant. Sitting on a wooden bench at the back of the shop. He feels a bit uncomfortable about it, but he doesn't say so out loud. He doesn't know what she wants. Inge doesn't know either.

"A frozen roast is the body of someone who's died from severe burns. Sometimes they're not buried, they're frozen and brought out when you want to have someone declared dead who isn't, or isn't yet, or will be very soon, but not in the way you want the world to think."

Aha. Very interesting. How exciting. I had the feeling the man was taking the piss.

"Listen, this's my proposal. We arrange the death of Inge Schulz as the result of a fire in her room, leaving behind a thawed-out frozen roast of the same sex and height. You take your Sofie with you, across the border—and that's the last we see of each other."

It slowly began to dawn on me that this man didn't need to be bribed because he'd already been bribed long ago. The telephone rang. Endewitt picked up the receiver; he seemed really exhilarated. "Aha? Good. Hold her there."

"Time for your big scene, Herr von Brücken. Take her with you and leave the rest to us. Have you a passport for Sofie?"

"Of course." I said it like a travelling salesman trying to convince someone of the quality of his goods. And suddenly fears one little detail will ruin the whole deal.

"I thought you would. May I see it?"

"Go ahead."

He slid his fingers up and down it, even smelled it. "Great. You'll have no problems at the border. Don't make the poor thing spend all the time in your trunk. And don't mess up. What I wouldn't give to be with you. Just one more thing: in case Frau Kramer should ever be difficult over there . . . however much time has passed, the matter can always be resolved *in a different way*. Tell her that. With my best wishes. Good luck."

"Eh? What am I to do now?"

"Shouldn't you be going home, Inge dear? Aren't you cold? Oh, I see, hey, you can't just open the schnapps like that. I have to put it on your slate."

"So you don't love me after all?"

"Within limits, Inge, within limits."

"Just like everyone here. Shall I tell you something."

Fritz Langenscheidt has to serve a customer and asks Inge dear for a brief postponement; then he turns to her. "What?"

"D'you know, Fritz, during a bank robbery in West Berlin I handed out chocolate marshmallows. You know, the ones they used to call negro kisses."

"That's just like you, Inge."

"I know that it's not like me. To tell the truth, it was another woman. She was called Inge too. We thought it was a great idea and wanted to copy it. But then I dropped all the negro kisses, I mean the marshmallows. I wonder what would have become of me in the States?"

Fritz Langenscheidt has trouble following her train of thought.

"In the States? In America?"

"Exactly. Or if I'd stayed in that castle with the ambulant violinist. Wow! How rich in possibilities life is, even if the fact is you only get one, and once upon a time my sister, my stepsister that is, I was adopted, was so hard, so radical and then the money came, that spoiled her, I wonder if she's happy?"

"You needn't go into all that detail, Inge."

"In the late afternoon Endewitt dropped me at my bed and breakfast telling me to pack my things, get in my car and drive to an address where I could pick up Sofie. No, not pick her up, the expression he used was *take into custody*. All kinds of thoughts came to me, especially bad thoughts. By the way, there's something you must promise me."

"What?"

"When I'm dead you must ask Lukian if he had anything to do with it. He wouldn't tell me and I can understand why he wouldn't tell me. But someone had a hand in it. Who else if not Lukian? I'll presumably never know, that's the price I have to pay. But if you find out it'll be as if I knew. Will you promise me that?"

I promised.

HANDOVER

Inge Schulz is horrified beyond measure when the customers are waved out and the shop is cleared.

"This shop is closing. Inventory. Please leave the premises." From her place Inge can only hear voices and the sound of the door closing and a key being turned in the lock.

Fritz has grassed on her, is her first thought, but she can immediately tell from the way he goes white that that's unlikely to be the case. Three Stasi types come around the counter and stand there, legs apart, saying nothing except that Inge should keep quiet, just sit there and keep her mouth shut.

Fritz L.'s wondering what he's got into, how he's going to explain it to his wife in the evening. A few snowflakes are drifting down outside.

"What am I charged with?" Inge Schulz keeps whispering to herself. Fritz L. has to hand over the shop key, then he's allowed to go, of which permission he immediately avails himself, though not without a worried, apologetic glance back at his best customer. Then all's quiet in the room.

The Security Ministry agents light cigarettes and give Inge Schulz one without her having to ask. Otherwise they behave as if everything's as it should be and no explanation is necessary. They talk about a film that's on that week and how well people think the main actress has played her role. Inge Schulz thinks they're exchanging coded messages, but it's just idle chatter, a lubricant for time. Whenever she tries to stand up, a hand on her shoulder pushes her down, so she stays sitting, asking questions no one answers. Suddenly there's a knock at the shop door. Again the sound of a key. A man comes in, he seems uncertain, his brow's covered in sweat, as if he needs to make sure he's got the right place. Inge's stood up. This time no one's stopped her.

Who is it? She knows the man from someplace or other, even though he's changed. Where has she met him? The man, middle aged but sinewy and slim, average height, clears his throat and says to the room in general, "Well then."

Well then what? What's going on here? No one answers the man. Is he perhaps the executioner?

"I'll take care of Frau Schulz."

The man with the toneless voice doesn't look at all like someone from the Stasi, even though that's not always obvious. What exactly is it that makes the Stasi look like Stasi? The man turns to her. Why does he seem so hesitant, almost embarrassed?

"Frau Inge Schulz."

"Yes?"

"Will you come with me, please."

She knows this man. She rummages in her memory. She's met him someplace.

Inge takes a few steps toward him. The three Stasi types don't stop her. don't lift a finger. The man holds out his hand to her. She leaves his hand unshaken, hovering horizontally in the air.

"Frau Schulz, I've come to collect you. Come with me, please. Trust me."

I didn't know what to say. Every moment I expected some kind of intervention, some *partypoop*, if the word exists. It doesn't? No matter. Even though if I'd sat back and thought about it I could have told myself: I'm Alexander von Brücken, no one can do anything to me without precipitating a diplomatic crisis. But what could I say to Sofie? I could see that she was scared to death. But still . . . still it seemed advisable not to come out with the truth straight away. And that was assuming I knew *which* truth. She'd clearly had something to drink, her steps were uncertain, but in her mind she seemed clear and sober.

I asked her to get into the passenger seat of my car, which was in a narrow garage belonging to the shop. It was already getting dark. "Listen," I said, "you have to trust me. Do you remember me?"

Inge Schulz does remember, though she doesn't admit it and shakes her head. It's that Boris from way back, the taxi driver—so he was a *Stasi agent?* Sad. It's clear to her that this is it. So why all the fuss? Why all this pointless talk?

She doesn't reply. The melancholy in her expression—her face was music, full of fear, expectation, hope, despair, everything, and this music was for my ears alone. I didn't want to say anything, so as not to destroy the music with words. Until I realized I *had to* say something, anything. No, not *just anything*. That was the last thing I should say.

"Listen closely. We're going to drive out of the city and to West Germany. Unfortunately you can't sit next to me. No one's to see you with me. Could I ask you to get into the trunk? It'll be a bit tight but it won't last long, you can trust me on that. As soon as we're out of Leipzig you can sit up here, where you are now. Is that OK with you?"

"I've to get in the trunk?"

"Just for a quarter of an hour. Please."

You have to visualize it. The garage door was half open and the three Stasi thugs were standing there, hands in their coat pockets, watching us with interest. It was a situation in which you definitely don't want to make a mistake.

"I'm to crawl in there?"

"Please, Sofie, just do it."

"But I don't want to."

330 · HELMUT KRAUSSER

"I can understand that perfectly. But do it all the same. It's in your interest. *Your* interest."

She looked at me, wide eyed. It was all I could do not to cry.

Sofie looked around, like an animal looking for a way of escape. Finally she got into the trunk. It was as if she were saying farewell to the world.

To have to do that to my beloved! Eventually I burst into tears, silent tears. The Stasi could see the funny side. They asked me not to stop unless it was absolutely necessary. I set off. I was so tensed up I could hardly hold the steering wheel. Never have I felt closer to Sofie. No, never. Even today I don't know how I managed to get through the evening rush hour in the center of Leipzig, it took ages, it felt like hours, in reality it can only have been twenty minutes, but eventually we were on the edge of the city, eventually the street lights became sparser and I stopped, out in the fields. Opened the trunk. The fear in the eyes I looked into! She was certain she was going to be shot. She continued to think so, even after I'd asked her to come and sit in the passenger seat beside me. We drove on, along a poorly lit country road, I thought music might relax the tension, the Beatles' *Abbey Road* was on the cassette recorder, outside the drizzle gradually turned into a heavy snowfall. I had to concentrate very hard on the road ahead.

"Where are we going?" She was the one who broke the silence.

"To the border. There's no need to be afraid. Really. In a few hours you'll be on the territory of the Federal Republic."

"It's too good to be true."

"It *is* true."

"What then? Over there? Will I be arrested?"

"You could be, but not right away. I mean not to start with. Perhaps never. It depends on you."

You see how clumsily I expressed myself? I handed her her

passport. She took it, opened it, read the name she'd had as a girl and didn't know what to think—no, that's my interpretation, rather: I didn't know what she thought, but she gave a quiet sob, presumably she was finally convinced she *wasn't* going to be shot. At least that it didn't seem quite so likely anymore.

"You're Boris, aren't you? I recognized you right away."

"You have a good memory."

"You never were a real taxi driver, were you?"

"No."

There was a pause. The snowflakes were whirling around in my head, not letting my thoughts settle. No, I decided, I wouldn't tell Sofie who I was, at least not now. Not yet. She should make her own decisions without me interfering in her life. Once we were over there, yes, then, there, I'd make her an offer, that was clear, that was a matter of course. A simple offer without conditions, obligations or ulterior motives. After all, she had to find somewhere to stay, with someone or other, at least until something could be arranged so that she could live in safety at a place of her choice, somewhere, anywhere in the world. That was the way I saw it. And then, going around a bend I stepped on the brakes and the car skidded, not much, not badly, black ice had formed, we could only go on at walking pace, if at all, and the snow was getting heavier.

Just imagine, we were somewhere out in the sticks, darkness all around. Should we perhaps take refuge in a village somewhere? With a West German car? And all the questions that was bound to lead to? And some tragic quirk of fate that might possibly prevent us leaving the country? I had taken on a lot and achieved a lot. Was I threatened with failure just because the November sky couldn't hold its water? If God does exist, then it was too cruel a joke. I found a place we could park off the road and stopped.

"No point in going on, we'll end up in the ditch."

"So what do we do now?"

"Wait?"

Unfortunately—no, not unfortunately but because of my stupidity the tank wasn't full, only half full. There was enough gasoline to reach the border, easily, but not enough to keep the engine running all night. And it was cold, around freezing point. There were blankets in the trunk and I fetched them. While I was doing that, Sofie opened the passenger door and ran off, across a plowed field with deep furrows, covered in snow. Fortunately she didn't get far, she stumbled and twisted her ankle. I managed to pick her up and carried her back to the car. If you're not quite that cruel, God, and the snow was only an excuse for me to hold Sofie in my arms, then I forgive you.

She sobbed, hiding her face behind her fists, which were quivering with cold. And not just with cold.

"Who are you?" she screamed at me. "What are you going to do to me?"

I put both of the blankets we had over her trembling body, pushed the tangled, damp strands of hair back out of her face and tried to calm her down. "Don't be afraid," I whispered, "Don't be afraid."

What would you have said? Would anything better have occurred to you? The music was still playing, the cassette had reached the last song *and in the end the love you take is equal to the love you make* it said and I had Sofie in my arms, a lover trying to keep his beloved warm. It was such an undecided moment, at the same time wonderful and terrible. She was crying and I was crying; eventually she stopped crying and started to wonder why *I* was crying.

I felt her fingers in my hair, the back of her hand against my temple.

"Who are you?" she asked again, calmly this time, almost tenderly.

I kissed her, only once and very briefly, on the lips, but I didn't say anything.

Even today I don't know whether she recognized me in that moment or not, I thought her face twitched slightly, it could be, I don't know, but that kiss, my God, that kiss—

After a minute's pause the bonus track rang out from the tape: *Her Majesty Is a Very Nice Girl*—not at all in tune with our mood, but still. In every life there's at least one second of divinity when, as you might put it, the *other*, that which is usually hidden, reveals itself, takes on sensory form—and there's the moment *after* when everything is as it was before. We were saved by a warm front from the west. Now it wasn't snowing, just raining and soon even that stopped. I got the car back on the road and, driving slowly, we reached the border around one o'clock in the morning. I handed our passports to the border guard, he checked them, had a look at both of us and gave us the passports back. I gave them to Sofie to put in the glove compartment. She glanced at mine, saw that I had, or at least had assumed the surname she'd been born with and gave a laugh, a laugh such as I've never heard from anyone before or since, toneless, hoarse, almost a whimper, it's almost indescribable, but you'll describe it for me, you'll explain it all to me, won't you?

On the other side, on the territory of the Federal Republic, Sofie asked me to stop the car. I thought she needed the toilet, so I drove to a service area. She got out of the Opel, took her passport, stuck it in her pocket and said goodbye. Quite unemotionally, almost as if it was of no significance.

"Thanks."

"Where're you going? Do you need any money?"

"Don't worry about me," she said and vanished around the corner.

I spent hours waiting for her. I looked for her, got out and screamed her name into the night.

It was the last time I saw her. A truck driver probably gave her a lift.

In the morning there was a report in the Leipzig local news that Inge S., an employee of the Dimitrov Museum, had died as the result of a fire in her apartment. There's a grave with her name on it.

I returned to the Owl's Nest and waited for Sofie to get in touch, waited and waited. But she seems to have managed without me. It's almost fifteen years ago now.

Sofie Kramer was never caught. After the collapse of Communism it came out that she had been Inge Schulz and Inge Schulz was dead. The Federal Bureau of Criminal Investigation had their doubts, the body was exhumed and DNA compared. I sorted that out. Since then she's not been on the wanted list. She's living somewhere, perhaps, I've made no more attempts to find her. What she's living on, if she is alive, I don't know. It's nothing to do with me anymore. Yes, that's it. Were you hoping for a happy end?

"But that is a happy end."

"Yes? Probably. You're probably right."

Von Brücken seemed exhausted. He laid his head down on the pillow and closed his eyes. It was a while before I roused myself sufficiently to ring for the doctor.

That evening Lukian said there was no need for me to stay any longer. Apart from wishing me all the best, there was nothing more his master could tell me, the rest he left to my imagination. I was to change all the names, wait for a few years before publishing the book and, please, not forget the note that all the characters and events were fictitious. The fee would be paid, I needn't worry about that. I was given—*on loan*, as was emphasized—two leather cases with notes, transcripts and tapes. Lukian drove me to the station himself.

"May I ask you a couple more questions?"

"No." And that was his last word; he shook my hand without even a "Goodbye."

Strange Turning Points

Von Brücken wrote me one more letter, in which he thanked me for the way we had worked together.

His handwriting was shaky, scarcely legible, but the tone of the letter was cheerful.

There were strange turning points in life, he wrote. It was some people's destiny to sit in the audience while others were born to be actors, and even now it wasn't clear to him which was the more desirable. The most astonishing thing for him was the fact that no one could be sure what their ultimate function would be in this great theater. Art had the ability to make ushers into heroes and vice versa. Life was just a pile of material out of which this or that developed, sometimes nothing. But he was content, even though there were things for which he had to reproach himself. His life had been determined by Eros, who wielded a complex, many-faceted power; at the end it ground you down, but always leaving you with the feeling of not being entirely alone and unimportant. He had been delighted that I had listened to him.

I hope all goes well.

Some Little Thing

A few months later I was invited to the funeral. I could afford to take a taxi from Munich and I had a guilty conscience because I hadn't yet started the novel. There was something missing. Some little thing.

The taxi went up the drive. The Owl's Nest had had a new coat of paint, it really shone, just as I had imagined the Ice Palace shining. The park with its little birch groves looked wonderfully arcadian, the delicate green of the new grass had a bluish tinge. It was already late in the afternoon, beyond the trees the edges of the clouds were turning red.

No one greeted me or even seemed to notice me. It was an unspectacular funeral. A little taped music ("A Day in the Life", "Fool on the Hill" and "Long, Long, Long") was played, no one made a speech, following the wish Alexander had expressed in his will.

The coffin was deposited in the tomb by means of a hydraulic lifting platform. In all there were scarcely a dozen people present, without exception oldish men in black suits looking like a matched set. Some threw a rose on the coffin, others didn't. Lukian stayed some distance away, strolling to and fro among the trees with their new leaves, lost in thought. It was mild and sunny on that day in May. Those who had attended the ceremony stood around for a while, then left the park one after the other, heading for the castle; hardly anyone spoke. It was not clear to me what I should do next, whether there was anything more to discuss or not.

Suddenly someone was beside Lukian among the poplars, a

woman in a black dress, black hat and veil. Lukian took her by the hand and the two of them walked slowly to the tomb and the woman, from her movements an old, frail woman, threw something in. I couldn't tell what it was, but it was light, it fluttered a little in the wind before floating down onto the coffin, a piece of colored paper perhaps. The two of them must have stood there for a quarter of an hour before, at a gesture from Lukian, the stone doors of the tomb were closed. Full of curiosity, I had gone closer, step by step, without a sound, until I was only six feet behind the pair. Lukian turned around and gave me a wink. The woman placed a hand on his shoulder, she seemed tired, I couldn't really make out her face behind the veil. I said my name and bowed, but she just nodded and walked past me without a word. As if to make it clear, that that was the end of the story for me.

CODA

Contrary to von Brücken's express desire, I have reproduced almost everything he recorded on tape for me verbatim. I felt the way he *didn't* describe some things, or refused to describe them, said more than any invention, however much embellished, could have done.

Years later I sent a typed manuscript of the completed novel to Lukian. He was welcome, I said, to add anything he liked. This would be the last opportunity. He did not reply.

Instead I received a very friendly letter from Asunción in Paraguay. It was Constanze da Ponte who wrote, exceedingly amused at what I'd made of the story. Unfortunately her brother Alexander, she said, had not told me the whole truth. That didn't mean I had to alter my manuscript, on the contrary I must not do that on any account, but she felt it was important I should know the truth. Because it was important for an understanding of what kind of person Alexander had been. She supposed he'd thought he had to show consideration for his sisters.

Her father, Knut von Brücken, had killed himself and his wife—with her agreement, that was made clear in a farewell letter—because as a convinced National Socialist he had not been able to contemplate a world without Hitler. His children, however, had been flown, on Keferloher senior's initiative, via Italy to Paraguay; that included Alexander, who had later broken with his family's past, a past which had been a cause of unhappiness to him for the rest of his life. In 1950 he had returned to Munich to take over the firm. Keferloher senior, whom I had depicted as an arch-intriguer, had never offered violent resistance to Alexander, only doubted his competence, that was all.

She was not in a position to judge the rest of the story. Alexander had come to a very generous settlement with her and her sister Cosima (d. 1991); they had both stayed in Paraguay and been happy under their new name. As far as that could be said of human beings.

This is a novel. All the protagonists are fictional, their names were changed several times.

Certain historical events provided a backdrop for the characters; sometimes the backdrop had to be changed slightly to fit in the demands of the novel. The author begs his readers not to see this as showing disrespect towards people who lived through this time. My thanks to Dr. Susanne Müller-Wolff, Leipzig, for advice on everyday life in East Germany.

The first version of Eros *was written in 1997, the seventeenth and last in 2005.*

Helmut Krausser is a novelist, poet, diarist, dramaturge, composer, and screenwriter. His novels *The Great Bagarozy* and *Fat World* have been adapted for the screen, both starring Jürgen Vogel. He lives in Berlin.